D1526255

Also by Gay G. Gunn

One Day. Someday. Soon: Book I, Culhane Family Saga
Might Could Be: Book II, Culhane Family Saga
Nowhere to Run
Pride and Joi
Everlastin' Love
Dotted Swiss and Gingham

By GiGi Gunn

Never Been to Me
Cajun Moon
Rainbow's End
Living Inside Your Love

May
We
All

Gay G. Gunn

May We All is a work of fiction. Names, characters, business organizations, places, events and incidents are the product of the author's imagination or are used fictitiously. Any resemblance to actual persons, living or dead, events, or locales is entirely coincidental.

2017 Different Drummer Trade Paperback Edition

Published in the United States
by Different Drummer, LLC

ISBN-13:-978-1979143141
ISBN-10: 1979143145

To all my fellow G.R.I.T.S. (Girls Raised In The South),
And all of our "ace boon coons" north, east and west of the Mason Dixon Line…
We Are One.
May We All: Coming of Age in the 60s
Culhane Family Saga

Book III

Culhane Family Saga

Coming of Age in the Sixties

1

Los Angeles, CA
1955

Jaz, born and delivered in this, the eighth year of her existence, sat in the back seat of the gray Dodge directly behind her father. Her older brother, TC, rode shotgun. As the L.A. heat poured through the open windows, Jaz couldn't contain her excitement. This was her rebirth, only this time, instead of butt-naked she wore a striped frock with a matching tam from her Aunt Selena who lived in Paris, France. She smoothed her dress down in front and unsuccessfully tried to hide her inner glee. Escaping the captivity of being with her mother and sister, Mel, on their various girlie activities, Jaz was relishing her moment with the guys in her life. Finally. Headed for the Watts Police Boys Club where her father, Coach Culhane, reigned supreme and TC heralded as captain of the Dragons football team. For Jaz, Christmas had come early this year. Once they reached the club, Coach drove his car into his reserved space and the father and son popped open their doors as Jaz waited for her father to unlock hers in the back. Immediately surrounded by the other Dragons, Coach Hep Culhane managed a decree before he left his daughter, "Stay where I can see you, Jaz."

"OK, Daddy."

"Over in the bleachers."

"OK."

Jaz meant to obey her father but the lure of the chain link fence surrounding the club dared her to take a victory lap. She had finally pierced that all-boys club bastion even if only as a

2

one-day observer. Not knowing when the stars and moon would align for her like this again, when her mother and sister were consumed with rehearsals and fittings, Jaz's PF Flyers found themselves on the threshold between the club and the sidewalk. She looked up into the crystal clear blue sky and let the sun rain down on her achievement. Feeling energized, she began to walk away from the club, letting the rays encapsulate and protect her as she planned to go just once around the coveted, legendary club before her father knew she was gone. With one foot in front of the other, she began a digital accompaniment with the tips of her brown fingers bumping along the metal fence. Halfway to the corner, she stopped and drove her hand into her goodie bag, drew out a squirrel nut, unsheathed the nutty deliciousness and popped it into her mouth. She continued to circumnavigate the club, houses on the left, cars passing, guys on bikes going to and from the doors of the club. Around to the bottom of the U she turned up and proceeded around the perimeter.

She heard a whistle's frantic blowing then one distinct, familiar piercing summons, produced by her father's two fingers and his tongue. She looked to see him in the middle of the field surrounded by a passel of boys who also stopped to look at what distracted their coach.

Ugh! Jaz thought, *Already banned and haven't even gotten in good yet.*

Her father stood akimbo, one strong arm pointed to the gate's entrance directing her with his irate body language. Apparently telling the boys to run laps, he waited until she crossed the threshold and whisked herself up into the stands.

She waved weakly knowing she'd gone too far. Sitting at the top of the bleachers, her hand disappeared into her goodie bag of penny candy, this time retrieving a Pixie Stix. Biting off

3

the top, she let the powdery grape contents spill over her tongue. She watched the Dragons go through their paces at the direction of her father. She looked at the other sports occupying the field, eyed the water fountain but decided to wait a few minutes before going for a drink. Her gaze fell on a boy sitting on the first plank of wood and decided to saunter down.

"Hi," she said, approaching the boy who looked to be a few years older like her brother.

His eyes shifted as if she wasn't speaking to him.

"Hi," she repeated and went to sit beside him.

He looked around, then at her and finally replied, "Hey."

"Are you a Dragon?"

"No. If I were a Dragon I'd be on the field," he snapped.

"You could've gotten hurt, suspended or something."

He rolled his eyes in annoyance at the pesky little girl.

"Want some candy?" Jaz asked.

He eyeballed her again as she opened her bag and rummaged through the sugary contents.

"I got some Mary Janes if you don't mind the peanut butter and taffy sticking to your teeth. My favorite is Bit-O-Honey but they were out of those." She offered him the square confection.

He reluctantly took it and mumbled, "Thanks."

"Sure." She closed the bag, gathering it around its neck and looked out on the field. "How long does the practice last?"

"Coupla hours."

"Umm. My name is Jaz Culhane," she introduced herself.

"OK," he said. She turned to face him full-on and it was the first time he noticed her eyes. She had unusual light eyes, a color that he had never seen. Cat's eyes his father would have called them. His own eyes began to levitate in response, like he didn't know where to look at her. She had smooth skin, and

4

curly hair peeked out from her tam. Her eyebrows—thick, deeply furrowed and her lashes seemed as long as her hair.

"Well, what's your name?" She asked.

"Dickie."

Her piercing-light eyes challenged him for a last name.

"Peckinpah," he answered.

"Pleased to meet you," she said and returned to watch the guys on the field.

He looked around again to see if she were by herself. Surely a little girl like this at the Boys Club must not be here alone. She looked out at the field and he looked at her. She looked older but acted young, yet she had stepped up to introduce herself and offered him candy. She looked bright and smelled clean, unlike the girls who populated his life. He tried to make sense of the getup she wore: the polka dots and stripes like she couldn't make up her mind what she wanted to wear so she put it all on. She fished in her bag again and asked, "Want another piece?"

"Yeah."

"How about a Jawbreaker? They last a long time."

"OK. You got a red one?"

The Dragons ended their practice running laps again as Coach Culhane came over to Jaz.

"Hi, Daddy. This is Dickie—"

Dickie smiled weakly as her father said, "Yes, I know Dickie." He smiled curtly. "I'm going to check in the office. Can I trust you to stay here?"

"Yes, Daddy."

"Hmm. Can you watch her for me, Dickie?"

"Yes, sir."

She looked mortified that her father had asked him that.

"So, you're Coach Culhane's daughter?"

"Yep."

Well that explains a lot, he thought.

TC ended his laps at the bleacher where his sister sat and the guys followed. "So, how'd you like it, Jaz? Worth it?" TC asked.

"Oh, yeah," she lied but thought it still beat being with her mother and sister.

"Hey, Dickie," TC greeted.

"Hey."

As the other guys filed in, Jaz noticed everyone acknowledged Dickie. Of course, she knew TC's best friend, Scoey, and some of the others who had come by the house on Saturday mornings to watch Westerns, but she'd never seen Dickie or this one guy who ran up and slapped Scoey on the back of the head and said to Dickie, "Hey, Smelly."

Jaz looked at the guy who looked to be TC's age or older. His skin, a rich, Hersey-dark-chocolate and his coal-black hair was cut short to the scalp like most, but she noted his nose: sharp enough to cut a piece of bread. Jaz thought his looks were appealing in an unusual way as his even-teeth blazed white against his dark skin.

"Something smells like a outhouse pit," he joned and fanned his hands in front of that perfect, keen nose. Jaz didn't know what an "outhouse pit" was but she didn't think it was a good thing. "Who could that be…huh, Smelly?"

"Cut it out, Carter," TC admonished.

"Your name is Dickie, right?" Jaz asked her new friend who nodded. "Why is he calling you 'Smelly?'"

Dickie hunched his shoulders to answer as Coach Culhane returned with a roster of phone numbers for each of the team's members. As the coach began to pass out the info, Jaz watched the handsome Carter transform from a cute guy to

6

just ordinary looking. She and Dickie, the only non-Dragons, stood off to the side.

Jaz asked, "Why do you let him call you Smelly? They all smell."

Dickie laughed and said, "Carter Hix is just kiddin' around."

"I think that's mean."

"C'mon Jaz," her father called.

She followed TC and Scoey to the car. She looked back and said, "Bye, Dickie!"

"Bye, Jaz."

Jaz listened to the male banter of three guys as they drove to eat before going home. "Captain, Tavio Culhane, and co-captain, Ellis 'Scoey' Scofield of the Dragons... you all will have to decide," her father said.

"He's too young," TC stated. "That little curly-headed boy should be a Bobcat."

"Too good to be a Bobcat, son. Not fair."

"OK, he can be a Cougar then."

"That boy can outplay the Cougars, too."

"Soon we'll be going into basketball season," TC dismissed.

"Supposed he can do that, too? Scoey, what do you think?"

"I think he should play where his skills say," Scoey answered. "Regardless of age."

Hep flashed a smile at Scoey through the rearview mirror as TC sucked his teeth in disgust and snapped, "Why have rules at all then if anyone can be an exception?"

Little curly-headed boy didn't have a friend in TC, Jaz thought.

At Tops Drive-In, Coach ordered cheeseburgers all around, a Coke, a chocolate milkshake for Jaz, two orange freezes for TC and Scoey. As they ate and discussed other boy stuff, Jaz listened and reveled in eating store-bought burgers, fries and onion rings on a weeknight.

While eating, TC recalled how the curly-headed boy had come to him once after practice, stuck out his hand and introduced himself. "Hi. My name is Quinton Chandler."

TC looked at the other Dragons and thought, *This kid just walks up to me?*

With no response, the boy continued, "My friends call me Qwayz."

Not used to such brash directness, TC responded by shifting from one foot to the other and asked, "Why?"

"My sister couldn't pronounce Quinton, so it became Qway-z. For Quad-C. I'm the fourth. Quad. Last name Chandler. C. Became Qwayz."

"Humph," was TC's disinterested response.

"Well, see you," the boy said, jogging off.

TC offered a nervous laugh to his fellow Dragons who watched their leader for his reaction to the stranger in their midst. They all knew each other from school, the neighborhood, the club, and none had taken to the interloper. When TC turned around, his father looked him dead in the eye. TC, unsure of what his father had overheard or what that stare meant, knew he hadn't heard the last of it.

"Is Dickie a Dragon? "Jaz asked the trio as she positioned her hamburger for a bite.

"Humph," TC scoffed.

"He's a little too thin, Punkin," her father offered. "He might get hurt."

"Besides he has no talent for football," TC said, as he chucked another French fry smothered with catsup.

8

"Unlike 'the curly-headed boy'?" Jaz asked.

Hep and Scoey chuckled at her observation, seeing what her brother failed to.

"Well, since I have the captain and co-captain of the team here, you two decide. But let me say this." Hep turned sideways to TC so Scoey could hear. "I've seen that little boy try hard to be your friend and for a reason that I cannot figure out, you, my son, seem to shun him. Let me tell you this, he is going to do what he wants to do with or without your friendship or approval. He came to the Boys Club a few years ago after his father died and wanted to join a soccer team. We don't have one. He was so young I took him home and his mother told me what a good soccer player his father had been and since his passing, her son wanted to hold on to that tradition also, as 'man of the house,' he took on a paper route and a weekend job as pin boy at the bowling alley. I think that's commendable. So that boy, Qwayz, is doing this for his father. You and the Dragons don't matter. If he doesn't get what he needs here, he'll go to another rec center and you'll have to face him on field anyway… on the other side."

Both TC and Scoey remained quiet as Jaz asked, "Can I have ice cream cake for dessert?"

Hep carried Jaz, piggy-back, into the apartment as TC disappeared to his room. "Brush your teeth, Jaz."

Obeying, she slept-walked into the bathroom, slept-walked down the hall to her bedroom, shed her outfit, put on PJs and climbed into bed.

"Did you say your prayers?" Hep asked, as he entered the girls' room to tuck her in and kiss his already sleeping daughter, Mel, on the forehead.

When she finished, she snuggled under the cover and Hep kissed her. "Night, Punkin'."

"Night, Daddy."

2

Mel belted out the last note and struck a pose in the full-length mirror on the back of her bedroom door. In her mind's eye, the crowd jumped to its feet and went wild. She bowed deeply, curtsied, threw a kiss and skipped off—all of her signature moves—to Jaz's bed, out of the mirror's view. Sometimes the imaginary audience called her back for an encore. She would feign surprise before launching into an even more powerful song. She had won every vocal competition with that routine. None as illustrious as the $2,000 prize she won on "The Ted Mack Amateur Hour" when just six; her bank account continued to grow. Nothing compared to the way she felt on stage with all the attention, the awe, the adoration. When she stood on that stage and sang, she felt alive. Even at ten years old, she recognized the control she had over the audience… her voice… the outcome. She alone. So powerful. So loved. She was good at it. Set for life. Jaz's bed, over by the window, her dressing room. She looked at her sister's neat bed in comparison to her own. She eyed the two pictures thumbtacked to Jaz's headboard: one of her sister and Aunt Selena taken at The Satin Doll one New Year's Eve before their famous Aunt moved to Paris and opened a nightclub; the other a picture of an *Ebony* magazine cover featuring Dorothy Dandridge.

On Mel's side of the room, there was no window but a wall covered with all manner of ribbons, plaques, pictures of her receiving checks and awards, and trophies that spilled from the dresser onto the floor. She felt sorry for her younger sister, content with playing games with friends like Echo Blake, jumping double Dutch, playing kickball, eating candy while waiting for the ice cream truck's bell when she'd take the Buffalo nickel from her socks and buy a Popsicle or Dreamsicle. Jaz drank water from the spigot, stayed outside all day until the streetlights came on. *Echo Blake,* Mel thought absently, *wasn't even her real name. They called her Echo because she went around repeating everything her older sister said. What was Echo's real name?* Mel tried to recall. Her own real name was Brittany Melba Culhane; she preferred Mel right now, but practiced autographing all of her names on a loose-leaf notebook page just in case.

Mel glanced outside to see Greg Minton sitting next to Jaz on the steps. Mel noticed how he always managed to get next to Jaz. Greg was a year younger but his older brother, Maurice, was in the class ahead of Mel. Seems one of them should be angling to get next to her. They were a natural match. Together, the Minton Brothers were a tap dancing team whose family owned Minton's Playhouse in New York City where Aunt Selena played when she was in the States. The Minton boys always went to New York for the summer and most school vacations and Mel should be going with them. She could sing and they could dance. Mel hunched her shoulders and shook her head free from the thought.

Her brother TC had talent. He had already written five songs for their Aunt Selena, which she had recorded and used in her Paris nightclub act. TC's bank account was bigger than Mel's and he never performed like she did. TC was set for life because Aunt Selena said when he graduated high school she wanted him to come to Paris and be her "arranger," whatever that means. Her brother could not only play anything he heard but also make up songs. Mel liked it when her brother played for her, usually during their stay with their grandparents in Colt, Texas for the summer. Mel thought him gifted in the

12

"boogie-woogie" he played and the way he'd "go to church" with his gospel flair. When he and his boys came home from a movie, TC would always sit at the piano and play the theme song; If a Western, they'd reenact all the parts. Jaz always liked him to play "Canadian Sunset" while she'd strike the two lower notes. TC played all around her, letting their baby sister think she was doing something, but it was only two notes.

Mel pulled out her notebook where she practiced her autographs: Mel Culhane, Brittany Culhane. She loved being alone, having the apartment–or at least the bedroom–all to herself. Her mother was up front but she didn't bother her. Her mother was always with her and knew of her talent, understood her, but other folks distracted Mel. They didn't share her likes and loves; they weren't musical at all. She preferred it when she didn't have any auditions, shows, fittings, hairdresser appointments or voice lessons. She liked to sleep and imagine her grown-up life with her own room and maids to clean up after her and cook anything she wanted. There would be no one to tease her about not going outside, or being messy, not making friends or using big words. She and TC would be simpatico, they'd be rich. Jaz… poor thing, had no talent. All she had was being pretty. "I'll probably have to take care of her when I become a star," Mel thought out loud as she filled another page with her autographs and flipped to a new one.

~*~

After the playoffs and the Dragons won the tournament in their age group, TC went to wait for his father in the office and spotted Qwayz, dribbling, posting and darting by imaginary opponents on the basketball court. TC, ready to go home and sleep, watched the boy go through his own paces by himself.

His sneakers squeaking on the polished gym floor, he made few baskets but he tried for them relentlessly.

He turned to see TC watching, so the older boy went over to him. "Hey."

"Hey," Qwayz said, and never stopped dribbling.

"You were good on the football team but you are terrible at this."

"I know. That's why I'm here. Practice makes perfect." Qwayz bounced, turned and shot at the high basket. Missing, he chased the ball and tried again. "You any better?" Qwayz asked, power-passing the ball to TC who caught it and threw it back.

"Football's my game."

"You a little small for football, aren't you?" Qwayz noted.

This little pip-squeak challenged his ability. As team captain, TC harnessed his anger and replied, "We'll see next season who's what."

"Naw. I know football isn't for me. That's why I'm switching to basketball."

"Giving up?" TC gloated.

"Expanding." Qwayz tried another shot and made it. "Just a matter of practice. Don't like my butt being on the ground. Not a lot of skill there anyways." He posted and missed. "Just be big like Scoey who can take the hits."

TC watched the boy remain in continual motion.

"What are you, a midget?"

"Don't call me that."

TC meant it as a compliment because the boy seemed so mature, but maybe you get touchy when your father dies on you. None of the other guys were as direct as this boy. He didn't care that TC was Coach Culhane's son or that he was captain of the team. His father was right as usual: Qwayz holds

14

himself to a higher standard. Most of all, he believes in himself.

"'Sides, I'm 'too pretty' for football," Qwayz said and laughed like it was a private joke.

TC stayed watching the cocky boy go through his own basketball practice, not minding the audience he generated.

Coach Culhane came into the gym. "Ready son?"

"Yeah."

Seeing Qwayz on the court, he said, "Qwayz, it's getting late. Almost dark. You want a ride home?"

Qwayz glanced at his watch. "Sure, thanks. Time got away from me." He threw the ball into the collection basket and joined the pair.

"Let me call your mother and let her know we're going to get a bite to eat before I bring you home."

"OK, thanks," Qwayz said, as he went to pick up his jacket from the corner.

TC went to get Scoey and they stood at the car as his father and Qwayz approached. TC rode shotgun, Scoey took his usual seat as Qwayz climbed into the backseat behind Coach Culhane. The ride to Tops Drive-In was quiet and, knowing what TC and Scoey's orders were, Coach asked Qwayz what he wanted. Qwayz ordered the Tops cheeseburger and an orange freeze, and TC and Scoey started chuckling.

"What's so funny?" Qwayz asked.

"They're both partial to orange freezes," Coach Culhane offered. "Welcome to their group."

On the ride from Tops to Qwayz's house the car filled with banter about everything from school, classes and teachers to favorite television shows and athletics. As the car slowed, both TC and Scoey eyed the neat two-story corner house with the door open and the porch light on. Scoey also lived in a house full of women sans his father. Ma Vy met her son at the door and unlocked the screen.

"Hey, Ma. Thanks Coach Culhane," came out in one stream as Qwayz jogged up the walkway.

"You're welcome, son."

"Yes, thank you," Ma Vy echoed from the porch. She recalled Coach Culhane's kindness when she'd gone to the Boys Club seeking an adult male mentor after her husband died, but was told her son was too young and there was no soccer. A couple of years later her son had made the same inquiry with similar results. And now, it seemed he was accepted by the club and the boys who frequented it. For a concerned, single mother with a rambunctious male child, this answered her prayers.

"It'll all work out," Hep had said to Ma Vy. "In due time," he had told her then and now.

"Just as you predicted," she shared a smile as he came to the door. "Thank you."

"Oh, he's good athlete," Hep said as he saw Qwayz get the trash can to take out for next morning's pick up. "You got a good kid," he told Ma Vy.

TC and Scoey waited in the car, when a cute girl turned the corner on the walkway and headed for the door.

"That's Denise Chandler."

"Sure is."

"You think that's Qwayz's sister?"

"Might could be."

"She is one fine motor-scooter."

"Better than the Byrd sisters?"

"Piper and Wren? Heck yeah. Denise got that cute, little turned up nose."

"She's too old for us. Must be in Carter Hix's class."

"A man can dream, can't he?"

16

"We know she ain't interested in Carter Hix."

"No doubt."

"Stix Hix." They chuckled at their friend wanting everybody to call him by that nickname now that he'd taken up the drums. "Is he any good?"

"To hear him tell it, he's the best."

Hep returned to the car and TC asked as nonchalantly as he could muster, "Has Qwayz got sisters?"

"Yep. Like you and Scoey, two. But Qwayz's in the middle—one older and one younger."

"Yeah. I recognize Denise. She's real smart."

"Yep. I think the whole family is. That was her coming from the library."

3

Selena Culhane Fluellen flipped through the paper as she lounged on her back terrace relishing the tranquil quiet, inhaling the intoxicating fragrance of flowers while gazing out at her back garden. She savored being here instead of the hustle and bustle of Paris. With all the unsettling news coming from America, she stopped to admire the blooming hues of her back pasture down to the ornate, white gazebo, a scene worthy of a Monet painting. The comingled splashes of color, reds, purples, pinks, oranges and golds peacefully coexisting—why couldn't the U.S. take a lesson from nature? She never tired of this chateau she and Zack had bought outside of Paris. Their haven, retreat, and sanctuary all rolled into one panacea for the ills of the world. Blessed and lucky to have worked hard to obtain it, she thanked God for her voice and its five octaves, which surely came from Him. With her club appearances and after-hours soirees, she spent less time here and more in the tiny apartment above her club, SELENA'S, on Rue Simone, unable to make it out here and back in time. She finally agreed with Zack that they needed a larger, "in-town" apartment but only if they could keep this fifteenth-century, stone, country estate, plucked from a fairytale. Chateau Jazz she'd proclaimed it and hoped her nieces, Mel and Jaz, would have their weddings here.

Lisette interrupted with more tea and the mail.

"Merci," Selena said as she went back to the paper.

Despite the disturbing news from home, she soldiered on. On the heels of the Emmett Till murder, national and international outrage still dominated the papers. A young man from Chicago, TC's age, visiting down south in Mississippi

18

just as her nephew visited Colt, Texas, beaten, shot and murdered for allegedly wolf-whistling at a white girl. Selena had read the writer William Faulkner's speech, "Can We Survive?" where he questioned his native state of Mississippi, and she would attend the rally that Josephine Baker organized here, but knew it wasn't enough. Simeon Booker snapped a picture of the young boy's bloated body, which appeared in *Jet* magazine juxtaposed to one of him smiling, confident, a teenage boy with light eyes and a fedora like Jaz wore…his life snuffed out—and for what? Selena wondered if the Culhane children were even aware of this atrocity. Her brother, Hep, and his family, like many others, lived well in California with perpetual sun, expansive beaches, palm trees and amusement parks—so far away from the South with its leftover venom and angst for a war they lost in 1865. Selena couldn't blame Hep and Lorette because if Selena had children she would also want them shielded from all this racial strife… if she could; lock them up and let them out when they reached 21. Then the world could unleash all they had against the armor of built-up confidence and esteem. It worked for her when she left Colt, Texas as a new bride with her then husband, Hoyt Colson. Not growing up with white folk in their all-black town, she paid the see-through, clear race, no never mind. But her own people served her a perpetual plate of curiosity: the hair texture, skin color and class thing. The Negroes in Chicago's South Side and Harlem, New York, so different from the black folk in Colt, Texas she knew and loved. Hoyt had helped her understand and negotiate it all. Once he was killed in World War II, it all became too much: whites hurling insults and mental injury, the continual, consistent dealing with outright, blatant and entitled prejudices… her treatment in Las Vegas being the last draw.

19

The cumulative reason she expatriated to France in the first place: It became psychologically grueling to live in the United States of America. Here she could breathe and live without overt racism, among those who only cared about talent and the color of interest was green—the color of money. From these European shores, the U.S. looked like a sick-puppy dying of a terminal illness. Choking on injustice, gagging from its own festering hate. Her daddy, Papa Colt, said it began with Truman's Executive Order integrating the armed services in 1948. Selena thought that the 1954 *Brown vs. the Board of Education* Supreme Court case had thrown white folks into a tizzy whereby some chose to close white schools to avoid integration. The racial strife remained an oozing sore left open from slavery, and whites actually believed they were superior to blacks. The audacity or stupidity of thinking they had the right and duty to decide the fate of Negroes—preposterous. Absurd that after slavery, whites tried to force blacks back into de facto slavery or get rid of them altogether once they had outlived their usefulness to them. *Well, we not only survived but prevailed and whites just can't take it,* Selena thought. White folks—still fighting the Civil War hoping for another outcome. Papa Colt, a slave who proved them all wrong and founded his own black Texas town where the Culhanes still visit every summer and at Christmas. *I guess every time a white person runs up against a Culhane, they learn about perseverance and excellence,* she thought.

"My daddy, his children and now grandchildren are just the ones to teach 'em," Selena said out loud. She hoped her sister Star had taught some folks some things. Selena's thoughts on Emmett Till and her sister collided. Star had left home in 1932 and hasn't been heard from since. It unnerved Selena to consider all the people in between her racial benchmarks, including the two lynched in Mississippi before

20

Emmitt Till boarded the train south. Selena had planted the seed for TC to come to Europe after he graduated high school if he didn't want to attend college. Brilliant and handsome, he deserved to be judged on his musical genius not the color of his skin, and not to be yanked out of a car and beat up and left for dead... Yes, even in L.A. Anywhere in America.

"Madame," said Lisette, interrupting Selena's inner reverie, "Zazu wants to know if you still want the crème fraiche brioche torte with fresh fruit poached in white wine for Sunday luncheon dessert?"

"Oui," Selena answered, thinking of her good friend Miles Syphax who loved that fruity dessert. "And the chocolate cake with the crème cheese icing."

"Of course," Lisette demurred with a smile.

Zack was right, they needed a place in Paris-proper. Doing a show and traveling out here was becoming a logistical hassle. Her rock, her husband Zack, kept her sane. She questioned how anyone would live in America if they have the means not to. Emmitt Till. Zack had held her through the tears over a boy she didn't know, yet knew too well. After sixty-seven minutes of deliberation, a jury of twelve white men acquitted the two other white men. Rigged. No women on jury, and no blacks were registered voters so they could not be called for jury duty. Acquitted of murder, and the grand jury decided not to even indict them for the kidnapping charges. Southern justice done and dispensed with left a bad taste in the mouths and hearts and souls of black folks everywhere. That's why on this day, Selena felt pride in Dr. T.R.M. Howard of Mississippi, a medical doctor and leader in the community, who had the money, prestige and guts enough to stand up and speak out. On November 27th in 1955 at Dexter Ave. Baptist Church, Dr. Howard was introduced by Reverend Martin

Luther King, Jr. and gave a fiery speech and, in the audience, sat Rosa Parks. Four days later, she thought of Emmett Till when she refused to give up her bus seat to a white man, thus sparking the Montgomery Bus Boycott. The climate of the nation and the world stood ready and waiting for a change. Enough was enough.

Selena admitted that she neither had the courage to participate in the movement nor the faith to allow her children, if she had any, to do so. Whether the Culhane children knew about civil rights or not, it was with great pride that Selena would call her niece long distance and wish her a happy birthday and tell her of this momentous occasion that occurred on her birthday, December 5th. Selena would assume the role of civil rights touchstone in their family and keep her nieces and nephew informed of the struggles and progress of their people.

~*~

Jaz chose to forgo the fancy outfits her Aunt Selena sent her from Paris, like the one she wore to her father's swearing in ceremony when he became captain of the LAPD, but she wouldn't give up going to the Boys Club. She continued to enjoy her forays into the all-male dominated world. Only now she dressed in her usual playtime clothes–shorts or pedal pushers, a matching top, Keds sneakers–all crowned with her signature hat, her dad's old fudge-brown, 1940s fedora. In her hand, her constant companion, a goodie bag stuffed with both Mary Janes and red jawbreakers for Dickie, although he was not always there. Not until her fifth visit did she notice a cute older girl with an upturned nose sitting on the first row opposite her and Dickie.

Good, another girl, Jaz thought as she adjusted her fudge fedora and sauntered over to greet her. *She must be here to see TC,* Jaz thought. She was his type.

"Hi," Jaz said approaching the girl.

"Hi," she replied.

"Here to see TC?" Jaz offered knowingly.

"Who?"

"My brother."

"No, my brother. Over there in the red shorts."

"Oh," Jaz eyed the curly-headed boy. "Figures. You two look alike. My brother and I, not so much." When she didn't reply Jaz forged on. "My brother is TC."

"Hmm," the girl replied absently.

"Want some candy?"

"No thanks."

"What's your name?"

"Denise. Denise Chandler."

"I'm Jaz Culhane."

"Oh, Coach Culhane's daughter. Nice."

"Yep." Jaz wondered if she'll ever have an identity all her own.

When practice was over the curly-headed boy jogged over to where his sister sat and pulled on a sweatshirt.

"Qwayz, this is Jaz. Coach Culhane's daughter."

"Hey. TC's sister," he said, further identifying her.

"Yep," Jaz said.

"We got to stop by the store and get lettuce," he reminded his sister.

"And those things for Melie," Denise teased.

"Denny. Dag. I'm not going to get—"

"I'm kidding, that's why I'm coming along," she said as they began walking off. "Oh, bye Jaz, nice meeting you," she managed before scurrying to catch up with her brother.

~*~

"Not a decision that should be left up to an eight-year-old," Lorette pressed as she passed the wet dish to her husband to dry.

"She's the one who'll have to adjust," Hep countered, drying and putting the dish in the cupboard. "Getting up hours earlier to get the bus before school and getting home late. Adding hours to her day. She won't be able to play outside with her friends."

"Oh Hep, she'll change friends a million times—"

"But not now, so young. It's up to her."

"Maybe I can pick her up after school if Mel—"

"Let me stop you right now. No. It just takes one time for Jaz to be waiting for you and you aren't there. Trauma."

"Trauma is not getting into a good college—"

"I don't think we'll have to worry about that. It's her decision."

Jaz had heard all the adult banter before about her, Ian Cummings, Echo Blake and Greg Minton going to another "better" school, Einstein Elementary. The four had vowed to stay at Park View with each other, where they ruled the math and science classes.

"Jaz?" her father called and laid out the familiar scenario. Jaz listened to the end and then replied. "I want to stay at Park View."

"But Jaz—" Lorette began.

"I want to stay."

"Alright, Punkin," her father decreed and looked from his daughter to his wife.

After the new school year began, only Echo Blake followed her mother's wishes and attended Einstein Elementary. Jaz recalled going and knocking on the door after school for her friend. Mrs. Blake indicated that either Echo was not at home yet or she was doing homework.

24

"She has a lot of homework Jaz because she is *going to be somebody.*"

"Thank you, Mrs. Blake," Jaz replied. "Tell her I said 'hi.'"

As Mrs. Blake closed the door without responding, Jaz glanced up to Echo's bedroom where her friend waved. Jaz smiled and returned the gesture. Mrs. Blake scowled at Jaz through the glass.

I am somebody already, Jaz thought. *Grown-ups sure have a thing about children "being somebody." Heck, we are children and have all our lives to grow up and figure out "what we're gonna be."* Mrs. Blake's strange statement reminded her of Lorette's reaction to Dickie when he came to apartment #3G to hang out with TC and the Dragons. "What's his claim to fame?" she asked and Jaz thought that an odd question.

"What do you mean?" she asked Lorette.

"He doesn't seem like the other boys."

Jaz hunched her shoulders as she walked back to Alvaro Street, thinking of how weird her mother was…as weird as Mrs. Blake. Adults.

~*~

On a typical hot, dry California day, Jaz and her friends were picking the players for double Dutch. They all offered one foot as Arnisha touched each one chanting, "Engine, engine, number nine, shooting down Chicago line. If the train should jump the track, do you want your money back?"

"Jaz, would you come up here please?"

Jaz's head jerked up to the window from which her father summoned her. *When did he get past me?* She thought. "But I'm up next on—" Her father's gaze stared her quiet. "Dag."

Jaz stomped in protest up the steps but getting to the final flight, she thought better of her insolence.

"Yes?" she asked, tempering her impatience.

"I wanted you to meet Gladys Ann McMillian," Hep said.

Jaz looked over to the couch and a girl about her age she hadn't noticed. "Hi," Jaz said and then smiled to Mr. McMillian, her father's old partner.

"We, Truck and I, thought it was time for you two to meet."

"Ok," Jaz said but the girl, Gladys Ann, failed to speak. "Wanna come outside with me? We're getting ready to jump double Dutch. You like double Dutch?" Jaz wanted to get back outside as quickly as possible.

The girl stared out the window speaking to no none. Jaz looked around and shrugged her shoulders. "What gives?" she mouthed to her father.

The girl bolted from behind the couch, ran into the bathroom with her father in hot pursuit. He knocked on the door and entered.

"What happened?" Jaz asked her father.

"Hmm. Perhaps, it was still too soon."

"For what?"

"C'mere Punkin." Hep sat facing his daughter on the couch, sunlight streaming through the window. "Gladys Ann's mother died a month ago and they were very close. Did most things together—"

"Like Mel and Lorette."

"Yes." Her revelation took Hep by surprise but, for expediency's sake, he agreed. "And this has made Gladys Ann very sad and we thought that if she met new friends and was around people who don't remember mother and daughter, it would help her move on."

Jaz nodded.

26

"So, this is where you come in. If anyone could be a good friend to a girl in need of one…it's you Punkin.'"

"Suppose she doesn't want to jump double Dutch or meet the girls in this neighborhood?"

"Who wouldn't want to be your friend?"

Jaz smiled. "I'll do what I can, Dad."

When Gladys Ann emerged from the bathroom with her father, Jaz asked, "Do you like jumping rope? Would you like to go downstairs? I could introduce you to my friends."

"No, thank you."

"We could play jacks on the stoop," Jaz tried. "Or go to the skating rink. Could you take us Daddy?"

"Sure can."

"No thank you." Gladys Ann nixed that plan.

Jaz was running out of ideas.

"Do you play Chinese checkers?" Gladys Ann asked.

"I'm the best in the family," Jaz teased, not wanting to stay inside, but she imagined how she'd feel if her father had died like Gladys Ann's mother. Jaz suspected the girl didn't want to meet anyone new right now. "I'll set them up."

Turned out Gladys Ann was in the other fourth grade class at Park View; and although they didn't share the same lunch and recess, and lived in opposite directions, they began meeting after school. Gladys Ann eventually met the girls in Jaz's neighborhood; Jaz relieved that Gladys Ann could almost jump double Dutch as well as she could. Almost. She seemed to fit in well with the "new" girls and Jaz eventually met Grandma Mac, the grandmother, who lived with Gladys Ann and her son in a nice house; each had their own bedroom. But Gladys Ann's neighborhood was dead compared to Jaz's Alvaro Street, populated with kids playing games, riding bikes and the ring of the ice cream trucks bells. Jaz predicted they could be friends with her missing her mother and Jaz missing Echo Blake.

"This might work out, Dad."

"Things usually do, Punkin.'"

~*~

Two men stood casually beneath the garage sign, "Red Ball Express," posing for the camera with cold beers in their hands. The camera snapped the picture as the men clicked the celebratory beers, drank a swig, toasting "To Range Criqui" as they saluted the sign.

"He shoulda been here," Skeekie decreed after a giant swallow.

"He is," Hep said with a wink.

Skeekie Benton, owner of Red Ball Express, and Hep Culhane, Range's childhood friend now police captain, remembered their mutual friend; one, a friend from his early years, the other from his last years, and both still missed him terribly.

"And to Mr. Walt Disney." Skeekie toasted again.

In '55 when Disney was behind schedule and hell-bent on finishing his theme park on time, Disneyland hired cadres of workers, black and white, to complete the project. Skeekie Benton was one of them who parlayed the salary and overtime and, after paying off his house, where Hep had arrested him two years before, bought this auto mechanic shop off Slauson. Skeekie poured all he'd learned compliments of the U.S. Army in World War II when he and Range Criqui ran the Red Ball Express carrying weapons, bombs, ammo, and whatever to the front line. Over the years, Skeekie Benton's Red Ball Express earned a reputation as the best mechanic shop in all of Watts. Captain Culhane had thrown business his way when the department's mechanic failed to tune the patrol cars to his liking. He had already entrusted his wife's Cadillac to

28

Skeekie's care. Hep hated that car as, initially, it had compromised his integrity, because no one could afford and maintain such a luxury car on a police department salary. The rumors of his being "on the take" flew until they discovered that his sister, Selena Fluellen, the wealthy chanteuse, not wanting to take the automobile to Paris, gifted the car to her sister-in-law and updated it every two to three years. Hep only drove it to Red Ball for maintenance and otherwise preferred his Dodge. The car was the one material thing Lorette loved, so he acquiesced since there was no house in the foreseeable future—not one that he wanted his family to inhabit. The Culhanes drove two cars when most families had none, a distinction that failed to impress Hep.

What began as a July vacation jaunt quickly became a tradition over the next few years when the Culhanes made an annual sojourn to Hep's home town, Colt, Texas for the entire summer, after school and the teams' playoffs ended hopefully in time for Founder's Day. That June day, set aside to honor Papa Colt and his boys, Micah Rudd, Joaquin Criqui, Josiah Pincus, Durango and Banyon who founded the small Texas enclave, served as a refuge for all. On that day, the town center–embellished by a manicured park with benches and a plaque gifted by "home-girl, woman," Selena Culhane, where the statue to the founders was erected by the townspeople years ago–pulsated with parades, fanfare, and speeches. The following Sunday the church service was crowned with a bazaar full of games, races, food, fun and other festivities.

Each year Coach Culhane made the pitch to Mrs. Scofield, Scoey's mother, to include him in the trip to Colt, Texas, offering to bring him back after a week if necessary. Every year she declined. When only nine years old, Scoey's dad left one night for cigarettes and never came back, and his mother was not taking any chances with her baby boy who, now at nearly thirteen, towered over her but she still wanted him close. Even his older sisters had said, "Let him go;" but Mama Scofield wouldn't hear of it; since Emmett Till's murder, no one even asked. So Scoey supplied TC with comic books for the trip and would wait for his best friend's return in August.

Now, the three Culhane children could stay all summer while their parents returned to L.A. after a week or so, sometimes with Mel, depending on her engagements.

Grandpapa Colt told Jaz that this time together was her parents' "second honeymoon." Jaz hated losing her father but readily adjusted since Lorette went back to L.A. with him, freeing her to have Big Fun. Grandma Keely wanted her grands to attend Vacation Bible School voluntarily, so the "heathen Culhane children" were not forced to attend and instead opted to sleep late, horseback-ride or meet friends at the swimming hole. However, Sunday mornings, they occupied permanent seats at Mt. Moriah Gethsemane Baptist Church where Keely reigned as resident organist and choir director. Mel started compiling her repertoire for Sunday services at Mount Moriah Church, selecting two hymns for every Sunday she was in attendance, adding a third song just in case she was asked. TC relished watching his grandmother operate the pump organ, and by that first mid-summer, he'd mastered it. Jaz adored sitting under Henley's steeple, so named for her uncle, her Dad's brother, who died as a child. The Culhanes had commissioned and imported a golden steeple that pierced the crystal blue sky; and for Jaz, sitting beneath it and watching the fractured sun prism through the stained-glass windows to kaleidoscope on the white walls proved exciting. She likened the entire church to watching a movie, only the actors were her grandmother, sister and brother...and her best friend Reba Gassaway, daughter of Reverend Gassaway, who could really sing.

When TC first heard Reba's soulful, powerful voice, it lifted him right out of his seat. He stood without realizing it, clapping at the end like it was a concert and the congregation indulged him with a slight smile as they were used to Reba's vocal abilities. TC could only imagine how she'd sound in a few years...with a mike in a studio. Reba wasn't the least bit interested in her gift, unlike his sister Mel who criticized

Reba's lack of professional training. His sister had a beautifully trained voice but Reba…was pure soul and all feeling. Mostly Reba and Jaz played like the childhood friends they'd become, while Mel worked hard to dazzle the church audience with her vocal acrobatics. TC thought if he could find Reba's voice in L.A. and introduce it on his own label… it'd be a hit. That's what he sought. TC had big plans he'd kept to himself as he had no time for naysayers who'd proclaim him too young and ambitious for such dealings. He coveted his dreams, held them close to make them come true.

TC learned to appreciate the various interests of his life and, once back in L.A., he adjusted to things he couldn't change and zeroed in on things he could. Mainly music. He and Scoey fell back into their best-friend rhythm but at his tender age and burgeoning stature, Scoey continued to be courted by various recreation centers in and around L.A. for football teams. Not only for his current moves but his evident potential. Often mistaken for Coach Culhane's son due to his size and complexion, Scoey took a quiet pride in the error though TC, built like an elegant Javier, bristled every time it happened. TC also didn't like that his father, now promoted to Captain of the LAPD, spent less time at the Boys Club and more at work, always going to or coming from the station. Hep carved out time on the weekends for them but the assistant coach ran the weekday practices. His father still used the club's conference room as an extension of the station as the gangs' informants preferred the Boys Club to downtown. TC knew his father continued to hold gang summits and receive info in that room because when TC came to practice after school he often heard, "Your dad was here earlier." With Scoey being so good at football and his father no longer coaching football, TC thought he'd try basketball, using that athletic interest as a decoy for his real love—music.

As a newly minted thirteen-year-old with a gleaming red birthday bike, his favorite color, TC took advantage of the freedom to explore his environs, riding out of the neighborhood, finding and taking new routes to the Boys Club. During these solo treks, TC thought of how to further his musical agenda: Find a voice like Reba's and record it. He decided that next year he would beg, borrow or steal a recording device—or perhaps ask his Aunt Selena to bring one with her. She wanted him in Paris after graduation. His father wanted him in college…but TC had other ideas. His exposure to Capitol Records recording sessions to witness full-blown orchestras accompanying his aunt, Miles Syphax, Nat King Cole, Frank Sinatra and other luminaries, solidified his dreams into achievable realities. TC soaked it all up like a sponge, flattered when he made suggestions that the musicians took and used. He had his idols like Ray Charles, who had kept his own masters, and Jackie Wilson's showmanship was inequivalent, but the incomparable Sam Cooke reigned at the top of his list as he'd not only moved from church to secular music like he hoped Reba would do, but he'd embraced the business aspect of the industry.

"Shit!" TC exclaimed, swerving and just missing an old man who swept his front sidewalk. The man cursed him. TC cursed him back.

TC saw and heard music everywhere. At basketball practice, he liked the resonant rhythm of the ball bouncing against the hardwood gym floor. When jettisoned to the outdoor courts, the ball's reverberating sound was missing, and he noticed the condition of the pocked asphalt, the tired posts, baskets without netting and how the rims dipped to one side.

"This is atrocious," he said to Qwayz.

"Use some of the change on that five-dollar word to pay for it," Qwayz quipped, posting and the ball went through. "All net—if there was one."

"Smart-ass," TC mumbled and then like a bolt, the idea came—an event to benefit the basketball court and raise money for equipment, a talent show where neighborhood kids could sign up and audition. It was only October with a few months until Christmas. That'd be how he'd find his Reba Gassaway now, for his later career. They could use records and a sound system or the Dragons who played instruments could be the backup band. Excited, TC asked Mel first.

"What's the prize?" she asked.

"What? It's a benefit for the Boys Club."

"Umm," she replied, uncommitted.

"Exposure," he added.

"I'll let you know."

Taking a cue from the movies his mother watched, TC obtained permission to "put on a show" for Christmas break and set about staging it himself. Unlike his sister, the other guys and gals shared his enthusiasm and then some, clamoring to be included. TC set up after school auditions, plowed through the list to decide who would and would not perform. For the band, TC had Scoey on sax and Carter Hix on drums. He played keyboards himself but had no guitar, which he could do without. From a distance, Qwayz watched the commotion with some interest and simply said, "Good idea, man. Let me know if I can help."

TC never did, but later, he noticed how Qwayz controlled the flow of contestants, and how he negotiated the additional chairs needed once Aunt Selena and Uncle Zack volunteered to do a song or two. Sales soared and Qwayz, without being asked, procured the roll of tickets to sell and later handed off the money to TC.

34

"Thanks man. Never thought of half this stuff," TC admitted one day.

"You got a lot on your plate, man," Qwayz said and walked off.

He is a midget, TC thought.

The First Annual Boys Club Benefit went off without a hitch. No Reba among them but there were first, second and third place ribbons with plenty of bragging rights. TC'd had a taste of production. Selena Fluellen, as mistress of ceremony, kept the audience off balance between laughter and awe, electrifying the crowd. To close the show, she forced everyone to stand and sing "Lift Every Voice," at the end of which she said, "OK, there were a lot of mouth-fakers in the audience. I'm putting you on notice that next year when I come back, you all better know the words."

The crowd laughed, whooped and hollered at the prospect that there would be a Second Annual Boys Club Benefit. "I'm inviting some of my friends next year and you all will *not* embarrass me!" she sassed and then bid everyone a "Merry Christmas."

She knew the folks of Watts would buzz about the event for months to come as few could neither afford a ticket to hear her sing here at the Hollywood Bowl nor fly to Paris. "Ah, one more thing," she announced, snatching back the mike from its cradle. "Me and my man have a check for these hardworking fellas." She summoned Scoey who brought a mock-up check for presentation to The Watts Police Boys Club. "This ought to buy you a few new uniforms. Pick something pretty. I'm partial to purple but you all decide. To the Dragons… job well done."

TC, along with his boys who strung across the stage posing for a picture for a *Jet* magazine photographer, accepted

35

the check. TC looked down the line of his teammates who'd made his vision a reality. "Hold up," TC said. "Where's Qwayz? Is Qwayz out there?"

Qwayz appeared from the sidelines and watched TC summon him on stage. Qwayz ascended the steps and went next to TC. "Now you can take the picture," TC said. As the camera snapped amid the crowd's loud applause, TC asked, "You play an instrument?"

"Yeah. Guitar."

TC's face beamed. "Cool beans."

5

Nothing titillated Jaz and all her senses like going to the movies. Heaven on earth. She loved plunking down her twenty-five cents in exchange for a full day of enchantment. She bought popcorn with a squirt of real butter for an extra ten cents, took a plush velvet seat, and vanished into the quiet where her world expanded by leaps and bounds. Partial to Westerns with the wide-open spaces and men and women in clearly defined roles–reminded her of Colt, Texas–and she could get lost for hours. She would get there in time for the previews of "Coming Attractions," followed by the main feature and then a second feature and, on Saturdays, cartoons. Whether by herself or in the company of the friends she met there or with her family… it was magic. When she went with her family, Lorette and Mel talked too much like they were riding in a car going someplace. But when she went with her father or got a ride with TC and his friends and they went upstairs to the balcony, Jaz had the downstairs to herself and total peace. Dickie also talked too much but eventually got the message and he would leave and come back. Jaz, absorbed in the dialogue or the places the movies took her, ignored him. None could compete with the houses, cars and clothes… Jaz wasn't in Watts anymore.

Once her father got the promotion, the movies defined their private time. TC found his stride in basketball and girls, not necessarily in that order, and Mel still preferred no other company but her own. That left Jaz and her father to do what they loved: going to the movies. Quiet claimed them during the show, and they used lunch afterwards to discuss the issues.

Once all things cartoon-colorful and Disney were seen, her father branched out to movies he wanted to see and were appropriate for his young, inquisitive daughter. He was impressed with Jaz's comprehension of *Giant,* amazed at how well she understood the racial and prejudicial overtones. How she liked Elizabeth Taylor's role because "she was her own woman and didn't care what the men said or thought about her." Yet, Jaz couldn't grasp *Raintree County* at all. Hep treated Jaz to her favorite–Dorothy Dandridge in *Carmen Jones*–and afterwards, suggested that she not tell her mother that they saw it; neither Lorette nor the "Catholic Standard's Legion of Decency" would approve. Over lunch, usually at The Lobster House on the Santa Monica Pier, Hep would field all the questions from his daughter.

A lot of the Dandridge movie went over her head. "Why did Joe kill her?" Jaz asked.

Hep explained to her satisfaction and relayed that *Carmen Jones* was a remake of an opera by Bizet. "Was Dorothy Dandridge in that, too? Did you see it?"

After dissecting the Western, *The Big Country,* they volleyed into a discussion of how it was for him and Selena growing up on a Texas ranch. Jaz shared how much she looked forward to returning this summer and her plans. The father and daughter talked from one meal to the next, often walking off one and starting all over again with a different menu at a different place. Jaz savored the time with her Dad who made her feel listened to and important. Dad and the movies, absolutely the most perfect day!

Lorette often complained of the living room of apartment #3G being "Boys Club West," at least for Saturday mornings when all the boys seemed to congregate in front of the floor model, console TV to see *Monster Mash Theater,* Western serials, and *Sky King* with his niece Penny. Jaz, partial to the

38

later, had no interest in monsters or scary movies, although
Gladys Ann and Mel loved them; Jaz thought real life scary
enough. She often disappeared into TC's room to look at his
little portable set on top of his dresser with frequent visits from
Dickie, Gladys Ann and Qwayz when commercials came on.
She looked at the movies and Dickie hung in with her the
longest until he started asking questions and she put him out.

"Commercial over!" would summon her visitors back to
the monsters. Jaz hung around the guys for the eventual trip to
movies. Older by a few years, Carter Hix was the first to have
a car, paid for from his after-school job at Briscoe Printing
Company. He and his girlfriend, Lorraine, piled in the front
with TC riding shotgun on the outside, while Jaz and Gladys
Ann sat on Qwayz and Scoey's laps in the back squeezed in
with two other Dragons.

"God, your boney butt is cutting into my leg," Qwayz
complained, shifting Jaz to one side.

Jaz and Gladys Ann, knees touching, faced one another
with their heads pushed up into the roof of the car. They both
watched as Carter Hix's right hand disappeared up Lorraine's
skirt. They eyed one another with sheer horror scrambling their
faces. Eyebrows raised to the top of their foreheads and their
mouths formed a collective "O." When they lit from the car,
she and Gladys Ann often met Dickie in the lobby, and when
the guys and girls went upstairs to the balcony, Jaz and Gladys
Ann couldn't wait to comment.

"Did you see that nasty boy and girl?" Jaz asked Gladys
Ann.

"Can you believe that? Disgusting. She's going straight to
hell."

"She didn't even sock him in the face!"

39

When Jaz went to the concession stand for a Mr. Goodbar, she slipped upstairs to the balcony to see just what those boys were doing with those girls.

"Hey, TC man, your sister's up here," one of them said, breaking suction with their girl long enough to tattle.

"Jaz! C'mon now! You want to go back home?" TC admonished.

Wordlessly, Jaz scurried back down stairs and assumed her seat just as Gregory Peck, the dude from back East, beat the snot out of Charlton Heston, the tough ranch foreman in *The Big Country.*

At the end Gladys Ann asked, "Can you believe old man Hannassey shot his own son?"

"Can you believe that he went on to be 'The Rifleman' on television?"

"I guess that's what they call 'acting."

After the show, the guys headed to the beach, Part II of the girlfriend dates, so Jaz and Gladys Ann were dropped off at home. "I guess we're too young for the beach," Jaz smirked.

~*~

TC continued to come into his own as he sped about on his red bike. Scoey continued to be pursued by various football teams in and around Watts. "Maybe my ticket to college, man," Scoey said to TC, who liked "men" who had plans for their futures. TC sped his way to practices in his red chariot, down the sidewalks, weaving in and out to avoid pedestrians and other obstacles. He used this time to not only explore his environment but also his mind as he searched for meaning and pondered his future, positive his father had done the same at his age. Now a bike, later a car…where all men contemplate the trajectory of their lives.

Even with all the pomp and circumstance at his father's swearing in, TC couldn't shake the undercurrent he was sure

40

his mother and sisters did not feel. A man thing. Unlike music, TC couldn't put his finger on it but knew his father's acceptance in LAPD was minimal. He felt the white cops waited for his father to fail. But they didn't know his Dad. Hepburn Henley Culhane didn't fail. He converted folks to his way of thinking.

TC ventured on that male path to adulthood. As a bona fide teenager, soon he'd be in high school. Although his parents spoke of college, TC failed to see the need to spend four years unlearning and relearning a system that obviously he didn't need; Things he wanted to study and explore could not found in college. The offer from his Aunt Selena and Uncle Zack to live in Europe stayed in the back of his mind, but he wanted to stay in the USA, to make his mark. He studied the American recording artists he admired, and he not only wanted to write and arrange but sing, create groups and single artists, while maintaining complete control. As the wind blew in his face, he added owning his own studio and label, eventually branching out into jazz. He grew excited by his pet innovation, the one element missing in today's music: a boy and girl duo. Listening to the songs blare out from Jaz's transistor radio, Fats Domino, Chuck Berry, Sam Cooke and Jackie Wilson… few female voices gathered some acclaim. But he figured Jaz's entire group will be in their teen years soon and want to hear their voices represented; their puppy-love feelings sung about and then beyond that… a male/female thing. All these ideas swirled in his head which he shared with no one.

TC zoomed around a slow couple on the sidewalk. He got so fired up when he thought of all he had to do and probably only three or four years to make it happen, to be taken seriously by his parents. He needed revenue to set up his own

41

studio. That's why he paid special attention in Mr. Goldstein's Economics 101 on stocks and bonds. TC recognized that the stock market was how white folk made money. When Goldstein asked the class, "Who has a social security number?" TC was the only one to raise his hand to which Dickie quipped, "My daddy don't have a Social Security number." TC chuckled with everybody else but paid close attention to the special project to pick stocks, make fake investments and chart the gains and losses. TC selected International Business Machines and Coca-Cola and mapped their progress intently. He stuffed the *Wall Street Journal* under his bed the way his friends hid girlie magazines. Back when he had more car time with his dad riding to and from practices or to the beach, TC shared the stock market info with his impressed father. TC got an A in the class. Because of his interest, excelling on the project and having a Social Security number, Mr. Goldstein suggested that TC actually invest in the market. TC told his father and asked his Aunt Selena and Uncle Zack to help him find a broker to buy shares with his own money from the song and his allowance. His father consented and after a year, the three adults and TC were amazed at the stocks' progress with no added attention. The shares had "split," multiplied and grew in value. Eventually, TC returned to his main interest in basketball, music and making his dreams come true and forgot about his portfolio, only looking at it once a year to ensure he wasn't losing money, only gaining. He also remained preoccupied with improving the Boys Club Annual Benefit and finding an untamed voice like Reba Gassaway's locally. That voice haunted him. Mel's voice soared and rattled the rafters, readying her for what she wanted—to star on Broadway. But Reba? That girl could shake, rattle and rock your soul; "squalling" like they do in church.

"Shit!" TC skidded almost hitting that same old white man sweeping the sidewalk.

"Hey. Kid. Look out!"

TC needed to concentrate or he wouldn't live to accomplish any of his dreams. As he eyed the fortress into which the man disappeared and shut the door tight, he read "West Coast Studios" on the sign over the door.

With the five hit songs he had composed for his aunt which had already been covered as standards by noted singers, TC had been reading liner notes and album covers since he was six. Now he was acknowledged on them. He wondered if this West Coast Studios was the famed studio on all the old records. *Couldn't be,* TC thought, as he made the light and raced to the Boys Club. That rundown building where that old man swept every day about this time was hardly a place where old musicians and vocalists recorded and taped classic records and held legendary session gigs. TC made a mental note to stop and ask. Right now, he would be late to basketball practice.

Every chance he got, TC changed his schedule to go to Capitol Records with his aunt and uncle and witness her record duets with Miles Syphax, Johnny Hartman, Frank Sinatra, or Tony Bennett—that more valuable than a college education. TC loved to watch the star vocalist amid a full orchestra. The sound, the swell and feel of violins reverberating and swirling around you, absent in today's music. "Blueberry Hill" didn't have strings—great piano, no violins. He relished his aunt and Joe Williams or Billy Eckstine singing to each other, even better than seeing them on Miles' television show because at Capitol they did several takes. TC envisioned that kind of connection with a guy and girl of his sisters' age. *That'd be sweet!* TC thought as he barreled through the club's fence and parked his bike by the gym.

The next day, TC raced his bike and, upon seeing the man in front of West Cost Studios, stopped.

"You're a menace!" the man shouted with raised fist.

"Is this *the* West Coast Studios where Coltrane and Ray Charles cut their records?" TC asked.

The wizened old man eyed this young whippersnapper and asked "How do you know about that?"

"I read. Well, is it?"

"One in the same," the man said proudly.

"Can I see inside?"

The old man huffed an audible response, made gestures and finally said, "OK. I've got to be careful. A lot of hooligans in this area." As he opened the door, TC dismounted his bike and rolled it on behind the man. "You can't bring that bike in here!"

"Why not? Can't leave it outside. Might be stolen by some 'hooligans.'"

"Ah, a wisenheimer, huh?" He motioned TC in then closed and locked the door behind him. "Put it over there against the wall."

"Why is it so dark in here?" TC asked.

"What do you need light for? All fortressed up from the outside so nobody can get in. There are some windows up near the rafters." He pointed. "C'mon then."

"I'm TC."

"Your parents named you TC?"

"Yep."

"I'm Mr. Alperstein."

They passed one small room off on the left side where TC glanced in at a single bed where apparently Mr. Alperstein sometimes stayed. The entire entrance smelled like musk,

44

canned food and old man. An ample reception foyer with a broken-down couch and Studio 1 straight head. They walked past a Studio 2 on the way to Studio 3 which TC liked immediately. They walked into a large anteroom with some seats before getting to the largest of the studios. Tucked at the very end of the hall, this would be his private world. The equipment was as old as Mr. Alperstein, but TC could tell the layout had good bones and a boatload of potential. Behind the exit from Studio 3 was a back door that led to the alley.

"What's upstairs?" TC asked.

"Another floor and a bunch of junk."

"Where do you live?"

"In the front room we passed on the way here."

"No house?"

"My wife passed. Lost it and moved in here. Don't need a whole house. Got a bed and a hot plate."

"You got no family?"

"Not to speak of."

That's how it began. A knowledgeable and inquisitive boy stopped by a lonely old man's studio. TC returned often, especially on the rare occasion that someone booked time to use the facility. He tried to engage the man in what he could do with the place: Spruce it up, replace some of the equipment gradually, charge competitive rates for cutting a demo, providing studio time or just rehearsal space, since there was no place like that in Watts for musical acts. Musicians often rehearsed at Shanghai's and Sugar Dee's, providing a free concert for the neighborhood. Alperstein balked and gradually relented since the boy said, "Wouldn't cost you nothing."

They split the take 60/40 until clients started asking for the "young brother."

"He's in school," Alperstein would tell them.

TC started hanging out more at West Coast Studios, making recommendations, re-interpreting music, essentially arranging and re-arranging the musicians' old pieces. When TC's schedule became dominated by basketball games and he didn't come as much, Alperstein hated to admit he missed the young brash boy. He was good. Alperstein liked watching his brain work and his suggestions were right on the money. Slowly, TC brought other guys in, introducing them to him; and Alperstein begrudgingly recognized when they weren't around, it was lonely.

Soon even more musicians came in specifically for "Youngblood" and his guys who played instruments for solo vocalists. "The acoustics here are boss!" TC decreed and then negotiated a change in the split so he could pay his session musicians: Carter Hix, Scoey, Qwayz, Zion Blassingame, and Jaxson Henderson who, with the improved acoustics, could sound like a full orchestra. TC realized that Scoey's and Qwayz's interests in music wasn't as strong as their desire for college, so he made few demands on them. Often TC doubled up on keyboards, organ, sax and guitar if necessary, but mostly he worked around them and laid their tracks later. Basketball and staging the benefit remained important but this music, played in this studio, reigned supreme… It was all he could do to make believe he cared about school and graduating, not knowing how to fake three more years. He had found his career niche. Loved and enjoyed and was validated by it. Teachers admired him as he knew some of the Cs should have been lower but he didn't have the interest. He took the average grade with gratitude. But when his idol Sam Cooke walked in one day to "check it out"–a sign from God that he was on the right track–TC was done!

~*~

"You must go to school, Jaz," Lorette said. "You cannot stay home and lay around. You say you're sick, but have no fever. Where do you hurt?"

Jaz breathed pure exasperation. She went to the bathroom again, came back out and flopped on the couch.

"This is totally unacceptable," Lorette continued.

"I want my father."

"What?"

Jaz repeated herself and Lorette dug in. "We will not be disturbing your father at work for this nonsense."

"It's not 'nonsense.' I'm dying and I want to see my father."

"I'm not so sure just who is the dramatic queen of this family. You or your sister. But his day will not be interrupted by an eleven-year-old girl—"

"You don't like me. I don't like you. I don't know what I ever did to you but be born. Please, just call my daddy."

The words slapped Lorette in the face like a wet, dead fish. The truth stung Lorette's ears. She had never talked to her mother like this. Never known any child who had been so... ungrateful. "You are the adult," she heard her husband's words and began, "Jaz, I love you. You are my child, my second daughter—"

"Save it for the eulogy, Lorette. Shall you call my daddy, or will I?"

Lorette returned to the living room and said, "Your father will be here as soon as he can."

"Thank you," Jaz managed, wondering if Lorette had really called. She crossed her arms over her stomach and rolled onto the side of the couch cushions away from the sight of her hypocritical mother.

Dealing with such a headstrong, smart girl like Jaz is trying in more ways than one, Lorette thought, just as Hep came through the door. Upon seeing Jaz stretched out on the couch as he had never before, he eyed his wife and went to his little girl.

"Oh Daddy!" Jaz released all the pent-up turmoil she was holding inside. She choked on tears and held him around his neck.

Lorette cut her eyes at the showy display.

"Punkin' talk to me. Where does it hurt?" He gingerly felt her bones. "Do we need to go to the doctor?"

"No, it's too late for that," Jaz sobbed and Lorette actually felt her daughter's pain. "I'm going to die. I'll never graduate from high school or college. Or fall in love, or get married—"

"Jaz!" Hep caught her attention. "Tell me where it hurts?"

"I don't hurt but I'm bleeding."

"What?"

"I'm bleeding and it won't stop. I can't make it stop. I'm going to run out of blood."

"Where are you bleeding?"

Jaz couldn't speak. Embarrassed, she finally pointed down toward her legs. Hep whipped back the comforter, looked and didn't see any blood. She leaned in and whispered in his ear.

Relief washed his face, he smothered a chuckle before soothing her with, "It's alright Punkin'. What you are experiencing is normal and natural for girls to go through. I assure you, you are not dying."

"Promise?"

"I promise. Now, go into the bathroom, take a shower and your mother will come in and talk to you."

"Why can't you—"

48

"No, Jaz. This is your mother's domain."

Jaz rolled from the couch and made her way to the bathroom. "If you are wrong, will you have TC play 'Canadian Sunset' at my funeral?"

Hep answered her with a reassuring smile and said, "How about I stop off and get some ice cream on the way home for dessert tonight?"

"If I'm still here." She closed the door.

Lorette's voice lilted in laughter. "Can you imagine? She is so young. Mel didn't get her—"

"Lorette, Jaz is not Mel or vice versa. Do you think you can give her what she needs in terms of instruction and equipment or do you want me to stop off at the drugstore on my way home?"

"No. I can handle it from here."

"Are you sure?" He tempered the edge on his voice, the disappointment still evident.

"I didn't know and she wouldn't confide in—"

"I will see you all tonight after work." Hep picked up his hat, opened the door and left, reminding himself that he will have to have "the talk" about the birds and bees with his daughter. He could not leave it to his wife.

6

The gray Dodge, weighed down with the Culhane family plus one, Quinton Regis Chandler IV, left Los Angeles for Colt, Texas. On the heels of the *Look* magazine article in which the two white men, protected by double jeopardy and paid four thousand dollars for the interview, freely admitted to murdering Emmett Till, Mrs. Scofield unequivocally would not allow Scoey to enjoy the wide-open spaces of Texas for any part of the summer. But Ma Vy said "yes" so fast Hep's head snapped. Qwayz was the one with reservations and concerns—not about going Down South but leaving his post at home as the "man of the house" and protector of the family of women. He'd quizzed Coach Culhane about the logistics and, after being assured Hep would bring him back in a week if he needed, Qwayz consented. Ma Vy whispered to the coach, "Keep him," and gave him a gift to give her son later on his twelfth birthday that she intended for him to celebrate in Colt, Texas. "I will miss my boy like gangbusters but he really needs this. Thank you, Coach Culhane."

Qwayz then carried Amber, his Dad's guitar, past the adults standing on the porch. "Qwayz, I don't think there is room—"

"We'll make room, Ma Vy," Hep said.

She smiled in reply and added, "He seldom goes many places without her. My men love that guitar."

When all finally settled into the Dodge, TC behind his mother, Jaz behind her father, Mel in the middle with her train case, movie magazines and cat-eye sunglasses, and Qwayz on TC's side sharing the window, they bid final goodbyes.

50

"You have the number to Cherokee Ranch and Qwayz'll call you in the evenings," Hep repeated.

"That's fine. Have a good time, son," Ma Vy said, waving and throwing a kiss. Once the car turned the corner, she wiped away a tear or two. "Lord, watch over my boy."

With all that TC had to show Qwayz the first week whizzed by. TC enjoyed his old Colt friends but relished having a like-minded individual with him. Unlike his Colt buddies, Qwayz was also blown away by Reba's voice on that first Sunday and looked forward to a repeat performance the following Sabbath. Qwayz took to horses, their riding and their care; and both L.A. boys schooled Colt guys on the art of basketball with the hoop that Hep and Papa Colt erected for their pleasure. As usual everyone took to the outgoing, easily likeable Qwayz and Papa Colt waited on the front porch with his liquid refreshment every night for Qwayz to play something on that guitar. The young boy accompanied himself, to which TC noted, "You got a good voice, too."

"It's no Reba and it's gonna change," Qwayz quipped.

"I got time," TC said.

As the weeks went on, Qwayz's calls to his mother were predictably distracted as Colt, Texas brimmed with fun at every turn. With his looks, he'd won the affection of many a Colt cutie of all ages; and because of his impeccable manners, Keely playfully confided to Selena, "I'm in love." If around, Qwayz offered to carry the wash or volunteered for other chores without being asked, and Keely proclaimed, "raised well."

Mostly, the male pair lived at the swimming hole, everyone's favorite place to pass the hot, days of Texas. Not quite sure how to carry himself with TC and the older guys around adoring girls, Qwayz preferred the water and racing, since he didn't know much about girls who were not like his sister, Denny.

"Watch you doing?" Qwayz came over to Jaz dripping wet.

"Look at you. All pruney." She brushed water from her towel. "You having a good time?"

"Am I ever. I never knew a place like this existed." He plopped on the grass by the bank of the water. "Well, maybe one. My dad would talk about Myrtle Beach."

"In the Caribbean?"

"Naw. Making his way to L.A. he stopped and worked awhile in Myrtle Beach. He loved that place. Said one day we'd go back. Just the two of us. Man to man, you know."

Silence claimed Jaz. She knew they never made it. The quiet deafening, she finally said, "Maybe one day you'll get there."

"Yeah. Hope so. Won't be the same."

Jaz wasn't used to this Qwayz.

"Look at Miss Thang over there," he teased, looking at Mel to get off of the subject.

Jaz eyed her sister who sat well away from the water and screamed bloody murder when anyone came near and threatened her hair or movie magazine with a drop of wetness.

"She just has to be a star. I hate to think what will happen to her if she doesn't 'make it'," Jaz lamented.

"Already has. How many girls or even adults have achieved what she has?" Qwayz pondered.

Jaz hunched her shoulders and asked, "How is she in school? You all are in the same class?"

Qwayz thought as if he hadn't realized it. "We're not in the same classes. I don't see much of her. She keeps to herself. They think she's stuck-up, but I just think she doesn't waste her time with classmates who don't share her interests."

52

"Yeah, I'm sure TC has the same thing," Jaz remarked.

"I guess anybody can seem stuck-up if you don't know them. But everybody loves TC!"

"He has a winning personality."

"Qwayz you coming back in?" someone yelled from behind.

"My fan club awaits," Qwayz teased and cannonballed back into the water with a splash.

After Reba finished "Old Rugged Cross" in church that Sunday, TC told Qwayz, "Next year I'm going to bring a recorder and get her voice on tape."

"What about Yvette? She's got a good voice, too."

"You can record her."

Qwayz smiled at the thought of his coming back to Colt, Texas next year. As per their nightly tradition, they sat on the porch to watch the sun set. TC played the piano, accompanying his own voice, joined by Qwayz on his guitar, Amber.

"You all are good enough to be on the TV like Selena," Papa Colt enthused.

The next morning the boys woke to wolf-down and satisfy their ravenous appetites with Keely's breakfast. "Did you all taste it?" she asked and warned the boys to complete their chores before hopping on horses and riding range. Selena came up behind her brother, knowing he was thinking about the carefree days when he and his buddy Range Criqui did the same things.

"Getting ready to head back?"

"Yep. Duty calls."

"Well, I can see the pink train case is ready but don't see Amber," Selena chuckled.

"Surprisingly, Qwayz is staying."

"It's good for him. For them. Who would want to leave a place like this?"

"We did. Three of us did."

"I'll be back in a couple of weeks. You'll still be here?"

"That's the plan. Summer and Christmas, I come home. Get my fill, do my do, and then head back to Paris."

"Works for you."

"Yeah, it do," she teased.

Selena watched the boys gallop all over the prairie, kicking up dust, before taking their horses into to barn to cool them down. Next, they would head for the swimming hole. Knowing their routine, she poured a glass of sweet tea over ice and sauntered out back and caught the last of a porch-step conversation between Jaz and Reba.

"Pinky-swear. Brown skinned beauties we are," Jaz and Reba repeated simultaneously as they interlocked their little fingers and pulled them apart before dissolving into laughter and running off to share more secrets.

Selena stood there and let her eyes fill with tears. Not only TC and Qwayz reminded her of Hep and Range, but now these girls made her think of herself and her sister Star who had invented the saying.

"We're leaving, Sis," Hep interrupted her reverie. Seeing the tears, he asked, "What's the matter?"

As he caught the last glimpse of his daughter's disappearing sneakers, Selena shook her head wordlessly, not trusting her voice. She leaned her head on his shoulder for an instant as if to calm her thoughts. "They just did a pinky-swear. Brought back memories. Plus, I hate to see you go," she tried to cover.

"You care as much as my children do," Hep teased. "Except Mel. She's ready to go. Bigger fish to fry."

54

"I miss Star more when we are here. At Cherokee Ranch where we last saw her. She's everywhere around here." She hugged her baby brother once before releasing him. "You think we'll ever see her again?"

"We'll find her. One day."

"You can't believe that, Hep. With all our money and efforts, we haven't so far. We'll find remnants of her."

"C'mon. Is it your time of the month?" he teased and she slapped him playfully on the upper arm.

"I love you," he said.

"Back atcha, my brother."

"Bye, Selena," Lorette said as she came into the kitchen.

"Safe travels." Selena walked the pair to the porch and car, Mel already ensconced in the back seat with a scarf tied fashionably over her head, and waved as the Dodge disappeared over the horizon.

~*~

"Listen," TC paused and Qwayz stopped his advance.

"All I hear is crickets and the waterfall calling, man."

"Shush." TC crept slowly like an army soldier advancing on a target. "It's Reba."

They waited to identify the song. "Who's that singing with her?"

"Don't know."

"Oh, Mary, don't you weep... Tell Martha not to moan." The voices blended and soared, becoming absorbed by the canopy of trees. The girls had slowed the hymn down to a mournful, soulful rendition that filled the hot, still air. The two guys peeped up and saw Reba and her friend with eyes closed, backs against the boards of the wooden shed.

"It's Jaz!" TC announced.

"Really?" Qwayz looked up and then ducked back to incognito status.

Reba wailed to a closing and Jaz accompanied her with rhythmic claps and woeful runs. "Who knew Jaz could carry a tune?" TC asked his friend.

"OK," Jaz jumped up at the end. "Now it's water time."

"See, she has no interest in singing. She did that so Reba would go swimming."

"Fair exchange ain't no robbery," Qwayz quipped. "Cool water awaits us, too. Let's go."

After dinner, Papa Colt sat at the piano and tinkled with the keys, a flat out full invitation for his grandson to join him… and the party began. In earlier times they passed the night by watching the sunset from the porch swing but that developed into an impromptu concert between grandfather and grandson trying to outdo one another on the 88s.

"They both play like they're in a Texas whorehouse in 1940s," Selena said to Zack.

"And just how would you know?" Zack teased.

Once they'd worked up a sweat and Grandma Keely could stand it no longer, they asked Qwayz to play something on Amber and sing. Keely liked that. No matter what Qwayz sang, Papa Colt liked him to finish with "Danny Boy" and he'd slap his knees with all the trills and runs the young visitor did with his voice. TC delighted in seeing his boy sing it like Jackie Wilson himself. "Qwayz's a ham," TC interjected with admiration.

"How do you know how Jackie Wilson does it?" Selena asked.

"We've seen him. Dad took us."

"For real?" Jaz challenged. "You lie."

"Square business. Dad takes us to some of the shows with Scoey, plus Carter Hix."

56

"Oh, I wanna go," Jaz enthused.

"No, you don't. It's rough there. Not a place for my sisters."

After a few weeks, Jaz found Qwayz on the side porch with a speckled black and white composition book and a pen. "What you doing? Practicing your autograph?"

He quickly closed the book and asked, "What?"

"That's what Mel does. Practices for when she's famous. What are you doing?"

Qwayz looked over at the corral and then around before confiding, "I write lyrics."

"What?"

"Music. And words to go with the songs."

"For real?"

"Yep."

"Anything you want to share?"

"Nope.

Jaz took no offense and said, "I wish Denny would come."

"Fat chance. She's not leaving that house. Or rather our mother. She thinks if she does, Ma will die. She thinks if she'd stayed home the night of Daddy's death he would not have died."

"Really?"

"Yeah. It's complicated."

"Good SAT word." Jaz continued, "It's a game TC and I play about the SATs."

"Qwayz can I see you for a minute?" Hep asked, sticking his head out of the screen door.

"Sure, Mr. C."

Jaz watched him leave and wondered what he did wrong to get a private audience with her father.

The pair walked past the mammoth fireplace with Papa Colt's treasured heirloom relics: the Winchester rifle, pearl-handled Colt .45 guns, the eagle feather symbolizing his father, the cowrie shell from Africa brought by his mother threaded through worn, leather string. Qwayz followed Mr. C into Papa Colt's study on the side of the house, where Hep, Selena and Star used to listen to secular, contraband jazz records; the room that housed all the classic books Colt Culhane read over the years on the trail and beyond—thanks to Gideon who taught him to read at twelve years of age. Qwayz looked around the room and Hep invited him to sit as he explained the significance of the room, the artifacts in it and on the fireplace they passed.

"Where and who you come from is very important," Hep began.

"Yes, sir."

"We all have a rich heritage. Some we know of and some we don't. Things that tie us to the past, sometimes determine the future. Or at least anchor you in ways that remind you what you're made of, what you can withstand. How valued you are as a person."

Qwayz looked at Mr. C and nodded in polite agreement.

"I know it's your birthday today."

Qwayz's face split into a wide grin.

"Your mother gave me something special to give to you on this day. She knew you'd stay the whole time."

"I like it here. I guess I'm trying to figure out why you ever left."

They both chuckled.

"Becoming twelve years old is important for a boy. You stand on the threshold of manhood." Hep knew twelve to be the age when his father lost Aunt Pearl and was left in the world alone, to fend for himself. Hep couldn't recall much

58

about his twelfth birthday, except that it was two years after Star left; she'd sent him birthday cards from New Orleans. "Your mother gave me a gift for you from your father."

Qwayz looked at Coach C, the reference to his father, Quinton Regis Chandler III, taking him by surprise.

"Your mother said it was important that you get it *on* your actual birthday so, you can receive it like he did from his father." Hep handed Qwayz an exquisitely wrapped box.

Qwayz took it, opened it and immediately recognized the contents. On a bed of cotton lay a solid gold St. Christopher medallion that his father always wore. "I wondered what happened to this," he said quietly as tears sprang to his eyes. Qwayz ran his thumb over the engraved relief. He didn't speak and Hep didn't interrupt the apparent memories of his dad, flooding back.

Hep stood and said, "I'll leave you to—"

"Would you put it on me first?" Qwayz stood and turned his back to Coach C.

The round gold piece dangled mid-chest and Hep said, "You'll grow to it."

"I will," Qwayz declared, fingering his father's gift.

"He'd be mighty proud of you, Qwayz. The man you are becoming."

Qwayz bit his lip, shook his head in agreement but could only voice, "Hope so."

"Stay in here as long as you like," Hep said as he opened the door.

"Can I call my mother?"

"Sure."

"Where's Qwayz?" TC asked, trying to look past his father as he closed the door behind him.

"In Papa Colt's study. Leave him be. He'll come out when he's ready."

Qwayz managed a private call to his mother and slipped pass the kitchen to take a walk. His father had been on his mind recently more so than usual and Qwayz thought it was because this place reminded him of the Myrtle Beach as his dad had described. The young man-child walked with his father and the medallion he wore before returning to the Culhane house. When he did, "Surprise!!" almost knocked him back through the screen door. The Culhane family and all the friends made during this summer surrounded him and sang "Happy Birthday" as Keely walked into the room with the biggest coconut cake he had ever seen.

After consuming homemade ice cream, playing games and finally quieting down for the night, Qwayz said, "Grandma Keely. That is my favorite cake of all time!"

"I know," she smiled.

"Thank you! I really appreciate it."

"My pleasure." She ruffled his curly hair.

"It's the cooked, marshmallow icing that makes it," Selena interjected. "No one does it better."

"I don't think I've had a birthday party since... I was six," he pondered aloud. "This was real special."

"You all better go to bed," Hep said. "We're getting an early start back to L.A. tomorrow."

7

As Captain Culhane offered a smattering of applause for the most recent distinction, he thought of how much Lorette would have loved to be at the Fraternal Order of Police Awards Banquet, held in the posh Ambassador Hotel's Grand Ballroom. She would have been the Belle of the Ball in her new dress, as they all loved her and she had been looking forward to dancing the night away to the live band. He always admired her ability to captivate men and women of any race with her Southern drawl and gracious personality, but cramps claimed her earlier, though she had fought the good fight and loss. He promised to get her new bottle of Midol and hand-packed butter brickle ice cream on his way home. Hep glanced at his watch just as an officer approached. "Excuse me, Captain Culhane. Would you follow me please?"

Hep did as requested until they left the ballroom proper and headed for a nearby elevator. Clearly, he was not getting a "surprise" award. "Where are we going?" he asked the officer he did not know or recognize.

"Your indulgence, sir. All will be revealed."

"You tell me now or we go no further," Hep boomed just as the elevator door slid open on the eleventh floor. He knew he had enemies in the department as did most black policemen at the LAPD. With the ding of the elevator, the suite door opened and the officer allowed him to enter first into a quiet almost reverent interior where three officers stood. They stepped aside to reveal a lone, white girl, dressed in a filmy negligee, her dry, dyed-blonde hair strewn along the white porcelain floor between the sink and the bidet. A vial of presumably cocaine in her hand, the powder dusted up her nose.

Hep bent over, grabbed her wrist and searched for a pulse he knew would be absent. "OD?" he asked.

"Apparently yes, sir."

"You call it in?" Hep asked as he stood.

"Not yet sir."

"What's the delay?"

"I believe that's my call," a voice said from behind.

Hep turned to face a man he recognized as Senator Prentiss Fitzgerald Eagan of Massachusetts.

"Afraid I don't follow," a nonplussed, unimpressed Hep replied. "A dead girl means a 911 call ASAP."

"There are extenuating circumstances," the senator said. "Captain Culhane is it?"

"It is. I'd like to hear what you think these 'circumstances' would be. That a married senator, running for president of the U.S. is in a California hotel room with a hooker who OD'ed on coke? I don't see the conflict?" Hep noticed an elderly man out of uniform and asked, "You are?"

"Dr. McIntyre. The hotel physician."

"Why invite me to this little party? This is not my jurisdiction. Commander in Chief Wentworth is just downstairs as is over half of the LAPD muck-d-mucks."

"Your reputation proceeds you. A man of fairness, courage, action, impartial to a fault. Steadfast, integrity, discretion—"

"Enough. I get my stroking from home." Hep walked around to where he faced the door. "Your research no doubt revealed that I will not do anything to compromise or jeopardize my job or reputation."

"I understand and would not ask you to but I need someone who can handle a 'delicate' situation such as this with a wider vision of its impact upon history."

"Like you did when you sought to entertain an underage hooker in a hotel room?"

"Touché. I have been separated from my entourage and am in need of safe passage out of this hotel and back to a more hospitable environment."

"Aren't you supposed to be in Palm Springs with friends?"

"Ah. You are enlightened and up to date on politics? Wish that I were," he said, unleashing a Hollywood smile that did not faze Hep Culhane.

Unimpressed by this rich, entitled, privileged white man-boy "Fitz" from Massachusetts used to getting things the wanted, when he wanted, Hep folded his arms across his massive chest.

"Regardless of what you think of me personally. I am the best man to lead this country, these people... *all* people to a better life. My opponent would make matters worse for everyone but the wealthy. How this is handled can affect the outcome of the election. The fate of the United States. All of it rests in your capable hands."

Hep cut his eyes away from the candidate who had managed to comb his thick, blondish-colored hair. Hep looked over the gathering to the sky beyond the balcony and weighed his options for himself and his career first. Then begrudgingly realized what Senator Eagan said was true. This candidate was the hope of this country. Would it be his civic duty? It's like Selena always said, "Sometimes you got to do what's best... not what's right." This is an opportunity that can change the world or plummet it deeper into Jim Crow darkness. Bigger picture. Bigger responsibility.

"Get dressed senator," Hep ordered, and directed the officer to bring Officer McMillian to the room, as he snatched up the phone. "Outside line, please," he said to place a call to Skeekie Benton.

Twenty minutes later, Captain Culhane stood at the door directing Truck McMillian to escort Senator Eagan down the rear service elevator, through the kitchen to freight delivery where a Red Ball Express tow truck would be waiting to take the senator to its garage. "Do we take him home?" Truck asked his former partner. "Let him find his own way home the way he found it here. We're not his babysitters."

"Thank you," Senator Eagan said with a mixture of relief, contrition and gratefulness.

"I'm not doing this for you, Senator Eagan." Hep lit a cigarette. "Let's be clear, after the autopsy, if I find out there was some negligence, coercion or irregularity. I will be in touch with you, personally."

"Fair enough," the senator replied.

Once Truck and a disguised senator left, Captain Culhane mandated, "Now go get the chief."

The two officers looked befuddled. "How do we do that, sir?"

"I don't care, get him up here. If this is his daughter, she's been missing for months and his first sight of her shouldn't be on a slab in the morgue."

The chief came to the suite in an outraged huff, noticing Captain Culhane immediately up entering.

"What is the meaning of this?" he assaulted the man he abhorred. The man who received the captain post he vehemently fought against so hard and long. This uppity Negro whose men, both black and white, respected. The chief

64

couldn't understand it or how he won the Precinct Delegate, a secret ballot, which began the slippery slope to his rise. This man was after his job.

Hep said nothing but stepped out of the way.

"You bring me up here to look at a dead hooker?" He spat indignantly. "I'll have your badge for this, Culhane!"

Hep remained silent as the doctor introduced himself and asked the chief, "Can you identify the young woman?"

"Have you also taken leave of your senses? A white man buying into a nigg—his tirade!" The chief glanced down and noticed the features of the face—the eyes of a little girl to whom he'd read bedtime stories... and attend tea parties... dance recitals. As recognition stabbed his heart, an inhuman wail emanated from his lips and he staggered against the cold porcelain wall, sliding down to the floor until they were there together as they had not been in years. Father and daughter. Side by side.

Truck entered with a nod, indicating to Hep the senator was on his way. Hep turned to leave the saddest of scenes... a man crying over his dead daughter's body. A man, who years ago, may have chosen his job and his position over spending time with his baby girl.

As Hep stepped to the door, Truck asked, "You just going to leave—"

"Not our problem. They'll handle it as they see fit."

The pair walked to the elevator and after the ding, eased into the open cubicle. "Is the party still going strong?"

"A bunch of overly familiar, drunk, white folks. Want to get something to eat?"

"Naw. I'm going home and hug my daughters."

"Not a bad idea."

Hep glanced at his watch and knew it was too late for any hand-packed ice cream tonight. Driving home, he spotted a late-night corner store on the fringes of Watts and pulled into a space. The bell above the door tinkled as he entered the bodega, with two guys following close behind him. Hep looked at the male cashier and headed to the Sealtest sign near the small store's coolers. The two males fanned out, one taking one aisle and the second taking the other. Hep unhooked the safety of his gun as he reached in for a half-gallon of chocolate ripple ice cream. The two men hunched down, simultaneously approaching the unsuspecting cashier. Reaching for chocolate syrup for Jaz, he assessed the situation: The men seemed totally unconcerned with his presence in the store. Hep approached the counter with his items.

"Give us your money!" the guys shouted at the cashier.

Startled, the cashier froze, then laughed when he recognized the pair. "Stupido…"

Hep watched them crumble into laughter.

"You didn't see us, did you?" the laughing pair asked. "We came behind this big man. How tall are you anyway?"

"Six-four," Hep answered giving the cashier a five and, adding a bag of barbecue potato chips, waited for his change.

"Your parents big?"

"Not especially."

"You eat good, huh?"

"I do. Friends of yours," Hep verified with the cashier before he left.

"My stupid brothers. They come to walk me home," he said with a Spanish accent.

"Good looking out," Hep complimented.

"Hey, you know. Family. This a bad neighborhood."

Hep chuckled, "Later."

Before Hep could clear the door, they turned the OPEN sign on the door to CLOSED.

Hep got behind the wheel, opened his bag of chips and started the ignition. He popped the salty spicy goodness into his mouth as he eased onto the tranquil streets. He could not shake the image of the girl on the floor. He never wanted to see either of his daughters like that. He hoped he had been a good father while he pursued his career. Equal amounts of home and work. Not as concerned about TC since his birth, he noticed his boy had always been introspective with a mind of his own. He'd already chosen his path—music. Luckily, he was good at it. "A genius" was how other musicians and trade magazines described his young son. It had been he and TC all along. He had taken him to the Boys Club to register him in recreational activities and from there, Hep became a coach for his son and for other boys who had no father or whose dads worked.

When his son took an interest in an economics class and wanted to invest in the stock market, Hep participated and encouraged him, as another way to for them to connect on a different level. Hep loved the way "the men in the house" read, shared and discussed the *Wall Street Journal,* learning about stocks and their symbols... together. TC graduated to music, basketball and girls, forgetting about the market, but a hooked Hep continued with the stocks his son had selected, International Business Machines and Coca-Cola, both had taken off. Hep began to dabble in the market even more; he diversified his holdings and, when the stocks grew in value and yielded dividends, he reinvested and his portfolio grew in leaps in bounds—so quickly he didn't have the time to keep up with it, beyond making sure he paid yearly fees and taxes. He and TC called the stock market "white boys gambling," and since Hep didn't play the ponies or poker, or frequent casinos, he let the account "ride." In a few years, without any effort on his part, he accrued an astounding cache of money.

Hep began to invest in commodities: tin in Sumatra, a coffee plantation in Kenya, bauxite in Jamaica, then foolishly, he lost big on speculative new stock. He never planned to share any of these market speculations with Lorette, as they had no effect on their household income and, upon losing over half his portfolio, he was relieved he never had. His decision maintained family harmony. Like he wouldn't mention how badly that incident just now at the bodega could have gone wrong. Or a million other times when his cool head and judgment saved him. No need to worry his wife. With no formal business education or the benefit of counsel from friends who dabbled in the market, Hep had learned an expensive lesson and began to buy real estate. *God ain't making no more land,* he realized and bought property in Geyserville, Ojai and Sonoma, partial to that area of the country that reminded him of Tuscany. Maybe he would become a vintner somewhere down the line and join the Orsinis and Vittadinis in a U.S. enterprise. Hep remained open to options and bought land, until tax time when it became apparent he had to buy more. Knowing how Papa Colt felt about drilling on Cherokee Ranch, Hep bought land northeast of Cherokee Ranch near the old ghost town of Rimrock; the folks who had tried to chase Papa Colt off his land and were flabbergasted when his daddy dynamited them away. Knowing his father cared nothing about Rimrock, Hep purchased those acres, which produced two dusters before the third well produced a gusher. Hep popped another chip into his mouth, chuckled as he thought ironically of Rimrock, which had given Papa Colt water, and his son oil. Now, Hep had a steady income stream, apart from his LAPD salary, that he didn't know what to do with but watch it grow. A delicious dilemma.

The second time a good deed proved lucrative for Hep was when he volunteered to pay passage for seven Orsinis to bury their grandfather in his native Italy. While there, Hep arranged for the Vittadinis to show the Orsinis where Hep had buried Tavio during World War II. Vetoing Selena's desire to buy a new car to replace the Cadillac, Hep used those funds for their plane and train tickets. Seven Orsinis went over, only two returned. The remaining Orsinis stayed to revive their pre-War olive oil business and Hep insisted that they allow him to invest only on the contingency that he become an absentee partner until they could reimburse him from their profits. Once they agreed, Hep felt as if he'd fulfilled a battle-front promise made to Tavio. If not for Tavio sacrificing his life for Hep, he would not have had the life or money to gladly loan the Orsinis. Over the last few years, the Orsinis partnered with the Vittadini Vineyards and built an alliance in their native country with plans of exporting their products.

But now with all the accrued revenue, the time had come for Hep to make the dream of Culhane Enterprises a reality. In this initial phase, real estate would get him in the game but he knew that would not be his only interest. Money gave him the freedom to play and enjoy. He would have to make plans sooner rather than later. What began as a solution for how to provide college tuition for his three children so they wouldn't have to drop out like their parents had, took on a life of its own and become a profitable lifestyle change instead.

TC would not be interested in any business venture devoid of music or its production, so Hep would give him a lump sum to use in any productive way he chose. Hep wasn't worried about TC and his future. But his daughters—Hep had no experience with raising girls or seeing them raised. In his childhood home, his mother and his sisters, Orelia, Star and Selena, formed a female counsel. He doesn't recall any of the details as he was always ripping and running with Range Criqui. "From womb to tomb," or "cradle to the grave," they used to say, not knowing how soon the latter would come for one of them.

Hep put another chip in his mouth and made a left turn. The girls fell under the mother's domain and, as far as he could tell, Lorette seemed to have it under control. He hoped. She had her hands full as his girls were so different. Mel craved being alone with no interest in cultivating a relationship beyond her art; a different kind of genius. Good for an adult but questionable in childhood. And Jaz, Hep cleared his throat and shifted in his seat remembering the one major argument he and Lorette had ever had when she suggested that a third unborn child would not fit into her scheme of things. With her ridiculous suggestion, Hep had invited her to leave. Instead he left, as for the first time in his life, he almost hit a woman. His wife. That major shift in values produced a marital hurdle that questioned whether they would make it. They did; although a tangible strain remained evident between mother and daughter, one he thought he couldn't do anything about. Encouraging Lorette to spend more time with Jaz only seemed to infuriate them both. Hep thought it would all work out, eventually.

Hep crunched on another chip, relishing this ride home when the streets calmed down, however briefly, and the beauty of L.A., of Watts, shone through. He did love it here as much as Colt, Texas and the combination of both made his life a good one. Striking a balance like Selena speaking of Paris and U.S. with all its flawed elements. He had taken the formula from his father's life, in which the love of a good woman running his home and hearth had been paramount to his family's success. Lorette had been a loving, attentive wife, partner and mother. This was not the life she had envisioned as he had never become mayor of a major U.S. city. Not yet. Having TC, their "honeymoon baby," present as their first anniversary gift hadn't allowed time for both of them to graduate college and establish a career. All his wife really wanted was what they both had had—growing up in a *house.* The fact that they had been the first inhabitants of apartment #3G or that it was larger than many houses didn't matter. Scoey's mother had a house and a husband before he walked out on both of them years ago. Eunice Byrd's two-story house on their same block of Alvaro Street, with her daughters, Piper and Wren, was paid for by her husband, Nash Byrd, who was always away traveling with Duke Ellington both domestically and internationally. Ma Vy, Qwayz's mother, had a nice, two-story corner house in Compton. Even Hep's partner, Truck McMillian, shared a house with his mother and daughter. So many examples of home ownership abound, but Hep wanted more for his family than just an ordinary house.

View Park and Baldwin Hills had been integrated areas set aside for middle-class blacks, but Hep wanted Beverly Hills, Brentwood, or Hancock Park—neighborhoods not welcoming ownership to blacks, only open to their service to the whites who already lived there. Hep rejected the notion of being told where to live. When Hep bought a house for his family it was going to be one of his choosing regardless of racial covenants. But time seemed to be the killer of dreams as it sped by, oblivious to his goals, moving the home farther away.

Soon TC would be leaving home, followed by Mel, to Julliard, leaving only Jaz for a very short while. Lorette expected college for TC; Hep knew better. Truth—with his investment portfolio alone, Hep could afford a nice house in Compton now, but he'd promised himself, when they moved, it would be out of south central L.A. altogether. He'd get Lorette a house unlike those in the black neighborhoods, finer than any she'd ever seen or could imagine. She deserved that much but it looked like she'd be the only one who'd really appreciate or live in it for long.

The door to apartment #3G squeaked open and Hep entered, slid the ice cream into the freezer and headed down the long hall, eyeing his son's empty room as he passed on his way to his daughters'. He bent over Mel, kissed her cheek and whispered, "Night, Princess." Mel did not move.

He went to Jaz's bed and repeated the exercise. "Night Punkin'."

Beneath the veil of sleep, Jaz raised her arm and patted his cheek. "Night daddy," she said as she rolled over without fully waking.

Lorette met him coming up the long hallway. "Everything OK?"

"Yep. Just wanted to say goodnight to the girls."

"How was the banquet?"

"Fine. Everyone asked about you. How are you feeling?"

"Much better. Thanks for the ice cream." She looped her hands in his.

"You're welcome." He kissed her forehead, just then remembering that he hadn't picked up the Midol.

"Let's get some and you can tell me all about the party."

"Sounds good."

8

In apartment #3G on Alvaro, Lorette held the letter in her hand, tempted to open it. But it was addressed *Signore Hepburn Culhane*, not Mr. and Mrs. Each year she vowed to take an Italian language class and open the next one. But each year she placed it aside and waited for her husband to come home and open it himself in her presence.

The letters started coming at their first apartment and continued up to now. First cards and then letters in Italian. Hep would open them, smile, place them on their dresser and often reply to the sender… in Italian. Initially, Lorette worried but she asked and Hep showed her the letters, written in a language she couldn't read but he translated for her. Christmas cards, birthday cards, congrats on your new baby cards in honor of the births; TC, Mel and Jaz. A few times a year, Hep would ask Lorette for the flowery stationery she used to write her folks and sisters. Hep had kept up a relationship with the Orsinis, Tavio's family, in Brooklyn, New York and recently some letters came directly from Italy with the fancy stamps and foreign postings. Over the years, she became used to them.

But now, to that mysterious pen-pal bunch, came a new entrant. Only at Christmas a postmark from Massachusetts to apartment #3G in Watts, California from *Senator and Mrs. Prentiss F. Eagan* to *Captain and Mrs. Hepburn Culhane*.

"Do you know him?" Lorette asked when her husband came home.

"Who? Ah. Met him once," Hep said, untying his shoes.

"How'd he get our address?" Lorette asked.

"I'm sure he has his ways of getting any info he wants." He kissed her quick on the lips. "What's for dinner? Smells good and I'm starving."

The next day after depositing a perp in Emergency, Hep glanced at his watch and hit the elevator button for ICU Pediatrics. He asked at the desk and was referred to the waiting room further down the hall. As Hep approached with his long-legged strides, the off-duty officer in civilian clothes couldn't believe his eyes. He rose and intercepted his fellow officer. "Culhane," he identified aloud almost sheepishly.

"O'Malley. Just thought I'd stop by and see how your boy was doing."

Stunned by the presence of this Negro cop, O'Malley's lips parted, "I...he's about the same. No change. I sent Mildred home to get some rest. We got other children."

"Four, right?"

O'Malley couldn't believe Culhane knew that.

"I know it's rough on the entire family. Years ago, I lost my brother when I was a child but now with modern medicine, your boy is here in a hospital getting excellent care. He'll pull through."

O'Malley bit his lip, squelching back tears. They stood at the window looking at his son hooked up to machines and watched a nurse go in, check his IV and leave again. In all the time Culhane was there, no other patrolman showed up. Then O'Malley realized that in all the time he was there, few of his buddies had come by to stand vigil with him. The minutes snaked on slowly and the interminable waiting remained tedious, but this man, this Negro cop, stopped by like he had been doing it all along. Like they were friends. They were not. In fact, O'Malley had led the charge that the Cadillac Culhane's wife drove was part of a bribe. He had anonymously sent that lie onto the chief. He and some of his cohorts, none of

74

whom had stopped by, fueled the lie to mar Culhane's reputation and prevent him from getting the respect and promotions he deserved. Hepburn Culhane rose above it. Once in the cloakroom, Culhane caught him red-handed with a black marker in his hand and "nigger" scrawled across his locker. Culhane looked at him and the marker in his hand, open and closed his locker and never said a word. Now, that Negro man stood in this hospital hall and inquired about his son.

"Can I get you anything from the vending machine or cafeteria before I go?" Hep finally said.

"No. But… I thank you for coming by."

"Sure. I can't imagine if this was my son." Hep looked at the small boy lying helplessly in the bed surrounded by monotonous monitors. "Let me know if I can do anything for you," he said, clapping O'Malley on the back.

"You've done more than most. And I appreciate it."

"Brothers in blue."

Hep took the elevator down and as he approached the hospital's front door, someone said, "Hep?"

A woman's voice, not his wife's, called from behind. Used to Coach Culhane, Captain Culhane or just plain "Culhane," he could tell from the greeting how he knew a person. He turned around, just as the loudspeaker paged a doctor.

He looked at a woman standing akimbo some distance away. Her nurse-white shoes squeaked toward him. As she approached, he recognized her. "Inez Foster," Hep identified, a huge grin plastered on his face. "What are you doing here?"

"I work here." She flicked at her badge: Inez F. McLeod, R.N. "I know why you're here. I've been keeping up with you. Your progress in the LAPD, impressive. I knew we'd run into each other sooner or later. We're all proud of you."

"You get to Colt, Texas much?"

"No. But I know all about you taking your kids there during the summer. Making time for—"

"Home."

"I call a lot. My hours are screwy, vacation isn't a priority these days." She paused to listen to the overhead intercom and when it wasn't for her she continued, "I left you in that cemetery by Range's grave and went to L.A. like I said. Finished nursing school, married a doctor, had three kids. Here I am."

"That is great, Inez." Although Hep thought of Range often, he hadn't heard his name spoken out loud unless it was from Skeekie. Range, more brother than friend. Inseparable since childhood, even went to Northwestern together where the partying and clubbing on Chicago's South Side took its toll on their grades and they ended up volunteering for World War II to save face after losing their free rides. Range Criqui made it home only to be killed in an automobile accident before Hep made it back so they could finish up their education at Howard University as they had planned. Now Hep looked into the eyes of a girl who loved him most.

"Last time I saw you I was in bad shape," she said.

"We all were. That's the only thing Range Criqui left us… a big hole to fill."

She returned the wave of a departing patient. "I still think about him."

"Me, too. Every promotion or hard time… or good time…He's always there."

"I guess we never get over those we love." A student nurse requiring Inez's signature, interrupted.

"Well, look, it was good seeing you, Inez. Great talking about him out loud."

"I bet he is laughin' his butt off."

76

"Probably."

"We should get together with our spouses. We live on Chelsea Avenue."

"View Park," Hep replied. "Nice."

"Yeah, it is. Good schools. Who woulda thought it, huh?"

~*~

"Say what?" Selena inquired as she spooned more ice cream into a waiting dish. "Are you jivin' me?"

"I am not. He offered me a Chief of Protocol position in Washington, D.C., which I haven't seriously entertained."

"Have you ever met President 'Fitz' Eagan?"

"Once." Hep spared his sister the details.

"You must have made a hell of an impression."

"You know Culhanes do that to regular folk."

"You've got to take it."

"I don't have to do nothin' but stay black and die."

"This is an opportunity of epic portions with broadening influence and ramifications." Selena grabbed a handful of her hair in excitement. "Do you realize all you can do? The lives you can touch?"

"I do that now as captain—"

"But this is a game-changer, my little brother. With this appointment your stage grows. Your responsibility magnifies. Your range of exposure quadrupled. This is such a coup for our people, Hep! Jesus!!" She put her hand over her mouth trying to contain a yelp. "Oh My God!! Your platform, the power and the folk you'll influence just by being there. Being visible."

"More like a target with a bull's-eye on my back?" he quipped. "Seriously, it's bad timing. I have the funds necessary to begin my business venture. Get Lorette the house she wants and—"

"Eeee," Selena screeched with exasperation. "C'mon, Hep. Where's that 'citizen of the world' Hoyt said you were? You are looking at this all wrong. Put your business off for a couple of years and do this first. It's your civic duty. Eagan won't give this position to another Negro. It's you he wants and nobody else."

"Do you know him?"

"Well, no but you made the mark, the distinction, the impression on him. If you say no, some white boy's gonna get it like they always do. Don't you see? If you don't take this, the entire race misses out. It's your moral and racial obligation."

Hep shrugged his shoulders nonchalantly and Selena thought she'd lose her mind with his irritating, blasé attitude. She wasn't getting through to him. "What's Lorette say?" she asked, seeking an ally.

"I haven't really told her. I know what her vote would be. Go to D.C. yesterday."

"Hell Yeah!!" Selena clapped her hand once. "I knew I liked that girl."

"I have my own plans: Work a couple more years here and then begin Culhane Enterprises. That's how I'll help my people: building. Affordable housing, education, scholarships and intern programs—"

"Small potatoes, my brother," she dismissed. "I can see you've been wrestling with it. You've made your decision and we're just supposed to go along with it. I know your moves. But… this is colossal."

"Don't want to uproot my family."

"What? TC ain't going anywhere. Mel's headed for New York. Jaz will be at Berkeley in a couple of years. I am not seeing any conflicts."

78

"I'm used to being my own man. Being in charge of me and my family. I can depend on me. And you know white folks—they give, they take away on a whim. Like offering me this in the first place; he admitted it'd take a while to put in place. Needs Senate approval. I have no guarantees or credentials, not even a college degree. He or the senate decides against it after I quit my secure job and then, where am I? Can't jeopardize my family's security like that."

"Good point," Selena paced a bit. "Hell, if it happens I'll take care of you all."

"Not funny," Hep gaged. "Eagan's also appointed a black astronaut and some other 'Negroes.' I'm just waiting for someone in his cabinet to tell him he cannot do this willy-nilly. He's appointed his brother Attorney General. That ain't gonna fly. I can't let go of the secure for insecurity. For a title. That ain't gonna feed my family. I'll keep my day job until the offer is firm."

Selena couldn't contain herself, "You don't think this man has checked you out, up and down? You don't think you have been vetted to death and he's decided on you, Hepburn Heath-Henley Culhane? You must be someone he thinks he can trust to do the job…and if you're a Negro, all the better."

"He did mention that in a phone call. He needed some help with the 'Negro perspective' on things domestic and international."

"He's calling you? On the phone? Got-damn." Selena shook her hands as if they were burning.

"I must admit if it were just me. I'd take this dog for a walk. Try it on for size and if it didn't fit… leave it be."

Selena grinned from ear-to-ear. "Yes! Yes! That's what I'm talking about. That's the Hep 'citizen of the world' I know. Try it out. No fit… just walk away. No harm. No foul.

Then you can start your business. If you don't at least try, you will always wonder… Besides, how good will this look on your resume?"

"I must admit that more than the chief of protocol salary for a couple of years, it's the national and international contacts and exposure that will serve me well in my private enterprise."

A knowing smile spread across Selena's face. "Yes! That's my boy!" A spent Selena collapsed with relief that she was finally getting through to him.

Hep's laugh boomed across the room.

She eyed him. "Ah! You were jivin' me all along?"

"Hey, our Daddy didn't raise no fools."

She playfully threw a napkin at him. "Boy, I could've had a heart attack."

~*~

Later that evening, Hep told Lorette who, predictably, loved the notion as she hopped up on the bed and jumped on it like a trampoline.

"If I take it—"

"When," Lorette corrected excitedly.

"I'll have to resign with the department. Travel back and forth to D.C. for confirmation and orientation before being sworn-in. There will be big changes; you'll have the major responsibility for the kids for a while."

"Psh! I can handle that. Have been all these years."

"We'll have to buy a house."

Lorette jumped up again and gleamed, "In D.C.? I want Georgetown."

"That'd be nice and close to the State Department." He grinned enjoying that she was so thrilled.

Lorette teared up and cuddled against his chest. "Oh Hep. It's finally happening. We're finally getting everything we

80

wanted. Everything you deserve. You've worked so hard for."
She reared up at him and kissed his lips. "I can't wait to tell
my parents. Can they come to the swearing-in ceremony?"

"I don't see why not. I'm inviting my parents, though, I'd
be surprised if they came,"

"We can tape it and watch it with them during the Colt
summer. Oh, and the children!"

"I expect them all to be there. TC'll be happy for me but
he's not leaving L.A. Mel will like that we'll be closer to
Julliard."

"And Jaz," they said together.

"She is not going to take kindly to leaving her school, her
friends, her life here," he said.

"We'll tell her together. A united front with a positive
spin. She'll have Gladys Ann visiting her in the summers."

"I want to keep this all under wraps until it's finalized. No
leaks to anyone yet. Stuff can happen, and I'll resign from
LAPD after I help with the search for my replacement. I do
love that job. I suspect it'll take more than a few months;
government bureaucracy, confirmations and entertaining all
the objections to my taking the post. Might come to nothing."

"Impossible. You are the best man for that job or any
other," Lorette upheld her man.

"Understand, I'm only going to do this protocol gig a
couple of years, then I'm going into business for myself.
Culhane Enterprises." He smiled broadly. "In San Francisco
near Jaz and Berkeley."

"I don't care," she hugged him tightly. "You know I'll
follow you anywhere. "

"You have."

"Because I love you. Always have. Always will."

9

Fresh from the Statewide Science Fair, Jasmine Culhane and Ian Cummings won for the second time in a row. The first year for their elaborate lava exhibition and this year for the whirling tornado entry. While Jaz was running out of interest in the science fair, Ian kept going strong. Since grade school, because of their last names, Culhane and Cummings, they'd always been paired together alphabetically, enabling them to forge their friendship. Jaz hated that Echo Blake no longer sat on her other side. Wondering what happened to Echo, Jaz realized she knew even less about her best school friend except that they called him "Magoo" for his heavy, black horn-rimmed glasses. Like Dickie, she'd asked about them calling him "out of his name." "I've been called worse," he'd said. She knew about as much of his home life as she did about Dickie's. From what Ian shared while they ate lunch or worked on after-school projects, he wanted to go to Morehouse like his father and become an engineer or rocket scientist.

"Regardless, that's what I'm putting in the yearbook. They never check," Ian had said. With his dry and sharp sense of humor, he kept Jaz laughing most of the time. Unlike Dickie, Ian knew who he was and where he was going. He didn't live around the neighborhood; she didn't know if he had siblings, only that he was as Morehouse-bound as she was Berkeley-bound. They kept each other on track.

School percolated right along with few surprises, and Jaz's main activity remained the movies. She would run into Tracy Summerville from dance class and listen to her go on about the wedding dress Yvette Mimeux wore in "Light from the Piazza," and they gushed over the "boss" pink bathing suit.

Gladys Ann and Tracy's friends appeared unimpressed with their conversation, but Jaz liked a girl who enjoyed the movies as much as she did.

The discussion between Jaz and Tracy could not compare to TC and the Dragons losing their collective minds when they saw "The Magnificent Seven." Eight times. They claimed characters, acted out parts and when TC got home, he played the theme over and over again. Jaz thought it embarrassingly over-reactive for a group of boys until she saw the movie herself; pretty cool. In honor of his idol Paladin in "Have Gun-Will Travel," TC began wearing black clothing, which complemented his hair and eyes. Then after "The Magnificent Seven" in homage to Chris, Yul Brynner's part, TC started to wear black clothes exclusively. To seal their combined commitment to this movie, the Dragons changed their name to Mag 7 to signify not only cool but also growth and development. "There aren't even seven of you in the group," Jaz pointed out. "Doesn't matter," TC answered.

Nineteen sixty-one proved to be a pivotal year for them and the Civil Rights Movement. On that May 19th, the first of the Freedom Riders boarded a Greyhound bus in Washington, D.C with the purpose of eliminating segregation on public transportation. The integrated Freedom Riders took their seats, just as Jaz and Mag 7 took their plush red velvet seats in the Baldwin Theatre in L.A. and waited for the action. The Freedom Riders rode South expecting the worse but hopeful for the best. Jaz and her friends sat and watched the rumble between the Sharks and the Jets in "West Side Story," not knowing the melee on screen would be incomparable to the real life fight the Freedom Riders endured outside of Anniston, Alabama. Without police protection, the protesters were trapped inside a firebombed commercial bus, exits blocked, meant to be burned alive until they were finally allowed to flee. As Jaz and her friends lunched at the Hot Shoppes, sucking thick milkshakes through thin straws, the Freedom Riders dropped on the ground outside the bombed bus, gasping for fresh air to purge their smoke-filled lungs. The news reports of man's inhumanity to man were missed by Mag 7, who focused on exploring their girlfriends' bodies under beach blankets around bonfires. And Jaz? Busy talking on the phone with Ian about a school project. Only days later did the California teens see news reports on the Freedom Riders. Jaz and Mag 7 suitably abhorred the treatment of their people Down South. Feeling helpless, out of touch, and absolute rage, a tremendous respect for each and every Freedom Fighter swelled their hearts.

Although Jaz and friends had seen "West Side Story" twice as many times as her brother and friends viewed "The Magnificent Seven," Jaz branched out to lighter fare. "Rome Adventure" captured her with the scenes of Italy, but the song "Al di La" enraptured her. "I don't even know what they are singing but it is beautiful," she told TC. Upon his sister's recommendation, TC finally went to see the flick and admitted it was a "good song," but that doofus "Gidget Goes Hawaiian" made him never want to go to our 50th state. "Summer Place" had a good theme but the story was hokey, and "Lawrence of Arabia" was too long. "Didn't know you were into colonial history," he told Jaz.

"I'm not. I'm into Omar Sharif. That's one good looking guy."

"Jaz, you not thinking about dating gray guys, are you?"

"Neither Bernardo nor Omar are 'gray guys,'" she countered, remembering how berserk TC and his boys went when their idol, Sammy Davis, Jr. dated Kim Novak, "lost an eye," and now was on to May Britt.

84

"No more than you would date gray girls."

"Psh… hell no. Only thing a white chick can do for me is point me to a fine black girl. I come from a long line of black women. No white woman ever did or can do nothing for me. Ready for dessert?"

Jaz enjoyed these May lunches with her brother but missed her father. "So, what do you think is going on with Dad and all this traveling to Washington? You think he's a spy?"

TC laughed. "No. Kinda big and black for a spy. Has it been that often?" he asked.

"Says the one who's not left with Lorette," she said. She thought about how TC seemed exempt from a lot of scrutiny, and asked "So how goes your studio?"

TC's handsome face spilt into an ear-to-ear smile. "I'm getting there. Almost got the studios just the way I want them. Working on the upstairs now."

"What's up there?"

"My apartment."

Jaz was speechless and it showed.

"Alperstein had boo-coup junk up there. I finally cleaned it out. Going to be my office, a bedroom and bath," he said as he tapped the tip of her fudge brown fedora. "Close your mouth. I graduate next year. Eighteen and out. Can't live at home forever."

"When do we get the tour?" Jaz hid her distress and envy.

"You can see the first floor anytime. In fact, I made an anteroom for you, Gladys Ann and your friends so you all can come, hang out and watch us record. Always thought you all should have a girls' club like we have one for boys."

"Oh, really?"

"Girls need some place to go before you go home to homework and dinner. In fact, I'm going to build a club for you all. Great music. No liquor, age limit. Need a venue for that. That's way down the line. I got a few years before you and Mel will be getting boyfriends and all."

"It's later than you think."

That next month when Jaz went to Colt, Texas, those words came back to bite her in the heart. Had she never realized how much Joaquin Redbird looks like Omar Sharif? She tried not to stare first at the resemblance and then at his handsomeness. Joaquin, fine and black, and Omar, Egyptian—but that's black, too.

That year Mel also became smitten by one Clarence "Slick" Savoy, visiting from Chicago, bringing his beguiling ways and swagger with him, characteristics Mel had never noticed in L.A. guys. Jaz duly preoccupied with third generation, Colt native born and bred Joaquin to take much notice. What she did notice was how simpatico they were as he'd come over and they'd walk to the swimming hole or ride horses. How he bought her ice cream and they'd giggle between themselves.

"C'mere, Sweetie, let me show you my new Paris flat," Selena suggested one evening after dinner. "I'm getting it ready for you when you come in '65. That'll be here before you know it."

"No, it won't Aunt Selena. That's forever."

The anticipation of the porch swing and Joaquin called to her, but after the third picture showing Jaz her own room with the fairytale canopy bed, her Aunt Selena had her hooked. "It is beautiful!"

"You'll have your own bathroom and that one long floor to ceiling window faces out the front." She squeezed her niece and continued with excitement, "The wall of windows goes past the guest powder room, TC's room, your room down to the end of the hall where Zack has his music room—and turn

86

the corner and all that belongs to us. The master suite: another parlor, sitting room, our bedroom, bath and closets galore."

"Dag... Where do these steps go?"

"Up to the maid's quarters. Three more rooms. 20-foot ceilings and a elevator from the downstairs courtyard to the first floor of the apartment."

"A elevator *in* the house? 1965 can't come fast enough."

"These pictures don't do it justice." Selena gathered them up. "It beats hoofin' it all the way out to Chateau Jazz when you're dog-tired after singing all night."

"Aunt Selena are you rich?"

"Comfortable."

A handsome figure stood on the porch and rang the bell politely.

"I do believe you have company," Aunt Selena teased.

"Why, yes, I do," she said. "Excuse me." She floated to the door to let Joaquin in.

"Can we sit in the swing?" he asked.

Jaz felt especially mature that summer. Along with TC and Qwayz who had girlfriends, she had a boyfriend. A really cute, attentive boyfriend who, on the rare occasion they weren't together, she thought about all day and couldn't wait to see him after dinner. He finally kissed her after the third week. Boy, that was just as she had imagined. Soft lips, a little flicking tongue that initially shocked her, and if it wasn't Joaquin, she would have thought it unsanitary. But that's how she saw the guys "bust slobs" with the girls in the balcony or at the beach. Jaz was a woman now. After relaxing, she quite enjoyed kissing. Joaquin always tasted of peppermint and smelled so good.

"You talk to the girls about the birds and the bees?" Selena asked.

"Puppy love and cute," Hep dismissed.

"She stares at his big adoring doe eyes and he looks at her like he could eat her with a spoon."

Hep looked over at them and made a mental note to talk to her; he could already hear her chastise, "Oh, Daddy."

Love bloomed all over Colt, Texas that summer. Everyone relieved that Mel showed interest in someone and something besides her voice and what she could do with it. Slick Savoy apparently had the aptitude to penetrate her facade and get to the girl beneath it. Outgoing, funny and easygoing in a South-Side-of-Chicago-kind-of-way, noted Hep and Selena. "I'd worry more about him than Joaquin." Hep called him Clarence indicating, "I know your mother did not name you 'Slick.'"

"No sir," he agreed.

Hep learned that he'd been sent here by his grandparents who were having difficulty keeping track of the young boy's whereabouts especially at night when those nocturnal escapades ran him afoul of the law; Clarence came to Colt, Texas as they all needed a rest and vacation from one another. Learning that Mr. Culhane was former LAPD made Clarence nervous and overly respectful… none of which impressed Hep. Clarence's major attribute was showing Hep if Mel could handle herself in New York.

Jaz laughed into the Texas sunshine, triggering Joaquin Redbird's companionable reflexive response. They sat on the bank of the swimming hole pulling honeysuckle from a string and letting the single drop of sweet nectar tickle their tongues, while watching the rest of the guys finish out a race.

Jaz tucked her legs under her and rested her face on her knees. "You like it here?" Joaquin asked.

"I *love* it here. I can hardly wait to get here for the summer, especially after last summer," Jaz referred to the kiss

88

he gave her before she left. It had taken her quite by surprise but she thought of little else since last year.

"I was going to write you but—"

"You should have." She turned toward him. "I would have written you back." She smiled and lit up his world.

Jaz had only confided in Gladys Ann that the boy she had a Colt-crush on had kissed her on the side of the porch just before she climbed into the car to come back home. Jaz admitted he could be The One. *My very first boyfriend.* "He is *so* good looking I can't stand it."

"Good looking like who?"

"Psh! No one around here," Jaz had scoffed.

Jaz played it cool until her parents went back, leaving TC and Qwayz to their girlfriend agendas. Jaz and Joaquin were inseparable in an appropriate way, at least that's what Papa Colt and Grandma Keely told TC and Qwayz, "Leave 'em alone. It's cute. Both of your sisters are 'in love' this summer."

After his chores, Joaquin would come over and pick Jaz up at Cherokee, greeting everyone before the couple disappeared on adventures: fishing, riding horses, swimming, catching tadpoles by day and fireflies by night, walking everywhere. Joaquin often ended up eating with the Culhanes and, with advanced permission, Jaz would eat dinner with the Redbirds. And, they attended football games and county fairs where his mother's cobbler would beat out Grandma Keely's. Sometimes Jaz would go over and help Joaquin with his chores or take a ride with him and his father over to River Bend to pick up a steer. They sat with their families but near each other in church, glancing at one another when something agreeable happened, like Mel or Reba Gassaway just killing a hymn.

"Could you live here, Jaz?" he asked once as they flew kites in the back pasture, Keely keeping an eye out from the front porch. "I know you love it for the summers. What about for always?"

"I never thought about it. I have to go to college but maybe after that. I could be a doctor here."

"Would it bother you if I don't go to college?"

"Heck no. You got a ranch to run," Jaz said with a giggle. He fell down on the grass and Jaz fell playfully on top of him. They kissed again. "I love kissing you," she said.

"I love it, too."

In the distance they heard the chow-bell clang with Keely at the helm. "Guess it's time to go."

"Guess so." He stood and reached for her, pulling her up and into him. "I love you, Jaz."

"I love you too, Joaquin." She thought she would burst from pride. *Wait until I tell Gladys Ann,* she thought, as they reigned in the kites and he looped his hand through hers.

Mel undressed and dressed quickly so the contest she had swum in without a bathing suit couldn't be seen by anyone. Slick had talked her into it and she had done it, drenched clothes and all, but the family needn't know how crazy she was about him. She hadn't liked anyone this much since Greg Minton, who had a crush on Jaz instead of her. His older brother wouldn't even look at her so Mel knew there would be no Minton marriage; her singing and a built-in tap dancing career. But now she had Slick. Forget those Minton boys.

Mel could hear Slick and some of his boys waiting outside near the back steps. They were going to dinner and then for ice cream in town, so Mel pulled out a dress from the wardrobe.

"I love her big eyes," Slick was telling his friends. "The better to see me with." He laughed letting his signature toothpick rest on the side of his lips. "I think her baby sister is the for-real fox."

90

"Joaquin's girl?"

"Yeah. For now. She's a little young for my taste."

Mel listened as she pulled on her shoes.

"She's definitely more my speed. The eyes, hair, complexion and she got a sturdy body-in-the-making. Don't you country boys know nothing?" He sat on the steps and crossed his legs. "You always go after the uglier sister. Like money in the bank. That lil' Jaz'll have her pick of guys but Mel was a sure thing. Don't have to work as hard 'cause she's thankful for any attention."

Mel stood in the window. The hurtful words filling in, replacing the love she had for him. *"The uglier sister?"*

Slick went on, "Easier. Mel's not hard to please. And will do some things the pretty one won't. She don't have to. There will always be men sniffing around her. She just has to pick the one she wants."

Just then, Mel saw Jaz walk up the pathway. Mel immediately hated her. Jaz kissed Joaquin on the lips and sauntered past the boys who said, "Hey."

Jaz said "hey" back to them and came into the house.

"Hey Mel," Slick yelled upstairs not knowing that she could easily hear him. "C'mon. Let's go!" he said impatiently as the other guys peeled off.

Mel never went down. She closed the door and softly cried.

10

"You better straighten this out, Joaquin Redbird!" Jaz shouted at him, slinging a water-soaked braid over her shoulder.

Her directive met with a sheepish grin as his boys stood around him. All that could be heard was the rush of water over the waterfall.

"I told them nothing happened. That we didn't go 'all the way' but they won't believe me," Joaquin ambled with a wide smile.

"Wipe that stupid-ass, grin off your face. I wouldn't believe you either!" Jaz grabbed her towel and flip flops and stomped away from them.

"Jaz," Joaquin ignored the cursing and called after her.

Without turning around, Jaz flipped him her middle finger.

Joaquin and all the guys stopped laughing, in shock at the gesture, as one said, "That's fast, city women for you."

"Shut-up!" Joaquin barked at them.

For the first time since she'd been coming to Colt, Texas, Jaz was ready to go home to California where guys didn't lie on you. Unlike with Mel and Slick, who'd quietly returned to Chicago, everyone noticed the breakup of Jaz and Joaquin. When he came around, Jaz refused to see him. "I'm done," she answered Qwayz when told Joaquin was downstairs. Her first boyfriend wrote and left her letters, which she tore up without reading.

"OK, cinnamon sticks," Qwayz said to her at the swimming hole, referring to her legs baked a deeper brown by the Texas sun. "What gives? You all have a lover's quarrel?"

"We were never *lovers!*" Jaz seethed. "You didn't believe that malarkey, did you?"

"I was just playing, Jaz. You all are too young to even play at being 'lovers.'" He shook himself dry, preparing for another dive into the cool water.

"Answer me this," Jaz began, and Qwayz aborted his dive. "Why do boys lie on you? Say they do things with you and they don't."

"'Cause boys can be stupid. Always worrying about being cool in front of their friends. I betcha he didn't even say anything but his boys egged him on and he didn't deny it. He wanted them to think he was more man than he was. If he was a real man, he would have fessed up from the git-go."

Tears pushed up against the back of Jaz's eyes, her nose burned as wetness rimmed her pupils.

"What are you doing?" Qwayz went over and stood in front of her blocking their view. "Don't ever let them see you cry."

"I'm not crying. I have something in my eye."

"Now and forever, if you're going to fall in love, only let a guy ruin your lipstick not your mascara."

"What?"

Qwayz hadn't had this issue with his big sister Denny, although he planned to have issues with his younger sister Hanie, but not for many years. Qwayz continued standing in front of her so no one could see her emotions and the tears threatening to wet her cheeks.

"He could have been The One, Qwayz. If he'd been a better guy, we could have gone all the way. We could still be in love." She shifted her weight to make a cogent mathematical deduction in the sand. "We had it all. Not only the double Js in Jasmine and Joaquin both 7 letters long, but the double 7s again in Culhane and Redbird. First and last names…all lucky 7s. It was perfect." Jaz fanned her hands in exasperation.

Qwayz broke his gaze from her nonsensical litany and just shook his head. "You girls and the way you play letter games, cancelling out and counting up …who is 'The One.' All that, don't mean diddley."

She rolled her eyes at him for cutting up her scientific research.

"Jaz, c'mon, now. Don't beat yourself up. He's the idiot. Not you. His loss, not yours. Good you found out now instead of later."

Jaz thought for a split-second and said, "You're right."

"Damn-skippy I am."

"Better than pining for him and finding out later that he was a assh…"

Qwayz looked at her, raised an eyebrow, daring her to curse.

"He was not man enough for me."

"True." Qwayz moved to the side.

"I'm never dating a guy as cute as him again."

"He didn't know what he had when he had it. He's not worth another thought. Don't let him steal your happy. Now, I'll race you to the mesquite bush and back."

"You're on."

~*~

"Hey Sporty," Papa Colt said as he made space for his granddaughter on the on the porch swing. "Pretty ain't it?" he asked, looking toward the sun that was preparing to set with striations of red and orange painted along the horizon. "Is it this pretty in California?"

"Sometimes. We get purple, too."

"Umph, that must be quite a sight." He noticed Jaz's lack of spunk. "Sad to be leaving early?"

"I'm ready to go. "

"Really. I could take offense. Of the three of you, you the one who usually wants to stay. Hear your Dad is considering a job in Washington, D.C. That's a pretty big deal."

"It may or may not happen. Seems the president has a lot on his mind."

"That Bay of Pigs thing in Cuba."

"Yeah, and they went to that induction party in January."

"The Inauguration?" Papa Colt clarified.

"Yeah. If he gets this job, I hope it doesn't happen until after I graduate high school. Maybe by then you'll go to see him sworn in?"

"If I was meant to fly, I'd have wings." They chuckled. "Too far by train and horse is out of the question." He bumped his granddaughter's arm and got a laugh out of her. "Your dad knows how proud we all are of him," Papa Colt said.

"Whenever it happens, it'll be my first flight too. Unless Paris comes first."

"Sure 'nuff?"

"TC and Mel have flown before. TC went to Paris with Aunt Selena."

"I remember that. He met the Queen of England?"

"Yep. Played 'Rhapsody in Blue' for her for seventeen minutes; she gave him a standing ovation. A bunch of Negro stars played for her. There were pictures and a article in Ebony."

Grandson of an ex-slave meeting the Queen of England, Papa Colt thought. *And his son being invited to a Presidential Inauguration.*

"TC said he'd rather stay home and work on his studio. Whenever he goes for Dad's ceremony, I bet he's only staying a few days. He loves that studio."

"It's good to have a passion about something, Sporty. TC's lucky to have found his so young. Just so it doesn't cloud your whole life and you forget what's important." They fell into a comfortable silence. "Did Mel meet the Queen, too?"

"No. She went to New York and guest starred on Ed Sullivan. Then Aunt Selena took her to Paris for two weeks!"

"Well, I'm sure you'll get your turn."

"Aunt Selena bought a whole new house for when I come. Won't be until I graduate from high school. That's eons away. I get to bring a friend, so I picked Gladys Ann."

"That's your dad's partner's girl?"

"Yep. My best friend in L.A. If the ceremony happens in the summer, I get to stay with her for a while in D.C. Her mother's people are from there and she goes there every summer like I come here."

Silence claimed them again, unusual for Jaz, so Papa Colt asked, "Something else bothering you, Sporty? You homesick?"

"No, sir. Just disappointed."

"Ah," Papa Colt said knowingly. "Folks are going to do that to you from time to time. Put too much stock in them before they deserve it. You do anything wrong?'

"No."

"Then that's it. You know you didn't and it don't matter what they say. That's their problem. You move on and leave them in their mess. You not gonna like everybody and everybody not gonna like you. That's a fact. You keep on being you. You do like my mama told me, 'Be who you are.'"

She smiled over at her grandfather.

"This is your life. You answer to you," he said.

96

"They say I'm too young to really know."

"People gonna always have their opinions, asked for or not. Tried to tell me the same about one Miss Lucinda Purdy. I was about your age, I fell hard for that cute little girl." He chuckled. "What's that, 80 years ago? Still remember how I felt when her father rejected me. Thought I'd never get over her, but suppose I'd gone off with the Purdy's?" He looked over at Jaz. "Then you wouldn't be here?" Jaz squinted at her grandfather. "I would have never met your Grandma Keely and we wouldn't had your father who had you."

Jaz nodded.

"Everything happens for a reason even if you don't know the reason at the time. I felt as low as a snake's belly but I got myself up, dusted myself off, kept plugging away, so when I met your Grandma Keely she'd see my value. That Purdy rejection was permanent damage at the time but stuff that happens is 10 percent what it is and 90 percent how you handle it. So, her daddy did me a favor. I took that 90 percent and made me the man I'd want my daughter worthy to love."

The swing swung a couple of times.

"I think this Joaquin—"

"Papa Colt!"

"Not much gets by me, Sporty." He winked at her and she relaxed knowing that in the absence of her dad, Papa Colt was just as good.

"He just moved out the way so a real boy can come calling. I think you dodged a bullet."

"But he's so cute."

"Now, you do sound young. Ain't what's on the outside that counts… it's the inside. What he's made of. How he makes you feel. If he don't make you feel good about yourself–who you are–keep steppin'. Of course, I'd say you are a few guys away from getting hitched for good."

"Grandma Keely was almost my age when you all married," she teased.

"Yeah. Well, that was another time and place. And how could she resist me?"

"I'm not having sex until I am in college."

Whoa, pump those breaks, Papa Colt thought, but managed, "Whenever you do, make sure it is *your* idea. Don't let any boy or your girlfriends 'make' you do nothing."

"OK."

"Now, let's see what's left from dessert? Then we'll have one concert before TC and Qwayz go home."

Last year when the sixties rang in, they spent not only Christmas but New Year's in Colt, Texas instead of the Satin Doll, which served them well for many years. The Culhane children missed the cache of balloons and whizzing confetti but here, Mel sang her song and TC and Papa Colt played tunes on the piano. The 60s clamored in full of promise and wonder but also an undercurrent that Selena and the elders felt more than the children. During their lively adult discussions, Selena continued to credit the murder of Emmett Till, the outrage and having had enough of the second-class treatment. Followed by Claudette Colvin and then Rosa Parks, both refusing to give up their seats to a white man, but the latter chosen as the symbol who'd make more of an impact than the fifteen-year-old girl. The Bus Boycott lasted 381 days and almost bankrupted the Montgomery Bus Company. Nothing magnanimous about the decision to desegregate, all driven by economics. Alabama white folks only cared about money as they surely had no heart. The Freedom Riders challenged and won the end of segregation on interstate bus lines; Colored Only and White Only signs came down. At what cost? Can't

98

folks just treat other folks with dignity because that's the right thing to do? And now Selena heard rumblings about sending a group of men and women South to challenge voter rights so black folk can have a say in who governs them and sit on juries... like the Till trial. Selena'd heard about a postponed March coming up in Washington D.C. and her friend Harry DeLacosta had already briefed her on that. Selena told Zack and Hep, "Something's 'bout to happen. Black folks are sick and tired of being sick and tired."

~*~

Having survived the Bay of Pigs invasion with Cuba in April 1961, and a colossal broken heart from Joaquin Redbird, and less preoccupied with her brother's adolescent trajectory out of the house, Jaz focused on her first year in high school. Ninth grade. She only had one year with TC before he graduated. Roosevelt High School, finally. Jaz was immediately challenged by Warlene Copley, who thought Mel was uppity and her newbie sister could be no better. On the third day, Warlene stepped to Jaz who didn't back down. The girl proclaimed, "Damn girl. No need to get your butt on your back," walked away and spread the word that Mel and Jaz may be blood sisters, but they didn't share personalities. At fourth period lunch when Jaz and Gladys Ann walked to the cafeteria line, a girl called, "Jaz Culhane. So good to see you again."

"Tracy Summerville," Jaz identified. "Haven't seen you since 'Light in the Piazza'."

Jaz reintroduced Tracy to Gladys Ann and, over a 37-cent hot lunch of Salisbury steak, mashed potatoes with gravy and peas, the pair related their dance escapades to Gladys Ann who joined them in laughter.

"We got put out," Jaz ended.

"Figures." Gladys Ann chimed in and told Tracy, "Jaz has more mouth than brains sometimes."

"That's what makes her so fun," Tracy laughed.

"Here, Squirt," Scoey interrupted, handing Jaz a notebook. "TC said you left this at the studio last night. Later."

"My brother, bless him," Jaz said clutching it.

Tracy watched the handsome, big, black guy leave. "Is that your boyfriend?" Tracy asked Jaz.

"Who Scoey? Heck no. One of my brother's best friends."

"He's positively dreamy," Tracy gushed.

Jaz and Gladys Ann eyed each other wondering about Tracy with the Sandra Dee words.

"Does he have a girlfriend?" Tracy asked.

"Several. They all have several. Quantity not quality seems to be their game which is why you are too nice for any of them," Jaz said protectively.

"So, you left Catholic School, huh?" Gladys Ann asked as they left the cafeteria for the fresh air of the bleachers. Tracy relayed how she'd had enough of nuns and priests and told her parents she didn't want an all-girls high school. It was time for a coed experience. They agreed only if she kept up with her dance and violin lessons and club memberships. Tracy looked at Jaz sheepishly. "I went back to Mrs. Therell."

"That's why you have good posture," Jaz joked.

"Hey, hey, hey. Who have we here?" Ian came and sat beside Jaz and her two friends.

"Well, this is Gladys Ann McMillan," Jaz teased. Ian smirked as Gladys Ann rolled her eyes. "And this is Tracy Summervillle... fresh from prison."

"Magoo," Ian introduced. "We have a couple of classes together."

"Yes," she demurred. "Pleased to meet you, Magoo."

"Really?" Jaz accosted him. "Magoo? I like Ian."

100

"I ain't dating you."

"You ain't dating Tracy either."

"So cold," he said to Jaz, pushing his black, horn-brimmed classes up on his well-defined, nose.

"She's spoken for." Gladys Ann, Tracy and Ian eyed Jaz. "Scoey."

They all laughed.

"Damn, she just got here," Ian lamented while Tracy blushed, loving the sound of that.

By the third week most male students referred to the three new freshman girls as Bronze Beauty, Black Beauty and Brown Sugar. Jaz's pedigree had been both challenged and verified as TC's sister. For the first time, freshmen were allowed to participate in the Harvest Assembly because Gladys Ann had talked his sister into reprising their hit singing the Ronettes' "Da Do Run Run," where they won third place and a lot of attention at the Boys Club. When Tracy learned that Scoey would be on sax, she volunteered to take Arnisha's place. A reluctant Jaz acquiesced once she knew Carter "the Styx" Hix, the reason they won in the first place, would be on drums. They won third place again and all the notoriety Gladys Ann wanted; "Hey I needed that. My brother doesn't go here." Tracy fell more "in love" with Scoey once she heard his wailing sax and, saw him on the football field, claiming him as "my future husband."

"Does he even know your name?" Jaz challenged.

"Doesn't matter," Tracy replied. "He will."

Walking to the studio after school one afternoon, a car horn tooted. Jaz ignored it as she always did. Then the car followed close behind as the driver offered all sorts of inappropriate banter. "Hey, pretty lady. Hey, girl. What you doing walking all alone? Don't you know that's dangerous?"

101

Jaz didn't pick up her gait, just put one foot in front of the other cursing Gladys Ann for joining the Latin Club. "Hey, girlie. Cinnamon sticks. Want a ride?" He switched to a Caribbean patois before zooming his car ahead of her and stopping. "You've learned well, grasshopper."

"Whose car?"

"Mine. Bought it. You like?"

"What is it?"

"Fire-engine red, Karmann Ghia. My Corvette will have to wait."

"It looks like a baby Porsche to TC's black Porsche... sorta."

"Nah. Hop in. I'll give you a ride."

"How many other butt cheeks have been in this seat before me?" Jaz sassed, as he placed Amber in the back.

"None. Yours will be the first. But not the last." He grinned unabashedly.

"I know that's right."

~*~

Sitting in the gym stands during a basketball game, Jaz became impressed. She'd witnessed TC and Qwayz, one-on-one, shooting hoops in Colt, Texas, but she had never seen them, the Dynamic Duo, in fierce competition before. She watched her brother command plays up and down the court as he dribbled the ball. And Qwayz, right there, to make it happen. The no-look, power passes whizzing by their opponents so fast they couldn't see them to intercept them. From the knot of players Qwayz would spring up as if on a trampoline, almost hang mid-air, and sink the ball through the hoop... all net. One of them would break away with the ball bouncing beneath agile hands and make a run for the basket only to stop, side-shoot to the other who would complete the set-up and get the points. It's like the article said, "One mind

102

and two bodies. Moves between them were instinctive, requiring no conversation." TC and Qwayz made the Roosevelt Rough Riders look like the Harlem Globetrotters out for benefit game to help sick children. The reason they were All Met two years in a row…their names were Culhane and Chandler.

From the bleachers, Jaz surmised this as one of the reasons they had girls always on the sidelines, waiting for a chance with either of them. After a break up, they could return to any former girlfriends because these guys knew how to treat the girls, especially those lucky enough to be dating them during their birthdays or the holidays… always bearing good gifts. Culhane and Chandler's unwritten edict— basketball and music came first. Being named "their girl" was status enough to make the girls special to the larger community. Complaining about time spent apart? A death sentence to the relationship. That was the secret to the longevity of the relationships between TC and Tiffany Thorne and Qwayz and Cherish Harley—they knew their places. Jaz liked both girls and thought the foursome well-suited.

TC's studio was christened as the local watering hole for fresh music, old blues standards and R&B. The session players at Champion Studios reputed as top notch. Artists continued asking for TC's arrangements and Qwayz's background vocals. Adding Yudi Hodges on trumpet had been as genius as letting Qwayz experiment with the electric guitar—cutting edge innovation. *The things that boy could do with six strings whether acoustic or electric is mind-blowing,* thought TC. On visiting Studio 3, passing through the anteroom, established artists asked for "Heartbreak and Dimples."

"Who?" TC asked.

"You know, those young girls who dance in the anteroom."

TC realized they were talking about Jaz and Gladys Ann.

"We know if we hit a groove by watching them. If they're dancing up a storm, we got a bona fide hit. If they just sitting there… we got some work to do."

TC had never realized that his sister and her friends had become a barometer for the patrons of Champion. He'd just been giving them a safe alternative after school haven.

On the rare downtime between sessions as they all fiddled with their instruments, Scoey asked, "Man, what's happening with the lawsuit?"

"Squashed," TC answered. "Alperstein sold me the studio for a hundred dollars in exchange for his remaining in the office out there was all legal and he was of sound mind. Plus, I arranged for his funeral and burial. The judge ruled in my favor and lectured his family on how they should be ashamed of themselves for coming all late to just collect on his estate."

TC remembered the old man fondly. "Old school." Alperstein just wanted to feel useful and respected, and TC was eager to learn; a perfect match. Alperstein shared inside and trade info with the "Youngblood" that Selena, an established star with "people" to handle everything, didn't need to know. Currently, TC seemed satisfied with conducting sessions, artists using the studio to rehearse, record and do simple sample mixing, but Alperstein knew of TC's ambitions. Told him about the business: producing, distribution contracts, local and national sales, deliveries to record shops and radio stations, bookkeeping, producer's fee, publishing income, writers' and artists' royalties. He told TC the key remained— to have control of it all. The old man wanted to impart his knowledge and expertise on willing ears … and to look at

LeLani Troop all day long. But she could handle him and anything that came her way.

"Yeah. Where was the family's concern all along?" Scoey asked.

"Took them a year to even realize he'd died."

"Having Selena and Zack's attorney and Hodges Funeral Home was a good move."

"I employ *my own,"* TC stated.

"We bury regardless of race, religion or national origin," Yudi quipped.

"Man, we've outgrown Mag 7," Scoey posed.

"I was thinking the same thing," TC agreed. "Not doing cotillions, teen house parties and store openings anymore."

"Need something sophisticated that sounds good when they announce us over the radio."

"No lie."

"Since it's your voices, how about Culhane and Chandler?"

"Naw, man that don't pop. Sounds like a law firm," Carter Hix noted. "How 'bout The Hix's."

"No!" Everyone pounced at once.

"Shouldn't be last names," Jax said.

"I got it. Even though TC looks all suave and debonair, he sounds rough and raw, raunchy even. And Qwayz's got that slick soaring tenor all up and down the scale. Raw and Silk."

"Yeah, I get it," Z said.

"Yeah, yeah!!" Excitement sent them all to their feet. "And now number one by Raw Silk…"

"That's a stone groove!"

"One more evolution. Since our lead singers' names both start with C…spell Silk with a C. Raw Cilk."

"Hot damn! That's it!!"

11

The two girls looked up at the lit-up apartment knowing just where they were headed, hardly hearing the thump of the cab door as it pulled off.

"Success," Jaz said as she and Gladys Ann walked the steps to the second floor. They'd pulled it off, each telling their parents that they were spending the night with the other. No one suspected, not Lorette, not Grandma Mac.

Jaz pushed open the ajar door and into the faint smell of weed.

"Uh oh," Gladys Ann said.

"C'mon," Jaz egged her on. "We're here now."

Junior Walker's "Road Runner" blared from the stereo and Jaz thought how TC would love this equipment. *Probably top of the line, probably stolen or bought with profits from ill-gotten gains,* Jaz thought, then stopped thinking about her brother as she knew he wouldn't approve any more than her father.

"Well, well, well, "Warlene approached them slowly. "What you all doin'? Slummin'?"

"Hey," Jaz offered hoping Warlene and her girls would behave.

"Want a toke?" Warlene shoved reefer near Jaz's lips.

"Not right now. Thanks." Jaz dared not look at Gladys Ann, as the pair slowly entered further into the crowded apartment, sensing, but not ready to admit, they'd made a mistake.

Having already dismissed the cab, Jaz and Gladys Ann tried to act as if they belonged at the party where they knew very few people by face or name, and those they recognized

106

were not any their fathers or her brother would endorse. They went over to the portable bar and took the proffered drink, choking on the grain-alcohol disguised as some sort of punch. The smell of reefer and unwashed bodies grew more pronounced as they danced to the Marvelettes' "Too Many Fish in the Sea," giving them time to eye one another with a "how the hell do we get out of here?" glance.

C'mon, Jaz, it'll be fine, she told herself, just as a guy grabbed her hand they danced to the Contours, "Do You Love Me?"

She fast danced to the Miracles "Shop Around" followed by their "What's So Good About Goodbye," hoping to cha cha her way to the door so they could saunter out, possibly unnoticed and walk a few blocks to a major street and hail a cab or just keep walking.

"Looka here, looka here," Satan, the leader of the Disciples, pimped toward Jaz. Sweating, drooling and sniffing around her. "Never thought I'd ever get this close to this piece." He grabbed her hand and threw her body up against his. "Dance with me girl. Ump, Ump, Ump you feel and smell as good as you look."

As James Brown lyrically told Satan it was "A Man's World," that would be nothing without a woman or a girl, a horrified Jaz couldn't keep her eyes from fluttering while they smarted in the cloud of Mary Jane swirling around her. Through the haze, she saw a terrified Dickie.

"What the hell are you doin' here?" he assaulted her as she danced.

Ecstatic to see her friend, she hunched her shoulders in answer causing Satan to open his eyes.

"Go head man. I'm dancing here. Ump, sure feels good to me." James conspired against her again at the record's end. As she tried to leave, "Try Me" came on and Satan held her tighter. "I need you," he sang with James flattening his body against hers. He breathed his hot reefer breath on the side of her face and into one ear. *This is disgusting,* Jaz's only thought.

Jaz felt his nature rise along with her inner thigh. *Oh, damn,* she thought. She saw an agitated Dickie go over to Gladys Ann, engage in a brief discussion before he disappeared altogether. Jaz wished she could tell Gladys Ann to leave and wait outside, but every little movement caused Satan to react.

Across town at the Studio TC, Scoey, Qwayz, Carter Hix and their girls were breaking up for the night. They'd spent a day laying tracks, gone to the beach and were heading upstairs for a tête-à-tête with their women. The phone jangled just as TC's pant leg disappeared up the spiral staircase.

"House of Love," Qwayz answered as Cherish Harley laid up against his stoked body. "Umph, umph, umph," Qwayz wasn't even listening, anticipation had seized his body, soul and good sense. "What? Slow down. Who is this?"

Cherish watched her man's face show exasperation, disappointment and then duty. "Baby, I got to go out for a few ticks."

"What! Now? You know I got a curfew."

"I know," he looked at the vacant stairs, thought of telling TC, then thought better of it. "I'll be back as soon as I can. Promise. It's an emergency. You know I love you." And he was gone.

Qwayz jumped into Reds, revved the engine and spun his wheels away from the curb. Didn't know which was hotter, the burned rubber or his temper. He was pissed.

When he arrived, there was no question as to where the party was happening. He took the stairs by twos, pushed open
108

the door and entered, surprising everyone with his presence. Rocket Chandler at a party in the Boondocks? Has hell frozen over?

"Hey man. I'm here to get Jaz and Gladys Ann." Spotting them, he motioned, went over and said, "C'mon. Let's go."

"Hold up man. You can't just come up in here and take the two finest women at Roosevelt High School. We just getting this party started."

"Look man, I don't want no static. First off, look again. These are girls. Jailbait. Whose fathers happen to be LAPD. I'm an errand boy, just picking up for Captain Culhane and Lt. McMillian who want them home. Past their curfews. Plain and simple," Qwayz said, holding Satan's gaze just as his Disciples gathered around their leader.

Gladys Ann stood on one side of Qwayz just as Jaz let go of Satan's hand and flanked Qwayz on the other side. "Don't start none won't be none, man," Qwayz said evenly.

After what seemed like an eternity to Jaz, Satan finally said, "OK, man. You keep winning those games. You are good."

"Thanks," Qwayz said as he turned the pair around and steered them toward the door and fast down the steps. "Get into the car."

Jaz threw up.

"Damn. How attractive. Don't throw up in my car!"

On cue, Gladys Ann added the contents of her stomach.

"Get it all out of your systems, ladies." He waited by Reds, one eye on them and the other on the steps making sure no one followed them. Up on the balcony, Satan looked down on the scene.

Qwayz just shook his head. "Girls," he reiterated to the gang leader as he told Jaz and Gladys Ann, "Rinse your mouths out at the spigot over there."

Gladys Ann climbed into the back, Jaz rode shotgun as Qwayz gunned his engine, shifted and tooted his horn to Satan, still on the balcony.

"You two may be book-smart, but your common sense ain't worth jack-shit."

Jaz could count on one hand the number of times TC, Qwayz or Scoey cursed in mixed company. However, she didn't think this was the time to bring it to his attention.

He glanced at his watch as he'd expected to be sliding between the creamy light thighs of Cherish Harley by now, instead he was out here with these two knuckleheads. "Did you two ever think about what could have happened if Dickie hadn't called me? Hadn't reached me? You were seconds away from a ringing phone with no one to answer. There are consequences and repercussions to everything. You sure as hell didn't think this through. What was the goal? Just the thrill of what? Going to a Boondock party? Cheeze. You all need to aim higher. Set better goals... 'cause these—"

"I'm sorry," Jaz muttered.

"You sure are," Qwayz said, downshifting to take a turn. Disappointment and disgust overrode his horniness. "Bronze Beauty, Black Beauty and Brown Sugar." He downshifted to turn again and asked, "Am I missing one?"

"She didn't come."

"Well, at least one of you had some sense. You better be glad TC didn't come. No doubt it would have escalated into something truly ugly." Qwayz spat outside his window.

Silence consumed the car with only the sound of whizzing rubber eating up the road.

110

"You can take me to Gladys Ann's. I'm supposed to be spending the night—"

"But you aren't, are ya? I'm taking you both home. Your parents can deal with you."

"But—"

"No buts. Case closed," Qwayz decreed, setting his jaw tightly.

Qwayz watched Gladys Ann stagger up her walkway into the glow of the lit porchlight, disappearing safely into the door. When Reds pulled up to Jaz's apartment building, she threw a quick "thanks" over her shoulder and bolted. She heard the car door thud behind her and pivoted, "You don't have to walk me to the door."

"Oh yes, I do."

Inside, Jaz took the steps by twos and fell once. Like a stalking monster in a horror film, Qwayz walked slowly but kept coming. At her door she fidgeted with her keys until she finally opened her front door and went in.

Qwayz shook his head, and thought, *I need to warn the poor sucker who ends up with that girl.*

"Jaz?" Her mother's voice came from the bedroom. "Did something happen? I thought you were spending the night over at Gladys Ann's."

"Obviously not," Jaz spat and headed back to her room.

~*~

"Here they come again," Gladys Ann said, warning Jaz of the press heading her way fresh from interviewing Jesse on the field. "You sure have been distracted since your Texas summer," Gladys Ann noted as Jaz's attention turned toward the oncoming press.

Fresh from her Colt, Texas pain–compliments of Joaquin Redbird–and the party in the Boondocks fiasco, she had said

111

"yes" when Jesse Ramsey asked her to "be his girl." Gladys Ann fixed her feminine wiles on Jehson Culbreath, and Tracy still tried to snag the attention of Scoey before he graduated. Jesse Ramsey, the star football player, had driven her home a few times—but nothing. Not a scholar, he'd garnered his popularity from displaying his football prowess and being a good dancer. He and Jaz enjoyed the banter riding to and from games on the team bus: the seasoned player and neophyte cheerleader. Unlike with Joaquin, Jaz's feelings remained in full control as she could handle Jesse.

But Jesse Ramsey always gave her credit for being his inspiration when everybody knew his main inspiration was to be the biggest, baddest running back in NFL history. To make it out of the ghetto and into the major leagues, the Heisman, a couple of NFL championship rings and after his NFL career ended years from now to be an announcer and even a leading man in the movies. He had it all figured out and intended to take Jaz Culhane with him ready or not. When Scoey, Jesse's upperclassman teammate, heard about their dating, he warned her, "Hey Squirt, watch out for him. The Marvelettes 'Playboy' had him in mind." Jaz figured Scoey would know.

"Which of you is Jaz Culhane?" The reporter asked. "You? Jesse Ramsey said the prettiest girl over there."

Jaz shrugged and placed an insincere smile on her face.

"So, you are his inspiration. The love of his life. The woman he intends to marry—"

"Too young to be thinking about marrying anyone," Jaz interrupted, knowing her father would have a fit with such declarations. She'd told Jesse a million times that she was going to college, Berkeley to be exact—just one more thing he objected to about their relationship. He suggested that she wait and see where he would be going on scholarship before she made her decision. He didn't like that she spent so much time after school and on weekends at Champion Studios with her brother and Raw Cilk when she should be supporting him at practices and games and, when not cheering him on with the squad, sitting in the stand or sidelines. He didn't like her shying away from his holding her hand or kissing her when they were out. He didn't like that Jaz loved kissing but grew pissed when his hands wandered out-of-bounds. "OK. I understand. As fine as you are, you're worth the wait," he had declared, "Not going to pressure you."

"Gee, thanks," Jaz had answered.

One afternoon, Jaz heard laughter tumbling down the hall from Studio 3 when she, Gladys Ann and Dickie entered Champion.

"What's so funny?" She eyed the guys who could barely stop guffawing.

Scoey spoke up, "Jaz, did you give Jesse Ramsey permission to sleep with whomever he wanted to?"

Qwayz, TC, Carter Hix and Z awaited her answer, verifying what their buddy posed.

"Well, he said he had 'needs' and since I'm not having sex at my age I suggested he get those 'needs' attended to by one of the many women interested in him just waiting for us to break up."

Laughter exploded anew.

"That's my sister," TC said proudly, slapping-five with the guys.

"Jaz Culhane, you are a humdinger," Qwayz added.

"We're just dating. No harm. No foul," Jaz said and unslung her shoulder bag and removed her hat.

Carter Hix stated, "You realize there may be a guy out there you'd be willing to, you know, 'do the do' with—"

"Hey!! Hey!!" TC, Scoey and Qwayz admonished him for that crack.

"No time soon," TC scolded.

"And when you do, make sure he wraps it up good and tight," Qwayz added with a wink.

"That's right," Scoey signified. "A couple of times." They all slapped-five in agreement. "Back it up with that anti-spermicidal foam."

"Cheeze," Jaz said to Gladys Ann and Dickie. "See what having three, nosey big brothers does. All up in my Kool-Aid and don't know the flavor."

While everyone appeared distracted with their own lives, Papa Colt decided to give the family and community a scare which cancelled the usual Culhane Christmas party. The prolific Texas spring had sent up the pollen from bluebonnets and Indian blankets, peppering the damp weather, not drying out in the summer, all challenged his constitution and filled his lungs, which hadn't cleared up by fall and into winter. The doctor diagnosed him with bronchial pneumonia, a virtual death sentence for anyone his age. His son and daughter flew in, overseeing his medical care and keeping Orelia informed and at the ready for flying in from Montclair New, Jersey, if need be. The Culhane children thought their parents waited too long before sharing his condition. The stalwart Keely fought to maintain positiveness and prayer but remained by his side except when the doctor made her leave for his examinations. Both Hep and Selena prepared for specialists to be flown in despite Keely stating her husband only needed her love, garlic tonic and God.

"You making too much out of this," Keely declared while cutting her eyes at her son, who called for the specialist anyway. Colt wheezed though an oxygen mask for three tortuous nights while his wife stroked his hands.

114

"How's he doing, Ma?" Hep asked.

"That contraption is too noisy," Keely snapped. "We hardly slept last night."

Keely climbed into bed beside her husband and whispered into his ear, "Don't you leave me, Colt Culhane." She massaged his laboring chest. "Don't you dare leave me now. I am not ready and neither are you."

On the fifth night, Colt opened his eyes, blinking uncontrollably until he focused lovingly at his bride.

"There you are," Keely smiled though happy tears. "Where'd you go without me?"

The doctor, amazed at his rallying, removed his oxygen, and tested the veracity of his lungs.

"What's all this?" Colt eased from a scratchy voice that hadn't spoken in some time. "Who died?" he joked weakly. Everyone in the room laughed as they wiped away tears. "Didn't think I was going to leave before my Founders Day celebration," he joshed. "One hundred years?"

"We know you love a good party," Selena teased as Keely brought him garlic soup and ginger tonic and helped him sit up in bed, propping him up on a mountain of pillows.

"Top Cat, Bright Eyes and Sporty here?" Papa Colt asked.

"No. We decided to let them stay in school. No reason to worry them."

"True that."

After speaking with Orelia long distance, Keely shooed them all out.

"Stop fussin' around me, woman," he teased and patted the side of the bed for her to sit next to him. "I saw 'em Keely."

"Who?"

"Everybody. My mama, Saida, my daddy, Lone Wolf, Aunt Pearl, Gideon, all my boys. Henley. They were all waiting on me." Keely smooth back his hair with her hands. "I almost went with them but I heard you Keely." She kissed his cheek. "And I didn't see her."

"See who?"

"Star. She's not there. Which means she's still here, Keely. I'm not leaving here or going up yonder without her being there."

Keely smiled and put her forehead to his. "I know you gonna do what you want, Colt Culhane. I'm awfully glad you came back here—to me."

"You my woman?"

"I am."

12

"OK, man that's it," TC accosted Carter Hix in Studio 3. "You're out."

"C'mon, man. Just a little weed gets my juices flowing," Carter replied.

"Your 'juices' are gonna flow out of Champion Studio. Get your shit and go."

"You're too uptight, man."

"And you're not tight enough. I told you drugs had no place in here. We don't create using artificial means."

"Hey, man. Herb is natural."

"Around my sister and these guys. No. I warned you twice this is it. Get to steppin'."

The guys waited for TC to yell "psych" but he was dead serious. Lethally serious. TC ran a tight ship and dared you to push his buttons. Everyone respected that… but Carter Hix.

"Man, this lame-ass group," Carter snatched his drumsticks from the stand and almost fell. TC eyed him patiently.

"I'll send for my drums," Hix said.

"You didn't buy these drums. They belong to Champion."

"Aww. Gonna be like that? You sorry Mothaf—. You'll be sorry. Later fellas." He staggered through the door then anteroom and out into the hall.

"Z, make sure he finds the front door and doesn't do any damage on the way?"

"Sure."

"Thanks. I know I don't have to reiterate my stance on drugs with the rest of you cats."

"Everybody who comes with you can't go with you," Scoey said.

"So, allow me to introduce our female lead. Ronnie," TC beckoned with his hand. "This is Veronica 'Ronnie' Alston and she is going to pair up with Qwayz's voice for the songs we've been rehearsing instrumentally, 'Just the Two of Us' and 'When I'm With You.' This combination is going to give Raw Cilk its first hit. Give Motown some competition." TC chuckled.

"Did you know about this?" Jax asked Scoey.

"Naw. His name is on the Studio and the checks."

With this one personnel addition, TC catapulted Champion Studios into a record company and the guys remained in awe of his vision and execution. After Ronnie's initial shyness, her voice meshed with Qwayz's in a way that made the session players smile. TC was right again. Motown, Stax and Chess records had solo acts or group acts. Boy and girl duos were rarely done, and TC intended to be the innovator. The hours were long, the tension high and TC never flinched. He knew what he wanted and when he exacted it from the new voices—it hit.

During their sibling date, Jaz looked at her handsome brother dressed in black, listening to him more than she talked. Right before her eyes he had become a man. Although it wasn't supposed to be until after his graduation, TC had all but moved out of his room and into his apartment on the second floor of Champion replete with an office and a bedroom with a round bed and adjoining bathroom. This development made Jaz sad; TC had always been there for her. And now he was gone. In the blink of an eye. Her father traveled most of the week now and Mel was never really there for her. It was a strange time–growing up–changing. She wasn't sure she was ready.

118

"So, what's the story on this guy Mel's been dating, Mickey Boulware?" TC asked.

"I'm glad she dating somebody. Seems nice enough. Works at Red Ball Express."

"No college?"

"Neither do you or Dad and you all seem to be doing just fine."

"OK. Miss Smarty-pants." TC spun his spaghetti on the fork. "Treats her well?"

"I guess," she teased. "Haven't seen her with any bruises." He rolled his eyes.

"And Jesse Ramsey?"

"Still Jesse Ramsey." Jaz shrugged her shoulders nonchalantly.

"Good player."

"Good kisser."

"OK. Basta."

"How about you and Ronnie?"

"What?" he screwed up his face. "Not my type. Too reserved. Too young. Nice girl, though."

"Well, she makes googly eyes at you all the time."

"She listens well. I am directing her."

"Sure. Don't piss on my shoes and tell me its rain." Jaz scraped up the last of the chocolate fudge from the cake. "What's up with Qwayz?"

"What do you mean?"

"Seems kinda preoccupied."

"Haven't noticed. I am recommending him for team captain when I graduate. He sure is hitting all the right notes on those songs. Maybe he doesn't like Yudi for Denny," TC guessed

"No. Nothing like that. Everybody likes Yudi for Denny. Finally, she has a cool and funny boyfriend whose family owns the best funeral home in Watts."

"C'mon, I gotta bounce," he said. She stood and he caught her in the crook of his arm like he used to do when they were kids. He kissed the top of her head, then let her go.

"I love you, TC," she said and put on her fudge brown fedora.

"Love you, too, Sis." He put the porkpie hat over his cold, black locks.

Jaz used her keys to open the front door of #3G, well-fed and dog-tired, she just wanted to review for her English test on "Beowulf," polish her saddle oxford shoes and go to bed.

"Wild as a buck you are," Lorette accused, as Jaz hung her jacket in the hall closet.

"Whatever," Jaz mumbled. Times like this she hated that her father was away. "Must we go through this every time I come home and you are bored?"

"You just wait. When we get you to Connecticut, you won't have these hoodlum friends. Running around at all hours of the night—"

Caught up in her own tirade, Lorette hadn't noticed the horrified look on Jaz's face.

"What did you say? Connecticut? What's that got to do with me?"

Lorette stopped, realizing she'd said too much, revealing partial plans to Jaz alone while she and Hep decided to break the news together. Lorette let out an exhausting breathe. "Your father and I were supposed to share this news with you together but…well, we're adults. Practically. And I think you and I together in Connecticut will be good. We may even become 'simpatico' as they say."

120

"What are you babbling about?" Jaz asked with a condescending air.

"You and me and a good school in a good neighborhood. If you don't like it, then a boarding school."

"You are demented," Jaz said dismissively, as she slid off her shoulder bag.

"Oh really?" The way Jaz spoke to her was abominable. *You messed up my plans once before by being born but it is my turn now,* Lorette thought. "TC will be here. Mel will be in New York and you, my dear, will be with me and your father," Lorette finished smugly, loving the feel of power and having the upper hand. "In Connecticut. In a private school for your senior year. Briarcrest Academy on your transcript guarantees you'll get into a great college."

Jaz stared at her mother unblinkingly. Her brain pinging inside her head. Jaz couldn't grasp a thought. She couldn't come back at her mother with a pithy retort that would silence her. "No," was all she could say as she shook her head. "No way."

"Oh yes," Lorette huffed. "It's my turn, Jaz! And you, little girl, will not ruin this for me. It's one year of your life. One measly little year…You'll be fine," Lorette declared. "Leave that hat, that hair and that crowd you run around with—"

"The hell you say!" Jaz shouted. She grabbed her jacket and shoulder bag, slammed open the front door and ran down the stairs into the setting sun.

Her beloved Alvaro Street bathed in an eerie mauvy red sunset more like Colt, Texas than L.A. She didn't' know where to go. Her father in D.C., her brother shut-away taping, Gladys Ann wouldn't understand as she loved her dead mother and her alive grandmother as did Denny. All these mother-lovers.

Jaz began walking, and walking with no set destination. She then caught the bus and got off at Santa Monica Pier. She walked passed the Lobster House where she and her father dined on their after-movie dates, heading straight for the carousel. Trying to making sense out of nonsense caused her head to ache. She climbed on the big black horse, the one her father said was alright over Lorette's objection when she was a small girl. Lorette wanted Jaz to join her and Mel on a tame, bench seat, while her father and TC climbed aboard stallions. Her mother. Lorette Javier Culhane had always been against her baby daughter. And now she thinks she has Jaz just where she wants her.

During their nightly call, Hep shared his evening events with his wife long distance from D.C. Who was there, who asked about his lovely wife—details that usually sparked her interest. This time was different. "What's wrong? Kids alright?" Hep asked his distracted wife.

"Why would you ask that?"

"I always do."

"It's Jaz," Lorette blurted out. "She left a few hours ago and none of her friends have seen her. Not Gladys Ann—"

"You told her," Hep exhaled on a breath of air.

"She got under my skin and I…" she stopped, realizing how feeble she sounded. That a child she birthed could push her buttons.

In a matter of hours Hep Culhane booked a flight home and upon his arrival found #3G all lit up like the middle of the day, looking like Command Central. Everyone had been called and Selena fought her brother to "stay put" before traveling from France. "She'll turn up," he told her. Not gone the requisite twenty-four hours yet, Hep pulled strings at the

122

LAPD, now headed by his former partner and buddy Truck McMillian. As everyone looked for the missing teen, Hep refused to accept the word "runaway."

People came and went from the Alvaro apartment and when all her known haunts were exhausted, Raw Cilk sat helplessly waiting for Jaz's appearance. Qwayz sat next to TC on the arms of the sofa, for once, with no objections from Lorette. TC bit his thumb nail as Qwayz rubbed his forehead and Scoey, overcome by exhaustion from a rigorous football practice and lack of action, had fallen asleep. When Hep entered the apartment, Lorette flew to him, rousing the guys from their confused stupors. Qwayz stood and stretched when a thought popped into his mind. "I'll be right back," he told TC who nodded in agreement. "You got something?"

"Maybe, maybe not," he said and left alone.

"C'mon girlie," he spoke to the gods as he steered Reds up and down the streets of Watts heading for the Santa Monica Pier. His eyes combed the beach and there, in the great distance, he saw a lone figure, sitting next to a wooden spike. "Please be her." He steered Reds between stanchions and onto the sand where cars were forbidden. This late at night he doubted anyone would stop him. When the sand softened and he couldn't get closer, he opened the car door and sauntered up to the lone figure which, with each step became Jaz; a fudge fedora hat clamped down over wild hair.

"Hey girlie," he said quietly. "What you doing?"

Startled by the intrusion, Jaz glanced up at him, contemplated leaving but thought better of it.

"You look cold."

"According to you, I always am."

Convinced she wasn't going to run, he slid down on the next wooden spike…both facing the rumbling sea. They sat in silence.

"So, what's up, Jaz? Why the unscheduled vacation?"

Her shoulders rose and sank in abject defeat; cold, tired and at a loss for words.

"Folks back at #3G kinda worried. Haven't seen or heard from you in a bit."

"Yeah, well if I had a passport and some money they wouldn't see me ever again."

"What would that prove?"

"That I can decide my own life without noise from the peanut gallery."

"That 'peanut gallery' is legally responsible for you until you're 18 and out. You got a few years."

"Always the lawyer. Is this why you're here? To badger me into submission?"

"Hey, I'm trying to placate and find a tolerable solution for everybody." He took out a roll of Cryst-O-Mints and offered her one. "That's what lawyers do."

Jaz took the offered Lifesaver and asked, "You got anything else? A hamburger or fries. A orange freeze?"

They both chuckled and Qwayz relaxed. "Hot chocolate would be more your speed."

He watched a small smile tug at Jaz's lips in the moonlight and fade.

After another silence, she sighed. "Know what it is…not just yanking me away from my home and plopping me down in lily-white Connecticut at some white boarding school with girls named Buffy, Muffie and Cottontail. It's not subjecting me to cold weather. Not even it being just me and Lorette for long stretches of time; I've made an art of avoiding her."

"Leaving all your friends?"

124

"Yeah, that too," Jaz said, unconvincingly before continuing, "It's that they never asked me about any of it. Never considered that I may just not like that idea. It's my life. Shouldn't I have been consulted? Even if they were going to do what they're going to do. Couldn't they pretend to care what I thought?"

"Your dad's got a whole lot on his plate lately and your mother—"

"Don't defend them to me—please." Her harshness surprised even her. "You know how TC and I used to play that 'look it up in the dictionary' game?"

"Yeah, he gave you your own for your ninth birthday." They both chuckled.

"It started with the word 'exasperated.' When Lorette was talking to her mother she said 'Jaz is just so exasperating.'" Jaz stopped talking and Qwayz heard the pain of remembering in her voice. "I was maybe four no older than five years old. So, when TC came home I asked him about the word and we looked it up. Surprise! Lorette wasn't telling my grandmother how wonderful I was at all. Ump," she huffed wryly. "That was the nail that sealed the coffin for us. A lot of folks loved me. I decided to just return the favor and none of them were Lorette."

A speechless Qwayz listened to the tumble of the ocean a few times as he had no idea what to say. His mother loved them all. While he had no opinion of Lorette, this certainly changed his view of her.

"So, you see, I'm not surprised by Lorette at all. But my Dad—"

"He probably thought this move was good for you."

"Well, I don't see how and I've been thinking about it all night. Can't make much sense out of it. So I'm out."

125

"What's that mean?" Qwayz looked at her with furrowed eyebrows.

"I'm not going to kill myself or anything like that. Not into suicide but I could do homicide... easily."

"You need to rethink that, too. You'd never make it in prison," he said, removing his red cap, running his hands through his hair and replacing it. "So, what you gonna do?"

"I've thought it all out and can't come up with anything lasting. I am not going to Connecticut. TC would jump at the chance to have me live with him but Dad would nix that big time. Like he would me going with Mel to New York or even going to Colt, Texas."

"I can understand that," Qwayz offered. "Sometimes after you all leave for dinner and homework, your brother starts a session at 6 and doesn't get what he wants from us until 2 am. He has no concept of time. Then he'll go a few more hours mixing and taping to his perfection. You should see him, Jaz. I mean that cat loves his music. He's the only one who can tell a G from a G flat and he means to get it. Sometimes you wished he'd say, 'Go home. We'll try it tomorrow.' But not him. He's incredible. Magic."

"That what he says about you playing basketball," Jaz confided. "A real mutual admiration society you all got going."

"All I'm saying is," Qwayz clarified, "I don't see how he'll be able to 'supervise' his little sister. And you and Mel? Here or in New York. Oil and water; don't see that at all."

"Maybe I can stay with Gladys Ann for that year, but Grandma Mac and I for a whole year? Ever since I gave Gladys Ann that Lilt Home Perm, the old girl has had it out for me. So, I thought about Paris with Aunt Selena and Uncle Zack. No one could refuse that. If I've got to go away, why not really go away. Another country. The experience of living abroad." Jaz beamed into the lunar rays.

Qwayz stared at her. "That's a long-ass way, Jaz."

"The farther, the better. I may come back to go to college, depending on my French experience. Or maybe I'd be an expat like they are. Then I'd *never* come back here. That'd show them. Hep and Lorette Culhane."

Never come back here, echoed in his brain, bounced off the skull and registered in his tired and weary mind.

"I heard Aunt Selena tell Uncle Zack that she got a call from Harry DeLacosta, which always means something civil rights. They're always looking for people. I know the Freedom Riders are over but there'll be a Voter Registration project next year Down South. I could volunteer for that. Or that Peace Corps I heard about on the news; I can sign up to travel throughout the world to make foreign countries better. For free—"

"That's no time soon. And don't you have to be *in* college to qualify for that?"

"Probably. Off by at least a year." Jaz shrugged her shoulders. "My timing is always off. Don't have all the details which is why Paris, France is the top winner now. A sure thing. You know how much my aunt and uncle love me."

"So do I," he blurted out. "So do a lot of people."

Jaz chuckled and playfully added, "To know me is to love me," she teased, unconvincingly.

Qwayz became embarrassed by his uncustomary but innocent declaration. He didn't mean it. Not in a romantic way. Did he?

Qwayz, consumed by stillness, caused Jaz to look over at him. "You'll come visit me in '65 with TC."

"Huh? The year you're collecting on your graduation present?"

"I've been waiting years for that trip. But now, I'll already be there. I can show you all around. Introduce you to my new friends... in French."

"Well, you've thought of everything," Qwayz said, in a daze. *All her solutions entailed going somewhere, going away,* he thought. He was going to lose his confidante and best female friend. Who would he tell all his deep dark secrets to, his dreams–Stanford, being a lawyer, Myrtle Beach–and not be judged or teased for it.

The entire dream of Paris faded with Jaz, the melancholia returned and she said, "I don't really want Paris... not without you guys in '65."

"But Paris can come here," Qwayz said and brightened. "You said it yourself. Your aunt and uncle love you. How about they come here to L.A. while you finish out your senior year? Then you go back with them for your senior trip and come back here for Berkeley?"

"But they aren't going to give up all—"

"Why not? They come a couple of times a year for weeks at a time anyway, more when Selena does guest shots on television. Zack is always talking about leaving your fans enough time to miss you."

"That's Uncle Zack, not Selena..."

"Don't know unless you ask. All they can do is tell you 'No.'"

"Then it's back to the drawing board."

"Look Gloomy Gus... Let's find out first."

Jaz smiled, rocked and said, "I like it."

"Yeah. Add 'brilliant' to my list of credentials." He stood and shook out his legs. "If you're ready to roll, I'm ready to ride."

128

"Where to?"

"C'mon, Jaz. Really?"

"Can we get something to eat first? The Waffle House is always open."

"I pity the man who has to feed you. C'mon."

"I will feed myself. That's what independent women do. Besides, being a 'runaway' works up an appetite."

Hands stuffed in their respective pockets, they walked to his car. As he was putting the top up, Jaz hauled off and kicked the door on the passenger side.

"Damn!" she released in frustration.

"Hey! My car didn't do nothing to you!"

"Sorry," Jaz looked and saw a crooked reflection of the moon in a dent she'd just created. Relieved when the door opened alright she climbed in and shut it, hoping Qwayz wouldn't notice for a few days.

They ordered and Qwayz went to wash his hands and called #3G, spoke to Hep relaying that Jaz was with him, cold and hungry but alright. He told him he would bring her home after they ate. Qwayz could hear the relief in her father's voice.

Jaz and Qwayz talked about everything and everybody as they devoured their breakfasts. "Wow, this is the second time I've ruined your Saturday night, huh?"

"That's what pesky sisters are for." He wiped his mouth. "Of course, this one wasn't as bad as the last." Qwayz thought of the party in the Boondocks where he rescued Jaz and Gladys Ann from Satan and the Disciples.

"Or maybe it was," Jaz teased.

"Last time you did have Gladys Ann as company. You've got to learn to shelter-in-place. Can't always bolt when things

129

don't go the way you want. And believe me they won't go your way a lot of the time."

"OK. Granddad."

"Ready to roll?" Qwayz asked, peeling off the money for the check and placing it on the tray. "Home?"

"Well, I ain't going to Connecticut," Jaz promised.

"You've made that abundantly clear."

They walked toward the door where he grabbed a toothpick and the waitress's attention. "Thanks for coming, do come back," she said, batting her eyes.

"Thanks," Qwayz answered with a quick smile.

"Cheeze, why are you all so unbelievably irresistible to women?"

"You said it best… 'to know me is to love me.'"

"Tsk," Jaz smirked.

"Maybe when you become a woman you'll find out." He winked and rotated his toothpick across his lips.

Silence replaced all the chatter and joning of the last few hours. Qwayz opened his door just as Jaz opened hers. "You don't have to go up."

"Oh, yes I do. You know the drill."

Qwayz followed her up the stairs. When they reached the landing and Jaz fished for her keys she looked over and said, "Thank you, Qwayz." She dove her head into his shoulder the way he had seen her do TC and her father—her act of contrition. Then she grabbed him and hugged him tightly and let go.

"Sure." The gesture gave him pause for the second time tonight.

The door swung open and her father filled the doorway, light etching out his massive form. Jaz dodged past him and went to her room as Qwayz began descending the steps.

"Thank you, Qwayz," Hep said with sincere emotion.

130

"You're welcome Mr. C." He stopped and looked at him through the bannister railings. "She was hurt you didn't consider her feelings about the move. If she'd had the resources, she'd be long gone. Goodnight."

Hep had thought of nothing else since he learned of her walking out. He was not prepared to lose another Culhane woman in America or beyond. His sister Star'd left in the Depression; he was not going to give his daughter reason to leave in the 60s.

Hep waited for Jaz to finish up in the bathroom and go to her bedroom. By the time he knocked and entered she was already buried between the sheets with her back to him.

"Punkin," he began. Jaz did not move at the sound of his childhood pet name for her. "Perhaps your mother and I didn't handle this news as well as we should have. But I thought we, you and I, could discuss anything."

"Then why did you make a decision without even consulting me," Jaz said without facing him.

"Parents are not perfect, Jaz."

She popped up and her eyes implored, "Like I'm a kid who just does what she's told with no input."

"I know. I apologize for that. I'm going to do my best to make sure it doesn't happen again."

Jaz looked at her father. Wanted to hug him around the neck and have a good cry, but she would be sixteen this December and wanted to be seen as mature.

"Thank you," she said and resumed her place on the pillow.

"I love you, Punkin'"

"I know."

The next morning Jaz spoke to Selena in Paris and, after promising never to give them a scare like that, Jaz proposed

131

their coming here for a year…her very important senior year and then she'd go back with them for the summer visit.

"We don't live in the real bad part of Watts—"

"Sweetie, I am well aware of where you live. Settle down."

Jaz sucked in her lips and held her breath. She had no plan B.

"Tell you what. I'll do you one better. How about Uncle Zack and I come and say, rent a beach house in Malibu and then when school starts move back to Alvaro?"

Jaz burst into grateful tears. "I think that sounds just perfect."

"I love you, Jazzy. Remember, I have your word that you'll never cut and run again. There is always a solution."

"Thank you, Aunt Selena."

From a crack in his bedroom door, Hep watched his daughter dissolve into happy tears. She knew how lucky she was.

13

That June, TC accepted his graduation diploma and assumed his place at the piano. His Indian-brown fingers struck a chord then a note as he accompanied himself on "Climb Every Mountain" and "You'll Never Walk Alone." Once his clear voice held the final note, not a dry eye could be found in Roosevelt's auditorium. Another milestone and passage for many in the audience, especially the Culhanes. With the exception of Papa Colt and Keely, who they'd see in a few weeks, everyone else attended: his parents, his grandparents Javier from Evelyn, Tennessee, his sisters, Aunt and Uncle from Paris and all of Raw Cilk. Somehow Jaz suspected that this upcoming trip to Colt Texas would probably be TC's last. As it was he wasn't staying long and with him also went Qwayz. She'd challenged them with a "be there or be square" to get two weeks out of them for the celebration. Neither she nor Mel moved into their brother's room. Leaving a place for him to return to or a shrine to his memory, it remained just as he'd left it.

A sign that read "Closed Private Party" hung on the glass door of the Satin Doll. Once inside, the revelers honored both TC and Scoey's graduation, partying in full swing. Not only the families Culhane and Scofield, but also the friends they'd known all their lives: from Dragons, to Mag 7 to Raw Cilk and surely beyond. Jaz eyed Mel as they glanced at all the decorations and even the confetti and balloons gathered for a future release, just like all the New Year's Eve parties they had spent there. Her big sister was next. *Not that Mel hadn't worked hard for it,* Jaz thought. *But things came too easily for her.* Lots of people have great voices and work hard for their dreams and many fail, but not Brittany Melba Culhane. She claimed it early and succeeded.

Jaz accepted a glass of punch and noted that her father and Lorette's plans remained to keep the small Georgetown house for Hep's residence while in D.C. but adding a sprawling mansion in Connecticut's countryside, which Jaz never intended to visit or see. Lorette had already scheduled visits for her parents, all of her sisters and their families and her old friends, Gay Iris and Effie. Now with plenty of room to invite them and staff to honor their every wish, plus a ride from the airport to their helipad on the south lawn, Lorette would finally live in the world she had always envisioned. Tenacity should be Lorette's middle name. Jaz had her aunt and uncle and TC down the street with Gladys Ann and Tracy still her ace boon coons. Jaz meandered the club and surveyed the celebratory nature of the party with Raw Cilk acting up, playing the white Baby Grand piano and enjoying being together now and in their future. Their released record, "Just the Two of Us" had debuted "on the chart with a bullet;" they were wild with unrestrained excitement. All of TC's old girlfriends swarmed around him, mingling with those hoping to be next. The couples huddled either dancing or watching others; Gladys Ann and Jehson Culbreath, Mel and Mickey Boulware and Jaz watched Tracy introduce her parents to Scoey. Jaz tried to forget the breach in her friendship with Gladys Ann who shared last week that she had slept with Jehson.

"What?!" Jaz exclaimed as she pulled her friend into a vacant classroom. "I thought we were going to wait until we went to college?"

"Couldn't. Things happen."

"So, the circle pins and our friendship pledge is a lie?"

"Let's just say I found my boyfriend irresistible."

"Oh cheeze. You hussy."

"I'm already sixteen. Wait until you find someone you're crazy about Jaz. You won't be able to hold back."

"Did you use protection?"

"Of course."

Jaz rolled her eyes against her friend's smiling face. "Well, how was it?"

Jaz smiled and accepted a crab ball from a roving waiter and wondered if this was what being a teenager was all about; half, feet securely planted firmly in quicksand and half, adrift. Somewhere betwixt and between was life… the way it was and the way it will never be again. A strange time. A changing time. How could she slow it down, fill in all the gaps and reboot it again? It's all happening too fast… time through the hourglass and she had no control. Trying to figure out when the last time was you did something for the first time.

She saw Qwayz with TC's old girlfriend Tiffany Thorne by the door.

"Hey?" Jaz sidled up to him just as Tiffany spotted that TC was free.

"She still chasing after him?" Jaz teased.

"Seems like. He's long gone," Qwayz quipped.

"Yes, he is. What about you?"

"What?"

"You seem preoccupied about something."

"Huh?"

Qwayz had never said "Huh?" in his life. Self-assured, decisive, Qwayz never had that word in his vocabulary. "You've been here physically but your mind is someplace else. It's not Ma Vy, Denny or Haine is it?"

"I wish."

135

"What?"

"I don't mean that."

"You just said it."

Qwayz shook his head in frustration and walked away.

Later, after the dinner, the dancing resumed, and while Dickie danced with Jaz, Qwayz cut in on the Shirelles', "Will You Still Love Me Tomorrow." Jaz loved dancing with Scoey, the way his height carved out a piece of the dance floor for them no matter how crowded, but she and Qwayz had a rhythm—a syncopation, a flow and he did a lot of turns, fancy footwork, hands drifts across the back and over the shoulders, double turns. Poetry in motion. When she danced with any of the trio, folks around usually stopped and watched. They volleyed in "Please Mr. Postman," followed by the Velvelettes' "He Was Really Saying Something"— Bop-bop-sookie-do-wah before TC cut the rivals and put on more Raw Cilk.

"Where's Jesse?" Qwayz asked.

"He left," Jaz said.

"You didn't go with him?"

"He should have stayed with me," Jaz sassed.

Qwayz laughed. "Joaquin would have stayed."

"Yeah," Jaz admitted wistfully and then added, "I might have left with him." Jaz chuckled.

"Well, Joaquin wasn't threatened by us like Jesse."

"No, Jesse's just a jealous knucklehead."

"No matter. Don't ever dim your own candle to make someone else shine."

"OK, Reverend Chandler," Jaz teased then asked, "Who's that girl talking to TC edging in on Ronnie space?"

"As TC will tell you, Ronnie has no space except six inches from the mike. And that girl is LeLani Troop, his newest permanent hire."

136

"Oh yeah? What does she do or should I ask?"

"She's the receptionist, office coordinator/manager. So far she's really good. Keeps everyone in line at the front door and accountable on task."

"I've never seen her. She's cute."

"Black father and Hawaiian mother. Hey, they're playing our song." He led Jaz out on the dancefloor again with Miracles' "Mickey's Monkey."

The following week at the studio, most of the guys sprawled on the couch waiting for TC to tweak the playback as Qwayz sat alone on a stool, thumbing the new electric guitar. "OK, what has Cherish done to you, boy?" Jaz teased trying to cajole Qwayz from his self-imposed melancholia.

Qwayz looked at Jaz long and hard, gauging the level of trust before finally saying, "Not Cherish. It's Breena."

Jaz looked at him and asked, "What's a Breena?'"

He chuckled and answered, "A girl I been messing with since Cherish. I don't even know how we hooked up. Next thing I knew, I was at her house... a couple of times."

"She put a voodoo haint on you?"

"Naw. It's all on me."

"So, what's the problem? Don't like her anymore? Move on."

"Not that simple."

"Why not?"

Qwayz's hazel eyes, flashing torment, embarrassment and guilt, pierced Jaz's light ones. He stared at her without speaking and she knew. "Oh, my god! No."

"Yep." He looked at her parted lips. "Close your mouth."

"Qwayz how did it happen?"

"I'll spare the details. But these last few weeks have been a living hell."

"How late is she?"

"Late enough."

She could see his nervousness, his blood shot eyes. His foot started fidgeting in a way she had never witnessed.

"There could be a lot of reasons she's late."

"Oh, yeah?"

"So, she making a trip to old doctor—"

"Wants to have it."

"Oh, Qwayz."

"My life is over. Not my plan at all. Stanford Law School, a great career championing for the underserved. Then marriage. Waaaay down the line and not to a girl like Breena Veney."

"Good enough to have sex with but not marry?"

"Exactly."

Jaz wasn't expecting that answer.

"I'm a guy, Jaz. A young guy. Marrying her never crossed my mind. Her mother came on to me. Imagine my child having that kind of a grandmother?"

"OK. Slow down. Maybe she isn't. Just wait and see."

"I messed up, big-time." He ran his fingers through his hair. "They got all these plans—"

"It's only been a few weeks. I suggest you wait it out."

"And then?"

"You deal with it. Right now you're wastin' a lot of energy."

Qwayz threw his head back and laughed for the first time in weeks. "How'd you get so smart?"

"See, I have these three pain-in-the-ass brothers, who wear me out about this stuff."

"Need to take our own advice. But I did. Makes no sense."

138

TC sat at the white Baby Grand and called for Qwayz. "C'mere man. Let's do 'Danny Boy' for Papa Colt."

Qwayz began to join him, stopped and said, "Thanks, Jaz."

"Sure."

You dumb-ass horny male, she thought. *It'd be tragic for him to become a statistic. Worse for the child… and who is Breena Veney?*

~*~

A few days later, Jaz entered the studio and watched TC and Qwayz shoot it out on the alley basketball court. When they hit a snag in either the instrumentals or the vocals, they grabbed a ball and went at it until one of them figured out the perfect riff or lyric. Their "busy the body and free the mind" technique might have been long and always smelly, but it worked for the two of them. After about an hour they came in sweaty, stinky and excited. Dickie handed Jaz the pink Hostess Snow Ball and, as she bit into the marshmallow gooiness, she asked Qwayz, "So, how goes it?"

"It goes Jaz." He broke into a huge grin of relief. "It goes and… flows!!"

They both laughed. Dickie eyed them and asked, "What's the joke?"

"No, joke," Jaz said, as Qwayz disappeared up the steps for a shower, leaving TC to make the final notations on the chart. Apparently, Qwayz'd solved the problem and got first dibs on the waterworks.

14

Even at ten in the morning, the air rippled Texas-hot and stifling. Colt Culhane sat proudly on stage as he had at all the Founder's Day celebrations before, but then he wasn't the lone founder. The variegated, crepe paper steamers and a Founder's Day banner flapped in the dry heat as the balloons tried valiantly to offer colorful relief from the monotonous green and brown, flat terrain. With his family seated behind him, Reverend Gassaway led the crowd in an opening prayer. Seated next to Colt—his wife and then his children: Orelia, Selena, and Hep. Behind each of them were their spouses and children. Colt's grands. Another generation.

Colt looked out over the smiling crowd in front of him to pay homage not only to this land but also to him for his 100th birthday. Not having a birth certificate on the settlement or in slavery, he was sure he was older by five years—but why split hairs at this point. It didn't matter; he'd beat pneumonia and was here.

Mel sang a song. Reba sang a song. The choir sang a song and there was more speechifying. A little boy read a poem and four little girls did some sort of tribute dance. *Whose children were these?* Colt wondered as he was ready to go home to the shade of his porch swing and enjoy the comfort of his liquid refreshment.

To stay alert, he watched a dot on the horizon. Then on the road by his house to keep focus. He would smile and quip every now and again to show he still had his sense of humor. He looked back at his dot. Was it moving? It was, but slowly. His daughter Selena sang and Colt patted his foot and nodded his head with the beat. Hep spoke and Colt agreed with a smile or two. Keely held his hand, he squeezed hers and looked back at his focal point. The dot had reached the gate by his house. Colt couldn't see around the tree branch that grew from the circle around the town center and the statute of the Founding Fathers. He wondered if they were waiting at his house or coming this way. Was it only one person?

TC sat at the piano and roused Colt from his vigil. If the person was coming to steal something, he would see him on the way back up road. He couldn't get away with much on foot. TC energized Colt with his rendition of "St. Louie Woman" and Colt thought of Fancy and Belle and those good old days. He supposed he wouldn't mention them in his speech. He wanted TC to play another tune, but he didn't. Colt knew they worried about the mayo in the potato salad and coleslaw for the picnic afterwards. He and his grandson, Top Cat, would make up for it.

Colt looked up to the house at the would-be robber and saw feet getting closer. It was not a *he* at all… it was a *she*. Tall, dark, big-boned, wearing cat-eye sunglasses like Mel, walking straight for them all. Like she knew them. Him. Like she belonged and didn't want to miss out. She stopped and stood on the edge of the crowd. Did anybody see her but him? His heart beat wildly. His breathing grew shallow. She removed her glasses and grinned.

"Star!" Colt stood straight up.

"Star!" Colt repeated and bolted upright, waking Keely.

"What is it Colt?"

He panted and looked about his bedroom. A pink dawn peeked over the quiet terrain.

"Are you alright?" Keely asked hoping he wasn't having a relapse. She had thought about canceling the children's visit this year but Colt so looked forward to their coming.

"I'm fine," he spoke quietly. "Just a ...dream."

"You want me to get the doctor?"

"No." He poured and sipped water from the nightstand's carafe. "Just a little excited," he assured her and patted her hand. "Go on back to sleep."

~*~

In a few weeks' time, Colt relived the exact experience he'd had in his dream. The only difference? Star did not appear. His eyes grew watery staring at the horizon and the road waiting for it to happen but it did not. The picnic and games on the church lawn, as they had always been, full of noise, old stories and fun with deference to the past and a vision for the future.

"How's Daddy?" Hep asked his mother.

"Fair to middlin'. That pneumonia kicked the stuffing out of him. But he's healthy for a old man," Keely teased.

"Maybe he'll come to Connecticut or fly to Paris."

"He's not going to do that. But you can ask. Likes being left alone. He is content." Keely used one of her husband's favorite words.

Proclaimed best Founder's Day ever, the revelers cut the lights, removed the last of the decorations and moved into the well-lit homestead. As they all filed through the front entrance, Qwayz grabbed Jaz's hand. She wrenched it loose and asked, "What's up?"

"A moment," he said, and as Aunt Orelia cleared the threshold, he closed the door.

"What's wrong?" *Hope he didn't impregnate another girl*, Jaz thought.

"I got some talk for you."

"Well, what? If I miss out on the last of Grandma Keely's chocolate fudge cake—"

142

"You always thinking about food," Qwayz said on a chuckle.

"What else is there?"

He sat on the bannister. She grew impatient. "Have you and TC been in that mulberry wine?"

"You know I don't mess with that stuff."

"Yeah, you all are 'athletes,'" she completed his and TC's creed and sighed with annoyed exasperation.

"You still messing with Jesse Ramsey?"

"Define 'messing with.'"

"You still girlfriend and boyfriend?"

"Yeah. Pretty much." *No one is gonna mess with Jessie's girl,* she thought.

"I just can't figure that one out."

"Co-captain of football team and cheerleader? It goes."

"Break up with him."

"What?"

"You don't love him."

"You don't love anybody at fifteen."

"Papa Colt and Grandma Keely would differ with you."

"That's old timey times."

"Gladys Ann and Jehson Culbreath."

"Well, they're special. Maybe even retarded."

"You don't want that?"

"What? Now? No. Too young. I'm not having sex until college."

"Still. You need to break up with Jesse Ramsey."

"And why would I do that?"

"You know how there's all this speculation about why I've been on my own for a while now."

Jaz smiled. *Yeah, you thought you got Breena pregnant so you're taking a breather,* she supposed but kept it to herself.

143

His boys continually speculated on who this new girl was that Qwayz was hung up on. They didn't know, but if Jaz could get the girl's name she'd win the bet. "Most say you had to get a much-needed rest."

He chuckled. "Well. What can I say?"

"Cheeze." She rolled her eyes. "You all are the conceited worst." She shifted her weight to the other foot. "Can't we discuss this while eating a piece of cake?"

"Resting is part of it but this next time I'm going for something… someone a little different—"

"Who is it? Does she go to Roosevelt? Do I know her?"

He chuckled into the moonlight and Jaz realized he wasn't going to give her any info. "You can't do better than Cherish Harley, anyway."

"Oh really? Sometimes you just get tired of the same-o, same-o. You know a cute girl, who does everything you want. Forgives you every little thing…Sometimes you want a girl with a little mettle. A girl who doesn't think you walk on water."

Jaz shook her head. "That's a prerequisite. You and TC don't date a girl unless she thinks you're the Second Coming."

"We are…but enough. I'm going to tell you who."

"Really? Who?"

He walked over to her and stood squarely in front of her so close that she backed away. He remained firm with a smile on his face and began to sing, ala the Shirelles, "Baby it's you. Sha nan a na na."

"Oh sh…. You play too much." She pushed him away. "If you weren't gonna tell me you don't have to mock me. Chocolate cake awaits—"

He stepped toward her again, cutting into her personal space, and grabbed her by the shoulders and sang the song again.

144

"What are you doing?" She wrenched away.

"I'm not kidding. It's you Jasmine Bianca Culhane. You are the girl I've been thinking about *all* this time."

Jaz just looked at him. "Tsk. Stop playing," she dismissed.

"I am not. You had no idea?" He tested. "I think TC had a inkling but hasn't said anything. And Dickie. I caught him one time just staring at me after you'd left. 'What's going on MF?'" He'd stepped to Qwayz who answered with a smile.

"Is this a joke? 'Cause I don't think it's very funny? And if I miss out on—"

"No joke."

"You cannot be serious. This is weird. We're like—"

"Brother and sister? But you are not my sister, Jaz. We, you and me, are *not* related."

Jaz stepped back again but didn't bolt into the house, which Qwayz took as a good sign.

"I know you Jasmine Bianca Culhane. I've seen you good, bad and ugly. With sleep in your eyes, a pimple on your nose and your hair wild and dirty with rainwater. But you are also my confidant, good friend and I trust you. You handled the Breena scare without flinching. I haven't even told the guys. They still don't know. But I told you. I had you in my corner."

Jaz stared at him trying to absorb his words, but couldn't. Was he speaking in Chinese?

"I know this is a new concept for you and you need to get used to—"

"I don't have to get used to anything because—"

He silenced her moving lips with one of his fingers. "When I found you at the pier after the argument with your mother, I realized come hell or high water, I was going to lose

145

you… to Connecticut, D.C., France, Down South, wherever—and for some reason that pained me. The thought that you'd be gone and I'd probably never see you again. That you'd go away and find someone new… I never worried about Joaquin or Jesse… both lightweights, and you'd still be around. But away… I'd miss you. Then slowly, I grasped how I really felt about you. How I'd really feel if you were gone for good. I didn't want to take that chance. And no matter who, what or which girl came upon me… none compared to the 'possibility' of you. Would this have happened if the threat of your leaving hadn't come up? I dunno."

Jaz eyed him with a stupefied expression turned to searching and trying to understand the sheer lunacy of his proclamation.

"Like I said I've had months to cozy up and really like the idea. You have not. So the ball is in your court. You decide whether we give this a go or not. If not we'll—"

"We'll what?" She assaulted. "We can't go back after you tell me this crap. You messed it all up—"

"Then why not just go forward?" He rubbed her arm. "What have we got to lose?"

Speechless, Jaz blinked a few times. He came toward her again. She did not back away.

She wondered if she was still breathing. Her mind tried to make sense of the ridiculous words coming out of his mouth. He was proposing incest. She waited for him to laugh and yell, "Psych!"

The world as Jaz knew it stopped spinning, stood on an angle and then disappeared around the edges, melting away like Tony and Maria at the dance in "West Side Story," and just she and Qwayz stood there on Papa Colt's front porch being serenaded by a chorus of Texas crickets. She inhaled rarified air, thin and not enough of it. Her heart beat faster and

146

her ears throbbed as if she were reentering the atmosphere after a long flight. Her entire body pulsated energy she'd never experienced before.

"You never thought of… us?" he asked.

"Never."

"Possibility. Ain't it great?"

Silence claimed them but Qwayz could see the wheels of her mind spinning.

"What if it doesn't work? What if it gets too weird?" *What if you break my heart? S*he thought.

"What if you were born for me and I was born for you?" He countered. "What if we were meant to be? What if our love becomes legendary?" He held her hand and rubbed her thumb with his. "What if years from now you take my last name? We have lots of pretty—"

"Oh Lord!" she anticipated his direction of procreation and became agitated and anxious again.

He chuckled and continued undaunted, "The point is that love is always a risk, Jaz. No guarantees. Take a chance. We'll discover together. Who knows? We might have the greatest love affair ever." He came close again. She recoiled when he reached up to push the hair away from her face. "I want to kiss you."

Oh, crap. Yuck, she thought as he came in on her left cheek and gave her a peck.

"Ready?"

She watched his face and lips cross to her right side.

"Set?"

He looked into her questioning eyes, held her face tenderly in his hands and said, "Go."

Ever so gently, he placed his lips on hers. Her mind echoed, *Ewww.* Her confused heart kept her eyes open looking

147

at his eyelashes covering his half-closed eyes, but her body stayed rooted to the wooden planks of Papa Colt's porch. He smelled of faded Jade East cologne and tasted of Cryst-O-Mints with chocolate notes from a Hershey bar. She wondered what her breath tasted like. Gently his tongue nudged her lips open and forced her eyes closed. She fell into her French kiss mode, tongue flaying every which a way. Qwayz calmed her tongue with his and established a rhythm of his own, a practiced, smooth, enjoyable rhythm she had never experienced. Pleasant, sensuously explorative and luscious without being overly wet. Her nervousness evaporated and her body melted into his like Joanne Woodward's into Paul Newman's in "The Long, Hot Summer," although she vaguely hoped she didn't look half as doofus. Then she didn't care, she was actually enjoying this little interlude. It wasn't Qwayz anymore, it was a boy she could kiss all day. She moaned pleasure. He broke the suction. Her lips throbbed for more, then she realized it was Qwayz again.

"Like I said. No rush. Break up with Jesse Ramsey and let me know when you're ready."

He embraced her, enveloping her body with his. His hands, hot and possessive, traveled across her back producing a strange sensation as she'd never before slow-danced with him or Scoey. Brothers they were— but Qwayz just upped the ante. He held, caressed and slightly rocked her and she thought he'd kiss her again but he released her and went to open the front door. "Your chocolate cake awaits."

"Huh? Oh. Right."

Jaz and Qwayz managed to finish out the remaining week undetected. When setting the table, beginning at opposite ends, they met up at a place setting and he'd rub his pinky finger across her thumb causing her to blush. No one noticed. She wanted another kiss from him but he didn't oblige. No one took notice of their walking to the swimming hole as they always did. Or sitting next to one another in church. They usually did. Riding horses or any number of other Colt, Texas activities... as they always did. Only they knew their status was in transition. Jaz relished that she could accept the newness without any comments from outsiders.

They were leaving Colt, Texas early this year. Everyone had something to do in L.A. before Hep's swearing in ceremony in D.C. Studio business waited for TC as did finalizing plans for Oasis, due to open in September. Hep and Lorette were readying for the occupation of the new house in Connecticut. Selena and Zack had gigs in New York City before going to D.C. for The March and returning to Paris and eventual relocating to the U.S.—Malibu and then Alvaro Street with Jaz.

Papa Colt managed to have one more knock-out porch concert before Top Cat and Qwayz left. Jaz watched two of the most important men in her life and wondered how her new relationship would play in L.A. As she spent time with Qwayz on the side porch, they stole a goodnight kiss before going to bed.

"Let it be known that I am ready for this to go public now."

"I've got to break up with Jesse first. That wouldn't be right."

Qwayz answered her scruples with a smile. "I respect that. We'll keep it between you and me. No one else matters anyway but you and me, Jaz-of-mine."

Jaz couldn't suppress her delight at him calling her that. Jaz-of-mine.

"You'll go on to D.C. for your dad's long overdue wearing in, spend time with Gladys Ann and come on back to L.A. To me. I'll be waiting."

15

The plane taxied then soared into the heavens and Jaz's entire body felt a rush with the take off, and seeing L.A. reduced to a small spot as the puffy-marshmallow clouds accepted them, thrilled her like the feeling she had when Qwayz first kissed her. A rush. She told TC most things but she kept this to herself. Lorette and Mel sat behind her and old flying veteran TC, having flown everywhere domestically and to Europe twice, seemed enchanted by his little sister's first experience.

"Like *the* best ride at P.O.P," she told him.

Five hours later, the same glee consumed her as she watched the approach to D.C. The wide boulevards splayed out around monuments and memorials reached up to greet her. The spike of the Washington Monument, the domed Capitol in the distance, the square Lincoln and rounded Jefferson Memorials rung with spent cherry blossom trees as they circled the Tidal Basin. The iron bird landed at National Airport. A car with a liveried chauffer held a placard— "Culhane."

The large limo snaked up the parkway onto the skinny streets of Georgetown, barely making a turn before stopping in front of a three-story, apartment building laid on its side.

"This is it?" a disappointed Jaz questioned. "Not much to it." Jaz climbed the few steps, entering into the cool air-conditioning and said, "Now that's impressive. It's not as big as #3G."

"Be nice," TC managed in passing, following his luggage up two flights to his room.

"I still have to share with Mel?" Jaz lamented of the tight little room with twin beds.

The ceremony installing her father heralded in pomp and pagentry, like Jaz had never seen. The State Department's reception room, imposing, showcasing opulence and dressed in patriotic regalia from the window treatments and chandeliers to the rugs and the chairs in which they sat; Grandparents Javier, Selena and Zack, Orelia and Sam from Montclair, Aunt Summer and her granddaughter who had accompanied her to Paris for a month to visit Selena, Gladys Ann and her D.C. family and an assortment of notables Jaz didn't recognize but knew her as Hepburn Culhane's third child. Two faces prominently placed: the President's and the First Lady's. Lorette sat on the podium next to her husband and the Culhane children remained duly impressed with their father's regal stature in his dark black suit, crisp white shirt and muted red tie. Handsome and articulate as he accepted the oath of allegiance to his country, he addressed the audience and thanked his parents who could not be present in the flesh but were always with him in spirit, acknowledging the edict "Be who you are," as his guiding principle. Glancing toward the back of the auditorium, he could envision his buddy Range Criqui, smiling with pride, toasting him with a long-necked bottle of beer like they'd last drank in Boot Camp. From this vantage point, he fully understood what Selena meant about duty and responsibility.

As TC sat in the first row, he noted a more sophisticated and gracious attitude toward his father missing at the captain's ceremony in L.A. He supposed that despite the delays, senate approval, administrative and scheduling glitches, his father managed to execute his job with aplomb and dignity that commanded respect. TC also recognized that this assemblage consisted of a better educated, generationally-connected, more

152

seasoned class of well-heeled people where diplomacy and correctness was paramount.

"Look at this spread," Jaz intoned as she picked up a gigantic prawn with silver thongs and placed it on her china plate with an ornate gold-gilt pattern. She sipped champagne from a flute as she and Aunt Orelia stood near the window and gazed at the nation's capital.

"Did you think your little brother would end up here, Aunt O?"

"Not at all. Maybe Henley but not Hep. But I couldn't be more proud," she replied. The camera man called to them, they struck a pose and toasted to Papa Colt and Grandma Keely, their glasses pointed toward the lens. "Life is full of surprises."

Yes, it is, Jaz thought. Qwayz, always on her mind, she looked objectively at Lorette and, for a moment, could see what her father saw in her. Radiant and charming as she dazzled the dignitaries and then posed next to the first lady, her mother the better-looking one of the two.

"Ma's in her world." Mel ambled up beside her sister, downing Beluga caviar on a toast point.

"She's a natural," Jaz admitted.

After the festivities, Hep took his entourage to his offices. "Bigger than that house," Jaz jibbed before being released to go stay with Gladys Ann and her aunt and uncle and cousins.

"I'll be talking to you, kiddo," winked Aunt Selena who was staying in the same northwest neighborhood.

The car traveled up 16th Street until they reached Colorado Avenue, made a left before pulling between two pillars and into a long driveway in front of an imposing Mediterranean house with a pink stucco façade and ivy climbing to its Spanish tiled roof. The gorgeous, stained glass cathedral window caught the sunlight and threw the colorful broken prisms back onto the manicured lawn.

Jaz lit from the car, mesmerized by the home. "This looks like California. Is that the famed Carter Baron?" Jaz asked about the park across the street.

"Yep."

Jaz had heard all the stories about D.C. summers from Gladys Ann over the years.

"Selena and Zack have played there almost every year," her Aunt Ivy offered as they walked to the door.

"I think I'm going to like it here," Jaz mused, walking through the door.

After the ceremony and festivities, TC flew immediately back to L.A. and her parents and Mel straight to Connecticut to the house that would be Lorette's base with Hep joining her on the weekends while keeping the Georgetown home for the workweek.

Jaz couldn't wait to confide in Gladys Ann about Qwayz.

"What? Is that even possible?"

"I didn't think so until he kissed me."

"Ew! Jaz."

"I know. I'm going to take it slow. Break up with Jesse--"

"He is not going to take that well at all."

Jaz shrugged her shoulders. "Has no choice. Then, I think Qwayz and I will go public."

Gladys Ann's face showed that she couldn't wrap her head around the weird concept.

"I figure. We'll date this year. I'll go with him to his senior prom and when he goes off to college... that'll be it."

"What you gonna do about right now? That brother like all of Raw Cilk is used to getting 'it' regular. You're not having sex until college. The math is not adding up."

"I can keep his attention until he goes off to college. Once he's up there—"

Gladys Ann didn't want to hurt her best friend's feelings so she shut up. No way was Qwayz going to do without for a year, but Gladys Ann wasn't going to tell her. "Well, you might want to give up the circle pin and join the club," she teased.

"No," Jaz stated simply.

Over the next few days, Jaz relished putting names of people Gladys Ann had talked about to their faces, and thanks to her friend importing the D.C. Bop to L.A. which she and Qwayz perfected, Jaz fit right in. She and Qwayz did the D.C. Bop instead of slow dragging, which Jaz had never done with any of the Dragons.

While Aunt Ivy preferred Modas hairdressers on Connecticut Avenue, Jaz went with Gladys Ann to the Cardozo Sisters near Howard University, afterwards, they strolled the campus pretending to be students. Gladys Ann, wedded to the idea of attending the university as her family had, proudly displayed the ins and outs and Jaz had to admit, "There are some fine brothers here!"

"And this is just summer school," Gladys Ann said and they slapped-five.

Summer in D.C. offered jammed-packed, nonstop activities. After sight-seeing with various friends, climbing the 555 steps of the Washington Monument, visiting the Jefferson and Lincoln Memorials and paddle-boating in the Tidal Basin, were crossed off the list, they visited the Smithsonian. Since Negroes were not allowed at the segregated Glen Echo Amusement Park, they took a Wilson Line boat ride down the Potomac River to Marshall Hall where Jaz won ten dollars from the slot machines. Prompted by an engraved invitation received weeks earlier, Aunt Ivy paraded the girls through the downtown stores shopping for semi-formal dresses, and Jaz became immediately impressed with Julius Garfinckel's at 14th and F Streets. She had gone to Woodward & Lothrop, Lansburg's, Kann's and the Hecht Company, but none held a candle to the opulent and classy Garfinckel's with its marble columns, sparkling chandeliers and elegant elevator operators; A gorgeous building, like a museum palace, but the clothes… unlike any Jaz had seen in L.A. or other stores, rivaling those sent from Paris by her Aunt Selena.

Donning their stylish new dresses, Jaz and Gladys Ann went to the Kappa Omega Psi Summer Simmer at the Presidential Arms Ballroom with music by the Carltons; a private birthday party at the Gramercy Inn; and a picnic in Rock Creek Park hosted by the Ingenues one week and Les Marquiis the next. Jaz especially enjoyed the Saturday parties in Howard University's Ballroom over the Punch Out where they did the Slow Fizz.

The food proved to be fabulous and dazzled Jaz's palate, whether a swirl of frozen custard at the Polar Bear on Georgia Avenue and Van Buren Street, luscious rum buns at Hogates or peppery shrimp gumbo at Billy Simpson's. Jaz savored waking on a Saturday morning after Gladys Ann's uncle and friends had traveled to the Wharf to buy Maryland blue crabs which scrambled across the kitchen floor like pets until gathered and steamed in a pot with copious amounts of Old Bay to be deliciously devoured on the picnic table in the back yard. Once they met Gladys Ann's uncle on Capitol Hill at his favorite pub, Gideon's, not knowing it was where Papa Colt had learned to read years ago; or that her grandfather had lived and Aunt Pearl had died just steps from the revered establishment with the historic plaque outside: Gideon's Livery. But the pièce de résistance? Being across the street

156

from the Carter Baron where you could hear entire acts. When Selena and Zack performed to a sell-out audience, Jaz and Gladys Ann went with a few friends. Then Selena wowed them with tickets to Johnny Mathis, and they lost their minds; loving his concert but fascinated at how shy he was when they met him backstage. Experiences like these registered as "old hat" to Gladys Ann, but she enjoyed sharing them with Jaz. What astonished the West Coast transplants most were the nightly calls from California to D.C. The first had occurred as a surprise to them both.

"There is a long-distance call for you, Jaz," her Aunt Ivy said right after dinner.

"For me?" Jaz wondered as she took the receiver. "Thank you. Hello?"

"Hey, Jaz-of-mine."

A big old blush-grin captured her face and held on for dear life.

"Who is?" Gladys Ann whispered.

"Qwayz,"

"In the flesh. What you been doin'?" he asked.

This became a nocturnal ritual and Gladys Ann finally admitted to Jaz," I think he really likes you, Jaz."

"Of course, I told you—"

"No. I mean *really*. Wow! Qwayz Chandler and Jaz Culhane. No one saw that coming."

Jaz had to admit that when he said "Jaz-of-mine"… it did something to her she could not explain; made her feel good and tingly and anointed. She missed him. The calls went from astonishing to anticipated to something to plan her day around. From "how are you?" and "What are you doing?" to "How was the concert?" "The boat ride?" "The party?" Qwayz had become part of her life.

From the California end, TC came to Qwayz and asked, "LeLani asked me who is making the long-distance calls to D.C.?"

"Me," Qwayz confessed. "That LeLani is a great office manager."

"Oh yeah. She's on it. I've met Gladys Ann's people. Nice folks. But nightly calls?"

"Just checking up on Jaz. Making sure she's OK."

"Really?" TC stared at Qwayz who stared right back. "So, is she?"

"Yeah. Fine. Going to the March on Washington tomorrow."

~*~

"If we get separated and trouble starts, you walk north and hail a Capitol Cab–they're black and orange–and go to Aunt Ivy's," Selena said, testing.

"Yes, I know, "Jaz said for the umpteenth time as she accepted the money and stuffed it into her sock.

"Your daddy would have a feces-fit if he knew I was taking you, but it's important, historically, that you be there. Easier to ask forgiveness than permission, so we'll wait until afterwards." Selena gave her some tissues. "If something happens to you—"

"Nothing is going to happen to me."

"I don't know how parents let their children participate in civil rights marches—"

"Aunt Selena. Calm down."

Jaz was excited to participate in this march organized by A. Phillip Randolph, who had organized the original March on Washington Movement for July 1, 1941 to agitate for jobs for Negroes in defense plants and the integration of the armed forces. Only after forcing FDR to sign Executive Order 8802, securing a major demand for jobs which led to the creation of

158

the Fair Employment Practices Commission, did A. Philip Randolph call off that march. But twenty-two years later, the need and demand continued.

When the car stopped on Constitution Avenue, Jaz noted the celebrities on hand: Paul Newman, Marlon Brando, Charlton Heston, Selena's buddy "Jimmy" better known as James Baldwin, Ruby Dee and Ossie Davis, James Garner and Lena Horne beside Josephine Baker, Mahalia Jackson, Dick Gregory and others Jaz did not readily recognize. Eyeing all the stars, Jaz thought, *Tracy would lose her mind.* Harry DeLacosta, who had arranged most of the celebrity presence and the plane that flew them from L.A. to National Airport the day before, rushed Selena and Zack, who were absorbed by the crowd of notables, immediately separated them from Jaz. Jaz walked toward the Lincoln Memorial and read the signs amid all the buses; L.A., S.F., Chicago, Alabama, each busload more festive than the last as they piled off singing. Songs she'd never heard before lifted her spirit in unimaginable ways, carrying her along with the tide of enthusiastic marchers. D.C. blazed hell-hot with a chaser of thick humidity you could chew and spit out, but none of that mattered. Among such joyous black folks–men in ties and women in their Sunday best, some with hats and gloves–Jaz felt the warmth of fellowship and felt loved and protected. She'd never been so proud to be a part of something before. Never been so proud to be black. Her heart swelled. Her soul lifted and everywhere she looked someone smiled at her. A sign–"We March for First Class Citizenship Now"–placed in her hand as the crowd gently nudged her forward. She landed at the base of the Memorial beneath a lone tree and perched above her like human leaves sat young boys in its branches. The program began late, delayed by a problem with the sound system.

159

Despite the cloying heat, Jaz felt as if she were inhaling consecrated rarefied air for the second time this summer and looked up into the cloudless, clear blue sky and wished Qwayz were here—and TC, Scoey, Dickie, Tracy and even Gladys Ann whose folks refused to let her go like so many others who expected trouble. Counter-protesters. The Klan. But for this indescribable experience, Jaz wished they all could share and participate. Jaz nibbled on the provided bag lunches consisting of a cheese sandwich, an apple and a slice of delicious homemade pound cake that reminded her of her Grandma Keely's or Ma Vy's.

That night Jaz relayed the entire experience to Qwayz who said, "I wish I could have been there with you."

"Me, too."

"This is the longest two weeks of my life."

"Me, too."

"I'll pick you and Gladys Ann up from the airport. TC's lending me his van. He asked about the phone bill."

"What you tell him?"

"That I was checking on you."

"What'd he say?"

"Nothing. You'll find that, despite the press, I am a man of my word."

"I know that already."

It was on the tip of his tongue but he didn't say it. It was too soon for "I love you." Not when she hadn't even fully consented to being his girl. Still getting used to the idea, he was there and had been for some time. But soon... very soon. He could tell. "I'm looking forward to seeing you tomorrow, Jaz."

"No, Jaz-of-mine?"

He chuckled. "You like that?"

160

"I love it. Better go now," she said in response to Aunt Ivy reiterating it was time for bed since they had a flight in a few hours.

"I love you" could have easily rolled off her tongue but she clamped her lips shut. "Tomorrow."

"Tomorrow."

Qwayz hung up the phone and TC stood there.

"You and my sister? When this start?"

"The night I found her at the pier when she ran away after the blowout with your mother. She started talking about her options. Leaving for good. Never coming back. Kinda threw me. Hadn't expected it. Had to think on it and decide how I really felt. Told her a few weeks ago on Papa Colt's porch."

"I can image how that went," TC said, stroking his goatee thoughtfully.

"I'll tell you, other dudes might have more money, some may be as fine as I am," he joked and then turned dead-serious, "but no one will ever love Jasmine Bianca Culhane the way I do."

TC stared at Qwayz and then said, "You know if you hurt my sister, I'll have to kill you."

"I expect as much."

"Well, you know more than most what you're getting into. You still want to. I can't stop a crazy man."

"She is my happy, man. No brag. Just fact. I knew it when just the mention of her name made me smile." Qwayz grinned. "She gives without taking. All those times I mistook lust for love. But this time it is love."

"For right now?"

"It's not like that."

"Hope not," TC said. "Sometimes love is not enough."

TC thought of himself now, when two grown people,

161

passionate about their respective careers collide, love becomes the collateral damage.

"And sometimes love is all you need," Qwayz smiled boldly. Realizing that his buddy was speaking of himself, Qwayz added, "I don't care how hard being together is; nothing is worse than being apart. I want to be the 'love of her life.' Not someone she 'used to love.'"

"Spoken like a young boy in love," TC agreed and slapped Qwayz on the back. "Glad it's with my sister."

"She got your nose."

"She has… so wide you can drive a Mack truck through it."

16

On the plane home, Jaz hated the thought that both Lorette and Mel were already at #3G sans her father. After Labor Day, she and Gladys Ann would return to their junior year; she to Jehson and Jaz to Qwayz. When they deplaned, got their luggage from Baggage Claim and headed outside, the first sight of Qwayz made Jaz's heart jump. She could see his wide smile from across the lot. She dropped her suitcase and ran into his open arms. He laughed into the California sunshine and held her. The feel of her in his arms made him hold her tighter and she did so in kind. They kissed.

"How sweet, "Gladys Ann interrupted sarcastically from behind. "No Jehson Culbreath?"

"He had to work," Qwayz said without removing his eyes from Jaz. "Says he'll call when he gets off. You and me. Let's go to a show tonight and dinner at the Lobster House," Qwayz suggested.

"Sounds good to me," Jaz agreed like a fifteen-year-old girl in love.

Unpacking, she realized that little had changed about her feelings for him. If anything, they had intensified like that old adage about absence making the heart grow fonder. He seemed equally as eager to spend time with her. In D.C. her stance solidified that she would give them a go. Worst-case scenario? She would date one of the best athletes on the West Coast, go to prom on the arm of the most popular, handsome, talented student at Roosevelt, they'd dance the night into dawn, and when he left for Stanford...it may be over...but she would have enjoyed a hell of a ride. With Quinton Regis Chandler

IV. He'd be a great memory; not the one that got away...but the prize she'd had... for a while.

Finding it necessary to turn Martin Luther King's hopeful "Dream" into a nightmare, 18 days after the March on Washington, on Sunday, September 15, the KKK exploded a bomb in the 16th Street Baptist Church in Birmingham, Alabama at 10:22 in the morning, killing four innocent little girls and injuring many others. The black community and some whites, appalled at the racist and white supremacist group, challenged the conscience and dignity of America with this heinous act.

"I cannot believe this?" Jaz relayed to Qwayz in their second week of school. "When will this stop?" she asked. "What do they want?"

"Us back in chains, or totally gone from these United States. Obliterated with no reminder of their 'original sin.' What they did to blacks and Indians in this country is unforgivable. Sick. And crazy. Like TC says, 'We ain't going nowhere. This is our country more than theirs; built on the backs of black folk with our blood, sweat, tears and freedom.' How can they possibly think they are superior to us?"

"Arrogant. Evil. Greedy to think you own whatever land you land on and the people already there."

"You sound like Papa Colt," Qwayz said as Jaz snuggled closer. "This time last year I thought we were headed for WWIII with the Cuban Missile Crisis."

"More white-boy posturing."

"They do seem amorally demented. They lie, cheat and steal so easily."

It became clearer to her why Selena, Zack and countless others left America. Jaz anticipated that Selena's involvement in the civil rights movement would probably increase if Harry DeLacosta had his way. Both TC and Qwayz wrote, produced

164

and released "Better Days Ahead" as an anthem and elixir for the ills of United States. The song became a healing panacea for the black community. The singer-songwriters knew there'd be no award in the future for this "message song," but it accomplished what they had in mind. "Better Days" and Sam Cooke's "A Change is Gonna Come" were constantly looped across the airwaves.

The football season began long before the first day of school and Jesse Ramsey met Jaz near the chain link fence, where he stood over her possessively, leaning in to her as she stood under his arm.

"Sorry I was away at training camp when you got back, but that was quite a coup for me, a high school senior, to be invited. We'll make up for lost time now."

Jaz looked out over the field nonplussed.

"Don't-give-a-damn-gorgeous," Jesse whispered with reverence. "God, I missed you... those luscious lips," he said watching hers and licking his own. "Wish I could kiss you right now. Waited all summer while you were in Texas and then D.C. but you're back now and all mine." He was making headway. Jaz Culhane loved to kiss. She just didn't allow much else. He'd continue his campaign to slow-walk her and she'd be his by Christmas, Valentine's Day tops. No doubt her watchdog brother, TC, and his boys conspired to keep her a stone-cold virgin until she graduated. They watched her at the beach parties until the Trio got with their girlfriends, and forgot about Jaz until after they'd been sexually satisfied themselves. Like all the other guys, Jesse wanted to be like them...but once he got Jaz, all his "love 'em and leave 'em days" would end. Once he made love to Jaz Culhane, he'd have her: Virgins always clung to their first loves. He knew it.

He would pop her coveted cherry and revel in the feel of her brown legs wrapped around his athletic haunches.

Jaz eased from under his arm and faced him, wondering if he even knew or cared about the Birmingham bombing. "I've been thinking."

"Yeah?" he grinned suggestively at her. "About what? You and me?"

"Yes." She looked off into the distance at the cheerleaders lining up. She should be over there before the official dismissal. "Good game, by the way."

"Of course, it was. Did I play? Now, with Scoey gone, I'm Top Dog."

"Jesse!" Guys called out to him. He waved them off.

"Let's talk about this later tonight. Pick you up about 7--"

"No. I think we should give each other some space."

"What?" He asked not believing what he'd heard. If anything, on the heels of this spectacular victory, he thought this night may be the one he gets to go further than before. A reward.

"You're right about us," Jaz continued. "Like you said before I left, 'We don't seem to be in sync. We seem to want different things. I'm not as supportive of you as I should be because I'm not that interested in football—'"

"Or me. Is that what you're saying? You all up into basketball."

"My brothers—"

"We ain't talking about them. We talkin' about us." He wiped his face with one big hand. Exasperation and anger consumed him all at once. "I've tried with you, Jaz. I've bent over backwards. Made you my queen—"

"I appreciate it all, Jesse but it's not working. It's too much of an effort—"

166

"Oh, wow. It's a 'effort' to be with me? Are you kidding me?" He looked up into the expansive sky. He wanted to smack her but he knew if he did he'd be beat into an unrecognizable pulp by her brother who would relish breaking his bones apart—then where would his football career end up? "It's not a 'effort' to be with Qwayz, is it?"

"What?" The question took her by surprise. Her breath caught.

"I see you all. I'm used to you preferring to dance with him and TC and Scoey 'cause that's how you learned and all. Didn't like when he cut in on me at the Harvest Ball, leaving me there on the sidelines like a chump. But I've seen something else lately."

"I don't know what you mean."

"I watch you, Jaz. You're *my* girl. I watch everybody who comes near you. I watch your reaction to them. There's something between you and that 'pretty boy.'"

Jaz stood speechless.

"Umhum." Jesse shook his head. "It hasn't always been there but it's there now. Ever since he broke up with Cherish Harley."

"I don't know anything about him and—"

"Are you the reason he quit her? Is it your turn now? I expected so much more from you, Jaz. You know they gonna get back together. They always do."

"Look, if you want to know about Qwayz and Cherish you should ask them. I'm talking about you and me and I think we should take a breather."

"For how long, Jaz? Until you find out that Qwayz's just a smooth-talking, good-looking guy who'll do you wrong? Dump you when the next cute girl comes along."

He stopped and just stared down at her, making Jaz uncomfortable. His nostrils flared and then the flush in his cheeks calmed. *She can't walk out in the middle of the dream I have for the two of us,* he thought. He looked over at his guys waiting for him and girls wishing for a chance with him— Jesse Ramsey; on his way to someplace special. He was going to be somebody *big.* But Jesse didn't want any other girl but Jaz; his complete package: looks, smarts, from a good family; she rode horses at her grandparents' ranch in the summer; her aunt, a celebrity—and they'd have such pretty babies. He wasn't ever going to find a girl like this again. He'd work hard for them… for her and his family. They'd be the envy of all others. The Ramseys of Hollywood Hills. But she didn't want him, wanted no part of the life he envisioned for them.

Jesse looked down at her and said in a quiet, almost inaudible voice that cracked with emotion, "Qwayz's going to make a mistake, Jaz. I hope he does something unforgiveable, where his 'sorrys' aren't good enough and he hurts you so bad…" He stopped. "That you'll come back to me." He walked off.

Jaz watched him go. His words punched her in the stomach and took the wind from her lungs. *How do you wish someone you purportedly love… hurt?* She wondered.

As Jaz meandered down the hill toward the bleachers, Dickie was coming up to get her. "Scoey said come on if you're riding with him."

Jaz shook her head.

"You OK?"

"Yeah." She braved a smile. She hadn't meant to hurt Jesse Ramsey. Beyond his conceit, he was a decent guy, but she finally knew what one of Aunt Selena's lyrics meant, "You can't make somebody love you… if they don't."

168

She continued walking down the hill when she heard her name called from behind.

"Jaz! Wait up." A tall boy with a camera ran toward her. "Hey," he said breathlessly.

"Hey," Jaz replied thinking she'd seen him before.

"Wanna know if I can get a picture of you in your uniform before I go."

"Sure." Jaz stuck a pose and smiled.

"No hat, huh?"

"Not regulation uniform attire," Jaz quipped with a smile. "It's in my locker."

"Sinclair Cosgrove," he introduced. "We took Algebra together."

"Sure," she said, acting as if she remembered him. "So where are you going?"

"Either Thailand or Vietnam."

"Where is that?"

"Southeast Asia."

"Ahh. Sounds exotic."

"Army. Besides buying my mama a house, I was wondering if I could call on you when I get back. Unless you're married to Jesse Ramsey."

"I assure you I won't be married to anyone," she smiled.

"Cool. Well, thanks for the picture. Check you out when I get back."

"OK, stay safe," she said, just as Scoey tossed her an evil look for holding him up.

Vietnam? Jaz thought. *Never heard of it. I'll have to look it up when I get home.*

~*~

Qwayz and Jaz operated away from the public eye. That no one seemed to notice any change in their relationship at the studio, testament to their closeness all along. Only Gladys Ann and TC knew, but he didn't acknowledge it. He was more preoccupied with the volley of Raw Cilk for top ten place over Motown, Stax, Chess or Atlantic Records on the charts. When Raw Cilk charted, TC was ecstatic and, instead of resting on his laurels, it speared his competitiveness, and he drove them harder, which didn't come close to how hard he drove himself. Already miffed The Drifters had added strings first, he'd trumped everyone with the boy-girl duo as Qwayz and Ronnie shone golden like he had predicted. He'd bought the stove factory next door and transformed it into Club Oasis, a posh teen retreat, to be completed in time for Jaz's sixteenth birthday celebration next month. TC's plate overflowed with his many projects and he loved it.

"I'll run her home," Qwayz often volunteered at the end of a session and he and Jaz would go off, usually to get a bite to eat before seeking the tranquility of the sea. Whether driving up the coast until there was only static on the radio, or to P.O.P. Amusement Park, Venice Beach or the Santa Monica Pier, their usual haunts, they talked about everything and nothing.

Jaz settled into Qwayz's warm embrace as they looked at the tumbling ocean like it was television. He kissed her temple. "Cold?"

"No. I'm fine."

"You sure are." They chuckled. No matter how hard she tried, Jaz couldn't harness her heart. She knew the plan; Qwayz until he graduated. She tried to control herself but could not. One touch, one brush of his lips across hers, one caress, one pushing hair from her face...and she fell deeper and deeper. He looked at her...within her... with reverence and respect, not lust and domination. He looked at her as if he could not believe his good fortune instead of the other way

170

around. While she had fought Jesse Ramsey's hands continuously, with Qwayz she wanted him to roam, to feel him touch her in places that no male had ever touched her before. They savored being in one another's presence and could do comfortable silence as well as frenzied excitement. He was just a marvel to her.

"You know what I don't get?"

"What?"

"You and Dickie?"

"He's been my friend for a long time."

"Yeah, but he was at Roosevelt when I came and he'll be there when I graduate. He must be twenty," Qwayz teased.

Jaz laughed out loud.

"Sure am glad he was there at that party in the Boondocks. If he hadn't called—"

"If you could've seen the sheer terror in his eyes when he looked up and spotted us."

"I get Joaquin and Jesse Ramsey… but Dickie."

"I never dated Dickie."

"Probably why he's still around."

"He's true blue. He is so funny. Makes me laugh all the time. Which is a sign of high intelligence. He reminds me of Ian."

"Ian? I see. You're both smart and could care less about what others think about you."

"Ian and Dickie are a lot alike. Two points on the same spectrum. Only Ian's parents took time with him. Exposed, challenged and supported him. Dickie didn't have that. He grew up in spite of parents not because of. If he had, he woulda been a force to recon with."

"A contender," Qwayz imitated Brando from "On the Waterfront." "Could have been somebody."

"You're pretty crazy yourself." Jaz kissed his luscious lips. "Please don't go all Lorette Culhane on me. Asking what 'his claim to fame' was. Snob. In her world now."

"You all getting along any better?"

"Peaceful co-existence with our eyes on the clock knowing it's just a matter of time before we are both rid of each other."

"We have to make sure our children, Quinton V and Shane, have a better relationship with us."

"I am not naming my son after a movie," Jaz giggled.

"You can name the girls."

"How many are *you* having?"

"That's not how it works. We'll have at least four. Two girls and two boys...to start."

The moon caressed their laughing images. "What time is it?" Jaz asked.

"Yikes. Time to get you home." Qwayz stood up and gathered Jaz to him.

"Before the 'wicked witch' rides her broom over the land."

"I love you, Jaz," he said simply.

Jaz blushed and grinned at the sound of this declaration, finally from someone she wanted to hear it. A breathless intoxication washed over her, but she managed, "Me too, you." They kissed again, two silhouettes etched against the backdrop of the sea and moon. The smell and feel of the salty air whirled around them.

"The stars are in their heaven and all's right with the world," Qwayz declared.

17

All decked out for its grand opening and Jaz's birthday party, Club Oasis was stunning. The bar stocked with all kinds of sodas, the sound system tops in the business, the Brawner Brothers posted at the door ready to bounce anyone without an invitation, and the cache of balloons in the center dancefloor just like the Satin Doll at New Year's Eve. Resplendent in an off-the-shoulder, semi-formal, pink chiffon dress from D.C.'s Garfinckel's, her hair swooped up for sophistication, Jaz didn't hold back when Dickie grabbed her hand and went into his crazy dance antics with the monkey, the jerk and boogaloo while the Contours asked "Do You Wanna Dance?" When the Drifters' "Save the Last Dance for Me" came on Qwayz cut in and they carved out space enough for quick turns, hand loops back over the shoulder, a little cha-cha crowned with the multiple spins of a Flamenco-gypsy. This time, despite the crowd they drew, they only had eyes for one another. TC, working in the studio with overdubs, took a break and used the cat walk from his bedroom above to see what was happening in Oasis below. He watched his best friend and his sister tear up the dancefloor as they'd always done. But something was different, something real. Something enviable.

"What's going on between Jaz and Qwayz?" Dickie saddled up to the bar and asked Gladys Ann.

"What do you mean?" She jumped from the bar stool when Jehson asked her to dance.

A few records later, TC pulled himself away from work to welcome everyone to a club especially for them. "The youngsters of Watts."

After TC's greeting, they rolled out a four-tiered frosted cake, devil's food with white icing, on a stand and sang "Happy Birthday" to Jaz. Qwayz, standing behind her, grabbed her hand and rubbed his thumb calmly over her fingers. She smiled but not at the singing or the sight of her parents and sister, aunt, uncle or friends, but that she had a guy she was crazy about. *This is what she'll remember about this night,* she thought. *When I turned sixteen and was dead-up in love.* Her father was saying something now and she tried hard to concentrate on his words but he was no match for Quinton Regis. Finally, they followed him outside where a pink, 1955 T-Bird with the wheel in the back sat next to TC's van and black Porsche.

"You'll need some mode of transportation from Malibu to school," Hep quipped. "Don't want you depending on *anyone* for a ride." He dangled the keys before placing them firmly in her hand. "No other driver but you. Be careful or I'll take it back."

"Yes, Daddy. Thank you!"

The rest of the night, a glorious blur. Laughing, singing, big fun as Qwayz whirled Jaz about the polished wooden floor, you would have thought there was alcohol in the refreshments. When the Impressions crooned, "I'm So Proud, Being Loved By You," Qwayz caressed Jaz's hand and pulled her body toward his. For the first time ever...they slow dragged, announcing to all that their relationship had changed.

"What the hell is that?" Dickie noticed first.

"What?" Ian asked.

"Jaz and Qwayz—"

A buzz zoomed around the room, they all noticed but Jaz and Qwayz did not notice them.

"Ain't this a blip?" Dickie jested. "When did all this happen?" Dickie asked Jaz pointing between her and Qwayz.

174

"Been awhile now," Jaz answered brusquely beaming.

"You could have told a brother. I mean, I should have known. I thought we was friends and all," Dickie said.

"We are. You're not going to make me and Qwayz split up, are you?" she teased.

"Naw. We, you and me, go way back. Take more than this jive-turkey to split us up."

The Boys Club Christmas Benefit topped last year's success. TC garnered stars from near and far who vied to be a part of the festivities, followed by the first Oasis New Years' Eve Party rivaling the Satin Doll. But Oasis was reserved for the younger set, the groovy set, especially since her parents hosted their own New Year's soiree in their Connecticut home, and were not traveling to L.A. or Colt, Texas that year. Jaz felt that change coming on her doorstep again; one she couldn't control or predict. But this, her first Christmas with Qwayz, proved to be spectacular. He gifted her a tan, fringed buckskin jacket and she to him, a dark brown leather bomber jacket which he immediately swapped out for his varsity jacket. "Every time you put it on, think of me wrapping you in my arms."

They rang in the New Year, 1964. TC continued making music his priority, every success buoyed by his drive, leaving little time for cultivating a personal life, although he had no problem satisfying his carnal needs. The more he succeeded, the harder he worked and loved it. Raw Cilk's "Fool for You," unseated the Miracles' "Tears of a Clown;" When Smokey's Pagliacci's clown succumbed to Qwayz's lyrics about Machiavelli's strings, TC was coolly overjoyed. Qwayz's lyrics remained inspired by Jaz. His "We'd Still Be in Love" (Better Man) from her youthful relationship with Joaquin bumped Jackie Ross's "Selfish One" and Gladys Knight and the Pips "Giving Up" from the charts. Raw Cilk, known for its mature themes, complicated melodies and lyrics by the young singer-songwriter, were like crème, always zoomed and settled at the top of the charts. TC re-arranged one of Selena's signature songs by slowing down the tempo, adding a melody to showcase her octaves, and the "old" song was elevated to another level, particularly when covered by Miles Syphax, Frank Sinatra and Tony Bennett who performed it from a male perspective; it was nominated for a Grammy. A new song by singer-songwriter Quinton Regis Chandler IV, "I Want to Be With You," had lyrics that professed that the vocalist would rather have a relationship of no sex with a woman he loved than have sex with anyone else. On "You Are the Only One for Me," Ronnie's voice charted at number 2 and then hung there for weeks. With "Our Day Is Here," "You Make My World Stand Still," "Never Gonna Break Your Heart," and "Keep Me in Mind" all charting, TC decided to put out an album for marketing purposes, despite the fact that none of Raw Cilk were free to travel and do shows as most were still in school.

That album release required a cover and TC used Selena's photographer to take a picture of Raw Cilk walking toward the camera out back in the alley. Qwayz and Ronnie in the middle; Qwayz holding Jaz's hand, who held Gladys Ann's hand. On the other side, Ronnie held Zion's hand with Jaxson who rounded out that side. They all looked youthfully jubilant as they walked toward the camera. At the last minute, Qwayz and Jaz looked at one another. That's the cover TC chose.

While the industry criticized the young mogul for his use of multiple leads for a group, TC remained undaunted. His let the lyrics and tone of a song dictate who would be lead vocal. He kept their voices fresh and unpredictable: male lead, female lead, duo lead…TC achieved mastery, results that no one

176

could argue or duplicate. Everyone in Raw Cilk who could and wanted to sing did. "Destination Paradise," was written by Qwayz for Jaz's voice, and TC agreed. Jaz balked, preferring to remain on background vocals but Qwayz and TC wanted her front and center. Qwayz refused to consider anyone else for the song. "Your song. Written for you." Finally, Qwayz consented to do the B side, "My First, Last and Only Love," with Jaz but she had to do side A.

Jaz did Side B hoping that Qwayz and TC would give up, but with Side B completed to everyone's satisfaction, they nagged her into Side A. Just to get them off her back, she relented. After several false starts, solo… Qwayz dismissed everyone and he and Jaz sang "Destination Paradise" to one another. As they all vacated Studio 3, TC left the recorder on and they got the take. Once Jaz heard her own voice, she conceded. "You can do it Jaz. I know you can," Qwayz pronounced. She acquiesced only if he and TC promised never to have her sing again. They did. The song was released and zoomed to number 3 on the charts. Everyone assumed it was yet another dimension of Ronnie's voice. Jaz let them.

~*~

Another tax bracket forced TC to buy a two-bedroom, mid-century bungalow where he never slept or visited and only Qwayz and Scoey had ever seen. His professional career gleamed pure gold and Jaz loved the artistic rendering of him in *Downbeat* magazine with only a few well-placed lines, they captured his essence: his porkpie hat, goatee and the Tootsie Pop, always in his mouth… symbolizing his technique, as he challenged whatever he was seeking–a lyric, a phrase, a note, a key change–before he got to the gooey center. Her brother had the world on a string and seemed fulfilled and satisfied, but Jaz wanted TC to find love as she had. "He's not complaining,"

Qwayz reminded her. "Never once have I heard the brother complain 'I need a woman.'"

"Oh, he has plenty of women but not a special one."

"Yes, he does. Music. She's number one."

Jaz relished her new status with Qwayz but her boyfriend always either defended or became noncommittal about his brother, TC. TC's women meet his needs but no "special woman" appeared to accept that she would *always* be second to his music. That's why Ronnie, poor thing, would never qualify, not even to be in his stable. TC hated the term and preferred to think he was being honest with women upfront. Eventually, the last one standing—LeLani Troop; ready, willing, able and accessible with no demands. It didn't matter to TC that he was her only one. "Her choice," he'd say and keep moving. It surprised Jaz that the beautiful LeLani settled for TC's shabby treatment. Smart, articulate and very much her own woman, LeLani took nothing from nobody—except TC. "Maybe this is a new kind of love," Jaz questioned Qwayz.

"Maybe it isn't love at all, maybe it's just sex," Qwayz countered. "They understand it and that's all that matters," he said as they turned and parked in a visitor's space in front of The Conservatory of USC. "Tell me why we are here again?" he teased, opening Jaz's door. "I planned on relaxing after the SATs this morning."

"To support my friend."

"Your friend." Once they entered the hall and took a program and then a seat, Mrs. Summerville nodded after eyeing Qwayz's Converse with a certain amount of disdain and then forgiveness that he didn't know any better.

Scoey slid in beside them, looking as uncomfortable as a whore in Sunday church.

"Well, look who's here," Jaz teased him.

178

"Listen Squirt, she asked and I said if I didn't have practice I'd come," Scoey nodded. "I didn't have practice so here I am. No big thing."

"A man of his word. Raw Cilk creed," Qwayz confirmed.

Jaz knew Scoey as well as TC and Qwayz... the trio, closer than three-part harmony. She knew he was falling for Tracy in an uncommitted way. By the end of the recital, Gladys Ann had arrived with Jehson Culbreath. A delighted Tracy smiled at her friends.

"She's really good," Scoey realized and when Tracy approached, he told her, "You can really play that fiddle."

"Thank you," Tracy demurred and blushed, fluttering her long black eyelashes.

"Thank you all for coming," said Mrs. Summerville.

"May I go with them?" Tracy asked.

"Maestro Burrage wants to meet you and introduce you to some of his proteges, and we have a small reception planned for you at the Satin Doll—"

"Helen, let her go with her friends," Mr. Summerville interjected. "Don't stay out too late." He looked directly at Scoey who feigned innocence as he'd never taken Tracy on a date.

"Thank you!" Tracey enthused.

Mrs. Summerville shot her husband daggers of disappointment. "She's a good kid. Let her have some fun. Only a year before she goes away to college. We ought to see what choices she'll make ahead of time."

"Give me a few minutes," Tracy told Scoey and the other four. "I have to make some introductions and get my violin case to my parents."

"Sure," Scoey said, wondering how he'd gotten hoodwinked into this six-some. "She's the only black girl on the program," he said quietly.

"Come home early, Tracy," Mrs. Summerville called after her. "PSATs tomorrow."

The couples dined at Luigi's laughing, joning and joking, and Jaz couldn't have been happier in the presence of her best friends and their beaus. Finally, she understood how Gladys Ann felt about Jehson and she was thrilled that Tracy had finally hooked up with Scoey besides just rides home from the studio.

"So, what's the Grand Dame doing now?" Scoey asked of Lorette.

"Oh, she's busy this weekend. Hosting her best friends from childhood in the Connecticut house."

"Ah, so your spot is free," Jehson noted.

"Not for that," Jaz blocked. "Every blue moon we get these free weekends before the official take over begins with Selena and Zack. We have folks popping over to check on us like we're children, anyone from Truck McMillan, TC, Shanghai or Sugar Dee. Lorette'll be back way too soon. Sometimes she comes home on the red-eye and only stays a day before she bounces back out. Like she's trying to catch us at something."

"And you better be home to get those nightly parental calls, too," Scoey reminded.

"What type of friends did your mother have back then?"

"Gay Iris and her family have just left and Effie, who lives in Vienna, is coming up after she finishes her gigs at Carnegie Hall and Lincoln Center."

"I'd loved to meet Effie," Tracy confessed, "Her voice is unbelievable."

"Lorette wanted Jaz to meet her, too," Qwayz teased.
180

"I'm not going to Connecticut," Jaz snapped. "'Sides, we have the PSATs tomorrow."

After dinner the couples went their separate ways to spend alone time before curfews were met. The rumble of the sea matched that of the blood racing though the veins of Jaz and Qwayz as they finished their "horizontal mambo," so named by Qwayz. He admitted thinking he was finished with these innovations after his first sexual experience at thirteen, the collateral perk of hanging out with older guys and gals.

"Thirteen," Jaz gasped.

"I was fourteen in a couple of weeks," he replied.

"Which means you were in Colt, Texas. Who was she?" Jaz asked.

"A gentleman never tells," he said, kissing her temple. "I told you, I'd rather have no sex with you, than all-day sex with any other girl."

"How do you know?" She asked as she gathered her hair and twisted it into a ponytail. "Maybe some you'd like trying out?"

"Don't want to chance us. The way I feel about you? The completeness. You satisfy all my senses and emotions."

"You just make sure you don't mess up, Mister," Jaz said, standing and tucking in her blouse.

He grabbed her hand. "You believe me, don't you?"

"Until you show me otherwise. Then it is over."

"Really? You can cut your love on and off like that?"

"Oh, I'd still love you," she admitted. "I'd miss you… but still love you." She laughed into the setting sun and ran to Reds. "Take me home, James. My dad is about to call."

"Nobody loves you like God, your daddy and me." He stood in the hall of #3G with the door cracked so she could hear the phone. "What is it about your goodbye kisses that make me want to stay?" He breathed the words over her face and they kissed fervently. "I love you, Jaz-of-mine."

The phone rang. "Gotta go."

"Call you later. Pick you up tomorrow."

"Hi, Daddy."

"Clairvoyant?" He asked, and then they discussed their respective days and he asked about Mel.

"Haven't seen her yet. Just came in. Tracy's concert was today."

Jaz hung up, clicked on the TV and sat in the chair next to her parents' room just as a dark figure moved stealthy up the hallway. It startled her motionless. *Oh, shit,* she thought, freezing, as her life flashed before her. The figure reached the living room and rounded the corner.

"Hey, Jaz," Mickey said sheepishly as he headed for the front door.

Jaz glared at him and said, "Not smart, Mickey."

A few minutes later Mel walked up the hall and disappeared into the bathroom. When her sister came out, Jaz asked, "Are you using protection?"

"Aren't you the little sister?" Mel clarified.

"Better than the pregnant sister."

"Yes, I am. You think I want to get pregnant by a grease monkey? Spare me the disappointed look, Jaz."

"You don't love him?"

"I love sex. That surprised me. Oh, maybe he's the best I'll ever have. Dunno. I'll be gone this time next year. Who knows what or who awaits me."

Jaz got up and went into the kitchen for a cold drumstick.

"What about you and Qwayz?"

"I'm not discussing him with you or anyone else."

"Are you going to tell Dad about this little soiree? I've never known you to be a tattle-tale."

182

"Not my news. You mess up… you'll be telling Dad."

"Fair enough."

18

Time sped like wind through a lattice trellis since Mel and Qwayz's graduation ceremony and the celebration party at Oasis; Mel sang at both. Selena and Zack rented the Malibu House and took possession immediately before the graduation festivities. With Jaz's transportation addressed with her new car, her parents and aunt and uncle decided to keep the beach house for the entire year and vacate next June when they took Jaz to Paris for her long-awaited trip. The new development satisfied Jaz…as most did since Qwayz'd become an important part of her life. Since no Culhanes would be returning to #3G, Hep and Lorette opened #3G to the neighbors to take anything they wanted. The Cadillac gifted to Lorette and expertly maintained by Skeekie was offered to the Fluellens, who declined, so Hep re-gifted it to Skeekie and his family.

Mel and her parents jetted off to New York City. No need for a car, Mel received a small, well-built, pre-war apartment building in the Village and selected the third-floor walkup with the picture window on the back. The other units, already rented, remained the responsibility of the first-floor resident manager who never knew Mel as the new owner.

Hep hadn't spent a full year as Chief of Protocol before President Eagan appointed him Ambassador to Italy and he and Lorette prepared to move yet again, this time to the American Embassy in Rome. The heavily lobbied President Eagan succumbed to the not so subtle pressure of the Orsini, Vittadini and other prominent businessmen who supported how perfect Hepburn Culhane was for the ambassadorship: He spoke fluent Italian, was already familiar with the culture, country and its people and had a vested interest since helping revive an old olive oil company, which now exports internationally. The Italian government and key dignitaries issued a proclamation crediting Hep Culhane's vision, foresight and financial backing for success with gratitude, making the Orsini symbol, a big O with the Roman numeral III inside, standing for Orsini Olive Oil and the Vittadini Vineyard in Tuscany, the double Vs logo, the most recognizable and prestigious in and around Italy and abroad. All to fulfill a World War II promise to a friend and a testament to his character and commitment. Their Tavio Reserve, which took years to cultivate, was now heralded as the ultimate Chianti in the region. Two Vittadini grandsons and a granddaughter completed university and employed mechanisms and machinery to elevate the business to new heights by implementing something as simple as electronic fencing to prevent the wild boars from eating the grapes. Despite the elders' protests that it was too expensive, the investment proved to be lucrative for generations to come. "All these successes stem from the influence and generosity of one man, Hepburn Henley Culhane, a friend of Italy," the proclamation read. "No better man suited to represent America in performing official duties or to handle dangerous threats with diplomatic confidence and flair. His temperament and respect of the larger community guaranteed his ability with domestic politics and foreign affairs." President Eagan could not refuse and knew that this would be one less thing to worry about if he appointed Hep as ambassador to the prolific, quixotic country of Italy who had run through three ambassadors in just two years. Never enamored with the post of chief of protocol, Hep jumped at the chance to become "His Excellency" at the same time he steered away from Wall Street

185

stocks and invested in technology and communications with his eyes still on Culhane Enterprises; his portfolio grew exponentially.

~*~

Their combined laughter caught the wind and carried it joyously down the beach. Two bronze bodies frolicking across a stretch of white sand not caring about anyone else because there was no one on this secluded stretch. They didn't need anyone else. Selena sipped juice in the air-conditioned luxury of the Malibu house she and Zack had selected.

"Look at them," Selena directed her friend, Miles, "The Tymes 'So Much in Love' should be their soundtrack."

"'Lover's Concerto,'" Zack interjected. "How gentle is the rain…"

"Too Young," Miles offered.

"Cynic. Ah. To be young and in love again when the world is yours for the asking," Selena said, recalling how her first husband Hoyt made her felt like that. She was twenty-one. Jaz is just sixteen.

"Imagine if I'd met you back then," she said to Zack.

"I'll show you some things those young pups don't know about," he teased.

"That you have." She kissed his lips lightly.

"They're having fun," Miles noted. "That's how I make my money… from love and love songs."

"Yes, you do."

Later, at twilight, Jaz entered the house. "Where's Qwayz?"

"He had a game at the Boys Club tonight. He'll call at eleven. Did they find them?" Jaz eyes pierced her aunts.

"No. Not yet," Selena replied.

"They're dead. Nobody disappears like that in Mississippi." Jaz knew about the Freedom Summer but with
186

the prom and Mel and Qwayz's graduation, Jaz didn't take notice until the three civil rights workers, James Chaney, Andrew Goodman and Mickey Schwerner, were arrested on June 20th and had gone missing since the 21st. On the 24^{th,} they found their burned-out station wagon in Neshoba County. The president then sent in the FBI to locate the missing men under the file name MIBURN for Mississippi Burning. If Selena hadn't come to take care of her, Jaz had considered joining Freedom Summer as an alternative to not going to Connecticut. She could have known these workers, could have been one of those risking their lives for voter registration, Freedom Schools, participation in a black boycott of a variety store and a myriad of projects in that third world country of Mississippi. Jaz prayed for them while trying not to be constantly plagued by their plight.

She sat with her aunt in the living room with its luxurious A-frame, floor-to-ceiling windows, pensive, quiet and waiting for Qwayz's call. "Remember when you told me about the Montgomery Bus Boycott in Alabama? When a fifteen-year-old girl refused to give up her seat and was arrested before Rosa Parks?"

"Yes, Claudette Colvin. They went with the middle-class, forty-two-year-old seamstress and member of the NAACP. Better test case."

"That girl was my age. And the boycott lasted for over a year?"

"381 days," Selena answered. "Because black folks stuck together. We walked, had carpools; many white women chauffeured their black maids. I guess they just couldn't clean their own toilets or cook their family a meal."

"So, these same lazy white women and their redneck, Klansmen killed those three workers."

"We don't know that Jaz."

"I think we do."

"Besides, not a bad deal for the black maids who got front door service *and* kept their jobs."

The phone rang and Jaz went to answer it. "Hey, handsome." She sank back onto the chair as Selena slipped away. "Just talking to Selena. How was the game?"

While Lorette helped Mel set up her Greenwich Village apartment, Hep flew to Malibu to see his sister and daughter. He watched her with Qwayz through the plate glass windows surrounding the deck. "Is he always here?" He asked Selena.

"Always," she teased. "Except when he's not."

"Humm. What do they do all day?"

"What you see. Bask in each other's presence."

"I hope this plays out when he goes to college."

"Fat chance. That girl and boy are in love."

"They have no idea what love is," Hep snapped.

"Do the name Feather Criqui mean anything to you?" she said in her best Kingfish voice from "Amos 'n Andy."

"We were children. I went to war and grew up."

"Well, Qwayz's going to Stanford, not war, and he can't wait to beat it back here to see your daughter."

"He doesn't spend the night?"

"And if he did?"

"Selena this is not what I had in mind."

"No. He either goes back to campus or to Compton. But he's here first thing in the morning." She stroked her brother's broad shoulder. "Relax. You know Qwayz is a good guy."

"That's before he started dating my daughter."

"You are going to have trust him…her…them. 'Cause next year we won't know what they are doing up there. I asked them to give me two things: responsibility and respect. So far so good."

188

"That's giving them license to—"

"To what? You can follow her around 24/7 but where there's a will... there's a way."

Hep went out on the terrace and whistled the special whistle he'd taught Jaz in Colt, Texas. She looked up and saw him, returned the whistle and ran toward him. "Surprise!" he said as she grabbed him in a bear-hug.

"The one swearing-in ceremony I wanted to attend and didn't get invited. I have a passport you know."

"I'll be in Italy a long time. When you go over next year for your Paris trip you'll swing by and stay with us a month."

"Deal."

"Hey, Coach C," Qwayz said, coming in with the blanket and towels.

"Qwayz," Hep acknowledged curtly.

"Congratulations on your appointment."

"Thank you."

Hep only stayed overnight and was off again. Jaz and Qwayz resumed their beachside residency.

"When are we graduating from the horizontal cha-cha to the real thing?" she asked him. "I want you and me to consummate—"

He brushed her sun-kissed hair back from her face. "I told you Jaz-of-mine. We are too special for backseat, sand dune, green grass motels or any hotel for that matter. You are only going to have one 'first time' in your entire life. I want it to be as special as we are."

"No one would believe we're not already doing the do."

"But you and I know. Told you I don't care about other folk. Only you."

She kissed his salty, luscious lips.

"You're the one with the big edict, 'No sex until college,'" he teased.

"I'm talking about making love."

"We do that."

"You are exasperating. How about on my prom night? I'll almost be in college."

"How about when we go to Paris?"

"*We* go to Paris? My 'plus one' is Gladys Ann."

"I know. Maybe I can give you a good send off."

"Happy bon voyage to me!" Jaz intoned as she traced the outline of his strong jaw. "Jeff Chandler jaws. Hey, are you all related?"

On July 2nd, 1964 the Civil Rights Act was passed. "Too little too late and still no civil rights workers found," Jaz stated. On July 4th, Jaz referred to Frederick Douglass' 1852 speech, "What to the Slave is the Fourth of July."

"What do I care about the 4th of July?" she said, as she surveyed the frivolity of those who gathered at the Malibu House for the fireworks and festivities.

"You getting political on me?" Qwayz asked with a kiss.

Night nestled in as Jaz and Qwayz remained on the blanket beneath the starry sky while the rest of the party gathered on the terrace and balcony soaking up the last of the summer they would all remember fondly. Their new stomping ground became Malibu, replacing the beach near the Santa Monica Pier. Fun, food and freedom rang around them as if they were privileged white kids on holiday. Sprawled out on the beach, Qwayz gathered Jaz into his arms.

"This is nice," he murmured into her ear and she moaned agreement. "Look at that thumbnail of a moon above."

"The stars seem so close."

"See that one right there next to the North star. Twinkling, sparkling to get noticed."

190

"Umhum."

"That's our star. Yours and mine."

Jaz smiled at it and then him. "I like it."

"So, no matter where we are or what we're doing, if you're here and I'm at school, or when you go to Paris…that will be *our* star, yours and mine shining over us at the same time. We'll remember this 'cause a day like today can give you comfort and peace for the rest of your life."

"Says my songwriter boyfriend."

"Always remember how much I love you, Jaz-of-mine." He looked into her honey eyes. "Don't ever doubt my love for you."

"I won't." She snuggled down into his arms and contentment rushed over her. "How can we be this happy?"

"Don't ask how…just savor that we are. I feel such peace and paradise when I'm with you."

"Amen."

At twilight the next day Selena instructed her photographer from inside the beach house looking out at Jaz and Qwayz. "So just take pictures, Cecil. No fake posing. Just snap them naturally."

She and Zack had decided to use photos of Jaz and Qwayz for her new album cover. *Malibu Summer.* Fans here and abroad would relish a gorgeous California sunset with two lovers.

Of course, when Cecil appeared, the couple began posing for him. A few days later when he returned with the proofs, Jaz's favorite photo of them was taken as she stood in front of Qwayz, his peach Banlon shirt offsetting their copper tones enriched by the sun, his strong arms wrapping her in his love as they both smiled into the camera. Young and in love. Qwayz's favorite was of Jaz by herself coming up out of the water wet and delicious like Botticelli's Venus. Selena chose the pose of the two of them perched high on a rock above the tumbling ocean, their profiles etched against a California twilight, a streaking sunset, looking toward their future. "We can make it a silhouette," Cecil suggested.

"Brilliant!" Selena enthused. "That's it."

They managed a few more weekends when TC would come alone, but Gladys Ann with Jehson, Denny and Yudi, and even Tracy and Scoey enjoyed the house. Dickie tagged along when he could catch ride. "So, what's this with you and Tracy?" Jaz asked Scoey as he reached for a beer from the outside bar.

"She's a nice girl," he said. *Easy to love*, he thought.

"I know that. When did this happen?"

He looked at Jaz and said, "When I saw her at the recital I realized that she's the kind you settle down with. She's cute, plays a damn good violin. Has two parents. Smart. Takes dance. And she loves me."

"So, she's wife material?"

"When the time comes. If we last that long."

"She's going to Pepperdine. 'Old Malibu U.' So, you better get her before someone else snatches her up," Jaz warned.

"Well, I got a few more things on my mind like keeping my scholarship with your boy Jesse Ramsey dead on my heels."

"Psh! You can handle him."

"I can and do," Scoey countered. "He's got something to prove. I just want a free four years before law school."

"He's not 'my boy,'" Jaz clarified.

"Use to be. I bet he'd take you back."

"Why would I do that?" Jaz sassed. "Go backwards?"

192

On August 2nd Qwayz's birthday was celebrated in style at the Malibu House. A Klansman and one of the participants in the murder of the civil rights workers was paid $30,000 and given prosecutorial immunity in exchange for information. On August 4th three civil rights workers' remains were found in an earthen dam and other culprits were identified. The state of Mississippi made no arrests.

September came all too soon and the beach parties ceased, replaced by all things academic; the last year of high school for Jaz and first year of college for Qwayz. The pink T Bird made its way to Roosevelt High each morning, while Reds' trips on the weekends became staggered as Qwayz's team responsibilities on campus increased.

"Once I get the lay of the land and the rules, I'll figure out how to circumvent them," he promised Jaz.

As a scholar-athlete, his season hadn't officially begun, but being confined to the jock dorm took getting used to for him. Regardless, like clockwork, he called Jaz every evening at eleven. "I promised AJ that I'd take him to P.O.P. this weekend as a reward for Ace-ing his test. Wanna go?"

"Absolutely! You are so good to him."

"I hesitate to ask you because you know he has a mean crush on you and I really hate to share. But a promise is a promise."

"Yes, it is. We, AJ and I, promise not to ignore you."

"Boy! I told you to stop jumping down those steps," Ma Vy shouted at her son, while Jaz and AJ laughed. Ma Vy used to yell at Qwayz for doing that when she came to visit Denny. Gladys Ann wouldn't come because all Denny liked to do was play board games. "Bored is the word for it," Gladys Ann used to say. But his "Uncle" Qwayz jumping the steps and incurring the mock-wrath of Ma Vy, cracked AJ up. Denny told Jaz that their father used to do the same thing. "Jump the last three steps from the landing to the living room. And when Qwayz grew up and found out he could do the same…he was thrilled."

Depending on how long Qwayz had, they would either drop AJ off at home if his parents were there or return him to Ma Vy's where he would sleep in Qwayz's old room and Qwayz would take Jaz to the Malibu house on his way back to Stanford. They would linger in Reds, kissing and fooling around before the final kiss when she would have to say goodnight. "You're a cool guy, Quinton Regis."

"He was born right after I came back from Colt, Texas that first summer. Wasn't gonna have anything to do with a baby but now—Glad he wasn't a girl."

"He's crazy about his Uncle Qwayz."

"I remember when my Dad died everyone came around to spend time with the widow and her children but later, they all went on with their lives except Aubrey. He and Melie were just dating then, but he'd come over and take me to the soccer field. Now that he's a busy doctor, I'm just giving back some of what he gave me. But Aubrey Jr's a cool little dude. Like I expect Q5 and Shane to be."

"I told you I'm not naming our son Shane."

"You can name the girls. Eh, the girls after Amber. We're going to have at least four you know. Two of each."

"Well, we better get started."

"Maybe we'll have two sets of twins."

"Perish the thought," said she as he inhaled her lips, kissing her long and hard. "Humm, you taste good. Cotton candy."

"Let me make it back up the way," Qwayz said.

"Drive carefully. I love you."

"Me too, you."

194

Jaz stood at the curb as he pulled away, waiting for his toot and wave, and then went inside. "I love me some him."

On Wednesdays, Jaz volunteered to pick AJ up from school and take him to a karate class that his Uncle Qwayz had arranged for him with his old master, Sensei Akira. Jaz watched AJ in his white *Gi* uniform then take him to dinner. "Boy, you can eat," she teased while quizzing him for a spelling test as she drove him either home or to Ma Vy's.

Once after dropping him off, Jaz drove by Alvaro and turned onto the dead-end street, pulling to the curb. She looked up at #3G, lit up by another family now. She wondered who and how many there were, and if they were as happy there as she had been with her father, brother, sister and at times, even Lorette. She thought better of stopping by Champion Studios, depending on TC's mood, he would either be ecstatic to see her or would just offer a casual wave before taking a break for a few minutes to see if she needed anything. Jaz didn't feel up to his distracted attention, so she headed back to Malibu. *There was no half-steppin' with TC. That's the reason he's a music mogul at such a tender age*, Jaz rationalized. "This Love Is Real," "Love You Like Crazy" and "You Belong to Me" had just bumped Martha and the Vandellas' "Nowhere to Run," The Temptations' "The Way You Do The Things You Do," and Marvin Gaye's "Pride and Joy" from the charts. Jaz had only talked to Mel twice since taking up her residency in New York, but she seemed happy, her studies challenging yet tedious. They would chat before Mel asked for Selena, and the two of them would talk for a while, with Jaz hoping that they would finish in time for Qwayz's call at eleven.

Life was good because of him.

19

On December 4, the day before Jaz's birthday, the U.S. Department of Justice indicted nineteen men for violating the civil rights of James Chaney, Andrew Goodman and Mickey Schwerner. It would take another three years before an all-white jury would find seven guilty, acquit nine, and deadlock on three others, a hung jury. Jaz's seventeenth birthday was celebrated at the Oasis with all her friends, Mel flew in from New York and her parents sent greetings from Italy. Qwayz showered her with love and gifted her with a solid, single gold star. "We have one in the heavens and now one encircling your neck. No matter where you look, be reminded how much I love you, Jaz-of-mine." She lifted her hair and he lovingly fastened it. "I'll never take it off." They kissed. As she fingered it she thought, *I love it and him.* "Can't we consummate our relationship now that I'm 17."

"You're not in college. Your proclamation, not mine," he reminded.

She settled for their horizontal mambo, which proved quite satisfactory; his gold medallion and her new star as tangled as their legs. "We'll work it out," they giggled

The next weekend they stopped by Champion Studios for Qwayz to run final tracks for, undoubtedly, the next Raw Cilk hit. They entered the building not knowing how TC would react to his idol, Sam Cooke, being shot and killed at the Hacienda Hotel at thirty-three, his musical genius silenced.

TC, hunched over the control boards, listened to a playback with Z and Jax for another group, all agreed the track was a go. "Oh, good you're here," TC greeted Qwayz and Jaz. "Ronnie, you ready?"

196

"Always am," she said as she approached the mike.

"Hey, man, how you doing?" Qwayz asked his buddy.

"Fine. Why wouldn't I be?" TC occupied himself with the recording set up.

"Sam Cooke—"

"His choice," TC blew it off. "I mean if the man had been home with his family or taking them to see Santa Claus instead of being at a motel with some woman, not his wife, he'd still be breathing. Hard to have sympathy, man. It's a great loss."

Qwayz eyed Jaz.

"OK. Cue up the music. Let's see if we can lay this down in a few takes. I know you and my sister have plans." He smiled that irresistible TC smile and Jaz relaxed, but recognized a disappointed sadness in his eyes.

Qwayz laid his soaring tenor around Ronnie's soulful voice, and even Jaz knew this was yet another hit.

Dinner found Jaz and Qwayz at the Lobster House devouring crab cakes, fries, onion rings, spinach salad and a chocolate milkshake for her and an orange freeze for him.

"I mean, nothing," Jaz was saying.

"You know despite his being a 'free spirit' as the magazines say, TC is really a very traditional guy with conservative values. At least morally." Qwayz buttered a roll. "Remember how outraged he was a few years ago when Sammy Davis Jr. married May Britt?"

"'No white women ever got Sammy where he is and when he makes it,'" Jaz said, quoting TC. "He reaches across the color line to take a wife. Not one of his own." Jaz continues, "Then Scoey instigated by asking TC, 'You wouldn't do that, man?' Then TC said, 'hell no. The height of disrespect to all black women everywhere. And when they break up… and they will, I hope he doesn't go crawling back to a sister.'" Jaz laughed. "He was 'done' with Sammy."

"I think he sees things in black and white because it's easier. And he believes it. Same way he warned Carter Hix about the drugs. Gave him a warning twice. Then boom. Out."

"When we went to see where the Baldwin Hills dam broke. They wouldn't let us get but so close and he just hunched his shoulders and said, 'mostly white folks' houses got destroyed. Wouldn't let me buy a house over there. God's wrath," Qwayz quoted.

"He said that?"

"Yep. We went on to the Studio. You can't fault him. He got his staunch prideful traditions from your father and Papa Colt. It's what he saw, what he knows. Strong black men who love themselves, their women and their families. Those are his examples. Pure pride in who and what they are; folks, black, white or otherwise, who don't share their pride? He has no use for them."

"I get it. I felt that way when President Eagan was assassinated. I didn't want him dead or anything; one white guy killing another white guy… But the first thing I thought was 'what does this mean for my dad?'"

"His administration had much to worry about besides an appointment to Italy."

"True. I wasn't that impressed with Eagan's slow response to civil rights issues anyway. He only sent troops Down South when he was embarrassed by European headlines."

"They made the man a martyr."

"Umm. Getting back to TC. When he makes up his mind…it's done. He seldom, if ever, reconsiders."

"It's served him well."

"I just wish he'd give Ronnie a chance."

"Really? Again? You on her family's side? She's not for him. You just said he seldom reconsiders. She is in the 'employee camp.' She's not getting out."

"How can a free musical spirit be so inflexible?"

TC no longer had time to stage the Christmas Boys Club Benefit, writing a check for anything they needed became his modus operandi. In October, he still produced the Fall Fling Talent Show at Roosevelt believing it benefited the students, helped their camaraderie, solidified school spirit and helped music in the schools remain important. Often, he contributed instruments to the music program and spoke there three times a year regarding the ins and outs of the music business.

Jaz spent Christmas with Selena and Zack at Ma Vy's. Scrumptious. Jaz returned from her long-distance call from her parents.

"You OK?" Qwayz asked.

"Of course. I have you." She kissed the tip of his nose and slid into his lap in the big chair by the fireplace in the living room, much to Hanie's delight and Ma Vy's chagrin. "We have another chair, Jasmine. Use it." Jaz jumped up and took her advice.

~*~

Jaz entered the Malibu house to a crumpled and distraught Selena with Zack on the telephone, attempting to comfort her.

"What's happened?" Jaz asked slinging off her shoulder bag and hat and going to her aunt's side.

Selena couldn't get it out. Couldn't gather words to speak. Zack hung up.

"Miles Syphax died."

"Aw. Aunt Selena. I am so sorry." She hugged her and Selena clung to her. "You were such a good friend," Jaz said.

Selena shook her head. "That was my buddy. I knew it would happen. When I went to see him last week his skin was blue from the cobalt treatments. We joked about how someone as dark as him could turn blue." She chuckled through tears. "I had no idea he was so close to—"

One of the smoothest male vocalists of our time has been silenced. One of Qwayz's idols. Jaz didn't want to think about losing anyone she loved, but only six days later on February 21st Malcom X was assassinated at the Audubon Ballroom in Harlem. Jaz had never met him but respected the charismatic leader's stance and ideology. Death dominated the 11:00 p.m. calls between Jaz and Qwayz for a few days. "I don't know what's happening in a world that doesn't tolerate differences of opinions."

"It was America last time I looked."

Two records were resurrected as the result of Malcom's murder: Sam Cooke's "A Change Is Gonna Come" and Raw Cilk's "Better Days Ahead," where Qwayz vocals rocketed high and wide eliciting, visceral emotional responses from all who heard; the "go to" songs to soothe the black community.

~*~

"No joke?" Jaz arranged the phone under her chin so she could paint her nails a pale pink for school tomorrow. Thankful that things seemed to be settling down on the national front.

"Told you the yearbook staff doesn't check that stuff. So 'rocket scientist' is my future occupation," Ian mandated and Jaz chuckled.

They were talking for almost an hour and had been most their entire lives. Ian called to let Jaz know he received his acceptance letter from Morehouse College in Atlanta and, unlike his father, received a full scholarship.

"So, you're not the only brain in the class," Ian teased.
200

"Never said I was," Jaz replied. "But a full ride is a full ride, be it Berkeley or Morehouse."

"Yep. It's boss. I'm asking Dreda to prom."

"A letter boosted your confidence, huh?" She switched hands to paint the other nails.

"Let's say we're not as stingy as you and Qwayz, keeping all the looks, smarts and dance moves to yourselves. We gonna spread our attributes around, share the wealth. Give ordinary folk a chance."

"Nut. You ask her yet?"

"I will. German-brown babies need love, too."

"I don't think she likes being called that. I wonder where she's going to college?"

"Ain't gonna be Spelman, so I better ask now."

"Hey," Jaz greeted Selena and Zack as they entered the living room after being out to dinner with Miles' widow and daughter.

"Look at you," Selena admired her saddle shoes all clean and polished for tomorrow.

"How was it?"

"Still raw, I'm afraid," she said, as she got a glass of ice water and went up to their bedroom.

"Hey," Jaz said to Ian, "I'm back."

"How goes it all the way out there in Malibu?" he joked.

"Not bad. I'm ready for college. How about you?"

"Yep. We've outgrown L.A. Although you're taking a side trip to Paree before you go."

"Yep. Only Gladys Ann's people are balking at her going. They want her in D.C. ASAP to attend pre-college summer classes."

"So, you're not going to go?"

"Heck no. One monkey don't stop no show. I've been waiting for this trip all my life. We're stopping off to see Papa Colt and Keely for a week and then onto Gay Paree."

"Life is so hard for you. Hey, Jaz... I see where Qwayz is tearing up the court up there."

"Yep. That's what he does. His schedule is so tight but we manage."

"I know you do. I still remember his last game at Roosevelt. People chanting his name at the end. *Qway-z! Qway-z!* Unbelievable."

Jaz and Ian both knew that neither of them would keep up with these calls nor write to one another. Neither were the type. Didn't mean they wouldn't miss one another. It just wasn't in their make-up to do so. The reason they had been friends for so long was because they understood one another. Jaz screwed the cap back on the nail polish. It was almost time for Qwayz to call and she wanted to change the channel from this tired black and white Nazi movie before he did.

"OK, kiddo. See you tomorrow."

"Okeydokey, Smokey." Jaz gingerly went to the bathroom, got a glass of water and sat next to the phone waiting for its ring.

"Hey, handsome," she said into the receiver.

"Suppose this was your father?" Qwayz teased.

"It'd work. He's handsome, too." Their mutual smiles collided across the lines.

"So how was your day?"

"Ian got accepted to Morehouse!" And they were off, sharing the time they spent apart and then discussing the pictures Cecil took that Selena wanted to gift them. They agreed on most of them, but Qwayz also liked the one where she jumped on his back piggy-back style and the camera snapped, capturing their eyes and unabashed feelings. Qwayz wanted the one of Jaz's eye, with brim of her hat slicing on an angle one way and her cheekbone cutting up the other way. "You can't even tell that's me!" Jaz joked.

"Oh, I know exactly who it is," Qwayz said. "That's my heart."

The pictures of them forehead to forehead looking into one another's eyes, and another one with their hats; the fudge fedora and the red baseball cap with the white script, also favorites.

"The one where I'm lying face down in the sand resting on my elbows and then you climbed on me lying face down and we're both looking at the camera and laughing. I want them all," he finally said. "Maybe he can make a little book of us." He chuckled. Jaz didn't. "Jaz?"

She stood with the phone in her hand before the great window with their star twinkling down on her. "Jaz?" he repeated.

Her eyes fixed to the television. Seeing something that her brain couldn't process, something registering horror. Unimaginable. Like a train wreck, she couldn't tear her sight away from the images. Black people. Her people, being attacked by German Shepard dogs. Being sprayed by water hoses, the force so strong they knocked down women and children and ripped the bark from trees. Hoses held by white policemen who laughed and made sport of a woman as old as Grandma Keely who fell to the ground under the watery weight. A child rolling over grabbed a branch and clung to it for dear life. "What is this?" she asked of no one as bile rose in her throat, tears streamed down her face and she couldn't explain it to Qwayz—the most heinous sight her eyes had ever seen.

Jaz talked Qwayz out of coming down and Selena echoed her sentiments. It seems that folks across America had reacted to the latest inhumane act against humanity. Seems that the cat was out of the bag and an uproar interrupted "Judgment at Nuremburg." Everyone knew it as Bloody Sunday.

The phone at the Malibu house rang all day and all night, mostly for Selena and Zack. Then her father called from Italy, calming her down over a long-distance call as much as possible, willing to come home to be with his daughters. The next day, Jaz went to see TC and upon seeing his face she ran to him and he accepted her embrace. Head first into his shoulder and then on the side of her face, like when they were kids. "Why?"

"Crazy white folks, Jaz. I can't answer it. Why they think they have the right to do this to us."

She went on to school and some people knew and others did not and it bothered Jaz that they went on with classes and the game as usual. It wasn't like the Bay of Pigs or the assassination on the President when they were sent home. *I guess black folks getting assaulted by white law enforcement in Alabama was not important,* she thought.

When she drove back to Malibu, she opened the door onto bags packed by the entrance.

"I've been waiting for you, Jazzy."

"Where are you going? Paris?"

Selena looked into her niece's questioning eyes without speaking. "I'm going to Selma."

With those words, Jaz burst into tears. She hated that her emotions always defaulted to crying. She wanted to appear anything but weak. "Why? You can't go!"

"This time I have to go. It's time for me to put my body where my money has always gone."

Jaz shook her head *no,* but nothing came out.
204

Selena took her niece's hands in hers and sank upon the couch. A perfect sunny day in Malibu never looked more inviting. "I've sent money for tickets and bail for the Freedom Riders, cheese sandwiches and toothbrushes, I charted the celebrity plane to take all the stars from L.A. to the March on Washington—but this time. I have to go. I have to stand up and be counted."

"Then let me go, too."

"No. Your dad hasn't forgiven me for taking you to The March. And this is no March. I want you to go and stay with Gladys Ann, Grandma Mac and Truck—and your father has already approved of it. I'll be fine."

"No. No you won't. I saw what they did to those people, my people. Those white folk are animals."

"Yes. Many of them are. But there are some going with us who are not. Good white people—"

"Oh puleeze!" Jaz spat. "That's an oxymoron."

"Every race has good and bad, Jaz."

"I don't have the time or inclination to figure that out." Jaz removed her hands from her aunt's. "I don't want you to go. Stay her and be safe."

"Sometimes you got to stand up—"

"Let somebody else do it. Not you and Uncle Zack."

"No, baby. It's decided. Go get some things together."

Petrified. Terrified. Jaz wasn't accustomed to these feelings.

The phone in the dorm hallway rang and when she asked for Qwayz, she was told he was on an away game. *Oh, right,* she thought. *I knew that.*

"You found me," Jaz said an hour later into the phone.

"I knew it was TC or Gladys Ann," Qwayz said. "You want me to come. I will."

"I know, but I'm in good hands," Jaz glanced at a surly Grandma Mac who couldn't understand any boy calling this late. "Besides, you cannot leave the team while you're on an away game."

"The time difference is messing with me, but all is OK. Have you heard from Selena?"

After an abbreviated discussion, Jaz returned his kiss into the phone and hung up. "Thank you, Grandma Mac," she said to the offended woman.

"He made a persuasive argument but this won't be a habit, will it?"

"No, mam. I'm going home tomorrow," she hoped.

Many equally horrified folks of all races, who could not remain in the safety of their hamlets, made their way to Alabama to fight the undeniable injustice seen on television at the Edmund Pettus Bridge. Viola Luizzo, a white Detroit housewife and mother of five, drove from Michigan to Selma, Alabama to fight for Negro civil rights. On March 25 while driving protesters to the airport, her car was ambushed and she was shot in the head by the KKK. She was thirty-nine years old. Reading that account, Jaz wept: *What of her husband and children?* To kill your own reeked of cowardice and a deep, mental and moral pathology. A southern sickness.

Standing in front of the TV at Gladys Ann's, Jaz watched the protesters march across the Edmund Pettus Bridge without incident this time and she bit her nail as they strode into Montgomery. Jaz nearly collapsed with relief and pride. Selena, Zack and all the marchers were all right. Tears spilled down her cheeks.

"It is exhausting being Black in America."

20

None too soon, Jaz pirouetted in the mirror in Selena's room as the doorbell rang.

"You look like a fairytale princess, Jaz," Selena said as Zack yelled up that Qwayz was here.

"Wouldn't I have a long gown on for that?"

"Your Prince Charming awaits."

Slowly, Jaz descended the stairs in her three-tiered, pink chiffon prom dress reminiscent of the Supremes and purchased at D. C.'s Garfinckel's. She noticed Qwayz's shoes before she saw his tux.

"Good googa mooga, Jaz. You look fine."

"You too." Her honey blazed on his hazel; their eyes, meant only for each other, met. After awkwardly looking for a place to pin the corsage, they decided on the wrist as Selena and Zack snapped a barrage of pictures before letting the couple go.

They danced the night away at the Hilton Hotel, went to Club Oasis for an after party and then on to the beach. The guys planted torches in the sand to attract grunions and lit the fire pits as the girls spread their blankets, so couples could make out at a respectable distance from their neighbors. Jaz and Qwayz, Gladys Ann and Jehson, and Scoey and Tracy, who'd snagged his heart. They cooked and ate fish, fell asleep and gathered together at the Waffle House for breakfast before returning to their respective homes to face the parental music.

A few weeks later at graduation as Jaz sat next to Ian on stage facing the crowd, she felt a pang of unexpected nostalgia. The friends side-talked, a feat they had mastered over their years of practice and friendship. Jaz noticed the absence of some of the older boys. "Where are they?"

"Received their 'greetings' from Uncle Sam. On their way to Vietnam."

"Oh, yeah." Jaz recalled Sinclair Cosgrove mentioning Vietnam when he snapped a picture of her in her cheerleading uniform. She intended to look it up but soon the "conflict" became the talk of the studio for a few days. It turned out that Zion's walking on his tippy toes wasn't bad but flat feet, which made him a 4F, kept him from taking Uncle Sam up on his invitation. Jaxson's color-blindness saved him. "They can't get TC, can they?" Jaz asked Ian.

"He got connections and can get out of it like them white boys."

"Hope you're right. What about Dickie? Too skinny?"

"He's got a job with Skeekie at Red Ball Express. After all these years, he just quit school and went to work." Ian said.

"... Jasmine Bianca Culhane, full academic Scholarship to UC at Berkeley."

Jaz stood to be recognized.

She looked in the audience and saw Qwayz beaming back at her. He held up his index finger and wriggled it like a naked sock puppet. When she sat down and faced him, she returned the gesture. He had started that when he sat in the audience watching her on stage at Papa Colt's Founder's Days celebrations, before they started officially dating. Now, Qwayz made this gesture whenever they weren't close enough to touch, when he wanted to really get close and couldn't. When she looked "irresistibly luscious," he'd tuck that sensuous bottom lip under even white teeth... but his eyes, the glimmering eyes, always gave him away. She loved that about him. Without touching her, she felt a rush.

208

"… Ian Lamont Cummings; full academic scholarship to Morehouse College, Atlanta, Georgia."

Ian stood to be acknowledged and sat and they resumed their conversation. "You can't go, right?"

"Naw. Got a student deferment unless I punch out."

Jaz thought, *Qwayz's safe.*

"Gladys Ann McMillian… Howard University. Washington D.C." Jaz and Gladys Ann exchanged congratulatory looks. After more speeches and a couple of musical selections, they posed for pictures on the lawn. That night they gathered at Club Oasis for the Class of 1965 celebration, dancing up a storm like it was the last day on earth that they would ever be together.

"I have something for you," Gladys Ann said to Jaz. "I know you're mad that I can't go with you to Paris."

"Disappointed," Jaz corrected. "Only dogs get mad."

"Yeah. But I have something for you." Gladys Ann gave her a little box, which Jaz opened to discover a keychain on a bed of cotton. It read, "Best Friends," which they'd been since they were eight years old. Gladys Ann snapped it in two and gave the "Be" and "Fri" to Jaz and kept the second part for herself. "No matter where we are, we'll always remember each other."

Jaz's nose began to burn and tears flooded her eyes. "Damn. Can't have a whole key chain, huh?"

"I love you girl. You are my best friend forever."

They stood on the sidelines recalling some of their adventures: the fights with Arnisha over turning the rope double-handed, the Lilt home perm, Jaz sitting outside the bathroom by the door while Gladys Ann tried to insert a tampon for the first time, Satan and the party at the Boondocks, Gladys Ann having sex before Jaz. They continued laughing until Qwayz and Jehson interrupted to resume dancing. Jaz and Qwayz owned the floor when "Save the Last Dance," "Road Runner," crowned by the Temptations "My Girl." TC watched from the catwalk above while Hep and Lorette observed from floor level.

At the Malibu House, the next morning as her parents prepared to go to Colt for a few days before heading back to Italy, Selena tapped on her juice glass to make an announcement at breakfast.

"I haven't given you my gift yet, Jazzy," Selena began, rearranging her caftan.

"But you have. You gave up an entire year—"

Selena held up her hand. "Hush child. That was my pleasure. Your day has finally come and you are going to Paris, France for the summer—"

"Minus at least three weeks you'll spend in Italy," Hep interjected.

"You hush, too. I guess this runs in the family," Selena teased. "If you recall, the trip was for two. You and your best friend. I'm not going to rehash all that with Gladys Ann but that leaves one ticket to use."

TC eyed his aunt and uncle while Jaz thought, *There's no one else I could stand for the whole summer.*

"So, I now know that you have a new best friend. I think you might want him to come. So, I've taken the liberty of inviting Qwayz who has agreed to be your escort about Paris when I cannot."

A stunned, surprised Jaz squealed with delight. "You kept that from me!" She mock-assaulted Qwayz.

"Selena threated to take it away if I told." Qwayz smiled, hazel on honey.

Hep bristled at the thought, but his sister had made a compelling argument: With Qwayz back here in the States Jaz

210

would be ready to leave after two weeks of sightseeing. With Qwayz in tow, they would stay the entire summer, splitting their time between both locations. "I can manage them here or there," Selena had continued. "Besides when they get back, they'll be totally on their own. Ready or not, your little girl has grown up, Dad. You are no longer *the* one."

Jaz disengaged from Qwayz long enough to turn to her father and say, "Thank you, Daddy."

"Your welcome Punkin'," Hep swallowed tears. "I love you." He said to Qwayz, "A vote of confidence for you, young man. Don't make me sorry."

"No sir."

"TC, I know I have you to thank for Dad's liberal stance," Jaz said to her brother as he stood next to his Porsche readying to drive back to L.A.

"Me?"

"You've always had my back. Been on my side. First time I remember is when you took me to be with your boys and they asked, 'Why'd you bring her?' And you said unapologetically, 'She's my sister.' I was *so* proud."

"Johnny Green was a yahoo."

Jaz embraced her brother. "I love you, TC. Now it's my turn to want the best for you. I want you to be in love when I get back."

"I am in love."

"I mean with a living, breathing female who loves and respects you and your music."

"See what I can do." She hugged him for the good guy he'd been to her all her life. "I'm happy I didn't have to kill Qwayz. He loves you, Jaz."

"I know."

"My ace boon coon became your man. Wow. Who saw that coming?" TC smiled toward the sky. "You two are damn lucky people."

"Yeah. We are… "

~*~

Papa Colt remained spunky, playful and full of moxie and sass with his sayings and advice. But something different permeated his being. More than the fact that pneumonia had knocked him back a little, he seemed a little worse for wear bodily but his spirit remained as strong and tough as ever.

"Maybe it's you," Qwayz told Jaz as they lounged in one another's arms near the big tire at the swimming hole. "You're older now, standing on the verge of full-blown independence."

"I don't know why Mel didn't come at least for a few days."

"New York can be far away."

"TC's only here for a week."

"So are we," Qwayz reminded.

That night TC and Qwayz performed their usual repertoire for Papa Colt as he sat on the porch swing. Sam Cooke, James Brown, Jackie Wilson and Miles Syphax. After they all went inside to bed, Jaz and Qwayz remained on the porch in the glow of the stars.

"There it is. Our star. Gonna follow us to Paris."

"Why is it we don't know when our last something is happening?" Jaz asked.

"Like what?"

Jaz thought awhile then said, "The last time I saw Echo Blake." He looked at her. "When we went to the movies and you were talking to one of your 'fans' I went around the side of the building to see the preview posters and this girl approached. She was on the verge of saying something but didn't. She felt familiar. Raggedy, unkempt, shabby clothes, smelling of urine. I said 'Hi,' but she didn't respond. I was haunted by that encounter. That night it occurred to me. It was Echo Blake. What happened to her?"

"Heard she'd had a beef with her family. Dropped out of school and got put out of the house. Living on the streets." He watched Jaz try to absorb it. "Education ain't all about just academics. Got to have some fun time. Apparently, she had none at Einstein."

"Her mother was so sure her daughter would 'be somebody.'"

"Echo got lost on that yellow-brick road; it wasn't her trip but her mother's." He brushed hair back from her face. "You think this is our last trip to Colt, Texas?"

"Don't know. Hope not. Trying to cherish the last of everything. The last time I danced on top of my dad's shoes at the Satin Doll for New Year's Eve. The last time he took us to Pismo Beach for clam digging. Last time I roller-skated at Kalorama Rink or had a long conversation with Ian or Dickie. The last time I saw Gladys Ann before she left for D.C. The last night I spent on Alvaro Street or the Malibu house for that matter."

"Yeah. But think of all the firsts that lie ahead waiting for us. Your first year in college. Your first college diploma. Your first wedding."

"And last."

"Another degree and our first baby."

"How about the first time we make love," Jaz speculated on something more immediate.

"You're going to lose your virginity in France with the 'love of your life.'"

"Who has the biggest ego I have ever seen. Such a control freak."

"C'mon. You know I've got to be good. The way I get you off and we're not even naked yet."

"Ah!" Jaz shushed him and looked around making sure no one heard.

His hands worked their way beneath her blouse so he felt her warm, supple flesh. "Umm. Can't wait."

"I dunno how you did this long. You are my first. Last and only Quinton Regis. When we're old and gray, I want all my lasts to be with you."

21

Jaz held Qwayz's hand as the Paris-bound plane skyrocketed and cut through the fluffy clouds. After devouring their four-course meal, the china and silverware were collected, the couple took blankets and pillows and napped, awaking in time for the hot towels, juice, croissant and apricot marmalade; their last airborne meal as they banked over Paris, France.

"I can't believe I am finally here," Jaz said, "and with you. It's surreal."

"We're magic Jaz-of-mine." Qwayz kissed her fingers gently, making her pulse rise even higher.

"I'm beginning to believe it."

A sunny, hot morning with the promise of more heat throughout the day greeted them as they descended the escalator with Selena's orders in mind: "Stay close now."

"Look at all those people," said Jaz. "I wonder what's going on?"

"Your aunt and uncle are coming home," Qwayz quipped.

Jaz hadn't thought of that. Zack and Selena, her relatives who gave up a year of their life so she could graduate with her class, were famous stars. Stewardesses had kept passengers wanting autographs out of first class, but, to Jaz, they were just people who loved her as much as she loved them. Now throngs of folks yelled from the fence beyond, holding up signs "Welcome Home!" and chanting "Selena! Selena!" As they entered the airport, crowds pressed in and newscasters shoved mikes in their faces to which Selena graciously said, "Good to be home!" Jaz watched them conduct interviews with bystanders in fluent French, well-beyond her comprehension. Once the police guided them into the limo, Selena made an introduction: "This is Emile. Our chauffer extraordinaire. He can take you anywhere you want to go and find parking for this big boat." Emile tipped his hat in greeting.

Selena retrieved a club soda and stemware from the limo's bar and poured a glass for herself and Zack. Qwayz spotted a Nehi orange soda next to a Royal Crown Cola. "Got it for you two." Selena smiled. "I'm so glad you're here!" she said, grinning even more. "All this don't mean dookey if you can't share it with loved ones." They clicked glasses. "Take the scenic route," she directed Emile.

The star couple took turns pointing out the sites: the Eiffel Tower, shops of the Champs, Rue du Faubourg Saint-Honoré "where most of your wardrobe came from," the Arc de Triomphe and Notre-Dame. The limo slowed over a bridge. "We've crossed to the Left Bank, the *true* Paris!" Selena proclaimed with the excitement of a child at Christmas. The wide boulevards of Saint-Michel and Saint-Germain gave way to slender streets jam-packed with people. The black limo squeezed into the shadow of the Saint-Germain-des-Prés onto the Rue Jacob, passed quaint shops and restaurants that didn't look any larger than the living room of apartment #3G on Alvaro Street. Emile swung wide, partially backing up into a one-way street and stopped in front of an immense metal gate. He jumped out and disappeared into a side metal door before opening the formidable entry.

"Oh, my goodness," Jaz exclaimed as the limo pulled into an exquisite inner courtyard around a fountain in front of three marble steps, crowned with double doors adorned with beveled glass. The gate closed automatically as Emile held the car doors open for his passengers. Jaz and Qwayz emerged with their mouths agape as they drank in the beauty of this fantasy

216

hidden by the ugly metal barrier. The explosion of colorful flowers surrounding the fountain matched those by the marble benches and grassy areas. The gravel crunched beneath their feet as they turned in a complete circle, noting the perfect square in which they now stood gazing up at a wall of interior windows on the floor above their heads.

"Nice digs," Qwayz said, finally speaking. "You live in one of these?"

"We live in all of these," Selena declared. "This is home!" Selena waved to a joyous white face peering down on them. "Follow me."

Selena pranced through the double doors into a cavernous foyer of marble before she began traipsing up the winding marble steps wrapped in wrought-iron balustrades. "There's the elevator, but I need the exercise." She paused at the landing by two stationary benches before climbing the next set of steps. "Come on. We need to catch up to Zack."

The ornate, gold-gilt, 20-foot mirror on the side wall captured the expressions of the California pair as they soaked in the massive hallway with lit sconces, a crystal chandelier and immaculate red carpet on which Selena paused momentarily before continuing her ascent.

"It's a museum," Jaz intoned.

"No mailboxes in the lobby." They heard loud greetings in fast-paced French as they continued the climb, peering into the gorgeously carved mahogany doors, purposefully left ajar. Qwayz looked out of the slender side rectangular window onto the Paris streets. "Who'd of thought that all this was behind that ordinary gate?"

"Come! Come!" Selena fanned them into the door. "This is my niece and nephew, Jaz and Qwayz from California," she said, introducing them in French, and both smiled as they recognized their names. "This is Lisette and Zasu," Selena said in English. "The best around. Been with me forever. If you need anything, just ask them." Clad in gray and white uniforms, the livered pair curtsied with enormous smiles and clasped hands.

"Be it ever so humble, there is no place like home!" Selena enthused. "Let me show you around your new home!" She stepped into a mammoth wash of light in an elegantly appointed room too pretty to sit in. "Formal parlor," Selena announced as Lisette interrupted her to decide on the meal for tonight. The room, as large as a football field with French-door windows from Jaz's waist to the ceiling, with sills deep enough to sit in. While her eyes were up there, she noted that room was divided in three sections, the ornate chandelier in the center flanked by two others on either side, each accented by an ornate plaster ceiling medallion. One hung over Selena's grand piano in the corner, placed on a diagonal towards the window; the middle one hung over a collection of Louis and Queen Ann settees with chairs, and the last over another a more casual antique seating arrangement. The room was divided by rugs over gleaming hardwood floors. On the causal side, an immense tapestry anchored to the ceiling draped dramatically down the wall to the floor. "That's a gift from Arabian friends," Selena said, resuming the conversation. "They're the only folks I know who can afford to give a twelfth-century tapestry to a singer they admire," she teased. "Let's start on this side." Selena entered the small dining room with one French-door window. "This is where you'll take any meal you like. In the mornings until noon or so, it's set up for breakfast. The food will be kept warm in the chafing dishes. If there's something particular you want, Lisette can make it for you. This room only holds eight comfortably, so anything beyond that is a buffet. Don't entertain much here. We have

218

two big parties at Chateau Jazz; one is the Fourth of July and you all will be here!"

"And this is the kitchen," said Selena as she guided them out of the cool green dining room. Qwayz looked around and panicked when he didn't see a stove or refrigerator. "Around the corner in a separate room, beyond the pantry," Selena answered his silent plea. "There's also an eight-burner stove and ample icebox."

"Where do these steps lead, Aunt Selena?" Jaz asked as they headed back to the entry door.

"Oh, that's where Lisette and Zasu live. Two bedrooms, one bath, the laundry room...it's easier for them, and a parlor with fireplace, TV and so forth."

Walking past the wall of windows that looked down on the courtyard, cars and the double doors, Jaz remarked, "I love all this light."

"We need breadcrumbs to find our way back," Qwayz teased.

"Now, the limo is Emile's baby. If you want him to take you somewhere, let him know a day ahead. The other two cars are for the girls for their various errands. You can use them anytime you want to. Just coordinate with them."

"I'll let my feet do the walking," Qwayz said. "I've seen driving in Paris."

"Right here..." Selena opened an over eight-foot door onto a small space, "the closet. When we have small soirees this is where guests leave their wraps. Next...guest bathroom." She opened the door to a room with intricate brocade and foiled wallpaper with a tray of perfumes, atomizers and a mirror before reaching the water closet itself. "Here's my guy's room. Yours and TC's." Selena flung open the next door and, in the middle of the room like a centerpiece, a sleigh bed perched on an Aubusson rug. She pointed out a huge closet and bathroom door but didn't open it as she led them back into the hallway into the next room. "Jaz's room." Upon opening the door, a fairytale princess canopy bed sprang into view. Jaz couldn't contain her glee, "And no Mel to share it with!" A white French provincial with a dresser and a wardrobe fit for a head of state welcomed Jaz. Like Qwayz's room, there was one French-door window next to a bathroom. Selena opened the door onto the long Jack and Jill bath with dual sinks divided by a slender stained-glass window allowing light while maintaining privacy. Selena walked through and opened the opposite door. The sleigh bed popped into view.

"Now, I trust that I can trust you two to share a bathroom," Selena stated. "I expect you to abide by the same guidelines as the Malibu house where you two did not live together. I want the same respect and responsibility this summer that you gave me all year."

"You got it," Qwayz said first.

"Yes, Sure."

"I need not tell you how much your daddy does not approve of this. He volunteered to get Qwayz his own room at The Ritz. If I have your word, that's enough for me. You two are not stupid or careless and have futures to protect. Enough said. Come…the rest of the house awaits."

"Where are they off to?" Zack asked Selena as she joined him in the front window near her piano, watching Jaz and Qwayz disappear up the street.

"They are young, in love and in Paris," Selena said, looking at the comely couple. "They are going to explore the City of Love." She kissed his cheek. "Me? I'm going to take a nap. Join me?"

"My woman in my own bed. How can I refuse?"

220

Jaz and Qwayz tore around Paris like sailors on shore leave with only weeks before they shipped off to certain death. They visited everything touristy, not minding the lines and getting no stares from their kissing and hugging—after all, they were where love was born, lived and expressed and they fit right in.

"Let's go see if the Hunchback is home," Qwayz said, taking her hand as they walked up the steps of Notre-Dame and looked at the city splayed out before them. Qwayz snapped pictures of Jaz beside the gargoyles, "Beauty and the Beast." He tried to coax her up the Eiffel Tower and she balked. "Come on, Jaz we're doing this together. You and me." Finally making it to the top, she held on to him like the life-preserver he was before being captivated by yet another view of Paris…higher and wider. Jaz preferred the walk up to the top of the Arc de Triomphe as the geometrical boulevards struck out from the arch like spokes of a bike wheel, appealing to her sense of order and symmetry. The visited Sacré-Cœur Basilica, perched on a hill in Montmartre, the neighborhood where many impressionist artists lived and "An American in Paris" was filmed. After climbing all the steps in the back of the Sacred Heart, they dissolved into laughter when they discovered the funicular out front. They ripped and ran for two weeks before settling into a calmer pace, living like Parisians or at least folks who had until August to explore. "We have to give Zack and Selena some time."

"I know. We haven't even seen their club."

"I don't think they can spare two seats for us."

The young couple always returned home to a note from Selena saying "If you want to come to the club, Emile will come and get you. If not, Zasu has food in the fridge if you're hungry."

Qwayz would rise earlier than Jaz, go for a run and come back to kiss her awake. They'd shower and eat in the dining room before setting out again. They had no set destination other than being in one another's presence. "No... not the Louvre again," Qwayz lamented. "We've seen it six times. Let's take the riverboat ride down the Seine."

"OK. Then the Louvre."

Often, they would stroll and blend in with the other lovers enjoying their picnics by the Seine. Salami and jambon sliced paper-thin from the charcuterie, along with the hunks of silky-milky purchases from the fromagerie to lay on crusty, freshly baked baguettes topped with desserts of artful, fruity tarts from the bakery as pleasing to the palate as they were to the eye. "Now this is a ham and cheese sandwich," Qwayz quipped. Rounding out their escapade with a bottle of red wine on a blanket, he knew once he got her by the river and supplied sustenance, she would acquiesce and forgo the Louvre.

"Our beach," Jaz declared as they fed one another while lounging on the grass. They could stay there all day until hunger grabbed them again.

"I'm crazy about you Jaz-of-mine." Hazel pierced honey with an intense sincerity.

"What's the difference between being 'crazy about' and being 'in love?' Which is better?" she asked.

"You love your daddy, your brother, chocolate cake--"

"I might be 'crazy about' chocolate cake," she challenged.

"Smarty-pants. Tickle fest!" Qwayz began tickling her and, despite her objections, she laughed so hard she couldn't catch her breathe. They settled down again and Qwayz continued, "See... 'crazy' is above and beyond love. I'm crazy-in-love with you. Stone-cold-in-love with you. I was

222

born to love you. Now that you've given me your heart… I'm never going to give it back."

"Don't want it back. You take better care of it than I do."

They kissed long and languidly becoming part of the Parisian landscape; No one noticing or caring about just another couple in love. He held her beneath the stark blue sky on the warm day in Paris along the Seine and said, "Wish I could hit pause and make this day last forever." They kissed again. "Another kind of day that will get you through the rest of your life."

"Making a memory," said she.

"No question. When the kids are driving us crazy and we're too busy to breathe with your doctoring and me saving the world in a court of law—we'll look at each other and remember when we had a simpler past. And know it'll all be all right."

"We'll schedule a babysitter and go off for the weekend. Just the two of us."

"Yeah." He smiled. "And remind ourselves that this was the life we wanted long ago when we were youngsters by the Seine River in Paris."

"And didn't have a clue. Before your stomach-paunch and gray hair," she teased.

"And your bones are so brittle we can't make love."

"Ah… Will we be back to no love making again? We better start soon." She rolled over on him. "No time to waste Jeff Chandler jaws."

They returned to the apartment, greeted by Zasu holding up the telephone, "Ah! Monsieur TC for you."

"Merci," Qwayz took the receiver. "What up, man?" He sat on the arm of the chair and slid into its soft center as Jaz went to the bathroom. "You on your way?"

"You left me in a lurch, man. The Latin group downright refused to tape when they heard you wouldn't be on percussions. But they seem satisfied with Jax now. The Watts Band was pissed you wouldn't be on bass. Now those brothers showed out. Said the only reason they delayed to summer was they knew you'd be back by then."

"So, they jumped to another label?" Qwayz joked.

"I'm doing it. A Grammy Award winner playing bass for a junkyard band. It could ruin me."

"Nobody'd believe it."

"So, you coming back like next week? Tell me Paris stinks and you hate being with Jaz 24/7."

"No chance." On cue Jaz returned to the room and Qwayz gathered her in his arms and kissed her forehead. "Where's LeLani? She usually keeps the natives quiet."

"They came on a day when she wasn't here. Worth her weight in gold. I really called to see if you got the tape? 'Night Moves?'"

"It's out?"

"Out? It's cleaning up. They're talking another Grammy, man—and it's only been a few days."

"Congrats. Your first jazz album."

"Been a long time coming. Thanks, man." You could hear his smile across the continent. "I sent it to you eons ago."

"I'll look for it. Can't wait, man."

They chitchatted amicably before TC asked, "Where's my sister?"

"Here she is." Qwayz handed her the phone.

"Hey, handsome," Jaz said and listened to TC wail about the bind Qwayz's holiday put on his enterprise. He moved on to Dad's usual visit for the Fourth of July at Chateau Jazz. "He's a wheeler dealer. Talked me into buying a bauxite mine in Jamaica and its making money. Talked to Papa Colt and Keely. She said you called."

"Yeah. Her best friend Ruthie Rudd Pincus Criqui died. You talked to Mel?"

"Yeah, I'll go see her when I get the time. She's got some play she wants me to see."

"Yep. She hopes Baldwin's 'Blues for Mister Charley' is still there for Thanksgiving."

"You going?"

"I was invited."

"You should. We'll do Connecticut for Christmas." He laughed.

"I prefer Colt, Texas for Christmas. A better party. You'll bring Ronnie," Jaz counter-teased.

"I'm about sick of her. She still has these headaches. I made two appointments for her, she breaks them. I arrange for a third and call for her mama and sisters to take her. They all forget. I actually go with her on the fourth and they cannot find anything wrong and refer her to a specialist, which I'm going to pay for. I make the appointment once, twice same old rigmarole with family. They break them. Like Qwayz says, I got no children. None I know of and she certainly isn't at 23."

"That's long distance," Qwayz reminds her as he downs an orange Nehi he poured from the bar.

"It's his dime," Jaz countered and TC misunderstood.

"It's 4 a.m., thought I'd take a break and call you guys."

"So glad you did. Usually we aren't here at this time of day. Have you seen Tracy?"

"Every time I see Scoey." Jaz smiled. "And Gladys Ann came by to say bye. D.C. bound."

"I'd love for you to surprise us with a visit on the fourth."

"Might could be."

"I know what that means."

"You two take it light and be good to each other."

"Always."

"Love you TC."

"Back at cha."

22

"It took them a few weeks but they really do exist. And are here tonight," Selena spoke into the mike at her club. "My niece and nephew Jaz and Qwayz from California. She's the reason I've been gone so long but as you can see... she's worth it." Jaz threw her a kiss. "She has a full scholarship to UC at Berkeley. She's going to be a doctor. He's already at Stanford and is going to be a lawyer. Right now, they are here and having the time of their lives. Help me welcome them!"

Jaz and Qwayz stood and waved to the appreciative audience.

"Before they go home, I hope they'll sing for us. I'll keep you posted," Selena sassed and volleyed right into "Too Young."

That weekend the family of four changed venues from their Paris city-center home to Chateau Jazz in the French countryside in preparation for the Fluellens' Annual Fourth of July celebration after which they usually flew to Colt, Texas. As Emile eased the limo down the narrow, tree-lined road, the chateau popped into view.

"Oh naw, not another mansion," Qwayz teased as the car passed a small house and took the circular drive that curved around an impressive stone statue and stopped at the front door.

"It's smaller," Selena offered as Zasu and Lisette, who had come a day early to supervise the additional staff the Fluellens hired for big events, welcomed them.

"What's that over there?" Jaz asked.

"The gatehouse. Unoccupied now but the caretaker and his family lived there years ago. Before security systems, dogs and nosey townspeople."

Jaz eyed Qwayz who returned the knowing gaze. *That's the place for my official deflowering,* she thought.

He smiled and touched her derriere as Jaz followed them all into the house.

The limestone outside with the long shuttered windows and climbing ivy reminiscent of every French mansion captured in the photos continued the theme on the inside. Immediately dwarfed by a cavernous two-story open atrium, the couple looked up at the bedroom doors, visible from the downstairs through the wrought-iron railing.

"Four bedrooms in four corners. Each with its own bathroom," Selena said. "No sharing." She smiled.

The same exquisite furniture and antique rugs, furnishings fit for royalty, and fresh flowers sprung from everywhere. The chateau, as elegant as the Paris flat, but with a more casual flair. With all the advance preparations, the house smelled as good as it looked. Groupings of furniture pushed aside to make room for the seafood table, with buckets in place for the iceman who would come from town with the family who does the fireworks each year. An immense buffet table , divided into sections like the stores of Paris, could satisfy each guest and their palates. The bar, laden with any spirit of choice from beer to champagne, had room for the attending alchemists to make any requested concoction come true. The kitchen, aflutter with activity, the liveried waiters receiving their last instructions, the valet and his staff talking with Emile, all taking orders like the soldiers they were. The goal… to ensure that each guest felt special.

The piano room, dressed in regal crimson, had the only comfortable spot in the house. As the Fluellens disappeared

228

fielding last-minute questions, Jaz and Qwayz followed Lisette upstairs and toured their rooms for the next week, smaller than their Paris digs but stylish and well-appointed. Qwayz and Jaz looked out the back window at a view plucked straight from a Monet painting. A small building on the right gave way to a gazebo over a bridge straight ahead, and a pond on the left. They met again in the hall, joined hands and went outside to survey their new environs.

Finding Selena, they asked, "Is there was anything we can do?"

"Get out of the way," she stated. "We pay over fifty folk in here to know what they're doing. Explore! Enjoy!"

"You see all the people in that house? This is before the guests arrive."

The little building shed could not be accessed. They traipsed across the bridge to the ornate white gazebo where they lounged and watched early arrivals. "Where are they all staying?"

"In town," Jaz said. "The local economy depends on this party and a few others. That's why they make sure this house is protected when the Fluellens are away. The young people love to work here, especially the guys who like the cars. The girls like the rich men. So, watch it."

"Not in the market, babe. Got my woman." He smiled and followed her through the cacophony of beautiful flowers both wild and trained on trellises. She almost plunged right into the pond. "Look at this."

"It's unfathomable."

"Think of all they give to civil rights causes and can still live like this." Nestled behind them in a cabana were towels and blankets, chairs, insect repellent, citronella candles, matches and stacked wood. They retrieved a blanket, spread it on the ground and lay there looking at the cloud configurations across the turquoise blue sky.

"So, tell me about TC's mystery woman," Jaz asked.

"Not much to tell. You know your brother. He has his secrets."

"Or priorities."

"They kept running into each other. She gave him his plaque at the NAACP Awards and then again at the Urban League. So, he asked her out and she said yes. A beginning."

"So, who is she to be giving out awards? What does she do?"

"A local L.A. network field reporter who seems to be as ambitious as he is."

"Well, that's good. She's no gold-digger. Got her own goals and life. Is she cute?"

"Haven't seen her. Apparently with their schedules, getting together is a challenge. But I got my own agenda right here."

"Yes, you do." Qwayz rubbed his lips across Jaz's when they heard people coming toward them, and fell silent as they passed. "Wonder if your parents are here yet?"

"I'm out here with you." She resumed kissing his inviting lips. "I suppose that fourth bedroom is reserved for them. Maybe something will come up and they can't make it."

Deciding to return to the house, they walked into a wall of people. "Is the party tonight or tomorrow?"

"Merciful heavens! Do you see who that is?"

"James Baldwin."

"Jimmy! Jimmy, come here," Selena called, summoning him. They shared a private, risqué laugh. "Oh Jaz, come. You remember Jimmy from The March? He has a place in Provence."

230

A star-struck Jaz began talking and once they got started, engaged in an enlightening conversation until interrupted by Fabrizio, "Divine! You are. You cannot be serious about being a drab old doctor."

As Mr. Baldwin peeled off, Jaz turned on Selena's fashion designer, responsible for all of her signature caftans and matching turbans. "Really? You chased off the best author of our times."

"Jimmy'll be here like us all… but you are a vision. Your coloring, bone structure, those eyes, that long waist and that don't-give-a-damn attitude. So refreshing. You have success written all over you." Jaz kept her eye on Mr. Baldwin as he was swallowed up by the crowd.

"Look Fabrizio, I've told you before I have zero interest in a fashion career." Qwayz sidled up to her. "I am going to be the doctor-wife to this man and have lots of babies."

"Oh, the horror! Such a waste." Qwayz shrugged his shoulders and Fabrizio continued, "But I can certainly see your point." He smiled at Qwayz and fluttered his eyes. "You too are delicious."

"Buzz off," Qwayz spat. "Really, you don't want none of this."

"But what if I do?" Fabrizio challenged, a pinky finger dangling provocatively from his mouth.

Jaz yanked Qwayz from the conversation. "I don't like that guy," he said.

"Yes, I know. You, TC and Scoey have a real thing about our…broken-wrist brothers."

Jaz watched Qwayz's jaw clench and release, clench and release. "Let's go check out the gatehouse."

"Oh, now you're talkin' my language."

They were waylaid from their gatehouse destination as Chateau Jazz continued to fill with people of all sizes, shapes, ages and ethnicities, some recognizable, others not: the royalty distinguished by the jewels and expensive casual clothing, some in full regalia and others in jeans with elaborate tops. "It's like a carnival of humanity," Jaz noted as the pair, intercepted and introduced to all, before escaping to their refuge, the gazebo. From there they could judge the comings and goings of the festivities, the orchestra, a band and the combo that rotated playing—all to provide non-stop music. The piano stood accessible to anyone interested in an impromptu jam session. "Isn't this wild?" Qwayz enthused.

"Like an Oscar Wilde party. We will not run our home like this."

"Aw. No fun."

Jaz and Qwayz, a self- sufficient couple, needed no outside assistance and remained in the gazebo taking turns to get food. Shrimp and cocktail sauce. Escargot. The melon and strawberries. "Watch out for Fabrizio," Jaz teased.

"Unfunny, Jaz."

Moments later she heard footsteps approaching. "Hey Punkin'."

"Daddy! You made it."

"You didn't doubt me for a second, did you?" She hugged her father and kissed his cheek.

"You look good."

"As do you. You must be enjoying your trip."

"I am." Jaz babbled on about all she and Qwayz had done and seen.

When she finished, Hep said, "Paris has nothing on Italy."

"I must admit I'm looking forward to it. Lorette with you?"

"Your mother's in the house. Holding court."

232

"Nice. Where will they have the fireworks?" Jaz asked, changing the subject.

"Right over there. You'll have company for them. The gazebo is a popular locale."

At about three, the mouth-watering aroma of roasting and grilled meats wafted over the countryside announcing that the Texas Barbeque was open. Both Jaz and Qwayz braved the crowd of grownups to partake of the Fluellen's signature cuisine. Jaz spotted her mother looking stunning in an Yves St. Laurent pantsuit with a matching scarf, handbag and sandals; her toes as manicured as her fingernails.

"My man is just scoping you out," Qwayz noted. "The Saudi prince over there."

"All that git-up freaks me out. He must be hot."

"Hot for you."

Did all guys have built-in radar when it came to their girlfriends, Jaz wondered, as she perused the room and found the Saudi Prince's gaze already upon her. Sometimes he just nodded royally and others times he just stared. She found it unsettling.

"No worse than Zsa Zsa over there who bounces her boobs off of you every chance she gets," Jaz countered.

"She's old enough to be my mother."

"She doesn't think so… 'dah-ling.'"

"Jaz, there is someone who wants to make your acquaintance," Jaz heard Selena over her shoulder and turned straight into the gaze of the Saudi.

"This is Crown Prince Omar. This is my niece Jaz."

"I'm pleased to meet you," he said with a slight bow. "I am sure you have heard before how simply exquisite you are."

Jaz looked at him with outright disappointment. "Looks are really a superficial way to judge someone, don't you think? As bad as using someone's bank account. Excuse me."

Finding Qwayz, they headed outside and were intercepted on the terrace where they engaged in a lively conversation on civil rights in America.

"OK, he's creepin' me out now. Those big, round dark liquid pools of ebony aimed right at me."

"He's harmless, Jaz. Can't help looking at a fine black woman."

Night progressed, showcasing spectacular fireworks lighting up the sky, exploding in a kaleidoscope of colors to everyone's delight. The orchestra cued up again, reviving the party and Qwayz held up the tape.

"Look what came today!" he said. "Time for a party of our own."

She took his hand and they traveled around the house into the parking area, found Selena's limo and crawled inside undetected. Qwayz popped it into the player and smooth jazz sounds flooded the car.

"Night Moves," he said, adjusting the volume. "Let's have some of our own."

They began nibbling one another with soft, supple lips. Playfully and then more intensely. The seduction of the French countryside, the soft mellow, lazy sounds of jazz, the taste of wine on their lips, and freedom made their usual moves unsatisfactory. Hands delved, clothes removed and Qwayz inhaled an erect, dark nipple. "Chocolate drops," he moaned and the sound of pleasure emanating from his throat, the feel of him on her nude skin, propelled Jaz to heights from which there was no recovery. Their star shone from high above christening their maiden voyage into their foray of lovemaking: their very first time. Organically, her cinnamon

234

sticks wrapped around his waist. She found and rode their rhythm to ecstasy. Blessed oblivion captured her in a vice and wouldn't let go. Time and space suspended her in a Neverland as Qwayz pleasured her in the most unexpectedly beguiling way. Afterwards, as they regained their breathing, they lay in a stream of moon light able to see out, but others could not see through the tinted windows. "Wow!" Jaz said smiling in the afterglow. "That was boss," she panted. "After all that waiting and anticipating, we still did it in the backseat of a car."

"Point of clarification. We are in France, it is a limo, not the backseat of Scoey's Impala and…I love you now more than I ever thought possible." He kissed her nose. "How was it for you?"

"Mama likes. Mama wants more."

"Please leave my mama out of this right now." They giggled and their sweaty stomachs made salacious sucking noises which tickled the couple even further.

"Every time I look into your eyes, I see heaven. But now, I've felt paradise."

"I love you too Quinton Regis Chandler. Now and forever."

"There's no going back now, Jaz-of-mine."

"I only want to go 'back' for more."

"You lil' vixen." He laughed into her neck and began kissing her anew.

Contented and satisfied, they fell asleep in one another's arms.

A car door slammed the couple into wakefulness. "Good morning."

"It was a better night. Chocolate drops for breakfast?" Qwayz intoned, kissing her lips then moving down to her breasts.

"You are insatiable and need a Junior Mint." Jaz began covering up.

"Joning on the love of your life?" He moved his dead-asleep arm. "Your breath is minty fresh," he teased sarcastically.

"I'm stiff." Jaz sat up and Qwayz waved goodbye to brown breasts and helped her put on her bra.

"Much more fun removing it. See ya later, ladies."

Jaz chuckled as she pulled on her blouse and Qwayz helped her with the buttons. "It was worth the wait," Jaz managed to say through love-filled eyes.

"You ain't seen nothing yet. Next time a bed. No more stiffness."

"The 'stiffness' is what I like," Jaz said naughtily, her hair tousled, lips rubied red, kissed into plumpness accompanied by a big grin on her face. "Do I look like a woman now?"

"Yeah. My woman." He kissed her again and moaned. A guest walked right by the car and seemingly glanced in but saw nothing. Qwayz raised his head like a submarine periscope and saw that the limo remained inaccessible by other cars, but this rendezvous was over.

"The continental breakfast must be over," he observed as he watched the catering truck leave. Using the plastic liner from the ice bucket, he began cleaning the remnants of Jaz's lost innocence.

Jaz held up the foil from the condom. "This couldn't pass for a Hershey Kiss wrapper if it tried."

"No lie." Qwayz grabbed it, popped TC's tape from the car's cassette and slithered out the side, and once the coast was clear, opened the door wider for Jaz. They circled the house and entered through the back door from the terrace.

"Oh, there you are," Selena said to them as they walked toward her. "Your folks were looking to say goodbye."

"We'll see them soon enough," Jaz offered.

"Some party, Selena and Zack," Qwayz piped up.

"Glad it's over. Now we sleep for a couple of days before we head back to Paris."

"And start all over again. Life is so hard," Zack joked

23

"What?" Qwayz asked.

"She just collapsed in the studio," TC said. "Called 911 and they took her to the hospital. She was pronounced dead. Results of the autopsy won't be available for a couple of days. The family is making funeral arrangements."

"You want us to come home?"

"Not for me. I've been told that I am excluded from the funeral—"

"What?! As good as you've been to that girl? That crazy-ass family."

"Hey, I guess folk mourn in different ways. I still offered to pay for it."

"I bet they won't refuse that," Qwayz spat.

"I'll keep you posted."

An incensed Jaz couldn't believe that someone so young could drop dead but the fact that her brother, who did everything for Ronnie and her family, was being shunned by the Alstons reeked of ungratefulness. The autopsy later revealed that she died of an aneurism, probably brought on by the beatings she'd received from former boyfriends.

"She did date some hoodlums," Qwayz agreed. "What her mama and them say to that?"

"Still blaming me for not taking better care of her," TC replied.

"So, you just supposed to baby-sit or love somebody you don't 'cause Mama say so? Absurd."

A few days later, TC advised, "Calm down, Q-man."

Qwayz raked his hand through his hair out of sheer frustration. "Sic LeLani Troop on them. She'll straighten them out. You're too nice, man."

"They're talking about suing. Legal said they have no legs to stand on and the fees will eat them alive. Champion has been quite generous."

"True that!"

"You're about to bust a gut. It's over. She's in the ground resting in peace. And I've got a date with my lady. We're going to New York to see Mel. So, everything is copacetic."

"I feel we should be there."

"To watch me go on a date? Don't need that man."

Qwayz broke into a big smile.

"You and my sister continue to enjoy Paris. If anything, we know tomorrow isn't promised."

"Yeah. OK."

"What's happening?" Jaz asked when he hung up.

Qwayz shook his head. "Your brother is pretty amazing, you know that?"

"Yes, I do." Loyalty was one of the things Jaz admired about Qwayz: If he loves you, he's all in. Always feels deeply and strongly. Perhaps losing his father at an early age and not being taught restraint, modulation and perspective was the reason. Qwayz felt if one of his boys hurts, it was his responsibility to do something about it.

Qwayz looked at her, hazel on honey. "Why can't family just take care of family; take care of their own. What a wonderful world that would be."

"True, but everyone doesn't have your values and traditions."

He gathered her to him. "Yeah. You're right." He brushed his lips against her temple. "Always ready to blame someone else for their problems."

"Let's take a walk," she said, guiding him out the door.

"Speaking of taking care of family, I told you Denny and I plan to send Hanie to college? We don't want Ma to mortgage the house."

"Maybe she'll get a scholarship like you and Denny."

"Have you met my baby sister, Stephanie Chandler?" He chuckled.

"You always said she reminded you of me."

"Yeah, she's cute, like you, has a mouth on her–writing checks that her body can't cash–but she's not focused on education."

"You're a good guy, Quinton Regis Chandler IV."

"Yeah? How good?"

"Let me show you," she began kissing him up against the garden wall.

"Umm. Have Mercy, girlie."

On that night, they synchronized their watches and met at midnight. The pitch-dark house creaked as they joined hands and crept to the side door. Like World War II reconnaissance, they snuck into the folds of darkness until they reached the gatehouse. Qwayz eased the door open and ushered Jaz safely inside.

Selena chuckled from her the second floor window.

"What is it?" Zack asked from bed.

"Qwayz and Jaz creeping to the gatehouse, thinking they're slick." Selena flicked cigarette ashes into a seashell astray.

"They think no one else in the entire world could feel the way they do," Zack countered.

"Young love. I'm just jealous."

240

"C'mon over here. I'll show you the skill of old love." Zack tossed back the covers on his side of the bed.

Selena dashed her cigarette and jumped in beside him like a twenty-five-year-old girl. "Don't hurt me now!" she teased.

Qwayz felt around for the candle.

"You can't light that!"

"It doesn't show on the outside. I came in earlier today and set all this up. There's champagne in the fridge, along with cold cuts, melon, chocolate covered strawberries and voila!" He swung back a blanket revealing a bed sprinkled with rose petals strewn all over it. "I promised you a bed."

"Oh, Qwayz!" Making love for the second time in a bed? Exquisite. She wondered if she could survive this much happiness. "I love the way you love me. I love loving you. It's heaven. No. Paradise. Oh, look!" Through the window the moon and stars smiled upon them. Twinkling in happiest— their Malibu star. "Can't nobody love me better."

"It followed us here, to bear witness to us," Qwayz whispered. "You're the best thing I never knew I needed."

Jaz still got a rush whenever she saw him or heard his voice and when he touched her... little micro-explosions set off all over her skin. Warm, tingly, in love, special and important sensations—all rolled into one.

"I'm addicted to the way I feel when I think of you," she told him.

"No habit I plan to break anytime soon. You're good for me. To me. To paraphrase Oscar Wilde, you don't love someone for their looks, clothes or fancy car; but because they sing a song only you can hear."

"Speaking of singing," Jaz began. "Your love is a Supernatural thing," ala Ben E. King.

"Interplanetary. Extraordinary love," Qwayz chimed in and they laughed.

After making love for their second time, they relaxed and reveled in the warm feel of one another. He rubbed her bare derriere as she snuggled beneath his satisfied smile. His St. Christopher's medal and her shining star resting against one another, cooling down like their bodies.

"I like the skylight that lets us see our star…and the beams are an authentic touch of France. All romantic," she said.

"Hungry?" he asked with his eyes closed.

"Not right now."

"What?" He felt her forehead for a fever.

"This is nice. I like falling to sleep with you."

"Jaz, I have a confession to make?"

"Hum?"

"You're my first one."

"What?" She raised up and scoffed at him. "Yeah, right."

"My first virgin. I started early and had sex often, but never with a virgin."

She smiled up at him. "I won't hold that against you."

"So, this is special for me, too. Magic. We are."

~*~

Chateau Jazz calmed down to a respectable foursome and the family floated around the house resting, eating, enjoying the peace and quiet the rural Parisian countryside offered. Near the terrace, one tree was surrounded by four others, each attached by a hammock like spokes to a wheel cog. The foursome had taken up residence there as a refugee from the heat to lounge in the cool of the leaves' canopy. At the base of the tree, Lisette supplied an endless amount of iced drinks, fresh fruit and cheeses in the chest-bar to hold their hunger at bay until dinner. Zack dozed and swatted an errant insect while

242

Selena hummed and swung in her latticed couch. Jaz rocked in her hammock while a thirsty towel drank in the last moisture from her freshly washed hair. The ladies listened to the restless Qwayz tinkle at the piano inside the house.

"Thank you, Aunt Selena. I cannot tell you how much this trip has meant... Will always mean to me."

"It's my pleasure, Jazzy."

Jaz got up and climbed into Selena's hammock allowing her aunt to embrace her as she had when Jaz was a young girl whose mother didn't know how to show her love.

"I can never repay you for all you've done. Sacrificed. It's incomprehensible."

Selena kissed Jaz's forehead and said, "When you love someone the way I love you, it is no sacrifice at all. I'd do it all over again."

"I think I know what you mean." She looked at her aunt.

"I bet you do," she answered. The reference not lost on her.

Jaz blushed. "We've always been so attuned to each other."

"Yes, we have."

"I think I love him."

"Psh! Think!" Selena teased. "I tell you what. Whether you do or not, that boy loves you."

Jaz grinned unabashedly.

"Even if he doesn't say it, you can tell by the way he treats you. He says it every time he looks at you. His heart has your name written across it."

"I don't know how not to think about him. It's so wonderfully strange."

"As it should be. Never heard of anyone dying from too much love."

"It's like I finally get it. Gladys Ann and Jehson, you and Uncle Zack, TC and whomever. I'm no longer on the outside looking in, wondering what the big deal is. Suddenly all the love songs are about us. Qwayz and I."

"You think the good times will come but you don't realize you're in them. Enjoy it all, Jaz-of-mine." They both chuckled at her use of Qwayz's sobriquet.

"I love you, Aunt Selena."

"I know, Jazzy."

They swayed and talked in hushed tones until they fell asleep in the comfort of one another's company, like they did when Aunt Selena babysat Jasmine Bianca.

The postman's bell rang, and Jaz went around the house. She waved to him, gathered the mail and went through the front door. Entering the room, she said to Qwayz, "You love this room because it's red." Rifling through the letters she sat beside him on the piano bench as he began to sing, "I Got You Babe."

Jaz joined in and Zack and Selena smiled from their hammocks. "They do have great voices."

"That's not the voices, it's the love pouring out and speaking," Selena postulated.

"I got a letter from Denny!" Jaz exclaimed as she opened it and then read and re-read it.

"What?" Qwayz asked.

"They're married."

"Who?"

"Denny and Yudi."

"What!" Qwayz stopped playing and swung his legs over the bench.

"Yudi is going to Vietnam and they wanted to get married before he went, so they did it at the courthouse."

"We leave L.A. and stuff goes crazy," Qwayz declared.

244

"Well, it's good news this time. No one died."

"Yet."

"Qwayz." Jaz sucked her teeth at the negative thought. "Seems more are going. Is anybody coming back?"

"Carter Hix came back but won't see anybody. TC said he's in bad shape."

"They bought a small house in Del Amo Hills, closer to school for her once he goes," she continued to read, self-editing. "Says he'll probably be placed in G to R because of his Hodges Funeral Home experience. 'Grave to Registration.' Sounds gruesome but at least he won't be fighting."

"No, just toe-tagging everyone who comes back in a body bag," Qwayz said.

"Married. A house? I guess the funeral business is lucrative. Going to start a family when he gets back."

"Ma Vy didn't say anything about it," Qwayz mused. "Maybe she wasn't invited. She likes Yudi well enough."

"Only guy Denny ever took a liking to. The family of one of Watts' premier funeral homes would be a good provider for her oldest daughter."

"Denny is in grad school. She won't need anything from the Hodges family." Qwayz glanced at his watch and asked to use the telephone to call L.A.

"There he goes," Jaz said. "Being the man of the house."

Once back in Paris, Jaz and Qwayz waited for the green light to run across the street.

"C'mon Qwayz," Jaz said, and he pulled himself away from the window and the adorable little dog whose tail wagged and barked excitedly at them both. They walked around gathering the last of souvenirs as the Parisian leg of their European trip wound down.

Ever since he'd seen the unusual, big playful dog in the park, he started to research the breed. "We don't have many Briards in the states do we? France gave Jefferson one back in the day."

"Which do you think Ma Vy will like?" Jaz held up a shawl for his inspection, as the vendor smiled. "I know something's up. Of all the bridges to take back to the Left Bank you always pick this one with that dog."

When they walked inside, the shop owner asked, "Monsieur Chandler you came to pick her up this time?" Jaz watched Qwayz's excitement and boyish grin just being in the cute puppy's presence.

"I always wanted a dog," Qwayz admitted. "An Irish Setter… but this one."

Qwayz, governed more by emotion than logic, left Jaz to pose the right questions: Would Selena allow a pet near her Louis XV furniture; could they take the dog to Italy and what type of paperwork was necessary to get it to America; and does his dorm at Stanford allow dogs? The crestfallen Qwayz understood. "Sure you don't want to be a lawyer? Culhane and Chandler?"

During their entire stay in Paris, the couple visited Club Selena only a handful of times. On one such occasion, Selena announced Qwayz's birthday and coaxed them both to sing "Destination Paradise." The delighted audience in turn sang "Happy Birthday" to Qwayz. Back at their Paris home, they enjoyed a lavish dinner of all Qwayz's favorites prepared by Lisette and Zasu, who replicated Keely's coconut cake with the cooked icing. He'd received phone calls all day from his mother, sisters, TC and Scoey, when Selena and Zack left the young couple looking at television on the front couch by the ancient tapestry.

246

"I almost forgot," Jaz said, reaching into her jacket pocket, presenting him with a small wrapped gift. On a bed of cotton, an ID bracelet from a French jeweler read, "Qwayz and Jaz" engraved on the face of it. On the back, it read "Until the end of time."

"Wow! Thank you, Jaz." He hugged her. "Thank you for loving me the way you do."

"You're welcome" was all Jaz could manage; she thought she should be thanking him.

"Tears?" Qwayz asked. "Not today." He held her tighter. "I will always love you Jaz-of-mine. You 'got me' like no girl has ever 'got' me."

Hoping they could make love one last time in the gatehouse, proved futile. Once back in Paris they'd settle for bathroom trysts.

"We were good for so long," Qwayz said as they embraced.

"You are always good," Jaz sassed. He opened the small stained-glass window behind her and the moonlight cut across his handsome, chiseled features onto his muscular, bare chest. He bent to kiss her and she always relished the feeling that when she looked up at Qwayz, he was already staring at her. He sat her on the counter and she shrugged from her baby-doll pajama top. He smiled at the sight of her chocolate drops and played with one before he suckled the other. She watched the St. Christopher medal dangle above her with every loving thrust, the usual visual being the moon, their star and St. Christopher blessing it all. She savored the unimaginable love they made, for he captivated, tantalized and ignited every feeling she ever had. Panting, sweating. Finishing with a crescendo and completely satisfied, he kissed her lips passionately as if they were just beginning before settling in beside her. Overhead through the skylight, they saw their star twinkling in agreement and farewell.

"I'm sure glad you came instead of Gladys Ann," Jaz said.

"Define 'came.'"

"You are so bad," Jaz twisted at his side playfully.

"You want a little 'bad' in your men. Keeps it interesting." He let his tongue reach and inhale a single chocolate drop, suckling her ripe nipple. "But, as much as *I loved* being here," he continued and Jaz couldn't believe his control. "I can't wait for our new lives to start in September. What an adventure we'll have. Our lives are magic, Jaz."

"I believe you. Our whole lives—an open road...Napa and Carmel on the weekends."

"Gotta study."

"That's what the weekdays are for." She smiled. "You know, a hotel with room service and a Do Not Disturb sign suits me just fine."

"I like the way you think," he said and began planting little kisses all over her. They made love again.

Four days later on August 6th, the president of the United States signed the Voting Rights Act of 1965 prohibiting discrimination in voting. "That's why we marched," Selena told Harry DeLacosta when he called her. Tears of resolute joy lived in Selena's eyes all day long as she took phone call after phone call. "Now we can have a jury of our peers... "

24

"I knew this day would come and I hate it," Selena said as she eyed the luggage piled up in the hallway awaiting Emile's expertise in packing and the ride to the airport, Italy-bound.

"Maybe we could run away," Jaz conspired playfully.

"My brother would just hunt us down." Selena hugged her niece. "We have one more night. Want to do something special?"

"I'd like to hang out. Just the four of us."

"Can't get any better than that."

They returned to the house after a farewell stroll around the neighborhood and flopped on the comfy couch near the bar as Zack flicked on the television.

Eyeing the chaotic images on the television, no one made sense of them, until Jaz noted, "Isn't that Lewis' 5 & 10?"

The store where she bought her penny candy and TC purchased the gold stars he used on the "homework" he corrected when she was four.

"Yeah," Qwayz piped up. "The shoe repair next door. Laundromat. Is this Watts?"

The foursome watched as looters smashed storefronts carrying everything from food and liquor to televisions. The sight of black people in full stride ran across the TV set, as they dodged fire and water hoses; police in riot gear and… a tank? A Riot. In their hometown?

Qwayz started calling everyone, from Ma Vy to Denny to TC. All circuits busy. The frustration on his face palatable. As he ran his hand through his hair, the phone rang and Selena yanked up the receiver. "Yes, Hep. We just got in. Yes, we see it…"

Qwayz paced as he listened to Selena's side of the conversation. He declined Jaz's offer of a cold Nehi orange soda, instead biting his lip waiting for Selena to hang up.

"OK," she finally said. "Your mother and sisters are all right. They're at that fortress of a studio with TC."

Jaz tried to reconcile her father's report with the images on the screen. It was Bloody Sunday all over again—only worse. *God gave Noah the rainbow sign. No more water, the fire next time*, she thought of Baldwin's words.

"We think Melie, Aubrey and AJ are alright in Baldwin Hills. Still trying to connect with them."

"What caused this?" Jaz asked.

"Traffic stop on Florence gone bad."

"Years of prejudice and discrimination and no jobs. Crowded housing bubbled over and exploded," Qwayz elaborated quietly. They watched the coverage until midnight when "static snow" claimed the television set, and started watching again the next morning when it came back on. The National Guard had been called in and things had calmed down after the bullets and tear gas.

"I'm going home, Jaz."

"We're going home," she corrected.

"No. I want you to go on to Italy. Your parents are expecting you."

"Are you kidding me? I'm going with you. No discussion."

"I have a home there. You don't."

"You are my home, Qwayz."

Hazel pierced honey. Tears stood in his eyes. He grabbed her and held onto her tightly. "I love you, girlie."

250

"He wasn't happy but he suspected as much," Jaz told Qwayz of her father's response.

"We should have told him together," Qwayz said absently, busy checking and making all the arrangements for the flight to L.A.

"We're a team, Quinton Regis."

Ma Vy's pleas that Qwayz stay and come home in a few weeks as planned fell on deaf ears. Qwayz finalized everything including TC picking them up from the airport when they arrived. Once Ma Vy and her girls were resituated at Aubrey and Melie's home, she tried telling Qwayz again that they and the house were fine, but Qwayz could hear the pounding of hammers onto stakes of the "For Sale" signs going up by white folks leaving the Compton neighborhood. "Everything's set, Ma."

"I just need to lay eyes on them," Qwayz confided to Jaz as the plane took off.

The Watts riots smoldered and claimed headline news for three more days with thirty-four dead, twenty-eight blacks, 1,032 injured, 3,952 arrested, and property damage estimated at $40 million. By most accounts, the spark that exploded into the slaughter stemmed from the arrest of a young Negro charged with reckless driving; a policeman drew a gun and an angry, short-fused crowd retaliated. This strong response, the result of being systematically demoralized and psychologically primed to lash out due to the overcrowded housing and unemployment situation in Watts, where 20 percent of the houses were dilapidated and one-sixth of Los Angeles' half million Negroes were forced to live in conditions that were four times as congested as the rest of the city. Discrimination prevented even those who could afford to live elsewhere from leaving. At the time of the riots, more than 30 percent of

251

skilled and unskilled Negroes were unemployed with no hope for work even in their own neighborhoods, where white store owners hired white employees, none of whom lived in Watts. For Jaz and Qwayz, the gutted, war-torn blocks smelled of charred wood, reeked of tear gas and resembled neither their childhood home nor the neighborhood they'd left in June.

On August 17th Jaz witnessed Qwayz's joy and relief when he grabbed his family in a group hug, Hanie hanging onto her big brother with no signs of stopping.

"Couldn't keep this boy in Europe, huh?" Ma Vy quipped through happy tears.

Jaz said, "You know how hardheaded he is."

"Just like his Daddy." She winked at Jaz.

"Where's Amber?" Qwayz noticed she was not propped up against the fireplace.

"At TC's. Safe and sound."

The tanks controlled by the National Guard remained in place and the stench of tear gas hung over Watts. A series of burnt out buildings with ravaged stores left folks without a source for groceries and other basic needs.

"Makes no damn sense. Burn down your own neighborhood. Where they gonna sleep, buy food? Need to go to Beverly Hills and burn it down," Qwayz fumed as he drove Reds through the battle-torn streets.

"There'd be more dead if they even tried going to Beverly Hills."

Qwayz, her brother and even Scoey could get bent out of shape by the darnedest things; Sam Cooke's senseless death and Sammy Davis marrying outside his race all over again. Traditionalists, were they?

Qwayz shored up the front door and one window as the Chandler house, like many others in the residential neighborhoods of Compton, was left almost untouched. Before

252

going to the studio to pick up Amber, Jaz had Qwayz take her to Alvaro Street to #3G, which hadn't fared as well.

Jaz and Qwayz ventured inside. The thick odor of tear gas, still apparent and shattered glass crunched beneath her feet. Jaz picked up a piece of familiar linoleum from the kitchen and made it back to her old room, freshly painted after they left but the holes, where she had thumbtacked the picture of she and Selena at the Satin Doll and one of Dorothy Dandridge's *Ebony* magazine cover, were still evident. Otherwise, she hardly recognized her childhood home… gone. She could never go home again.

~*~

Jaz climbed the steps of The Towers at Berkeley, her home for the next year. Greeted by a gaggle of girls introducing themselves as her suitemates, self-impressed that they had been chosen as the residents of this dorm for its inaugural year. Some girls' parents were still there and only then did Jaz realize she was alone. She left the common area and unlocked her bedroom door, smiling at the keychain Gladys Ann had given her, to find it superbly decorated. A curtain hung from the large window with a matching bedspread of flowers like those she'd left only a week ago at Chateau Jazz. A typewriter sat on a desk with her books for the first semester and toiletries and towels stood at attention when she opened her small bathroom door. A relieved and touched Jaz burst into tears as she read the note.

Hey Punkin',

Your mother and I couldn't be there in the flesh but we hope you like your new room. We love and are so proud of you. You always wanted Berkeley and there you are. The first of many of your dreams to come true. Call us anytime.

Love always, Dad and Mom.

253

A knock on the door summoned her, "Culhane? Phone."

Jaz took the receiver and immediately calmed as she heard Qwayz on the other end. "Hey girlie."

If she could have jumped through the phone into his arms, she would have.

She hung up and from the looks of the other girls in the living room, she'd talked too long on the communal phone. She returned to her bedroom and readied for the first day of class.

Freshman Orientation failed to leave Jaz with a warm and fuzzy feeling. Held in a large auditorium, the dean both welcomed and proclaimed, after looking to the right and left that one of them would not be there at the end of the semester. Later, seventeen-year-old Jaz Culhane opened the door to the Physical Science class and gazed at a lecture hall spread out below her full of over 200 chattering students. Pushed into motion from incoming classmates, she descended into the bowels of education, so unlike Roosevelt High's classrooms that only held thirty. She walked down the steps, taking a seat near the aisle, removed her hat and buckskin jacket as the professor walked in from stage left and a grad student passed out a thick syllabus. Jaz realized it wasn't just the sheer magnitude of the class or the self-absorbed coldness of the students… but they were white. All white? Mostly white? Not like Roosevelt; more whites than she'd ever seen in her life. *Gladys Ann or Ian aren't going through this at Howard or Morehouse,* she thought. She looked around. Few looked like her.

Tray in hand, she took a seat in the cafeteria by the window and began reviewing her assignments before going to her dorm to await Qwayz's call.

"Hey girlie, how goes your first day?" he asked.

"Interesting," Jaz managed, still in shock.

254

"Not like you thought, huh?"

"Not at all."

"Start with the fact that you have to share a phone and we're late," he teased.

"I know, but I couldn't get them off."

"I was just kidding Jaz-of-mine. I'm in college and know the deal." He didn't like the way she sounded. "You're not in Kansas anymore, huh?"

"No lie," she responded to the "Wizard of Oz" reference.

"It gets better. I promise."

"If you say so."

"How was the food?"

"OK."

"Tell you what. I'll come up this weekend and we'll do San Francisco. Pier 29, Ghirardelli Square, whatever you want. I need some new Converse."

"You always need new Converse," Jaz chuckled, relieved to hear he was coming up. *If we could just breath the same air, I'd be alright,* she longed to say but that verged on whining. Jaz hated that.

"Then, since I have to take my car for servicing next month, we'll drive down to L.A. to Skeekie's. Maybe Dickie'll be there?"

"I know AJ misses you."

"Yeah, we'll take him to the movies or P.O.P."

She hung up, amazed at how much better she felt. More grounded and more herself. The next few days dragged on like a cotton bag around an old slave's neck. She sat in her last class and glanced out the window. There, on the steps near Sather Tower, she saw him. A fine brother in a brown leather bomber jacket and a red Stanford cap. She couldn't calm her heart, the sight of him setting off the usual rush. She ran down the steps and ran into his open arms. "Oh, Qwayz!" She hugged him to ensure he wasn't an apparition. She kissed him hard and long, like in Paris, not caring who was around.

"Hi Jaz," a pretty student with sandy-colored hair coiffured in a flip and thin body said.

"Hey," Jaz recognized her as one of her suitemates but didn't know her name.

"My father keeps asking if I'd made your acquaintance yet. So now I can tell him yes. I'm Sloane Yeager. From Atlanta. Our fathers know one another."

Sloane kept looking at Qwayz, so he introduced himself, "Hi. Qwayz Chandler. Jaz's man."

Jaz chuckled.

"Pleased to meet you," Sloane greeted. "Any more like you? Brothers? Friends?"

"Really, Sloane?"

"No offense, Jaz."

"None taken. We're getting ready to head out. I'll catch you back at the dorm."

"Sure. Nice meeting you both."

"My man?" Jaz teased him.

"That's what I am. Your man. I hope to prove that during this visit."

"Oh god. I hope so too."

The couple devoured San Francisco as their time together seemed to evaporate with the setting sun. They ate first. Then Qwayz bought his Converse and socks before the intoxicating aroma of chocolate lured them to Ghirardelli Square. They nuzzled and nibbled on nuts and chews, sauntering around the corner and window-shopping on Antique Row, each discovering the others love of well-built, stylish, vintage furniture. They spent time dreamily selecting their furniture for their imaginary apartment: a hall tree from *Memories*, a

256

gleaming and heavy, big brass bed from *Heirlooms*. Not wanting to waste time in a movie where they wouldn't be able to talk to one another, they ate again before checking into Reasons, where they made love and slept. Jaz woke first, propped herself up on her elbow and eyed the love of her life as he slept. He was everything to her. Just his smile, a feel of his hand in hers, the touch of his palm at her back as they crossed the street. Without even knowing it, he always came to her rescue. His eyes fluttered awake.

"Hey, you," he said with a stretch that included her.

"Our first time really sleeping together," Jaz noted. "We can just lay here as long as we like. No sneaking, hiding or scheming. This is so rich."

"I love waking up to my best friend," Qwayz said, kissing her nose as he ordered room service for breakfast. For a change of venue, they ate dinner in the dining room, made love and, wrapped in one another's embrace, slept until check-out on Sunday when Qwayz dropped her off at her dorm. Like a mail sack hanging on a train platform waiting for pickup; she also picked up the melancholia she'd left at school when Qwayz'd arrived. "C'mon Friday" became her new mantra.

"Your father was looking for you," Sloane said. "When he couldn't find you he asked for me."

"What'd you tell him?"

"Nothing to tell. Yes, I met her. No, I haven't seen her recently I've been busy."

Jaz smiled. *You know you might work out alright after all, Sloane Yeager.*

Sloane in turn introduced her to Farrell Simmons, the other black suitemate, and Jaz began meeting them for meals. But Jaz lived for the weekends, muddling through the week

257

anticipating the nightly calls she knew would be less frequent once basketball season started.

"I'm going to invent a portable phone you carry with you everywhere and then we can talk anytime," he'd told her one night.

"I raised my hand and gave the wrong answer," a mortified Jaz confessed.

"Might be the first time. Won't be the last," Qwayz soothed.

"I felt so stupid. They looked at me like I don't belong here. A mistake was made."

"Listen up, girlie. You are where you are supposed to be. You earned your place; you got the SAT scores, the grades, the ability and desire. You got a scholarship, even if your dad gave it back. So, forget them. They don't mean diddley to you. What's that Papa Colt used to say, 'Consider the source?'"

"In order to insult me, I must first value your opinion," Jaz quoted.

"Yeah. The only relationship you have to worry about in a class of hundreds is the one between you and your professor. You don't understand? It's his job to explain it to you until you do. His responsibility. You hear me?"

"Yes sir," Jaz replied.

"Besides, every successful black person—you, your dad, your grandfather, your aunt—the lives they live… is a big middle-finger to every white man who thinks they are superior in any way. My life and yours, and our children's are gonna be the biggest 'F--k you white man' there is."

Jaz laughed. "You are crazy!"

"Crazy about you." *I will personally F-up any man, woman or child who dares to hurt you in any way,* went unsaid, but was fully understood. The fact that anyone could make Jaz feel "less-than" about herself inflamed him.

258

"I did make a 96 on a pop quiz."

Qwayz laughed. "See. You're just pulling my leg."

"Wish I could."

"Feel better?"

"Much. You're my 'Dr. Feelgood' and cover all my prepositions. You're good *to* me. *For* me, *by* me and *with* me."

"My name is yours alone to call, Jaz-of-mine. Whenever you need me."

"I love you."

"I know."

~*~

"You're Jaz Culhane," the girl accused as Jaz walked across campus to her next class.

"That's right," Jaz confirmed squelching her usual Watts-reply of "What's it to you?"

"Recognize you from your Raw Cilk album cover," she said.

"You're the one who bought a copy," Jaz teased.

"Oh, please. Raw Cilk is a phenomenal hit for a group that never toured."

Jaz stopped and looked at the girl who knew too much about her.

"I'm CC," the girl said. "Chaim Cooper. A student here but I live at home. Before you ask—my father is Black, career military retired from the Presidio, and my mother an East Indian housewife, which explains my very dark skin and long shiny, wiry-black hair. They say we look alike. We don't. White people think we all look alike. Pleased to meet you." Her words tumbled to an end.

"You, too." Jaz resumed walking toward her class.

"We certainly don't act alike. You know my whole life story and I know nearly nothing about you. Except your boyfriend is Qwayz Chandler who plays basketball for Stanford."

"Then you know everything that's important then."

"I hear you, sister. I tend to have a strong personality because I am the fourth daughter born next to the coveted child, a son, so I had to fight for recognition in my family."

"How's that working for you?"

"Just fine but exhausting. You can rest easy about Q Chandler, too. He's not my type."

"Good to know."

"Has too much hue for me. As you can see, I have enough for everybody."

This means what? Jaz almost asked but CC continued, "I date 'clear' boys to whom I'm an exotic conundrum with my 'polished mahogany skin.' I go where I am celebrated not tolerated. Besides, you'll find the Negro guys here don't give us a chance anyway; they date white girls and I will not be denied—"

"Or ignored," Jaz added as she pulled open the door to the building.

"Precisely. I can see you get me. We're going to be great friends," CC predicted. "Later."

You are too spaz-mo for me, Jaz thought.

It appeared that CC had met all the "sisters" including Sloane who didn't react as harshly to CC's dating practices and agreed that the high-energy girl was right. "You have a man, Jaz and don't feel the pain. Our time is spent with each other studying and playing cards. Not dating."

"We're here to get an education not a husband," Jaz said.

"Really? If we get a BA one week and a *Mrs.* the next... our parents would be ecstatic."

"Regardless, you should go to the Black Student Union meeting with us," Farrell said.

260

"We go there to try to pick up black guys."

"I'm meeting Qwayz this afternoon."

"Oh right, it is Friday. See you Monday in class."

"You got it," Jaz agreed.

Having found their weekend niche, Jaz and Qwayz never tired of and rarely varied their routine. Qwayz applauded its existence since he'd navigated his freshman year alone and loved that Jaz was in the vicinity, not in Malibu, for his sophomore year and beyond. Jaz savored that she had Qwayz to rejuvenate her for two days so she could endure the coming five; Eating, Ghirardelli Square and Antique Row their usual haunts. As a change of pace, they'd discovered an Italian Restaurant, Giuseppe's, to fill the void of the Italian trip they never had and Aloutte's, a French bistro, to remind them of their Parisian summer. Now they didn't mind going to a movie and once Jaz showed him a place off road she wanted to explore; he was game.

"There it is!" Jaz exclaimed.

"Damn! That's quite a turn." Qwayz made a U turn and went two miles up the road to approach it again without ending up in the Pacific Ocean. Reds skidded, Qwayz downshifted and slid.

"Well, don't kill us."

They rode on for about a mile and the highway disappeared as a narrow winding road rose to meet them. On the right, the expanse of an untouched Pacific Ocean became their escort.

"This is beautiful. So secluded."

"Yeah, that treacherous turn is the reason," Qwayz cruised in second gear before taking it down to first. "Oh look!"

Qwayz turned up onto an unexplored road that led to a tongue of granite protruding out over the ocean. He came to an abrupt stop only a few feet before the peninsula ran out. Jaz jumped out and stood over the blue abyss. "I bet this has a sensational sunset," Qwayz said joining her.

"Let's stay and see."

They gathered the blankets from the trunk along with a picnic lunch as they'd done in Paris and sat on top of that granite rock, ate, made love and waited for the sun to set and the moon to rise. They lay in one another's arms, and their star found them as it always did. "The stars are in their heavens and all's right with the world Jaz-of-mine."

"It's like we are in this world all alone. Just the two of us."

"You're all I need," Qwayz began singing. Beside the frigidity of the crisp nocturnal air and the bruises left on her vertebrae from the impenetrable granite, they vowed to visit often. "Our slice of heaven."

"Our Paradise. Paradise Rock."

"No one will ever find us here."

"That's the point." She kissed his luscious lips.

25

"You talked me into this," Jaz told Qwayz at the gate when they announced final boarding.

"It'll be good for you both. I think she's reaching out to you. Miss Thang probably needs her baby sister from home to ground her."

"I don't think anything good can come from this. Except the bruises on my back will heal from our latest Paradise Rock adventure." Jaz leaned into Qwayz and his nature rose.

"Sorry 'bout that."

"Don't ever apologize. At least someone will miss me." Jaz hoisted her shoulder bag into place. "Just know I'd rather be in L.A. with you, Ma Vy, Denny—"

"Only if we finish the game early. I'll call you."

"You better." She kissed him. "Will that keep you for Thanksgiving weekend?"

"It'll have to." He leaned in again for one more quick kiss.

"Wish you were coming with me."

"I'll 'come with you' when you get back." He kissed her again. "Love you."

"So, you say." She turned and wriggled her index finger at him and when he returned the gesture, she disappeared down the runway.

Jaz slept through the flight, and after arriving at LaGuardia, she got her suitcase from baggage claim and waded into the sea of humanity. *Suppose her sister isn't here to meet her?* Jaz thought and decided she would catch the next thing smoking back to LA. She didn't have anything but Mel's number. No address.

"Hey sis!" A girl with a halo of fluffy black hair styled into an airy Afro grabbed her in a bear hug. Jaz assumed it was Mel, but was not sure until released from her embrace. Jaz looked into her sister's big, bright eyes rimmed to perfection with mascara, eyeliner and shadow. A gold ball pierced her nose.

"Wow! You look great!"

"Thanks. A little different from the last time, huh? Follow me."

Jaz shadowed her sister, following her into a cab for a ride that took as long as her flight. She couldn't focus on the sights Mel pointed out as the congestion of human beings and buildings and trash and filth and darkness, even though it was daytime, assaulted the California girl at every turn. She wanted space, trees, a bird, not a pigeon, flying high and free. Deposited in front of a brownstone apartment building's stoop, they walked to the third floor where the door opened onto more confined space. To the right, Mel's bedroom, a nice brick wall her headboard. To the left, the living room with a big window where neighbors could look in if they so desired. Straight ahead, a tiny galley kitchen. "Home!" Mel exclaimed. "You can sleep with me or on the couch."

"Couch!" Jaz exclaimed. "As I recall you sleep in a ball."

"Still do. Make yourself at home. Bathroom is through my bedroom."

Jaz put her suitcase next to her "bed" and when Mel disappeared, she went into the kitchen for a glass of water and saw… no turkey. Not in the refrigerator. Not thawing. *Happy Thanksgiving,* Jaz thought.

The phone rang and Mel came into the room. "Guess who?" Mel dangled the receiver.

"Thanks."

"So how goes it, girlie?"

264

"There's no turkey."

"Maybe you all are going out to a friend's house."

"Your optimism is enraging at times."

They talked for a full five minutes before Mel held out Jaz's jacket with a "Let's go."

Jaz followed her sister into three different clubs that night: starting with Ramsey Lewis at The Cellar Door, Jimmy McGriff at the Blue Note ending with Nina Simone at the Village Gate. Brit, Mel's stage name, a celebrity everywhere they went, and Mel introduced her visiting sister to a bevy of "friends" whose names and faces were as varied as their races and genders. Entering a basement establishment for espresso and conversation, Jaz noticed a swarthy little nervous-type guy lurking around the bathroom and was astonished when she saw her sister talking to him involving an exchange of some kind. Jaz asked her about the guy Mel didn't bother to introduce and if she was dating white boys now.

"No that's not my bag," she said, light bouncing off her gold ball as she took a long drag from a short cigarette.

"When did you start smoking? Isn't that bad for your voice?"

"When I started drinking," Mel laughed and her groupies laughed with her. "Don't be a drag, Jaz."

Taken aback, Jaz fought the urge to cuss her out, go get her bags and catch the next flight out. If Mel thought Jaz was going to play the urban sophisticate to Jaz's unenlightened baby sister, Miss Thang had another 'thang' coming. They talked about Jaz as if she wasn't there:

"Are you taking her to see 'Blues for Mr. Charlie' and 'Slow Dance on the Killing Ground'?"

"No, I'm taking her to see 'Day of Absence' and 'Happy Ending.' She read about Small's Paradise in the

Autobiography of Malcom X and wants to go there," Mel said with a condescending chuckle Jaz didn't appreciate. But Jaz perked up when Mel said she was taking her to the new Black Arts Theatre that LeRoi Jones had established in his brownstone where he refused to admit "whitey."

They returned home, missing dawn by a few hours, and slept until noon. Qwayz had called and left a number with Mel's answering service but the line was busy when Jaz tried to return the call. "Rough when your boyfriend's a basketball star scrimmin' over the holidays, huh? Them's the breaks."

"I don't smell any turkey," Jaz said, ignoring her sarcasm. "Are we eating at a friend's house?"

Mel convulsed with laughter. "I don't cook and neither do my friends. How'd you get so square so fast? In New York, only poor people cook for themselves. We're going to the Coach House." She poured and took a sip of Chianti. "Tomorrow I'll take you to Balducci's to get you vittles that'll tide you over for your little visit."

They'd managed a decent dinner and conversation without her fan/friends in tow. Jaz asked if she had seen Dad recently. "More than I'd like. He's through here frequently handling his business for Culhane Enterprises with his 'white-boy' front."

"You met him?"

"Kylerton Tipton? I'm convinced that's what took Dad so long to settle that property in San Francisco. You know folks still don't want to deal with a black man with money. You need your white boy flunky for that."

"Just so he's not scamming Dad."

"Dad knows what he's doing and how to do it. Had dinner with them a couple of times." Mel shrugged her shoulders. "Old white guy. White hair. White skin with those little brown spots. Probably as rich as Cootie Brown, too."

266

It took Jaz seventeen years to have the worse Thanksgiving ever but she was not disappointed with Mr. LeRoi Jones' play where the black character kills the white one out of rage and anger and frustration; both cathartic and exhilarating. But Mel took her to another party and by the time Jaz threaded her way through the crowd, she knew the evening would be going downhill. Wall-to-wall people but no one was dancing. In fact, there was no music you could dance to. When looking for a bathroom, she inadvertently opened the door on a couple screwing, not making love; they barely noticed her and when they did, they smiled; Reminiscent of the kooky party that Holly Golightly gave in "Breakfast at Tiffany's." No food either. Spotting Mel from across the room she finally reached her and asked for the key. "I'm going home."

"Don't be such a spoil sport. Give me a few hours and I'll be ready, too. OK, baby," Mel touched Jaz's cheek and peeled off.

Who the hell is this heffa? Jaz thought. *Don't know or like her. Qwayz was wrong about this trip.*

Jaz found more amorous couples in the bedroom beneath the coats. They didn't mind her or she them, so she looked at television. When the "The Twilight Zone" went off Jaz went in search of the key; Mel could come or not. As she navigated the room it seemed like more people had come, and Jaz headed to the only open space in the room. Inhaling deeply, she looked down and saw the glass coffee table, covered with smudged white lines of powder, next to a neatly stacked bowl of joints.

"Aw shit!" she said aloud, cursing at how she could be so stupid. She hoped the burnt smell of pot was coming from outside. Jaz searched for Mel with a vengeance, standing on tables and window sills, headlines swirling in her mind: "Daughters of first Black Ambassador of Major European

267

Country Found at Coke and Pot Party, How Can He Rule a Country If He Can't Control his Children? Fired and Disgraced Because Daughters Found with Illegal Contraband at New York Party."

"What the hell are you doing?" Jaz said, yanking Mel's elbows, her cheeks sunken from a deep toke on a short reed.

"C'mon Jaz," Mel's speech slurred. "Lighten up." She laughed at her own pun.

"Gimme the keys." Jaz wanted to hit her hard.

"Oh, baby I don't know where my purse or my coat…"

"Are you coming with me?" Unconsciously, Jaz gritted her teeth like Qwayz did when he was livid. "What about Daddy?"

"Oh, is he here?" Mel laughed, salvia flying from her mouth. "Hi Daddy."

Too angry to feel the hawk rip though her thin coat, Jaz roused the resident manager, apologizing for waking him to let her in. She threw clothes into a suitcase and checked the flights. As if the gods conspired against her, there was not one seat on any flight to San Francisco or L.A. Maybe she would go to Colt, Texas.

A few hours later, Mel slithered in and a rested Jaz sat straight up. Seeing the packed bag Mel said, "Cutting the trip short?"

"You don't need me. Apparently, I'm in the way." Jaz's ice-cold tone sent shivers up Mel's spine.

"That's right, when the going gets tough, Jaz splits." Mel hid her fear by attacking.

"I am not my sister's keeper. In fact, I don't even know you."

"Well that's the first real truth spoken." Ebony blazed on honey until the shrill of the phone separated them. "Guess who?" Mel dropped the receiver onto the couch and went to the bedroom.

"Thought I'd try early today since I've been missing you. You all having fun?"

"It's been... interesting," Jaz said, as Mel reappeared and stood in the kitchen watching Jaz over the counter.

"You two have a tiff?"

"We never could share the same space for long. How'd you do? Beat the pants off of them?" Jaz listened to Qwayz relay the results of their victory, her eyes never leaving Mel's. After his litany, Jaz said, "I'm thinking of coming home later today."

"That bad? San Fran or L.A.?"

"Don't know yet. I'll either be in the dorm or at TC's."

"OK. Let me know. Remember you only have one sister. Love you."

"Love you, too." Jaz hung up.

"Thanks for not dropping a dime on me. You going to tell Dad or TC?"

"Dunno. Not sure I'd be doing you any favors. I cannot believe that you Brittany Melba Culhane use drugs. That you'd let me see it. That you don't care more about yourself as a person."

"Don't forget that Dad would be disgraced... his star daughter, the pothead."

"And coke," Jaz added.

"I don't do that."

"There was a time you didn't do pot either. Slippery slope. If it's attention from Dad you want...I can think of better ways."

"You ought to know. His favorite. The smart one. The pretty one. You didn't give a damn about anyone and they loved you for it." Mel slid into her chair near the sofa.

"Oh, please. Self-pity? That's amateurish."

"Didn't want dance? Didn't do dance. Didn't want Einstein for the gifted and talented? Didn't do it. Didn't want any part of the clubs, cotillions or tea parties? Didn't do it. Got to jump double-Dutch, skate, ride bikes—"

"I invited you."

"Got two iconic stars to give up Paris for Watts because you wanted to graduate with your class," she huffed wryly. "I used to envy you and Gladys Ann. I never had a close girlfriend like that."

"That's my problem… how?" Jaz watched her sister cut her eyes. "Gotta be a friend to have a friend. You had Lorette. A mother. I had Dad and TC. That's the way we divvied up."

"Did I have Mom? I did everything she wanted and all I heard was her agonizing over you. Jaz won't do this. Jaz won't do that."

"Ancient history. Let's talk about current events. Drugs. Why? You've been a child star even before you won that amateur hour and money. You did plays all over California and some in New York, did a movie and met the frickin' Queen of England. Wanted Julliard. Now you have it. Drugs don't make sense."

"It's lonely at the top. I know I don't have a *true* friend in that bunch. If my stardom and money faded tomorrow, so would they. I was thrown into this space and place and told to cope. I had Mom for a while until she went off to Italy."

"Well, I *never* had her, so consider yourself lucky." Jaz reached for a Hershey's Kiss in the coffee table dish and mused, "All I ever wanted was for her to just once, come down the hall, knock on my door and ask me, 'How you doing Jaz?

270

How was your day?' Just once, a little interest. Know what I got?… Directions. Orders. Know who I had? Know who came down the hall—my dad, my brother and my Aunt Selena. I jumped through hoops for that woman called 'Mother' but I was always too much for her…hair, mouth, hue—yet I was never enough. Couldn't hold her attention for long. So, I got off that merry-go-round early and went with those who didn't criticize me for having a mind of my own. Realizing I wasn't born just to be an extension of Lorette; to fulfill her vision of who she was supposed to be." Jaz unwrapped and chucked the candy into her mouth. "I cut her importance to me off and went with the sure love from Dad, TC and my aunt."

A flabbergasted Mel said, "I had no idea."

"Yeah. Well, you found your niche and own little world which was acceptable to Lorette. Good for you."

Mel had erroneously thought Jaz had it all. She wiped away a tear and said, "And maybe that's it. You learned self-sufficiency at an early age and I'm just learning it. Intellectually, I know if I'd been born into any other family I'd be cute. But I'm a Culhane and you and TC raised that bar. But emotionally, it hurt. I first realized it when I overheard Slick Savoy that Texas summer saying, 'Go after the ugly sister because she's grateful.' He talked about how fine you'd be in a couple of years."

"That's the year Joaquin Redbird broke my heart."

"I know," Mel said but thought, at the time, *I was glad.* "And boy, look at you now."

"You begrudge me a guy that makes me happy?" Jaz blush-smiled at the mere thought of Qwayz. "You got to think highly of yourself first. Surround yourself with folks worth your time, energy and love. Otherwise…why bother? You may be alone sometimes but that's why you have to like yourself."

271

"Easier said than done."

"It's habit like anything else. Rather be alone than with some of the doggish guys out here."

Mel disappeared and returned with weed and an assortment of pills and threw them in the trash.

"Noble gesture. You are in drama classes. Will it last?"

"You are a hardheaded, hard-hearted woman, Jasmine Bianca Culhane."

"But I like me. And I am not drowning to save you or anybody else. Not going to be less-than so you can shine." Mel looked at her thoughtfully. "Know who taught me that? Papa Colt, Dad, TC and Quinton Regis Chandler."

"I see a trend," Mel said drolly.

"You attract what you reflect." Jaz gave her sister an unyielding profile.

"I suppose I was a little envious of you," Mel said.

"Don't know why. Nothing I did."

"I guess I realize that now. Finally. Hell, like I said in another family I'd be the cute one."

Jaz shook her head and had to smile.

"I guess it is time for me to grow up. 'Buck up' as you always say."

"You are the oldest."

"Could you meet me halfway here? I mean we don't ever have to live together again. We're on the verge of for-real adulthood and I'd like for us to be friends. To be close as sisters."

"We have to accept ourselves as is—for who we are. No game playing or posturing."

"Agreed. You did stick up for me when Johnny Green called me gorilla nose."

"And now you have a gold ball in it."

They both chuckled. "Will you stay as planned?"
272

"If you take me to Small's Paradise."

"God, you are like a dog with a bone."

26

"Let's take it again from the top," Selena directed from the mike while rehearsing with her band.

Selena missed Jaz and Qwayz more than she imagined and immersed herself in her work, changing up on the repertoire and arrangements to spice up what had become a hum-drum life. No good at self-pity, she knew how lucky she was. As Selena continued to rehearse, from the stage she watched a young lady enter the club and pause to talk with Zack at his usual table by the door. It had started a week ago. This woman's visits. Selena waited for Zack to mention it but he never did. *Is this how it would end?* Selena wondered. After all these years some little young strumpet comes in and snags her man? Just like that? This happened to other people. Other couples. She expected them to share and lament about it before deciding on lamb chops for dinner, but he would never bring this woman up.

Selena didn't know how to handle this bad fiction. Someone you were so certain of... like the sun was going to rise the next day...throws you for a loop. *Why would he?* She wondered. Sure, there was more of her to love hidden under her gorgeous signature caftans, but that was nothing new. He, too, had gained a few pounds. Sure, they made less love but spent more time together—wasn't that the sign of a maturing, enduring love plus the blessing that they were so busy. They still slept side by side intertwined every night. When could he possibly have time for an affair? They were constantly together day in and out... except for her two hours on stage. She supposed a young girl like that had all kinds of tricks up her sleeve and in places she could surely expertly control.

Selena held up her hand and stopped the band mid-lyric. "Excuse me!" she interrupted the couples' discussion. "Am I interrupting your conversation?" she snapped.

Zack stood and led the woman out into the vestibule, Selena watchful that he did not take her upstairs to their club apartment or out the front door.

"Let's take it from the top again," Selena directed and tried to concentrate on the new arrangement of her classic signature song from TC, "Send in the Clowns." Her nephew had reworked the song, slowed it to a mere crawl to showcase all of her octaves. "…losing my timing this late in my career…" Had she taken Zack for granted? Why now? She knew her man as well as he knew herself…they were comfortable but maybe he wanted excitement that she couldn't give him. What he does *with* you, he'll do *to* you, she recalled the old saying. She had done this to his wife, Lucille, but they had been separated for years. At Zack's direction, he and Selena ignored and embarrassed Lucille, carrying on without one thought of her. Was this payback for Selena? Selena refused to show-out or act a fool. She had more going for her than Lucille, then and now. Selena would not stoop, threaten or grovel for a man. Any man—least of all the man who should know better. "Send in the clowns… they're already here," she sang.

Over the last few days Selena hadn't decided how to handle it. Should she just confront them and divide everything 50/50? Should she fight for Zack or let him go? They'd had a good run, maybe it had run its course. The girl was so young… but old age and treachery wins out over youthful stupidity any day. Times like this she really missed her buddy, Miles Syphax. He knew the ropes. He'd tell her. Or, if she could only talk it over with her sister, Star.

Zack came back in and assumed his seat at his table without a word, a smile or even looking at her.

~*~

Selena reviewed the week's menus with Lisette when the shrill ring of the doorbell interrupted. Already annoyed that someone had successfully breeched the metal gate, crossed the courtyard, entered their house and climbed the steps to ring the doorbell, she halted Zasu and said, "I'll get it," wanting to confront the interloper herself. "Zack are you expecting somebody?" she asked as she swung open the door.

"Huh!" was the only sound that escaped her lips on a breath of air. *There she is!* Selena stood tall blocking the entrance, fixed her eyes and folded her arms over her ample chest, staring into the woman's face. "You have some nerve coming to my front door. Uninvited."

The girl offered a nervous smile, fidgeted uncomfortably and inhaled to steady herself.

God, Selena thought. *She is so much younger up close.*

"I invited her, Selena," Zack said from behind.

"Of course, you did." Selena didn't remove her eyes from the girl. She had intended to flounce off into the living room and take a seat while young-girl and Zack proclaimed their newfound love and intention to run off together. But Selena stood face-to-face with her, her mind ablaze but not betraying the inner turmoil on her stoic features. Maybe she would fight for Zack after all. Maybe the girl was pregnant with his baby. They could afford to take care of a baby if he wanted to do that.

Suddenly, at the sight of Zack, the girl relaxed, blew out her breath and smiled.

Selena, startled by the brazen gesture, thought, *Oh, this bitch—*

The girl stuck out her hand, held up her crooked, little finger and said, "Pinky swear. Brown-skinned beauties we are—"

Selena arched her back, reduced her eyes to slits and said, "Is this supposed to be some kind of sick-ass joke? Not funny little girl."

Quiet filled the doorway before she gulped air and finally said, "No ma'am."

Selena's heart beat wildly in her chest. Her breath stuttered as her palms began sweating and she snatched her head high to clear her thinking. Her eyes betrayed her, for everywhere they landed on the young girl's face a memory formed… the nose, the cheekbones, the eyes, shape of the lips. All remotely familiar.

"You look like her," the girl beamed.

"I look like my mama, my daddy, my brother—"

"And Star."

The sound of her name filled Selena's ears. All these years wanting, waiting to hear it from someone, anyone who can shed light on her lost sister…and this girl's lips uttered it simply… without prompting. Her heart filled then spilled beyond its bounds, as she wrung her hands, not wanting to touch the girl. Not wanting to admit that this girl may know of Star. Selena's lips remained tightly closed but her heart yelled, "You knew Star?"

"My mother. Star. I am your niece."

With that simple admission Selena's resolve crumbled, and her eyes exploded tears as her restrained hands flung open to hold the piece of Star they had left.

"Why don't you all come in," Zack suggested. "Selena, this is Keely."

"That's our mother's name," Selena said as they entered the formal parlor.

"I know. My grandmother. I was named for her."

"Is this all legit?" she looked at Zack.

"Yes, I checked it out," he answered.

Selena looked at her new, full-grown niece and said, "I can see it all right there on her face. And brown-skinned beauties… "

Selena couldn't finish it. Instead, she grabbed the girl and held on to her for fear she would disappear, before pushing her back. "Where is she? Star? Is she here? In Paris?"

"No, ma'am."

"Is she?" Selena couldn't form the words.

"May we sit down?" Keely asked, as Selena's eyes devoured her.

"Yes, of course. Your daddy ain't no white man, is he?"

"No, ma'am. Just light-skinned."

"She reminds me of Mel," she told Zack. "That café au lait complexion," Selena interjected nervously, not sure she was ready for the news of her long-lost sister. "Where is she? Afraid I'd be mad?"

"I'm afraid she'd be mad at me. I hesitated contacting you. She made me promise I would not. But I think she needs you. She needs to reconnect."

"Praise Jesus!" Selena jumped up with hands extended over her head. "Call her. Tell her to come on, now. I'll pay for her plane ticket. Oh, I have to call Hep. Oh my God!!"

Zack went to Selena, calmed her and sat her back down on the couch while asking Lisette to bring tea. "Selena give the girl time to explain."

Selena took in a deep breath and then said, "Call Hep. Hep has to know now."

278

"Good Lord, woman you're going to have a heart attack before you learn anything."

"Is it bad?" Selena wrung her hands and then took three deep breaths as she followed Zack's advice.

Selena wiped her tear-drenched face and looked at the pretty, cultured young lady and said brusquely, "Proceed."

Keely admitted being in Paris studying art at the Sorbonne for a year before she decided to approach her with the news of Star. Once, after a car accident, her mother, deciding that if she died her daughter should know her people, confessed that at 18 she defied her father and left home to pursue a singing career in the middle of The Depression. But once she recuperated, Star blamed the episode on being sedated and drugged, saying she had made it all up.

"Where is she now?" was all Selena wanted to know

27

"Who is that?" Jaz asked of a tall, jet-black black man whose form, hidden beneath a colorful dashiki, called the Black Student Union (BSU) meeting to order.

"Solomon Noble. Ain't he fine? The reason there are so many ladies in the audience," CC quipped.

"Not really your type," Jaz countered never removing her eyes from him.

"I'll gladly make an exception. How about you?"

Jaz hadn't remembered a time when she was so visibly shaken by the sheer vision of a man. Not only his midnight-dark chocolate complexion, reminiscent of Selena and Gladys Ann, but when he spoke, the timber of his voice grabbed her body, shook it and wouldn't let go.

"Jaz, it's five o'clock," Sloane whispered.

"Uh huh," an engrossed Jaz stared but hadn't heard a word he'd said.

"Jaz—"

"What?" she asked CC who pointed to her watch.

"Don't you have to meet your man?"

"Oh crap!" Jaz jumped up and headed for the door.

She scurried across campus to Sather Tower, fell into Qwayz's arms and their lips locked sensuously. "Hey handsome, don't ever send me away again."

"I didn't send you this time, but seriously wasn't it worth it?"

"We did clear the air about a lot of things." They began walking arm and arm, snuggling, cuddling and basking in one another's glow.

"Is that the Wonder Woman bracelet your Dad sent? You need an armed guard."

"24 carat Italian gold cuff. It's so yellow no one thinks it's real." She held it up so the twilight bounced off of it. "You are my real prize in this life. You know that?"

"So, I've heard. But I have a surprise for you. A combo birthday and early Christmas."

"I love surprises from you. Can we eat first?"

Qwayz laughed aloud. "Don't ever change."

They dined at Giuseppe's, the little Italian restaurant where the owners had taken a liking to them; Mama to Qwayz and Poppa to Jaz. Once Qwayz remarked that the restaurant used Orsini olive oil and that Jaz's father was part owner, the couple was treated like family. On this night, learning of Jaz's birthday, they surprised her with a devil's food white icing cake with a candle instead of tiramisu and sang "Happy Birthday."

"Eighteen years old," Qwayz teased. "Might have to trade you in for a younger model." He kissed the tip of her nose as they left and began walking.

"I'm legal."

"Not until you're 21."

"Really?" They sauntered past Reds. "Where are we going?"

"Thought we'd walk off a meal like that."

"I got a better way to work it off," Jaz demurred.

"Too late for Paradise Rock now."

They tackled the steep hill that seemed to go straight up when Qwayz stopped at a beautiful Victorian House with stained-glass panes and window boxes holding an explosion of colorful flowers. The lamppost, entwined with climbing clematis until it reached the lit flame, resembled a gas lit glow.

281

Qwayz went up the steps and onto the porch then opened the door with a key. "Where are you going?" Jaz whispered.

"The surprise is in here. Three flights up. I'll show you. C'mon." He tucked his sensuous bottom lip under his even white teeth, the twinkle in his eye, irresistible. They tip-toed on the carpeted runners past the doors on the first and second floors. Once they got to the top floor, only one door faced them and Qwayz put in his key, opened it and invited her in.

She stepped into a massive room with a bank of windows across the back wall, overlooking San Francisco lights twinkling below them. "It's like Paris."

"I knew that wouldn't get lost on you. Unobstructed view."

"This is beautiful. Whose is this?"

"It's yours. At least for the next year." He held her. "Your own a two-room, one-bathroom flat."

Jaz looked up at him and he began to rock her gently.

"I know how much you hate being in that dorm. Sharing with and being interrupted and bothered by all those girls. I know how you like time to yourself so you can concentrate. Soon I'll be on the road with the team and might not be able to call you on time or even every night depending on where we're traveling. But if I can think of you here. Safe and sound and happy. That'll do until I come back."

"Oh, Qwayz," Jaz held him and thought, *this man of mine knows me.*

"So, you have this big room. The fully equipped kitchen with the little round stained-glass window that looks out to the front of the house so you can check on Pinky. Look up."

She obeyed and smile-cried, "Beams!" Jaz noticed a little side window to the left looking at the roof of the house next door and to the right. "A fireplace!"

282

"Yeah, it's a little challenging with the front and bedroom doors but it works. I'll want you and s'mores when I get off the road."

"You shall have them. The wall of windows extends to the bedroom?" Jaz pushed open the door by the fireplace and in the center of the room—"The brass bed from *Heirloom's*!"

"Surprise! Happy birthday, Jaz- of-mine."

Jaz squealed with delight and jumped onto the sturdy bed with a comforter and pillows.

"I love you but I just couldn't do pink or a canopy," he confessed. "The beams were the clincher."

"Like our first time at the gatehouse. C'mere." She fell on the bed and gave him a come-hither look. "You said you'd come with me when I get back. I'm back." She shed her hat, then her jacket and started unbuttoning her blouse.

"If you don't mind. I still prefer to unwrap my own packages."

He removed his cap, jacket, Converse sneakers and went to her.

"I don't mind watching Rocket Chandler. If you want to remove more. I can handle it."

"Yeah? You think?"

They began playfully at first, then urgently, then slowly again as if realizing they had all night and day…no check out time, no roaming housekeeping crew with their carts, nothing to destroy their flow… the freedom and ease of it ushered them on at their own pace.

"This is why I love you… because you love me."

"Always will Jaz-of-mine. My love will never run cold. Never run dry."

Their perch in the clouds, the mattress of the brass bed like a magic carpet suspended over all of San Francisco.

Soaring, exploring, summersaulting high above the city unencumbered. Together they flew in the quiet sky throughout the night among the stars, around their star; Qwayz loved her from the bottom to the top. As he raised himself above Jaz, she smiled as her moist center accepted him and the established rhythm echoed in the movement of his St. Christopher's medal reflecting the skyline, matching their passion-laden crescendos as they came together.

"This is a whole new level of loving, Quinton Regis."

"That was the point Jaz-of-mine."

She cuddled under his chin, beneath his satisfied smile. "Our first time in our first house. You did good." She liked the play of the city's light below illuminating his handsome face. "I like it here."

"I get good vibes all around."

"Our own Paradise Rock. You supplied the rock. Thank you for that."

They wolfed down the little supplies from the fridge as they sat at opposite ends of the bed, she at the headboard and he at the foot. Drunk with their carnal success, relishing that they had no set time to get back or vacate the premises. "We'll need one more set of sheets. More towels. A dresser for our clothes."

"I just did the basics. You do the rest. A little portable TV on rollers to push between the two rooms. One telephone with a long cord will be hooked up in two days."

"Can we afford this?"

"Oh, now you ask. And what do you mean 'we' white man? Have I asked you for a dime? Thanks to your brother being a stand-up, black entrepreneur, we get paid for sessions, songwriting credits, masters… We'll be fine. We just can't go overboard. Make sure we pick quality pieces for our first real home."

284

Honey melted into hazel. "You think of everything."

"This bed will be our marital bed one day." He rubbed the inset of her foot as they lay facing the headboard looking out at the dancing lights below.

"How did you decide on this location?"

"3523 Alta Vista? It's thirty-some miles and an hour to Stanford and only fourteen miles and forty-seven minutes to Berkeley. Given our lead-feet, it's a central location. Reds and I are used to going to L.A. for a visit. This distance is a piece of cake."

She held onto him tightly, wondering what could possibly make her any happier. Nothing. "Thank you, Quinton Regis. I don't want to sleep; I don't want to wake up from this dream. Finally, my life is just the way I want it. You and me...I wouldn't even know how to pray to get this. You've given me something I didn't even know I wanted."

"The stars are in their heavens and all's right with the world."

"Like you always say, memories like this will get you through the rest of your life."

28

The woman rolled her wheelchair to sit in the sun,
basking in its warm rays and daring to inhale deeply. She
glanced toward the entrance at the Information Desk gauging
if she could roll her chair down by the pond without being
detected. The nurse, in rapt conversation with a hoity-looking
woman and a dapper black man, proved to be just the cover
she needed. As she unlatched the brake on her chair she noted
the pair coming fast toward her. In one moment, she froze. In
one moment, after all these years, she realized the jig was up.
After all the bold-faced lies, near lies and subterfuge, her
world was about to come crashing in on her. Her eyes darted
wildly for a way out but there was no escape from their fast
approach. She pulled her short hair over her neck then held her
head on one side, shrunk in her seat, hoping they'd pass her
by. They had done it before. In seconds, they were upon her.
After the mad rush to get to her, the pair stopped.

"Star," the man's voice accused, while the female choked
back tears.

The woman did not trust herself to look up.

"Star?" the female tried.

The woman shook her head feebly. "Cher Anderson," she
said without making eye contact.

"Star Luna Culhane," Hep boomed distinctly, correcting
her claim.

With the sound of her given name coming from a man
whose voice she had last heard when he was a petrified eleven-
year-old little boy begging her to stay, the woman began to cry
softly. A lifetime of solid absence, of stoic deceit, began to
crack. Then shatter. Tears ran down her face onto the blanket

draped over her legs. Tired of denial, tired of covering up, tired of running away. Staying away. Her family name pierced her ears and fell on her heart, squeezed it like a vice, then massaged it like a mother's gentle hand. She finally looked up into her brother's and sister's eyes and said, "What took you all so long?"

They kneeled down and enveloped their sister, all crying tears of joy, happiness, relief …paradise found. The trio… together again.

~*~

"It came today. Mrs. Meucci let them up. That hall tree fits perfectly between the front door and the fireplace," Jaz enthused.

"I thought it would," said Qwayz.

"Can't wait for you to come home and hang your cap and jacket there. How's it going?"

Jaz usually drove down to the home games with Sloane or CC, either one would always be willing to ride shotgun to Stanford's gym to scope out an entire new crop of eligible men. From the stands, she would yell as if she were the coach and, after Qwayz found her in the crowd and wriggled his index finger once, he would go into a zone like she wasn't even there; having jocks for brothers, she understood. Sometimes Scoey and Tracy would come up and they'd all go to dinner afterwards. TC sometimes came with AJ on occasion but mostly he'd fly solo. Often it was just the two of them after a game. Whether Qwayz won or not dictated his mood for the first hour or so. She would wait for him to emerge from the locker room; sometimes there would be press there and sometimes not. Jaz thought of how Jesse Ramsey used to send reporters over to interview her. Qwayz didn't do that, but she wouldn't have minded. If Qwayz had won and was interviewed, he would give his usual credit for the victory to the team, and give her a nod, wait for her to reach where he was, grab her hand and they would split. Jaz loved those times when everyone sweated her boyfriend. She was so proud and he was so humble, that's why everyone loved him. Here at Stanford, they had begun calling him Magic Chandler for his moves… the power-passes, the fake-out shots, his speed and "natural ability." They all loved watching him and, like at Roosevelt, girls wanted to be with him and guys wanted to be him. He was just true to himself.

"You think you'll miss basketball when you leave?" Jaz asked as they cuddled in bed.

"Not really. It's a big man's game now and I'm barely six feet."

"But you have skills they only dream of."

"Not my goal. That's why I get so irritated when they pit me against that dude from Princeton. Midas. I can see what they're planning in a couple of years. He's about my height and build and they want us to square off like two field-bucks for Massa Basketball."

"You can beat him?"

"Oh, yeah," Qwayz laughed and squeezed her tightly. "Easy. But I guess that's entertainment. I'm saving all my moves for you and to Coach Amber and Shane's teams."

"Amber?"

"Oh, yeah. She's gonna be baller too."

"Ballet."

"She can do both. She is going to have two amazing parents."

"I'm going to resurrect Heath. My dad's middle name before his brother Henley died and he took it as his middle name. Heath got lost, but I think it is a cool name."

"Heath Chandler. I like it. Sounds like a for-sure athlete."
288

The next morning Qwayz went for his run as Jaz scooted deeper into bed and put the covers over her head. He returned with coffee and donuts. "We should go to Paradise Rock today. It's been awhile."

"We don't need Paradise Rock now. We have here." She went to him and squeezed him around his waist.

"No more Mr. and Mrs. Lucas McCain? Or Mr. and Mrs. Joe Cartwright? How we've grown up."

"I haven't talked to Selena in two weeks. That's odd."

"You need to give her a call when the rates change."

Just as Jaz smiled at his frugality, the doorbell rang and she darted for the bedroom. She dressed while Qwayz dealt with the intruder. When she opened the door, straight ahead, moving men set the large Chesterfield sofa built for two into place.

"Merciful heavens!" she exclaimed, rubbing her fingers across the nutmeg leather with brass nail trims, like a prop from a 1940s movie. "You are just full of surprises."

"I figured it was time to give her a home, we visited so often," he said.

Jaz jumped into its ample cushions and Qwayz joined her. They faced one another comfortably, their knees touching in the middle. "Ready for some serious studying. Dean's List here you come."

She went to him and lay on his chest and they rested in quiet bliss, the haunting foghorn below lulling them to sleep. Upon awaking from their nap, too late for Paradise Rock, they went out, got food to eat and makings for s'mores. He lit a fire as Jaz talked with Selena. "She is really campaigning for us to come to Colt, Texas for Christmas. My dad all but ordered us there. Everybody's coming, even Aunt O and Uncle Sam from Montclair."

"Wonder what that's all about? You think Papa Colt is sick again and they want us there for one last time?"

"When we talk, he sounds fine to me." Jaz was looking around. "Got it." She found the Ebony magazine. "She said there's a picture of Dad when he met with Vice President Anwar Sadat of Egypt. Oh, here it is. Aren't they fine looking? They remind me of one another."

Qwayz gazed at the picture, "Yeah, your Dad has a few inches on him, and a few shades of color and a full head of hair."

"Gimme that," Jaz snatched it playfully. "I didn't mean they were separated-at-birth but they are both so regal, elegant, handsome and so respected by the masses."

"OK, on that I agree."

~*~

"How you feeling?" Selena asked as Star approached the back verandah of Chateau Jazz.

"Like I died and gone to heaven," Star admitted. "I love this place. Glad you brought me here."

"Like I had a choice? Threatening to run away again is not an option for us. Capiche? That's dirty pool."

Star drug out a chair and sat as Lisette brought her a platter of fresh fruit, yogurt and freshly made croissants, her usual for the past few weeks they'd been there.

"Well, you're gonna have to meet them sooner or later. Preferably before they die," Selena sassed.

"Can't I just stay here in the Paris countryside?"

"You can always come back... but you got unfinished business, my sister. Buck up."

"Yeah," Star sighed.

"You look as good as you gonna look. Hep's handling all the Colt, Texas details. He's aiming for Christmas at the latest."

290

"I'm such a disappointment."

"You got a sister, brother and a daughter who don't think so. And a mother and father once they know."

"Just want to be well when I see them."

"You are. You haven't had any bouts over here. You take your medication—"

"So maybe I should just stay here in Paris. Why tempt fate?"

Selena eyed her wearily and said, "I can't believe I've kept you from them this long."

"I can't believe it was asthma brought on by a pecan allergy. A sinus infection. Sometimes I got antibiotics. Sometimes not. Couldn't breathe—like a fish out of water or struggling to get air through a straw. Tired and clogged up all the time. All I could do was lay down and hope for the best. They told me to move to Arizona but I sure didn't know no black people there."

"Well, I don't think the Negro hospitals and doctors in your town knew a lot either. That's the way of money and access. Pure and simple. Look at you, even your skin has cleared up."

"That's good nutrition, good sleeping. And no stress."

"Time to fill in the blanks," Selena mandated. She had treaded lightly and prayed each morning before going into Star's room that she hadn't bolted in the night. "Star?"

"Not much to tell… especially when you've spent most of your life trying to forget. I was holding my own and finally got a gig with Ivie Anderson, Duke Ellington's singer…by then I was Cher for Cherokee, but Duke didn't need two of us so he let me go with a reference. I just took her last name when the roadie got me a passport, Cher Anderson. We traveled all through Europe where I met Pax 'The Sax' Paxton, although

291

we didn't hook up until we got back to the states; off and on as only Pax knows how to do."

"Lord," Selena interjected quietly.

"I was doing pretty good, then I got pregnant. As you can imagine Daddy, Papa Pax Peques, was none too happy. Keely-J was born in New Orleans at a Catholic convent where I worked a while before going to Pax's mama and the Reverend Peques for some help while I worked at the shirt factory next county over. Supposed to be a temporary arrangement, but Mama Peques took to Keely-J, gave her a home, stability and so much love. She went to school and church with her grandparents. Eventually, I got a two-bedroom house across the tracks just before you get to The Bottoms. Using Mama Peques' address, Keely-J kept the same school, took piano and dance lessons. I became choir director, taught Sunday school even after I shot a man who thought I was a easy mark living alone in my house. 'Shot him. Should've killed him.'"

"Really?"

"That's what his wife said."

"Were you arrested?"

"Nope. They don't care what black people do to other black people down there. Now if he'd been a white man, I would've had a necktie party compliments of the sheriff's office."

"No love in your life at all?"

"Besides Keely-J? Sure as heck wasn't Pax Peques."

"For once I guess we had the same taste in men."

"I wanted to tell you so badly to run like the wind. But you got him but good."

"You heard about that?"

"I can read." The sisters crumpled in laughter recalling Selena's throwing him and his clothes out. "Thanks to Keely-J. I found out I had a reading disability. Remember when I told

292

you the words didn't line up on the page right? Got me the dyslexia."

"I wonder if I have it?"

"You'd known by now," Star said plucking another grape from the bunch. "I was in the kitchen the night you came by with him and brought KiKi the milk."

"You jivin'!"

"That was the hardest one. I wanted to just grab and hug you and then let you go on. But I knew that wouldn't happen."

"I would have dragged your butt back."

"Don't I know it? I had a good life. The life I planned? No. But things were going well. I couldn't go back to Colt, Texas with a baby born out-of-wedlock and face Mom and Papa Colt. I just couldn't."

Selena didn't agree but understood. She thought of her old friend, Zen, who'd had an abortion. Star kept her child. The strength and courage of her choice, staggering.

"I just keep doing what I was doing. One day at a time."

"Then you had the accident and wanted Keely-J to know her people."

"Yep. That backfired on me. I lived and she wanted to go to Colt, Texas. I convinced her not to but I could tell it was a matter of time before she'd disobey."

"I am so glad she did."

"You said that my visiting Mama Peques was the hardest. There were others?'

"Oh, yeah. Here and there. Once I served Hep with his entourage and all. He looked at me and I looked back him for just a second too long. He was being interviewed and they began asking him questions again... and when his eyes met mine again, I ignored him like the stranger he was. I saw him do another glance as he left the restaurant." Star took another grape. "Then I did a stint with Ella Fitzgerald, got on as her wardrober. We came to SELENA'S in Paris, France."

"What? You could have approached me… on foreign land?"

"I didn't but Keely did. She gave you your earring."

"The little girl in the club," Selena recalled wistfully.

"Yep. Girl, you blew them away. Your vocals. Your band. Your place. I *was so* proud."

"You could have stayed. We could have shared the stage. Still can."

"Nope. That life belongs to you, Selena Fluellen. You earned it. I worked in the club's kitchen for a while but Paris is expensive and then the government got me for overstaying my visa. I went on home where Keely-J belonged."

"No man-love, Star?"

"Who says? Psh! I had me a man once. A big, tree-standing black man. Big Beaudine, they called him."

Selena watched Star's face light up just talking about him. Star hunched. "He was married with five children and took care of every one of them. One day the wife hats up with the girls. Left the two boys with him. I never let him spend the night. Keely never saw him leave my bed come morning." She eyed Selena directly.

Selena noted that Star had developed a worldly edge from living on her own all those years. Juggling and struggling, just she and her little girl. She asked quietly, "What happened to him?"

"Dead. A proud, big, black man in the South makes a powerful target and ain't long for this world. He left the farm to me and later I turned it over to his sons. Growing up on a ranch… I taught them not to be scared of horses and how to ride them. How to tend livestock and plant a good crop. They're still working it and give me a little money every year.

294

Kept me going a lot of times. They're good boys… eh. Men with families of their own. I should let them know I'm OK."

"You're a good woman Star Luna Culhane."

"Tried to be. I remember the last thing Mama said to me, 'Don't let your praying knees get lazy.'" They finished together. "I guess we never found love like she and Daddy did."

"Speak for yourself," Selena sassed.

"I guess you're right. Zack seems like a good guy."

"He is."

"Even though we had no corral to test our men."

"What?"

"You know like Mom and Daddy. Before we were born, Mama would hear the thunder of hooves rumbling toward the house and know that was her man, Colt Culhane, guiding wild horses home. She'd pull on a robe, stick her feet in slippers and run to open that corral gate wide just in time for the lead horse to run the others in. Imagine her hair wild and uncombed and Dad galloping in and dismounting and they'd disappear into the barn and make love right there in the hay."

"You blaspheme," Selena reacted. "Where'd you hear such a thing?"

"From Mama. Said that first time, he didn't like her standing there in a robe and nightclothes in front of his boys but then it turned him on."

"Oh, Star!"

"Seriously. His boys stayed busy with the horses and knew not to go into that barn. Waited for him to come out and Keely to skedaddle back to the house."

"You jivin'!"

"If I'm lying I'm flyin'."

The sisters laughed. "And then she told me sometimes to mix it up a bit. She'd sleep in and he'd come trudging upstairs, his dusty boots clomping on the steps, to their marital bed. That took the good parts of 45 minutes of an hour."

Selena convulsed with laughter. "We never think of our parents 'doing it.' She never told me this."

"We got here some kinda way. No immaculate conceptions for Colt and Keely."

"You're forgetting Orelia."

They continued laughing at their prim and proper older sister.

"That was my sex talk. You didn't have one?" Star continued, "Oh, you left with a husband…so you probably had a different one and didn't recognize it."

They laughed to the rafters like they'd never been apart. "Now don't tell mama I told you!"

"Promise. Pinky-swear?" Selena stretched her hand across the table and held up her last finger.

"Brown skin beauties, we are."

They yoked their older, wiser pinkies just as Zack came around the corner. Seeing them with interlocking pinkies, he turned back around and went upstairs.

29

The two old friends spent rare and quiet time alone at the studio while Skeekie put new tires on Reds and Jaz hung out with Denny that day; Tracy the next. TC and Qwayz climbed the spiral staircase to TC's office outside his bedroom with the circular bed. With Qwayz on the sofa by the piano and TC in the big chair, they jaw-jacked, joned and caught up talking about everybody and anybody. TC seldom had any down time. "Haven't done this in long time," Qwayz said.

"Too long," TC agreed. "Things got real hectic. Man, not sure whether I was coming on going."

"That's what happens when you're an 'old man' with lots of irons in the fire."

"I'll be pushing up on what, twenty-three, soon? Damn! Almost a quarter of a century."

"Look at all you got to show for it, man. You've lived several lifetimes."

"Too much. Too soon."

"You burnt out?"

"Hope not. Did get some much-needed rest."

"So how are you and Bev Nash?"

"I didn't tell you her name," a shocked TC replied.

"C'mon, man it's me. I know your type and there weren't too many choices."

TC chuckled. "Yeah, you right." TC took another swig of beer. "My music, business and career are right on track but my personal life is nowhere'sville."

"Interesting choice of words. Knowing you could have any woman you wanted."

"Now see, that's a thought-provoking observation especially coming from you. I know I can and did and do have sex anytime I want, but that one 'exceptional woman' eludes me. Don't want a woman I can live with—I want a woman I can't live without. I want what you have with my sister."

"Ain't gonna lie, it is priceless, man. She loves me like there is no such thing as a broken heart." A big old smile claimed his face. "She's my cool and my crazy. I'm happiest when we're breathing the same air."

"Yeah. That's what I'm talking about. You all are too young to have baggage anyway." They chuckled. "I had three good women. Ronnie died; didn't even give her a chance. One left—no, two left; LeLani and Beverly. Now none. I want that connection. That no matter what goes down *we* can handle it. Just getting a woman for sexual pleasure? That's masturbation by proxy."

"So, you'll get that next time. Some find it right away. Some find it later. But you got to believe you will or it ain't never gonna happen."

"See. I know what it is to choose your passion over a mate; I did it enough. It's just the first time it's happened to me. I don't like it one bit. It's demoralizing. She left L.A. and chose the San Francisco market. We tried that long distance thing and it did not work for us. The missed dates. The emergencies. Contingencies. Making you feel like yesterday's news or an afterthought. Not a priority. That hurts. Intellectually, I know she didn't graduate college and begin a career just to give it up for me or any other dude. Not now. Not while she's young. But emotionally, it's a bad scene."

"So far LeLani Troop was probably your best bet."

"Yeah. At least, she understood. We had good times but I didn't love her. Not like you and Jaz."

298

"No one loves like me and Jaz. We're magic," Qwayz said, beaming.

"You all are on the way to legendary."

"You ever hear from LeLani?"

"Nope. Moved to Hawaii to be with her mama. Sent her last two checks to her daddy. She cashed them at the Bank of Hawaii. Guess she's still there."

"Aloha" they sang together and laughed, slapping five like the old days.

~*~

"Star!" Selena called out in exasperation. "C'mon. We'll be late! Star."

A surly "I'm coming" came from upstairs.

Selena stood in the middle of the room and looked up to where the voice emanated. She began to cry. Never in her lifetime, despite the expense and effort, did she ever think she would call out her sister's name and have her answer. She imagined, envisioned, wished and hoped, but never did she really believe it would happen. Selena wiped away her joyful tears as more poured out to take their place.

"Selena," Zack said coming to her.

"I know. It's silly."

"Not at all." He held her.

"Am I dreaming, Zack?"

"No, baby. She's here."

"Oh damn! Now I've ruined my mascara."

On the flight back to Texas, Selena suggested, "The sight of you strutting in there might kill Papa Colt… we'll tell mama. Surprise him."

"You sure it'll be alright? He told me never to darken his door again."

Selena chuckled. Then realized her sister was serious.

"You are jiving, aren't you Star?

"I didn't do what I said I was."

"Failure or not. A day doesn't go by when he isn't sorry he was so harsh. You have no idea how much we've *all* missed you. He's lived this long because he wants to see you before he dies."

"Is he sick?"

"He kicked pneumonia's ass a while back. But he's healthy as a horse. He's never changed the locks on the door. Your key still fits and I know he's hoping one of these days you'll use it."

"Really?"

"Square business.

"Ok, Mama first and then Daddy."

~*~

Cherokee Ranch wrapped itself in colorful lights that could be seen across the prairie, a beacon of Yuletide audacity. Hep allowed everyone to celebrate Christmas with their families, mandating that they should arrive at the ranch no later than the 29th in time for the Culhane Holiday Party. When the ambassador spoke, the family listened. The house rocked like the parties of yesteryear. All were in attendance and the vibe reverberated high, festive and strong up through the roof.

"Top Cat, Bright Eyes and Sporty," Papa Colt claimed them all. "You know my grands?" he said to a visitor. "That there hairdo is called a 'Afro,'" he informed a guest of Mel's hair.

The food abundantly good, the liquor flowed as did the flip he fixed for his boys before he went out to visit them and let them know how happy he was that everyone was home. Almost everyone anyway. When he returned to the house from his annual visit, Keely stopped him by the door while Selena removed his coat, passing it off to Hep who hung it on the hall tree.

"Time for our concert, Papa Colt," TC urged him to sit beside him on the piano bench.

Untrained brown fingers catapulted up and down the black and white keys, TC matching his grandfather with the honkey tonk he'd learned years ago at Fancy's. "Who is that pretty little girl right there?" Papa Colt asked of the only stranger in the room. "Who do you belong to?"

"My name is Keely Joy."

"Pretty name for a pretty girl. My wife's name is Keely. Keely!" he called out.

"I'm here."

"Her name is Keely, too," he said in way of introduction. "Who you named for?"

"My mother named me for her mother," Keely-J said.

"What you say now?" Papa Colt looked her dead in the eye. She smiled broadly. He recognized that grin right off.

"Where's your mother?" Papa Colt sprung right up from the piano bench. "Where's my Star?"

"Right here, Daddy." Star stood on the threshold from the dining room to the great hall. The room, graveyard quiet, watched the reunion in the making. Obsidian eyes locked with one another; father and daughter, spanning the distance of years apart. Years of life lived without one another. Hep held his breath; it had been Star's idea to have one meeting and then, as she said, "If he rejects me I only have to go through it once."

Papa Colt soaked her in—he would have known his second child anywhere. Face-to-face, heart-to-heart, soul-to-soul, they spoke without using words. He burst into tears and held open his arms. "C'mere, girl."

She ran into his arms like a little girl and their tears mixed and flowed between them.

"Welcome home, baby. Welcome home."

"Thank you, Daddy."

He opened his arms, summoning Keely to join them. "Our little girl's finally home." He gave his wife a salty kiss. "We're all together again. Our family."

Keely-J snapped all kinds of pictures in various combinations. Parents with adult children. Grandparents with grandchildren. Everyone with the last name Culhane. Then old neighbors and Star's friends with their families. The revelry continued for three more days with stories and reenactments from happier times; Keely-J treated to a family she almost didn't meet. "I guess not having a hotel in Colt, Texas has come to bite me in the butt!" Papa Colt teased, looking younger than any of them ever remembered.

Soon the holidays were over and it was time for everyone go back home.

"I'm going to stay here with Mom and Daddy for a while," Star said.

"I thought you would," Selena replied. "I'll miss you."

"Thanks, Hep for arranging all this. You got them all here." Star accepted his embrace.

"She's kicking me to the curb and staying here," Selena told him.

"As it should be." Hep stood in the middle and grabbed both of his sisters on either side and kissed them on the cheeks. "I love you. The trio!"

~*~

Once the door to Alta Vista opened Jaz said simply, "Home."

"That was a wild welcome to 1966. Imagine not thinking you're going to see anyone ever again and then—Bam! There

302

she is. Aunt Star and Cousin Keely-J. More family, just like that."

That weekend they drove out to Paradise Rock. Their jubilant voices funneled up the ravine from the private beach that disappeared with the high tide. They spread out the blanket and retrieved the picnic basket beside their texts books, which they never opened. "I love this place," Qwayz said.

"Your Myrtle Beach. Look at that water whoosh in. We made it just in time."

"Our timing is great." He stopped chopping on a chicken leg long enough to kiss her.

"How'd TC seem to you?"

"Fine. Better than the last time. He really enjoyed being at Cherokee. Seeing all his old friends, grooving with his Gramps."

"Mel told me she's going to finish out this year then drop out. Says she's tired of theory and wants to do plays. Now she can't do auditions 'cause if she gets a part, she can't take it."

"She said something about a play coming up." Qwayz downed an entire soda.

"Yep. If she gets the part this summer, it's sayonara Julliard," Jaz said eyeing a lone sea gull. "We have to do something for AJ's spring break."

"As long as his Auntie Jaz is involved he could care less," Qwayz said. "He's got a mega-crush on you."

"He's a cutie. We could have him come up here and squire him around. Drive him over to Sausalito, 17 Mile, up to Napa—"

"Not going to hold the attention of a ten-year-old boy."

"Humm. What are you going to do this summer? Basketball coach at the Watts Boys Club."

"You realize I did that to be near you. Shorter ride from there to the Malibu beach house."

They snuggled together as the sun prepared to set. "Dad asked if I was coming to Italy for the summer. I told him I was going to get a jump on Organic Chemistry. He was duly impressed."

"You should go for a couple of weeks."

"Italy is for you and me and our honeymoon."

"We got to wait that long?" He chuckled. "He won't be ambassador then."

"Oh, darn." Jaz laid her head on his shoulder.

"You need to take another easy-A elective."

"You sound just like him. I'd already thought of it; then I'll be seven credits ahead."

"Take an Art History course. Something that uses the fact that you spent last summer in Paris at the Louvre and Jeu de Paume. Let the impressionist painters help you get an A."

"I was thinking Stress of Materials, under the Architecture Department." Jaz slid her hand beneath his shirt for warmth. "What are you doing to stay up this way for the summer with me?"

"I'm a grown-ass man. I just stay. I got no one to explain anything to."

"We don't have to give up our apartment?"

"Not unless you want."

"It's perfect for us. You're perfect for me."

"We're perfectly imperfect for each other." He kissed her forehead. "Look at that!" he exclaimed. "A beautiful California sunset over the Pacific. Nothing better. You and me at Paradise Rock." His smile rivaled the setting sun. "I love you."

"I love you, too. I love us—"

30

Star held her face to the Colt, Texas sun reveling in the way it caressed her already dark cheeks. She inhaled the fresh heated air into her nostrils and recognized the mixture of manure, the fragrance of Indian blanket and blue bonnets, freshly turned hay and the underlying layer of humidity that would top the day off by this evening. Home. She sat atop the horse and let her eyes drink in the sight of as-far-as-you-can-see land. Culhane land. Cherokee Ranch. Her heart could not be stilled. She raced across the wide-open prairie with nothing but wild life scurrying and heavenly birds soaring above for company. Not another human being in sight. Not a road or a traffic light. Not a building. The view soothed her soul in ways she hadn't realized she had missed. The horse went to the swimming hole for a long drink and Star plunged into the cool welcoming water fully clothed. She touched the bottom, dead-man's-floated on her back, eyeing the lacy canopy above before she lay in the soft grass and fell asleep. She opened her eyes as birds skidded across a sun preparing to set. If she never left here again, she would be content.

She walked the horse into the barn, rubbed its coat and noted the irony of life: how maturity has a way of ordering things. The very place she couldn't wait to leave at eighteen, was the only place left on this earth she now wanted to be.

Unlike her sister Selena, Star relished rising early and spending her days helping her mother with breakfast, gathering eggs from the chicken coop, milking a cow, setting up the rolls for dinner that night. Carrying the wash for Keely from the machine to hang the freshly washed clothes on the line, anchoring them with wooden clothespins, to catch and dry in the hot Texas breeze…heaven. She savored going with Papa Colt to ride the range, whether a slow and steady gallop or on the buckboard to repair a fence. At about 105 years of age, he still discussed current events here and in the world: the price of beef or the Dance Theater of Harlem's debut that January, Indira Gandhi's election as the third Prime Minister of India, or Bill Russell with the Boston Celtics being the first black coach in the NBA. Papa Colt remained engaged. Before Keely-J returned to Paris where she declined the invitation to stay with her Aunt Selena, holding on to her Left Bank flat, the three women would clean up the dinner dishes and plan for the next day's meals. Twice a week Star would accompany her mother to choir practice, where Star had earned a prominent spot in Mt. Moriah's choir.

Star now content and blessed to sing for the Lord and the congregation of Mt. Moriah Gethsemane Baptist Church. Having reconnected with Delilah, Francie and their families, there was always something to do with either their children or their grands since Colt, Texas now had a movie theater, soda parlor and a restaurant, where she had accepted the invitation of the widowed Rufus Macklin who'd driven her to River Bend Station when she left so many years ago. They started keeping company, but the one company she seldom missed –a chance to sit with her daddy on the porch swing with his liquid refreshment as they watched the sun plummet behind the distant mountains only to splash up the moon and the stars. Star was home; never more to roam.

~*~

"OK Jaz, let me explain," Qwayz pleaded, standing in front to their apartment on Alta Vista, barring her from entry.

"What have you done?" Jaz wondered, pushing him out of the way.

306

She stood on the other side of the door. Her eyes grew saucer-wide. "What the hell?"

"I was thinking of you. Wanting to keep you warm. They had a good deal so I ordered a cord and then two."

Jaz looked at the wood that lined the circumference of the entire front room. Under the windows to the base of the sill, up the wall by the bedroom door. Up the three steps to the kitchen. Two logs deep; three in some places. Jaz began to laugh… and laugh.

"You know how cold you get. Luckily, Mrs. Meucci stopped them in time."

Jaz couldn't catch her breath and finally Qwayz joined in. "I guess we'll have to have a fire and s'mores every night to use this up by graduation."

"Oh Qwayz, how thoughtful. Is this my Valentine's gift?"

"Part of it," he quipped. "What do I know about wood?"

"Plenty," Jaz sassed and sidled up against him.

"Naughty. Naughty."

That night they dined at Giuseppe's along with other celebrating couples, each woman receiving a red rose. Upon opening the door, a pole lamp illuminated one end of the Chesterfield sofa and the Ponderosa pine coffee table, made of five big slices, placed in front of it.

"That's for us. We need more than the bed and hall tree. I have something else for you in the bedroom."

"I bet you do." Pushing open the door, she saw their images in a free-standing Victorian cheval mirror draped with a big red bow. "Like Grandma Keely's!"

"Besides the dresser mirror and the one in the bathroom, you didn't have a full-length mirror."

"I look at my reflection in your eyes to see if I look good."

"You mean I could have saved those duckets?"

Their lips met and wine-soaked tongues intertwined. "I'll have to figure out a way to aim it so I can see the action from bed."

"You are so bad…" They kept kissing and his hands roamed.

"And you love it."

"Yeah, I do." She let her tongue slip behind those pretty white teeth. "Oh, I almost forgot your gift. Wait here."

Jaz went out the front door and returned carrying a box. She set it on the floor and waited for Qwayz to return from the bathroom. "Happy Valentine's Day!" Jaz pronounced.

Qwayz looked at the big box with the holes on one side.

Jaz fluttered her eyelashes. A whimpering sound came from the box.

"Is that box moving?" Qwayz lifted off the lid and a beautiful Irish Setter puppy popped up on cue. "Ah! Jaz! Hey, girl. Is it a girl? Hey c'mere." Qwayz picked up the bundle of energy as Jaz went into the bedroom closet and brought out a dog bed, a clock, a bowl and dog food.

"I know you wanted a dog. And now we have an apartment for her."

"Oh, Jaz this is perfect. She has your coloring."

"You could have gone all night without saying that." Jaz watched Qwayz and his dog roll around on the floor. "One thing. Lips that kiss that dog will never kiss mine, and no sleeping in our bed."

"OK," he agreed without removing his eyes from his canine companion. Jaz wondered if she had made a mistake.

"Name?"

"Akira. After my sensei karate master."

"Irish dog with a Japanese name. How international."

308

And so, boy and his dog became inseparable. Akira ran with him each morning and sat up front in his car in Jaz's seat when she didn't occupy it herself. While on Antique Row, he bought Akira a vintage collar and leash and couldn't wait to tell AJ. They always stopped by *Rare Finds* for a sip of cappuccino from the ornate 1912 brass machine; the venerable object' de art pumped out an intoxicating aroma summoning folks for blocks. Jaz found an intricately made classic Victorian ecru chiffon dress with the leg 'o mutton sleeves and Juliet points.

"You should get it," a distracted Qwayz told her while he played with Akira. "How much?"

She turned over the price tag. "For that we could get your leather chair with hassock. Besides, where would I wear it? A costume party? It is gorgeous," she said sotto voce.

"It won't do for TC's award banquet? Is that black tie? Do I have to wear shoes?"

"It's the Fairmont Hotel. Probably. He'll be in a tux."

As they continued to introduce Akira to Antique Row, Qwayz said, "It's going to be a warmer than usual weekend. We haven't been to Paradise Rock in a while. How about we take Akira and picnic there tomorrow? You haven't seen it yet. Have you, girl."

Jaz rolled her eyes at both of them.

Blanket and basket in tow, Akira in AJ's seat, Qwayz took the turn like a seasoned champ.

"Uh oh," Jaz said as he slid along the road and up the path. "Did you see that stick with the two red ribbons attached? Means someone has discovered our Paradise."

Qwayz pulled Reds onto the peninsula of granite jutting out over the Pacific. Opening the door, Akira jumped out to do her own exploring. "She's a good dog."

"I'm just glad she's toilet-trained."

"House-broken," Qwayz corrected as the dog came back to him and Jaz threw open and spread the blanket.

After devouring the food, they descended the rocks to the right where they had blazed a trail, frolicked on the private beach, scurrying back to the top just before high tide submerged the beach.

That night, Qwayz and Jaz sat at a table of ten and watched Tavio Culhane receive yet another award for community service. He not only gave financial support but also lent his many musical talents to helping the youth of the Potrero Hill Projects. A handsome trophy for him to add to his collection, but Jaz couldn't understand why he came to San Francisco to receive it, as he usually begged off and organizations would send them to him. She thought nothing else about it until TC knocked on their Alta Vista door. "Who is it?" Jaz queried.

"TC."

Jaz thought she would die at the discovery. She ran to put on street clothes when Qwayz told her not to bother.

"He knows?" Jaz looked at Qwayz, astonished and betrayed.

"That we're in love and sometimes you stay over? Yep."

Qwayz opened the door and TC sauntered in.

"Kind of surprised to see you, man," Qwayz said.

"That makes two of us. Night didn't exactly go as planned." He sat on the couch, looked around and said, "Nice. Hey Jaz."

Was her brother drunk? Jaz wondered more than the discovery.

"Got any aspirin? Got a helluva headache working."

Jaz went to the medicine cabinet and brought him aspirin with a glass of water.

310

"She punked me again, man."

"Did she? Seems like she's been pretty clear all along."

"Oh, I'm the one with the hard head?"

"No. You the man who cannot believe that this girl doesn't want you."

They both chuckled.

"It was bound to happen sooner or later," Qwayz said.

"Why'd she accept the invitation to the banquet?" TC asked.

"She doesn't hate you, man. It's a chance to see you again. Maybe even make a little love—"

"A lot of lovin'," TC corrected with a stupendous grin.

"I'm sure you're good but throw-my-career-away good? Nope. You wouldn't respect her if she did. Later on, you'd both grow to resent each other."

"I came here 'cause I'm in no condition to drive back. Didn't want a hotel and sure as hell wasn't staying with her until 4 a.m. when she leaves for work."

TC stretched out on the couch, kicked off his shoes, crossed his arms and closed his eyes. Not used to overnight guests, Jaz went and took the comforter from their bed.

"Thanks," TC managed, "See you guys in the morning. Breakfast is on me."

"What is going on?" Jaz whispered to Qwayz.

"Tell you when I get back from walking Akira. C'mon, girl." Qwayz leashed her and opened the door.

When Qwayz returned, TC was snoring and Qwayz shared what he knew about TC and his lady friend. "Have you met her yet?"

"No. I feel like it. She's got your brother's nose big time. I never thought I'd see it happen. At least when it is unrequited, which might be part of the allure."

311

"She's using him. She went to the banquet on his arm, to work the room, and boost her career."

"Might could be. At some point he needs to cut his losses and move on. She's not leading him on. She's been consistent but it's leaving him in an insecure and precarious state."

31

Nineteen sixty-five proved to be a pivotal year politically and personally. The president signed a Voting Rights Act that July while Jaz and Qwayz frolicked in Paris and Star returned to the Culhane fold with her daughter Keely-J. Nineteen sixty-six followed with firsts, foundings and continuations. Jaz completed her freshman year, aced summer school and entered her sophomore year; Qwayz, his junior year; and Mel fell in love and contemplated dropping out of college for a man who hadn't attended college but deemed her his soulmate. Martin Luther King, Jr. spoke out against the Vietnam War at a Washington, D.C. rally; B52s from Guam bombed North Vietnam for the first time; and Howard University elected its first homecoming queen, Robin Gregory, who wore an Afro. Martin Luther King, Jr., who'd moved his family to a Chicago suburb, called off a march for open housing in the Cicero district when another more determined fraction continued: white folks threw bricks at peacefully marching black folks and, for the first time, black people chucked them back.

In spring of 1966 SNCC, under the leadership of twenty-three-year-old Trinidadian born activist Stokely Carmichael, traveled to Lowndes County, Alabama to help with voter registration. That June as Martin Luther King, Jr. maintained his peaceful resistance, Stokely marched to Mississippi and on June 16, first used the term "Black Power," while Sly and the Family Stone's "Don't Call Me Nigger, Whitey" blasted from the radio. Across the bridge from San Francisco in Oakland, Huey P. Newton and Bobby Seale adopted the "Black Power" epithet of the Lowndes County marches and founded the Black

Panther Party for Self-Defense to monitor police actions in their black community and develop a 10-point program, building a foundation to establish several chapters of the Black Panther Party in various cities, a national newspaper and a free breakfast program for school children.

Bombing in North Vietnam resumed after a thirty-seven-day pause. The number of troops in Vietnam reached 385,000. Yudi Hodges was one of them. Chicago ignited for four days with two people killed in July. The U.S. Supreme Court ruled that poll taxes were unconstitutional; and James Meredith, who enrolled in the University of Mississippi in 1962, was shot after beginning a 220-mile March Against Fear from Memphis, Tennessee to Jackson, Mississippi. LBJ, Premier Ky and leaders of five other nations involved in the Vietnam "Conflict" pledged a four- point "Declaration of Peace" and the war waged on… in the jungle, in the cities and in the mind of its citizens.

And then there was discovery…

After Mother Nature finally vacated the premises, Jaz made up for lost time all weekend finally releasing Qwayz to his classes. "Have I told you lately that I love you?" he said as he kissed her goodbye hard on the lips and eased out the door. Jaz stretched with fulfillment, raging then resting to a calm throughout her body, from the tips of her toes to the top of her head. Could she be any happier?

The man in the limo watched the man with the brown leather bomber jacket and red cap open the car door for a dog, get in and drive off. The man in the limo placed his hand on his door, opening and closing it himself. He looked up at the round stained-glass window on the top floor and walked through the front door just as someone was leaving. He looked at the mailbox with two names: Chandler/Culhane.

He climbed the two flights and stood at the door before knocking. He knew all would change with this one gesture.

Hearing the knock, Jaz chuckled and went from the bathroom, where she prepared to shower for her classes. She ran playfully to the door. "You never get enough, huh?" She swung the door open onto her father.

She screamed and shut it fast. She closed her robe to hide her nude recently satisfied body and knotted the belt tightly. "Damn, damn damn! Shit, shit shit!" she whispered then covered her mouth trying to harness her breathing.

"Jaz. I've seen you. Are you letting me in or not?" Her father's voice boomed from the other side of the door.

She quickly surveyed the apartment. *What am I doing?* She thought. The jig was up. Jaz opened the door for her father who walked in and looked around before being invited to do so. "May I get you some juice or coffee?"

"No, thank you." He looked at the view of San Francisco below through the wall of windows. "So how long has this 'arrangement' been going on?" He looked at her and tried not to notice her tousled hair, the ruby color on her still plump-from-kissing lips, the scent of recent love-making giving way to the humidity of a just-taken shower. He looked into the bedroom and saw the rumpled sheets on a brass bed. Jaz closed the door.

"A while now."

"Were you planning to tell me?"

"No."

"Humph." *My brazen, too-honest daughter,* he thought.

"Eventually, I suppose. Hadn't given it much thought."

"Ah! Because this is the way you were raised. To consort and live with a boy without the benefit of marriage." His words stung but Jaz didn't reply. "What do they call it? Shacking up?"

"I love him. He loves me. We don't call it that."

"Oh, so love makes the difference."

"Yeah, it does Dad, at least for Qwayz and I. He got this place for me because I was having some adjustment issues."

"Maybe if you'd told me I could have—"

"I'm eighteen years old now. Can't go running to my father every time—"

"So, you run to a boy."

"It's Qwayz, Dad. Not just any old 'boy.'" She watched her father stiffen. "I have a 3.5 cumulative average because he's there for me."

"Umph. Certainly you are not giving him credit for your intelligence!"

"No, but I am giving him credit for being here for me. For giving me what I need before I know I need it. For always supporting me, bolstering me up, reminding me I belong here just as much as anyone else. For loving me… unconditionally."

Nothing becomes apparent until you become a parent, Hep thought of his father's saying. His thoughts were consumed by Star's leaving Cherokee Ranch at eighteen, Jaz's age, but he didn't feel Jaz would leave college over their difference of opinion. His headstrong daughter would finish just for spite; re-apply for her scholarship and not miss a beat, but Hep had visions of, years from now, having to go through Qwayz to see his grands because Jaz had cut him out of her life like a cancer. She was good at that. Star was back home now after all those wasted years. Hep knew he should be grateful to Qwayz for being there. He knew him to be a good man who loved his daughter despite their youth. Hep was not willing to lose his daughter because of her current lifestyle choice.

With the air still tinged from laughing and love-making, silence filled the room. Hep thought while Jaz had her own internal conversation. How could she tell her father that she loved Qwayz beyond words? Sometimes they just stared at one another—honey on hazel without speaking… words too trite to convey the deep, abiding love they shared for one another. She couldn't tell her father how many times, with just one look, Qwayz had saved her without even knowing it. She couldn't tell her father how she loved how they made love, and relished the ripples of pleasure he sent through her. She savored each thrust of his strong athletic form and delighted in seeing the St. Christopher's medallion caught in his silky chest hair as he sank deeper into her body, her mind, her heart, her very soul, as they became one. *No Dad, you will not diminish what we have,* she offered him mentally. *You cannot make us cheap or tawdry. The way we feel about one another is not just for now, it is everlasting.*

She knew Qwayz felt that way about her. In her heart and bones, she *knew* she was loved by him; loved beyond the capacity of any language in the world to tell her so. But his feelings spoke volumes when they held one another's gaze. Quietly. Intimately. Priceless moments. Whether they made sweet, tender love or fierce love when he ravished her like it was the last chance he had or he just held her and they'd fall asleep. Any experience with him—other-worldly and exquisite.

How could she explain her addiction to the way Qwayz made her feel; loved, respected, cherished and important in his life. She saw it in his eyes, felt it in his touch, inhaled it in the essence of him before and after making love as they washed

317

their cars, strolled Antique Row or cooked in their kitchen. His love, incomparable and ever-present, remained in his eyes whether surrounded by adoring fans, giggly girls or reporters…he was the constant in her life. He made her feel anointed. There was no living without him. She was not confused.

"Don't ask me to choose, Dad," Jaz said, breaking the silence, as part warning, part threat, part declaration. *You'd lose,* was heard but left unsaid.

Hep stood and Jaz stood with him. He could barely look at her. "You have some nice pieces." He spoke of the classic Chesterfield couch, the oversized club chair built for two with a matching ottoman.

Jaz followed his gaze and thought of all the ways they'd made love on the furniture and said, "Built to last."

Hep proceeded to the door. "Neat," he said, grasping for neutrality.

"Mel was the messy one."

"Well, goodbye Punkin'," he said, the pet name slipping out before he realized it. She was a long way from his little girl. "Take care," he said stiffly, his disappointment fought the love and he patted her awkwardly on the shoulder before leaving.

"Bye."

When Qwayz returned that evening Jaz calmly said, "I had a surprise visitor today."

"Who? TC again?" He unleashed Akira who took her seat across the bedroom threshold.

"Nope. His Excellency. Hepburn Henley Culhane."

"What?" Qwayz's eyes grew Stepin Fetchit huge. "You're still standing. How was it?"

"Surprisingly calm. I've made my choice. It's you."

"Did he ask you to?"

318

"No. It was quite civilized. I'm with you now and he'll have to adjust or not."

"My woman," Qwayz grabbed her playfully.

"I am," she repeated Grandma Keely's response to Papa Colt.

Three weeks later, a letter from her father shared the mailbox with Gladys Ann's ten-page, front and back, yellow legal pad tome keeping her abreast of all the happenings at Howard University.

Jaz entered the apartment, poured a glass of grapefruit juice, sat on the couch and opened the one from her father. "Here goes," she said, recognizing his familiar scribble.

Dear Jasmine,

>*Blood of my blood, flesh of my flesh. Special to me from conception to now. I was ill-prepared for our last visit and, having time to think it over, I have begun this missive several times and it's still an inarticulate mess of words. You are not a parent and I don't expect you to understand any of this now until you are faced with your own children on the brink of adulthood. My father and I. TC and I... and now you. You only want your children to have it better and easier than you did. You want your children healthy, happy and eventually, financially independent. You want them to love and be loved in return. If my only objection is that you are too young, then I am ahead of the game. You have always been advanced. I will not lose you, your love, support or respect for a decision you make at 18. You've told me that I am the man by which you measure all others and I do not have to be told that about Qwayz. I know. Black, brilliant, principled, from a good family, great values, mature,*

319

*loving and will take care of you, as you will not freeze
to death with all that wood. I welcome him once again.
I could not choose a better man for you. You will never
be a father but perhaps Qwayz can project and
understand the crazies that beset a father when his
daughter replaces him for her "knight in shining
armor." It's a process and, as I've told you all your
life, you and I can discuss anything. As the father who
loves you, I cannot think of anything worse than to be
systematically eliminated from your child's life. That
will not happen. I will continue paying for your
tuition, book, allowance et al. but have released on-
campus housing for you next year so it can be
available for someone who needs it. Your mother
thinks you'll be staying off campus in an apartment or
sorority house with girl roommates. Please let her.*

*I have selected the location for Culhane
Enterprises office building which was covered by all
the papers as it will be the tallest and, upon
completion, the most exquisite office building in the
city. By my desire and design it will take years to build
as the imported Italian marble for the three-story foyer
will take that long to mine and quarry. I was not ready
to see you then but when I return in a few months,
barring any problems, I'd like to take you* and *Qwayz
to dinner, my treat. I'll share plans and blueprints
with you so you can follow its progress. Until then, do
forgive an "Old Fool" who only wants the best for his
daughter and realizes she already has it.*

*I love you, Punkin'
Always,
Dad.*

Jaz sighed with relief just as a teardrop fell.
"Love you, too, Daddy," she whispered.

32

Papa Colt's death came as a shock. Even at 100 years plus, no one expected him to ever leave this earth. With Star's return he had a renewed spirit and joie de vivre, and even Grandma Keely spoke of his friskiness. All the Culhanes rallied around him at Cherokee Ranch in life and so they did upon the call that he had fallen from a horse and hit his head. "There are angels in the room," his last words, and he lingered for a few days, seemingly allowing everyone time to arrive before he closed his eyes on this world to open them in the next. A contented smile graced his face. "Privacy please," Keely asked simply of her four children in his last moments.

Colt's breath grew ragged, raspy, then shallow and panting, and Keely knew the love of her life was struggling to leave her. She held his hand and climbed into bed beside him. Hooding his eyes, he looked up toward her, feeling her more than seeing her. She cleaved him to her breast. His eyes volleyed around the room as if he had no control of them. His lips moved but nothing audible came out.

"I know," she soothed him and smoothed down his locks. "I know. Leave in peace, Colt Culhane." Tears fell on his softly curled hair. "I'll be all right." She kissed his forehead.

Later, Hep and Selena came in to check on their parents and found their father had passed. His hands lukewarm to the touch.

"He's gone," Keely said. "It was his time." Keely removed herself from the bed. Pulled the covers up to his chin as if he were sleeping. "The only man I ever loved."

Selena and Hep, stunned by their mother's composed poise, watched her open the door and leave their bedroom.

322

They checked on their father. Keely told the doctor as she descended the stairs and passed him in the great room, "He's ready for you."

Keely walked out the back door as the doctor took the steps by two. As he examined their father, Selena stepped back and looked out of the window. "Hep look," she called her brother to view the scene. There at the corral, Keely opened the wooden gates wide as she had all those years for her husband to let the horses in—now she let the horses loose. "Run free just like these horses, Colt Culhane. You will always be the love of my life."

~*~

"Be who you are," the Reverend Gassaway began addressing the overflowing congregation. "That's what his mother told him upon her death. Made him promise. And he set about doing it. Wasn't but six or seven years old. His father, Lone Wolf, dead, and now his mama. Born free like his daddy and delivered back to the same massa that owned his mother, Saidah. After the Civil War freedom came and went again but he and his Aunt Pearl stayed until that old massa took a whip and carved permanent stripes on his back. He was nine. They left for Washington, D.C., and Black Pony worked three jobs to live in a filthy back-alley dwelling near the Capitol Building of the United States of America. A free man long before the War, Gideon, taught Black Pony to read just before Aunt Pearl died and he hopped a train west. On his own at 12 years old. A man-child with no family. Can I get a amen?"

The congregation gave him what he asked as he mopped his brow and continued, "The world told him that he was a 'throwaway child.' Insignificant. Disposable. No place for him, so why not just disappear or die. But Black Pony said 'not so fast.'"

"Well," a congregant testified.

"You not the boss of me. You don't define me. I am the decider of my fate—not you. I got plans and he rebirthed himself into Colt Culhane. Took that last name from the side of a barn that said 'Culhane Feed and Grain… Best in the West,' and he set about making plans and making them come true. Was a cowboy, then rode as a scout for a wagon train, then worked a ranch, which hit on what he wanted: a ranch and family of his own. As he crisscrossed the American West he saw and bought a sweet piece of land years before he was ready. Let that be a lesson to you young folks—"

"Amen," someone said.

"That piece of land is now Colt, Texas… our sanctuary. Our haven against the outside world. He moved here, built a ranch with the help of his 'boys' who live right up there on that hill next to the Cherokee Ranch house. His boys and their families are here with us today. They made this town work; Micah Rudd, Joaquin Criqui, Josiah Pincus, Durango and Banyon. Then he met his beloved Keely Ross, the woman he chose to make his dreams come true. The woman he chose to be the mother of his children. The woman he loved to the end of his days. The woman he still loves in the hereafter. May we all know love like that."

"Amen."

"Be who you are," Reverend Gassaway repeated again, wiping the white handkerchief across his dark face. "Colt Culhane. Not a tall man only 5'8" but a Big man. A good man. A true man. Cared little for what others thought of him. The most important person to him was himself—I mean that in a good way. Colt Culhane didn't care about things. Most important opinion to him was his own. He didn't cotton to lying or cheating. Raised his children up to be just like him. Married the right woman to help him do it. Keely Ross Culhane was his rock. Guess I should say they were each other's rock. Life wasn't no 'crystal stair' for them. Lost children; stillborn and death; the loss and return of their prodigal daughter, Star Luna; and their three remaining fine children: Orelia, Selena and Hepburn. And their children. Who will have children to carry on the legacy of 'being who they are.'

"You see, Colt Culhane knew his birthright—he was a American, more so than most, and despite what they tried to do to him… chase him off this right and legal land, Colt Culhane blew them and the horses they rode in on to Kingdom Come. The waterfall and swimming hole were God and his ancestors' confirmation that he'd done the right thing. For him, his family to come…for us. He continued working on his inheritance. His legacy. What he had here on earth and how he'd leave his family -- provide and protect them, while here and after he's gone on to Glory. You take care of your family even in death. Especially after your death!"

"Amen!"

"Colt Culhane cared about everybody's children and, because he was on his own at such a young age, he gave back to others without being asked. Dr. Seth…. for one, and every lost boy who'd come here from a northern city in the summer who needed guidance, discipline, a change and a chance, Colt Culhane gave them a job in the summer as long as they kept their noses clean."

Mel thought of Slick Savoy from Chicago who broke her heart and, momentarily, wondered what ever became of him.

"Colt gave back," Reverend Gassaway continued. "And kept giving in his own way. He was a man's man." The

325

Revered uncharacteristically choked back tears as if recalling a kindness Colt had given him. "We all have memories of this man. May we all live a life as good as his. May we all acknowledge what a fine example of a man with a plan, a mission, a purpose, can achieve when *all* the odds are against him."

As the light filtered through Henley's steeple, the reverend chuckled, "I just imagine him now, telling St. Peter he wants to see the Lord. 'We got some issues to discuss.'"

The congregation chuckled.

"I'd love to be a fly on Heaven's cloud to hear that conversation."

The crowd laughed.

"He was not an easy man. He didn't suffer fools well. Had no patience for them. Was not a rescuer. Said he was like the Lord, '*I help those who help themselves.*' Got to meet him halfway before he'd even bother with you."

The congregation signified and nodded in agreement.

"Didn't have much use for church," Reverend Gassaway continued. "But he lived the Ten Commandments. He kept them better than most who come to church every Sunday. Nothing hypocritical about him. He calls 'em as he sees 'em. Never known him to run from a fight or back down from any issue. He was a righteous man. Rest in peace, Colt Culhane. Thank you for all you've done for us. You will be missed."

The choir stood and Reba Gassaway walked forward. TC cued up the organ and she began, "Precious Lord." His daughters Star and Selena offered their rendition of "Amazing Grace" to TC's bluesy organ, jazzing it up just the way his grandfather loved, like they were at the piano at the annual Culhane Christmas party. The congregation rocked in their seats as the sisters volleyed into "Old Rugged Cross," their perfectly blended voices reminding all who knew them in

326

times of fellowship years ago. The music Black Pony learned from Fancy's Saloon years ago now holy. The music of Papa Colt, Star and Selena … the trio of musicians in the family. At the end, not a dry eye remained in Mt. Moriah Gethsemane Baptist Church. A celebration of his life, Colt Culhane… sent home in a fashion he would approve.

Buried with his boys out back, all attendants smiled at the fact that they rode together again— high on a cloud somewhere in the western skies of heaven. Whooping it up. Even Keely had to smile at the thought. "See you after while," she whispered.

After a scrumptious repast was devoured, the mourners, including Orelia and Sam, left the church and their families returned to the house they still owned where one of the twins lived with her husband and family. This left only the Culhanes standing vigil on the front porch as Papa Colt did every night. Star left to check on the corral gate and the horses.

"I look at her and see Dad," Hep said to Selena.

"Spittin' image. She even walks like him," Selena replied.

"When you going back?"

"Tomorrow after the will is read. They'll be no surprises."

The next day, predictably, there were none. Papa Colt had set up trusts for all his grands including Keely Joy Peques, his newest addition; Jaz and Mel were the only ones not yet twenty-one. *And to my daughter, Star Luna Culhane, who has impressed me immensely since her return, I leave the operation of Cherokee Ranch. She has the aptitude, interest, skill and the love of this land and its equine and bovine inhabitants; the job is hers as long as she stays. While the house proper belongs to my loving wife Keely, and our four children; Orelia, Star, Selena and Hepburn, I hope Star continues to stay, run and live here as she has been. Then I may rest easy and run with my boys. Thank you for being my family. I loved you all.*

Later, Selena found her brother by the freshly turned grave.

"Can't believe he's gone," Hep said.

"I know." Selena looped her hand though her brother's arm as they both stared at the gravestone:

Colt Culhane
Beloved and devoted
husband, father, grandfather
1861-1966
Be who you are.

"What's that old saying, having a child is like having your heart outside your body?" Selena began. "As long as Star was out there in the world, Daddy was going to stay vigilant in case his daughter needed him. I didn't have children but I can imagine the comfort a parent has in knowing where they are and that they are safe and doing fine. Daddy died of happiness."

Hep looked evenly at her.

"Better than dying of a broken heart. Papa Colt had nothing more to hope or wish for—he truly had it all once Star came home... safe and sound and brought him another granddaughter to boot."

"He did have a contented smile on his face."

The next day, Hep watched his daughter and her boyfriend walk hand-in-hand up to the gravesite to visit Papa Colt. Hep swung around and looked straight into Selena's waiting eyes. "It's your fault," Hep accused his sister for encouraging his virginal daughter to live with her boyfriend in a love nest.

Selena let out a hearty laugh. "You give me too much credit." Selena gazed at the couple and lit her cigarette. "Jaz and Qwayz are a force of nature like a tornado. No human being can stop that." Selena took a drag from her cigarette. "May we all be so lucky."

"Humph," Hep scoffed, still trying to reconcile the situation.

"Intimately intense. They're young so it might burn itself out in law and med schools. Or it might last like Mama and Daddy 'until death do them part.' I do know you're fighting a losing battle. They're going on with or without you." She flicked her ashes. "Like I told Zack, as long as they each think the other is the best thing to ever happen to them, they'll be in love."

Hep remained silent.

"They'll be fine. If I were you I'd concentrate on Mel."

"What's wrong with Mel?" Hep's concern registered on his face. "She's dropped out of school, hasn't she? She was talking about doing that at my last visit."

"I guess they figure their Dad has done just fine without a college degree."

"These are different times and honorary degrees don't get it."

"You had your chance. Made your mistakes. Let them do the same."

"I didn't have the benefit of someone like me warning me about the world."

"When will you learn that you can't control your adult children?" She tapped him on the shoulder. "Ask Star."

~*~

"I understand you and your Dad had words," Selena mentioned to Jaz as she stood on the front porch spooning her new cousin Keely J's peach cobbler into her mouth.

"Humph, that girl put her foot in this." Jaz savored the last of the confection melting on her tongue, and continued, "He had words. I just listened to what he said and didn't say." She took a swig of ice cold water. "I think we're all right."

"That's good. You thinking of marriage?"

"No time soon. Qwayz and I haven't changed our plans. It's Dad who has to adjust. When we get married, we'll do so because we want to not because Dad wants it."

"How mature." Selena went to her niece and hugged her around the neck the way TC usually does. "That was a damned good answer." She kissed her niece's cheek.

"A piece of paper won't make me love Qwayz any more or any less. I've seen people who don't honor the license when they have it and others who don't have it but love with all their hearts and soul."

"Who you telling? That's why Zack and I never bothered."

"What?" Jaz's eyes grew wide.

Selena realized her slip of the tongue. "Oh hell. You grown now. You know about Hoyt? My first love. Like you and Qwayz."

"Yes."

"Well, after he passed, I wasn't thinkin' on ever fallin' for anyone again and Zack just came into my life. He was just a mentor when his wife showed up and showed out. She was premature but prophetic. Propinquity breeds familiarity and eventually we did begin dating. The wife reiterated that she was not giving Zack a divorce despite the fact they hadn't lived together in five years."

"Why'd she keep holding on?"

"She was nothing without being the great Zack 'The Sax' Fluellen's Mrs. So, we just went on lovin' and living our lives. Finally, embarrassed, she filed for the divorce. Then,"

330

Selena hunched her shoulders, "when we could, we didn't. Didn't need a license. A piece of paper."

"You'd never know."

"Well, you're the only one in the family who does. Not even your Dad knows. He's very traditional. Do or don't marry. I'll always love you, Jazzy…and Qwayz of course."

Everyone lingered around Cherokee Ranch for Keely, who seemed to be adjusting well and had to tell Star to stop doting on her; she wasn't an old woman yet. "Besides, I couldn't have asked for more," she often said. Hep and Lorette flew back to Italy, and slowly everyone went back to their respective lives.

TC returned to music-making at the studio and, by request, arranging for established stars and some groups. Mel confided to Jaz that she'd left Julliard and snagged the lead part in an off-Broadway musical and remained dead-up-in-love with "Hud," an already popular actor who changed his name to Hud, confiscated from a Paul Newman movie, and because it rhymed with Stud. *Hud the Stud,* Jaz thought. Mel seemed as in love as she and Qwayz. The only difference?

Mel was pregnant.

33

In a 'big man's game,' Quinton Regis Chandler wasn't quite six-feet tall, but every member of his team, opponents and the crowd were forced to watch and marvel at him whenever he took center court. He'd jump up from the knot of players, seemingly pause in mid-air and sink the ball into the basket, mesmerizing spectators. In response, the crowd paraphrased the lyric from the Marvelettes' song, "Qwayz must be a magician, he sure has the magic touch." "Rocket" Chandler at Roosevelt High evolved into "Magic" at Stanford. His power, speed and focus defied odds of much larger men. From his vantage point, he'd eye the hoop, spring up and arc the ball over the court, while some players tried to swat at its trajectory, others were forced to watch it drop from an out-of-reach curve before it landed—all net—through the metal hoop. On the rare occasion it hit the rim, Chandler would buck and catch his own rebound and sink it. Swish. On his way backup court. "Hustle and Flow," one reporter named him, but "Magic" stuck.

Jaz admired his intensity. Once he spotted her in the crowd, wriggled finger offered, he entered the basketball zone. He'd told her he never heard the crowd, what they are saying or calling him. He barked commands to his team, sometimes running backwards to watch the team scramble into position ready to accommodate any plays he sent their way. The power passes, no-look over the shoulder, between the legs—one had to be ready for whatever he was about to dish out. When interviewed, Magic always spoke of a team effort. Team work. Always "we." Never "I." "Teamwork makes the dream work," his favorite quote.

Although he had another year, Jaz wondered what activity he would use for his focused intensity once basketball was no longer a priority. Relieved he had this outlet she had only seen him lose his temper once. An out-of-control Qwayz unsettled her, but reaffirmed that he was only human after all.

They had been at the studio when Ma Vy called him home. He headed out with Jaz in tow and, upon arriving, for the first and only time, Jaz encountered a distraught Ma Vy. "A boy is coming to the house to get Hanie!" A confused Qwayz didn't understand until he saw his baby sister, who had apparently gone off to the movies with friends after getting into Denny's makeup. She looked fifteen. "Go wash that shit off your face," he commanded. Hanie burst into tears and flew up the steps to oblige just as the bell rang at the front door.

A door Jaz realized she'd never seen closed. The screen was always bolted but the wooden door lay open so you could see straight through from the front porch to the backyard. Not on this day.

Qwayz opened the door onto Hannibal, a known gang member. A flick of recognition passed between them. "Rocket Chandler," Hannibal identified, when Qwayz's face registered with him.

"Yeah?" Qwayz countered.

"I came for Hanie," he said, rotating a toothpick from one side of his lips to the other.

Qwayz coolly looked out at the guys littering his front yard. "A lot of fellas for one girl."

"Well, you know. These my boys."

"Not going to happen today or any other day," Qwayz said. "She's too young."

"Says you. I say she just 'bout right."

At that point Qwayz stepped out onto the porch, closing the wooden door behind him. Ma Vy sprang for the telephone.

"Listen…" Qwayz began. "I didn't get your name."

"Hannibal," he offered proudly. "Hannibal and Hanie. It goes."

"Mr. Hannibal, my baby sister is not coming out or dating anybody for quite some time. So why don't you and your 'boys' vacate the premises."

Hannibal's eyes flashed heat. "I ain't going no place without her."

Qwayz's eyes bore into Hannibal's. "Hanie," Qwayz called to her.

The door creaked open and Hanie stood by her big brother's side. "This is my sister Hanie. She's twelve."

A visibly shocked Hannibal was taken aback at her freshly washed face.

"Seems to me you'd want a woman, not a little girl." Qwayz could tell this joker was about to say something stupid, even obscene regarding her virginity to save face, and big brother readied his fist for a fight.

Just then two police cars screeched to a halt, one jack-knifing to the curb as Truck McMillan lit from the opening door. "Well, what have we here? A meeting of the Gladiators?" He eyed each, taking a mental roll call. "A few missing. Oh yeah. They're in juvie. Aren't you on probation, Purvis?"

The boys snickered at the use of the name his mama gave him.

"I see the head honcho is here. Junebug. What's up?" Truck crossed his arms over his chest. "When did you get out?"

"Yesterday."

"And what you came over for tea? You a little far from home. Watts is over that way. Jail is that way. Either way, you're in the wrong neighborhood and white folks don't like you all straying."

"Later for all this shit," Hannibal spat. "Lil' girl ain't worth it." He cut his eyes. "Let's bounce."

"Not so fast," Truck ordered. "That house is a friend of the precinct. A hard-working mother and three good kids live there. My daughter comes to visit. If anything happens to any member of this household or that white Corvair, or red car, I'm coming for you first and then your boys. Locking you up six ways to Sunday until we figure it all out. Might take a week or two, you all know how that works, but I'm sure the boys in lockup will be real accommodating."

"That's harassment!" Junebug objected.

"Is it? So, if I were you I'd take real good care that nothing happens to these law-abiding folks."

Defiant silence.

"Did you hear me or do you want me to repeat it?" Truck loud-talked him

"I hear you, man."

"Good day," Truck dismissed.

While Truck went to speak to Ma Vy, Qwayz sought refuge in the corner of his front porch. Jaz touched his shoulder and he reeled around with such force and fury in his eyes, Jaz didn't recognize him. He grabbed and held her. His heart beating fast against hers.

Hanie came out onto the porch and ran to her brother. "What were you thinking, Stephanie Chandler?" he asked sternly.

"I'm sorry. I'm sorry," she sobbed. "Are they coming back?"

"I dunno," he lied, knowing that if they valued their freedom they wouldn't jeopardize it for a twelve-year-old girl.

"Do you still love me?"

"Always." He bent down to her level. "But that doesn't mean I like your behavior."

She looked into his caring eyes. This time not mad that he had the hazel and hers were just plain black. "Thank you, Qwayz. I love you."

"I apologize for cursing at you," he said.

"It's OK. I still love you; although, I didn't like your behavior," Hanie teased.

"Don't be in such a hurry to grow up." She shook her head in agreement. "Go rinse your face."

Jaz realized what a good father he would be. Qwayz took Jaz into his arms and held her again. His heart beat back to normal.

"Kinda like the rescue from the party in the Boondocks," he teased.

"I was older and had a friend," Jaz defended. "And you loved me."

"Not then. You ruined my date with Cherish Harley."

"Define 'date?'"

Qwayz went inside and Ma Vy came out on the porch and sat with Jaz. "That was enough excitement to last me for years." She fanned herself and offered, "Had two hot-headed men both name Quinton in my life, neither built for backing down. When men grow up without a father, the boy doesn't really know how to be a man. I love my son but I can't teach him how to be a man. Sometimes they go too far, other times, not far enough, but then he adopts surrogates. My boy picked good ones: Big Aubrey, Coach Culhane, Sensei Akira, a couple of teachers and formed good friendships with like-minded boys. My boy did good in all departments, plus he picked a girl who loves him. That's a win-win situation."

Jaz blushed.

"You know I think I'll make some blaff and bread pudding."

"I know who'd love that," Jaz said.

"Hey, Aunt Jaz," AJ greeted excitedly as he claimed the seat next to Jaz, bringing her back to the Midas vs. Magic game. Melie, Ma Vy, Hanie and Dr. Aubrey grabbed nearby seats. TC sat across the way. Z, Jaxson, Rudy, Raw Cilk, the Roosevelt High crew, and boys from the neighborhood rounded out the raucous cheering section while Tracey and Scoey waved.

"Is that Midas?" AJ asked Jaz. "Number 33? He doesn't look so tough."

"Can you believe we're here tonight for the Stanford/Tulane NCAA Championship, Bert?" Those who couldn't get tickets listened to the transmitted commentary. "An unlikely pair in this sellout crowd, here at the Sports Arena. 16,161 seats all occupied. This will go down in the annals of basketball history for many years to come. Stanford hasn't been here since 1942—Magic Chandler brought them here at the Sports Arena in L.A. today."

"A tribute to two outstanding college athletes who got their teams here today…that's Magic and Midas. Has all the hype… The Russell and Chamberlain of college circuit."

"Neither of these boys intends to go pro despite their phenomenal ability. They're relatively small men in todays' game when the players are 6'8'' and 7 footers. But the big-guys don't rack up an average of 25-30 points a game like Magic and Midas."

"Where's he going next year?"

"Magic Chandler has another year. Midas is graduating going to grad school. Princeton. You know that this is the first time in NCAA history that the five starter-players have all been Negro?"

Jaz, elated that she couldn't hear the inane banter of the commentators, helped AJ put on the Stanford T shirt which fell below his knees. "Traffic is a monster," Denny said, leaning in to kiss AJ's cheek, "Hey, Sweetie. "

"Congrats Denny. A master's degree. I've never had a friend to get one of those."

"Guess what else?"

"Yudi's coming home?"

"I wish. He hates it over there. I can tell. He's keeping his spirits up for me."

"That's what loved ones do. So, what then?"

"I've been offered a fellowship to get my doctorate."

"Oh, Denny!" The two friends' squeals went unnoticed in the basketball melee.

"Thanks. It'll help keep my mind off of what is happening to my man in Vietnam."

The crowd jumped up when they introduced the Stanford team. Jaz held her heart at the sight of her man. Number 24. After all this time, she still got a rush every time she saw him. He raised his arms, smiled at the crowd, did the finger-thumb gesture with TC and pointed at Jaz, wriggled his index finger and winked and entered his zone. Let the games begin…

Time sped like sand through a sieve. A flurry of activity, sneakers squeaking on court, the thwack of the basketball, and the roar of the crowd. Players sprinting up and down the court flinging sweat and talking trash. Qwayz and Midas traded shots for shots. Qwayz stole the ball from Stovall took it down court, pulled up… swish. All net. "That boy can shoot from anywhere!" the commentator spoke of Qwayz.

338

With time on the clock running out, Midas stood back ready to accept the pass from Stovall to stuff it in the basket, hoping for overtime. Qwayz blocked it, the buzzer sounded and Midas sunk to his knees, pounded the floor once, sprang up and jogged off court. Stanford triumphed over Tulane 110 to 108; Great game and no spectator disappointed. Throngs of folks waited for the emergence of Magic and Midas who spent easily over 45 minutes signing autographs while answering reporters' questions. Qwayz beamed at the sight of Jaz and slung his arm protectively around her as they waded through folks who congratulated and back-slapped him with all kinds of positive comments while the couple made their grand maneuver "outta here."

Qwayz and Midas approached each other from opposite ends of the lobby and Jaz watched the dance of the warriors as they walked nearer to one another. Two prized black men, tops in their athletic fields who baffled media by not making basketball their life choice. Two black guys who didn't know each other but respected one another's ability and prowess despite the rivalry the press tried to create between them. Magic and Midas maintained an unspoken covenant of privacy, keeping their interviews positive and dignified unlike their pedantic boxing counterpart, Muhammad Ali, who sought the limelight and self-promotion, or even football contemporary of UCLA, Jesse Ramsey, who had won the Heisman trophy in his sophomore year with talk of earning another one.

Jaz witnessed the jock "Hello." The reverse nod that begins low in the chin and jerks up. "Good game," they shook hands in passing, never stopping.

"Humph. Humph. Humph," Stovall said to Midas. "Did you see that, man?" he referred to the girl on Magic's arm with the brown fedora hat and crazy-phat legs.

"Hard to miss. A stone-fox," Midas agreed.

"New Orleans got no monopoly on fine ladies."

"No jive-jack," they slapped five as their eyes led to more black beauties ahead. "California girls."

But Midas back-glanced Jaz, who did not reciprocate as she walked off with Magic. *Doesn't seem quite right. Won the game and the girl,* Midas thought with a smile. "Right on, my brother."

34

On a typical, Northern California, sunny, spring day, five black women strode across campus to hear a speech to the Black Student Union by Dr. Martin Luther King, Jr. orchestrated by the now graduated but still fine ex-president of the organization, Solomon Noble. Like a breath of fresh air amid a bland, arid landscape, the five black students presented a hue-spectrum that amazed and confused most non-black students. They formed a sorority of sorts, not like the one Gladys Ann had pledged at Howard University with their pink and green colors, but one of similar souls and sisterhood. On one end was Farrell from New Orleans, who had taken Jaz's old dorm room, with fair skin, brunette hair and green eyes; next was sandy-colored haired Sloane, who was going home this summer to help with her father's second bid for mayor of Atlanta; Jaz in the middle, the natural bronzy skin deepened by the California sun; then came the browner Hilson, who had donned a beret to cover her natural at her father's swearing in ceremony as judge so that people thought she was a Black Panther; and last, but not least, CC. She and Jaz continued their heated arguments about her choice of beaus. CC, the darkest yet the most free, as the depth of her skin color represented the height of her perceived exemption from it. "It's no biggie," CC dismissed.

"This on the way to see Martin Luther King who sat-in, marched and was beaten up by whitey and you are fraternizing with the enemy. The oppressor's son!" Jaz ranted.

"I'm living his dream. Total integration. Dr. King marched so I can date whomever I please," CC countered. "We all can't get a guy like Qwayz."

Jaz's face split into a wide grin. "He's coming home tonight and we're going to Paradise Rock tomorrow."

"Ah, I get it…," CC said. "He's the Paradise with the rock-hard—"

"Something like that," Jaz interrupted. "You are so horny."

Qwayz'd gone down to play in a fundraiser exhibition game in Watts for AJ's school and the press still hounded him trying to start a rivalry between him and Midas. Qwayz gave no satisfaction, only saying "That game is over, man. Move on." So desperate for a story on him, a one-pager in *Sports Illustrated* entitled, "A Boy and his Dog," displayed a picture of Qwayz and Akira walking on Stanford's empty campus with a rehash of old info. Qwayz, livid at the invasion of privacy and the reference to him as 'boy,' barked, "This rival thing can't be over soon enough."

As they lay on the hassock roasting marshmallows for s'mores in their fireplace, Jaz asked, knowing her man and the answer. "Spring break. What do you want Napa or—"

"I want Paradise Rock. It's been too long and we won't run into anyone there."

Driving to Paradise Rock with Akira in tow, the couple spoke of how quickly the time was flying: He already registered for his LSATs. Jaz registered for her two summer classes, neither math nor science, but art history and architecture which she found inspiring, challenging and fun. She massaged the nape of Qwayz's neck as he drove, and he shared with her how he liked that she and Mel spoke regularly as well Selena, Keely and Star.

"They are family," Jaz said.

"Who are you?" He teased.

"The love of your life. I'm maturing."

After lending his voice to the Temptations' "My Girl," and "So Much In Love" by the Tyme, together they sang "You're All I Need To Get By," their voices blending perfectly; after which Qwayz informed her, "Jesse Ramsey is going to get his second Heisman trophy and is marrying Cherish Harley. What a pair. Both our exes. I wonder if they take turns being us?"

"You are so crazy!" she laughed then said, "Uh-oh," as he took the turn onto Ruidoso Canyon Road.

"What?"

"It's not good when they start naming streets. Architecture 101."

Sure enough they rounded the curve and paused at the paved driveway on which a house sat on their secluded rock. "How long has it been?"

"Apparently, too long," Qwayz said and drove up to the house like he owned it.

"Where are you going?"

"No one's home. At our home."

He hopped out of the car and peered through the sliding-glass doors. "Good googa mooga," he remarked of the interior.

Jaz looked through the other plate glass as Qwayz slid open the door.

"What are you doing?"

"Watts 101. C'mon."

Jaz couldn't resist the temptation as they stepped into the almost complete but empty house. "Get a load of this."

Standing on the floor they looked over at the floor-to-ceiling, split-rock white stone fireplace that sparkled in the sunlight and plunged into a sunken living room with built-in circular-seating.

"This is gorgeous," said Jaz, still awed by the living room, when she heard Qwayz call from a hallway. "Check this out." Jaz walked on the tiled floor through a short hallway and into the one bedroom with another sliding glass door revealing the fabulous scene. They became mesmerized by the tide coming in, crashing wildly against the rocks below before whirling with the outgoing water. The ebb and flow, like life itself. "I bet our star shines from right up there at night."

"We could lie in bed and watch it shimmer, assuring us everything is alright and telling us goodnight. We could write our names across the heavens after we make love."

"C'mon." Back out in the alcove he opened a door to the left onto another magnificent view of the angry sea below. On a raised pedestal platform sat a luxurious tub. "Can you imagine the things we could do in there without anyone seeing?"

"These views are magnificent. The architect took full advantage."

"Except setting that carport right out there."

"It obstructs nothing and they'll need a place for their cars."

In the alcove, a linen closet, another closet and the open kitchen with the basics, a little window over the sink and a back door, stood ready. Around the corner, a small area reserved for dining and the front door behind the mammoth fireplace and back around to the sliding doors through which they had come.

A threesome on the outside of the doors startled them and Qwayz slid open the door.

"Nice but a little small for us," he said to them, walking through holding Jaz's hand. "I suppose the search goes on, Lovey."

He opened the car door for her as Akira hopped in the back. He rounded the hood of Red's, got in, started her up and they spirited down the driveway leaving the trio baffled.

Jaz laughed at his audacity. "Gotta act like you belong, girlie," he said.

"Just keep an eye on the rearview mirror for the cops," she added.

"Naw," he drove further down beach but found nothing that rivaled Paradise Rock. "Damn! I never thought of it. I should have bought it. The land at least. So private, secluded… we could always build on it later."

"Like after law and med school?" She reached over and fingered the curls around his kitchen.

"We'll always have Napa or Carmel."

"And Myrtle Beach."

~*~

"Hey handsome. Welcome home," Jaz greeted Qwayz, coming in from a run with Akira.

He started shedding his clothes. "Bubble bath! Just what I needed."

"Ewww," Jaz protested until his manhood presented itself and she thought better of it.

"Don't you like me sweaty, girlie." He kissed her on the lips as he lowered himself into the claw foot tub.

"Only when I am the cause of the sweat," she sassed.

"We can work on that, too." He let his magnificent body become absorbed by pink bubbles. "I don't mind that you get your sweat working with the Panthers."

"Really?"

345

"Let me rephrase that. Volunteering with them." He put his legs on either side of her body. "How was it today?"

"Great. Too bad the Panthers don't get the credit they deserve for their breakfast program or the school. The kids are wonderful. They missed Akira today."

"It's good, you go when you can."

"I'll start doing more when you're otherwise occupied and not home."

"You mean when CC can get ahold of you on a Saturday morning."

"That too," Jaz smiled. "She was right though. Huey Newton is brilliant."

"Think they'll get back together?"

"No, they definitely have different agendas now," Jaz said of the old lovers.

"We've got to plan something super-special for this Valentine's Day," Qwayz posed as he pulled her toward him. "I'm graduating and will be in law school next year this time."

"Big time Stanford senior now." Jaz flicked his bottom lip with her tongue and began kissing him. "Speaking of which, Selena called to find out your graduation date. They'll be headlining at the Monterey Pop Festival from the 16-18th and are deciding whether to stay here when she comes in May for your graduation or go home and come back. Said we might want to come this year. Besides her and Dizzy Gillespie, they'll be other 'pop' acts."

"Anybody we know?"

"She didn't have specifics yet. Otis Reading and somebody named Hendrix."

"That's May-June. Back to Valentine's Day."

"I must finish my South Hall model for Stress of Material II class."

"It looks good to me."

346

"Maybe I should have opted for the paper instead of doing the three-dimensional model."

"You must be enjoying it."

She smiled in answer. "It's a nice diversion from math and science."

He reared back and restated, yet again, "If I'd bought Paradise Rock, we could go there for Valentine's Day."

"We didn't and we have Alta Vista. We do fabulous things here. I love it. S'mores and popcorn in our fireplace before and after our romantic interludes—"

"When did you fall so in love with this place?"

She sank back against the cool porcelain of the tub. "When I came home from class that day and you were perched on the hearth wearing nothing but a smile, stroking Amber."

"Yeah." His face broke into a huge grin. "I remember that."

"I knew this was home because you had Amber here instead of in L.A. or your dorm room."

"We do have good times, don't we?"

"We do and will…"

"Unlike Mel. She's had a couple of scares but apparently this time is for real."

"Seems like they need a better form of birth control. Two free spirits. One better get a clue."

"She told Dad, so that ship has sailed. It didn't go to well. I'm not surprised. "

"What'd he say?"

"Nothing to me. She's moved in with Hud now."

"Your poor father. Maybe we'll only have boys. You girls are giving your Pops the blues."

"Star isn't. She and Mama Keely are still going strong. Keely-J sees Selena frequently and is doing well with her culinary efforts. Got an apprenticeship with the chef she wanted. I don't know enough to be impressed."

"That's good."

"Grandma Fern refused to go to Italy with Lorette after Papa Javier passed last year. She didn't mind Connecticut or D.C. but she won't be leaving the country."

"I guess your Dad is happy about that."

"I don't think he's home enough to notice. From what I hear you don't know who's in that big-ass house from moment to moment." She looked at Qwayz. "Promise me that we'll never have a huge house. I want you always only a touch away."

"Yeah. Like Paradise Rock!"

"Ah! Cheeze Louise! Enough already—" Jaz climbed out of the tub. "Let it go!"

"Hey, where you goin?" Qwayz watched her nude form disappear around the corner.

~*~

Denny peered out of the window of their Del Amo Hills home into the bleak night as she had for the last three evenings. Absently, she touched her still tender but no longer swollen cheek, as the vigil for Yudi's returned proved futile. Instead of a blissfully happy early discharge, Yudi had drawn her into a limbo of sleepless nights and foggy days. The husband she had kissed goodbye less than seven months ago was not the man who returned. She expected a period of adjustment but, besides his looks, the man was a stranger. He didn't like going out, preferred the blinds drawn during the day while the television watched him. At night he paced back and forth and when exhaustion claimed him, he fell into a restless, fitful sleep full of guttural screams. He couldn't go on like this, not eating or sleeping, staying house-bound not getting help.

348

The stark reality caught up with them three nights ago when Denny asked Yudi how he wanted his steak prepared. Yudi focused on the glistening bloody knife in her hand, crouched and cowered in the corner before springing up and knocking her hard across her face. In a millisecond, he pinned her down and retrieved the knife, its steely edge poised against her throat. Unable to scream, she closed her eyes to accept her fate when Yudi recognized her. He backed away crying, apologizing and chanting "I'm sorry, I'm sorry, I'm sorry. I could have killed you." He shoved things into a duffel bag, ran from the house, leaving the door wide-open. His inner pain and turmoil evident to his wife who expected him to come home any day.

At the hospital where she'd done her master's practicum Denny sat in on a group of Vietnam vets, bitter, angry, confused, lost and frustrated about their treatment upon their return. These vets had seen combat, so Denny sought out a veteran who worked Grave to Registration like Yudi. Hank considered himself lucky as his G&R unit was bombed, he lost a leg and was sent home but he described the horrors of unzipping the black, plastic body bags not knowing what you would find. The sight. The smell. Cleaning partial bodies, limbs, sometimes only bones where the flesh had either rotted away in that devil-hot sun or eaten by wild animals.

"Sometimes the pieces didn't match...a black head with a white torso. Mostly the decaps were the worse," Hank recounted. "The heads the gooks sliced off and spiked to a tree as their calling card—you prayed folks back home wouldn't open the casket to find we didn't have enough body parts to send back. Hoping they just took the dog tags and personal effects and let the brother rest in peace. So, it don't matter that your man worked at a funeral home... I guarantee it didn't

349

prepare him for any of that." He fell silent and Denny's eyes filled with helpless tears. "Being isolated is bad, too. No one wants to hang out with you. They call you 'Dr. Death.' Your hands up to your elbows turn white from the chemicals, so even when you're off-duty...they know what you do. It's gruesome and grisly. Inhuman. The whole damn war is inhumane."

On the drive back home Denny had thought it couldn't get any worse than their first love-making attempt. Right after TC and Qwayz sang "Daddy's Home" a cappella to him, Yudi's eyes turned distant and strange so Denny cut his Welcome Home Party short, making excuses that Yudi was tired. On the third night when she put on her filmy pink negligee from Qwayz and Jaz–"a gift for both of you"–Denny had made undeniable advances, anticipating a tender homecoming rendezvous. He'd reacted... violently. After trying to avoid her gentle kisses, he swooped over upon her, his heavy body covering hers, his hot breath panting into her tearful face, until satisfied. He rolled off of her and slept on the floor where he continued to sleep until the day he drew the knife and walked out. "I can't stay here," he whispered. "I love you but I can't stay with you. It's no good." She'd asked Hank if Yudi would return to her.

"Dunno. Can't say yes. Can't say no."

35

Jaz walked Qwayz over to the School of Architecture lobby and there in the atrium on prominent display stood her model of South Hall. "Tah-dah!" she exclaimed to him.

"You won? First place? That's my girl!" He grabbed and hugged her. "Congratulations!"

"The first non-architecture student to ever win!' I understand there is now a petition that future winners must be an architecture student. Thank you."

"Thank me?"

"I had a boyfriend who had twenty-some games a year and left me time to devote to the meticulousness of it."

"Thank you," he said in return. "I loved watching you perched over the blueprints, rear-end poised mid-air; a pencil in your teeth, one in your hair and one in your hand…and the loving that resulted from those visuals."

"I guess we're a perfect match, huh." She kissed him quick on the lips.

"Let's celebrate at the Purple Hippo."

"Great idea." Jaz took one more lap around her model with the Blue-Ribbon flapping the breeze, grabbed Qwayz's proffered elbow and they sauntered out of the door. On their way back home, they passed the property of the future Culhane Enterprises. Once at their place, Akira beat them both to the top of the stairs and ran in first when the door opened.

Later that evening, Qwayz said, "Basking time is over. You'd better pick up that Advanced Anatomy book for tomorrow."

"And what will you be doing?"

"Right beside you with my LSAT prep."

"You decided on Stanford or Berkeley Law School?"

Qwayz redirected her without speaking. She climbed onto the sofa, assuming the study-mode posture; each with their backs at opposite ends of the couch, facing each other with only their calves touching. They managed to study for about an hour before Jaz cleared her throat and Qwayz began massaging her ankle absently. Once he turned his page, he put his book down and took her foot in his hand and began kneading… his thumbs middle up, over the instep toward the toes. Jaz tried to ignore him but this was foreplay to her. She opened the top of her blouse and began rubbing her upper chest… hoping some of the heat generated there would evaporate. She feigned reading without looking at him her thighs falling slightly open. Nothing could be seen through the jeans, but Qwayz knew what the denim covered. Jaz shot a sexy glance at him…honey on hazel and he was on her in a millisecond.

"You devil."

"You tease."

They laughed and kissed. Akira yawned.

"I got it. What we can do for Valentine's Day."

"What?"

"How about we get married?" He rolled back to his side of the sofa taking Jaz with him. Their eyes never left one another's.

She searched for a trace of playfulness, yet wanted him to be serious. Or did she? All kinds of emotions danced in her head but her gaze remained steady as she said, "All in due time."

"No time like the present."

"I think there are a few other things we can do to make this Valentine's Day super-special."

"Name one better than that."

"You are joking, aren't you?"

"Serious as a heart attack." He brushed hair out of her face. "Why not?"

"Why... now?"

"What would be different from the way we live now, except we'll be legal. Have a license."

"Exactly. Why do we need that?"

"'Cause I want the security of it. It's a crazy world out there, Jaz—assassination of a president. Medgar Evers shot in the back in his driveway in '63, riots in major cities, can't get through Sproul Hall without war protesters, police killing blacks in the streets and getting away with murder. It's an uncertain world these sixties. Totally violent and out of control. But you and me? We're golden. You are my safe haven and somewhere in the annals of history I want it written that despite all the lunacy swirling around us, we loved one another enough to commit forever." His eyes twinkled as he tucked his sexy bottom lip under even white teeth. "Life is short and true love is rare. What are we waiting for? My heart is yours—forever—if you want it."

"You are a diehard romantic and a puzzle, Quinton Regis Chandler. In a time when people are 'shacking up' and running from responsibilities including marriage, you want to jump in?"

"I do. And I hate that term 'shackin' up.' That does not and never will apply to us. I've never been one to go along with the okey-doke. Isn't that why you love me?"

"One of the reasons," Jaz gyrated against him.

"Hey, don't change the subject. What do you say? Is it a date?"

Jaz looked at him sideways and teased, "Are you pregnant?" They both laughed and then fell silent. A foghorn from the bay below bellowed and also waited for her answer.

353

"Girls like you make guys like me consider marriage. For me the search is over. I need to look no further. Like I always say, you are not perfect but you are perfect for me. Together—imperfectly perfect; made for each other. What you don't know, I can teach you, grasshopper."

"Oh, really?"

"Or should I say, what you don't know you make up for with innovation and pure enthusiasm."

She play-pinched his side.

"Seriously, whether we marry now, two or five years from now what is the difference? There is no reason for us not to. I cannot imagine my world without you in it. I'm asking you to share my life. I want Jasmine C. Chandler on the mailbox downstairs. 'Baby, it's you,'" he sang like the very first time on Papa Colt's porch.

Jaz smiled.

"I don't want to lie to our children that we lived together for years before we got married."

A speechless Jaz melted into his hazel gaze.

"I figure you can wear that Victorian tea dress from Heirlooms and we can drive to Vegas and marry in one of those 'tasteful' chapels."

They chuckled.

"TC could be my best man, Denny, your matron of honor and our parents—"

Jaz bristled and said, "I don't think my father would want his nineteen-year-old daughter marrying—"

"You'll be twenty by February," he interjected then fell silent and listened as it was the first time she seemed to consider the proposition. He thought Hep would like having one of his daughters marry, but Jaz knew he wasn't doing any of this for Coach C.

354

"Maybe we can keep everything status quo with the parents and marry for them later after we graduate… Do it up big time."

"Renew our vows in '69," Qwayz mused. "Go to Italy on our honeymoon."

"Sounds good to me, Quinton Regis. I'd be honored to be your legitimate and legal wife. 'Til death do us part." He brushed his lips across hers and she devoured them hungrily.

"We'll write our own vows," he said excitedly. "Invite TC, Denny, Scoey and Tracy—"

"Swearing them to secrecy," Jaz interrupted, thinking she would have to tell Gladys Ann, even invite her but her friend hadn't been back to L.A. since high school graduation.

"Wait, that's a yes?"

She shook her head as he wrestled himself from beneath her, exiting into the bedroom and returning with the Victorian tea dress.

"You devil," she said, running toward the beautiful frock.

"I know it fits. The right color, ecru and not white," he smirked playfully.

"Pretty sure of yourself." Jaz rolled her eyes in mock-disgust.

"I am sure I love you with all my heart, Jaz-of-mine. I just hoped you felt the same way."

His words dissolved her reserve and tears eked from her eyes. She watched him sink to one knee.

Qwayz took her hand and said, "Jasmine Bianca Culhane I want to spend the rest of my natural born days loving, caring and protecting you. Will you do me the honor of becoming my wife for the rest of your life?"

"Yes," Jaz sniffled. Like the Magic that was his nickname, Qwayz whipped out a small velvet box and a solid gold cigar band ring shimmered against the rays of the last twilight.

"This was going to be the wedding band. I thought we'd pick out the engagement ring together. But in view of it being a secret... I think this one could pass before a diamond solitaire would. Tell your Dad I got it to match the cuff bracelet."

"My man. You think of everything."

"I love you, Jaz." She planted kisses all over his face. "Afterwards we can have our initials carved into them."

"Mine will be the same. So, I'll have yours carved into mine...QRC."

"And I'll wear yours."

"I've peeked behind the curtain, Jaz. Know what I saw?"

"The wizard?"

"Us. Forever. That's all I want from you—forever."

~*~

Family, friends and neighbors enjoyed a wonderful Christmas in Colt, Texas, festive as it could be without Papa Colt, but his presence roamed everywhere. In the heritage relics on the mammoth fireplace, in the flip he'd always prepared for his boys and in the essence of the music TC played and Star and Selena sang. Jaz watched her father's face exude pure happiness while his reunited sisters sang. Keely-J had gone to see her father, Pax Peques, at his New York apartment before joining her mother at Cherokee Ranch. Like Jaz, Keely-J's voice was also exceptional but she had no interested in pursuing a singing career. Mel, with her petite frame, was hardly showing. She came alone and left early, having to return to her role in the off-Broadway play. As a gift, Aunt Selena gave Jaz and Qwayz a photo album with "Young and in Love" stenciled on its cover. Inside, all the pictures from the Malibu summer and Paris, France and a couple of

356

rolls Zack developed that Qwayz'd left behind. One with Jaz and her Aunt Selena napping in the hammock at Chateau Jazz stirred her memory. "What a treasure. Thank you, Aunt Selena."

Once Qwayz and Jaz quietly shared their news with TC and Mel; the elated best man sprang into action, taking his position seriously. TC changed the venue from gaudy Las Vegas to classy Lake Tahoe and set about planning an exquisite wedding for his best guy and best girl. It took some doing, but TC convinced Denny to go up for one night and volunteered to personally drive her back the next day, so if Yudi chose that date to return, she would be there. Once Akira settled in with AJ in L.A., all the pieces of their "happily ever after" were in place.

Now, as Reds snaked behind the black van to the Tahoe Regal, they sang all the way; Raw Cilk songs, old and new, then "You're All I Need," "You're My Everything," "Stand by Me," "Reach Out," "This Magic Moment" and anything else that came into their happy hearts.

TC orchestrated all the chapel arrangements, musical selections, and reserved all the rooms for the guys and girls, a suite for the dinner reception and the bridal suite for the honeymoon night, boutonnieres for Qwayz and Scoey's tuxes, and nosegays for Denny and Tracy's gowns. To augment her favorite perfume, Jungle Gardenia, Qwayz ordered a bridal bouquet of the fragrant flowers for his bride with a matching crown to rim her cascading hair.

While Denny and Tracy were radiant in their gowns, Jaz glowed in the tiered, ecru Victorian tea dress with the leg 'o mutton sleeves and the Juliet points. She walked toward Qwayz on a cloud of hopes and a headful of innocent dreams to Nat King Cole's "Too Young" then "Al di La" from "Rome

Adventure." Jaz smiled at TC for remembering. Qwayz held out his hand and Jaz slipped hers into his as she had done a thousand times. TC winked and Scoey smiled unabashedly. Handing off her bouquet, the minister began his words that meant little to anyone in the wedding party. Then it was time for the vows from the bride and groom.

"Jasmine Bianca Culhane," Qwayz began, as the love they felt in their hearts pushed up into their eyes, honey on hazel. "In this coo-coo crazy world out there, I needed someone special by my side. I can take anything this world has to dish out as long as I get to come home to you. All the negativity, all the press, all the nay-sayers—none of it matters more than you and me. You are my sanity, my refuge. My joy. The reason I want to do or be. There is no life for me without you. Twenty years from now we'll regret the things we did not do. I don't want to regret not making you my wife when I could. I could not conceive of any other woman alive who could make me feel the way you do. No one fills my heart, my mind, my soul or my hands like you."

Jaz blushed.

"No one better for me but you. I once told you to 'Be who you are.' But remember whose you are. You are mine, Jaz-of-mine and I am yours. We belong together. Now and forever. I love you."

He kissed her prematurely and everyone laughed, TC through tears.

"Jaz," the minister prompted.

"When you told me of your new feelings for me on Papa Colt's porch, I was both shocked and disgusted. Then my entire life changed with just one kiss. Finally, I rationalized that if the great Quinton Regis Chandler wants to date me in his senior year, I can do that until he moves on to the next girl. But you never did. Instead you proved to me each and every

358

day that I was the one. Worthy. Equal too. Not perfect, but perfect for you. You made me feel I can do anything. I belong to you and you belong to me. You will always be my FLO, Quinton Regis Chandler. As long as I live you will always be my First. Last. and Only love. I trust you and what I love most about you is that you say what you mean and mean what you say. Honesty. I know you'll both be there by my side, and be there to catch me if I fall. You are my man and I love you.

"From this moment on we'll go down in history as husband and wife… for our children and grandchildren and great-grands and on through our Chandler-Culhane legacy. We'll be together for as long as we both shall love."

"We don't know what the future holds for us, Jaz-of-mine. But together we can handle anything," Qwayz concluded with another spontaneous kiss on the lips.

The minister resumed his role and the couple exchanged rings, Qwayz surprising Jaz with a single band of diamonds to crown her cigar band.

"It's beautiful." Jaz held out her hand.

Qwayz chuckled. "This is where our happy ending begins."

Pronounced "husband and wife," they both laughed into each other's arms as the minister finally decreed, "You may kiss the bride."

Raw Cilk's first hit "Just the Two of Us," followed by "When I'm With You," and the one they sang to each other, "Destination Paradise," played softly in the background as they hugged one another and their friends right at the altar. They sauntered back up the aisle, and Qwayz cocked his head and suggested, "Listen."

Johnny Mathis sang "Twelfth of Never," and they both recalled the night he surprised his now wife, strumming Amber on the hearth of Alta Vista wearing nothing but a smile.

Scoey snuck out to tie cans to Reds, missing out on a few pictures from the photographer; which were re-taken with him present. They all drove back to the Tahoe Regal where they dined on filet mignon and lobster. TC tapped his glass to get everyone's attention. "As best man and brother of the bride," he began.

"You were brother of the bride first," Jaz clarified with a smirky-smile.

"Be nice Mrs. Chandler," TC said, "No secret I didn't like the cocky little curly-head boy. Mainly of course, because he didn't like me. Or he didn't care who I was or who my father, the coach, was. He was good."

"Thank you," Qwayz toasted.

"Got my goat but good. I knew back then he was a righteous cat. Years younger than us," he looked at Scoey. "But he kept up with us in every way but I knew, like we all do, that when he found 'the one,' she was going to have to be really special and one lucky somebody."

"Never thought it'd be your sister," Scoey teased.

"True that. I never thought I'd see that. Intially shocked, I wasn't sure how to feel about it. My Brother From Another Mother and my sister? That's ain't right," TC said, pouring Denny the last of the champagne, signaling the waiter for more. "But slowly... I saw there was no other way. If I could find what they both had...well, that'd be a stone groove. That's what everyone wants but few have."

"We have, Babe, don't we?" Scoey kissed Tracy on the nose.

"Well, you are lucky. I've seen folks marry, have children and still don't have what you all have. Never lose it!" TC

360

raised his flute for another toast. "I love you both!" he sipped again. "As a matter of fact, I love you all!"

"When did you know?" Denny wondered.

TC thought then replied, "When I first saw them at Oasis dancing to 'Save the Last Dance for Me.' Showstoppers. I knew it was more than just the usual Qwayz and Jaz pairing up as dance partners. I saw something else."

"It was love," Qwayz pronounced and kissed his wife.

"When you all hit a bump in that road. And you will— two stubborn, headstrong individuals like yourselves, are gonna have some times. But you will handle them together. Always look out to the future with the same view. Shared goals."

After dessert and after dinner aperitifs, TC dangled the bridal suite keys in front of the guests of honor. Qwayz lunged for them. "My wife and I are retiring to our boudoir to consummate our nuptials. You all are not invited but thanks for coming. That's what I intend to do now. Over and over—"

"Qwayz!" Jaz reprimanded her slightly tipsy husband.

The newlyweds staggered toward their suite, Jaz not realizing how much alcohol she'd consumed until she stood and the room swayed. After a few attempts to put the key in the lock, finally success. The door opened and Qwayz whooshed Jaz up in his arms, leaning against the doorjamb for support. Both sobered by the opulence of the decor. "Wow! TC don't play," Qwayz teetered into the room running with Jaz in his arms and falling on the round bed. They both flopped and stayed where they lay. Barely moving they looked up at the ceiling and said simultaneously, "Beams!"

Sloane, CC and Farrell spent the weekend with Jaz and Akira while Qwayz played an away game and thumbed through the photo album from Selena again.

"Umph. You and Qwayz are so selfish," CC proclaimed. "You all are too good looking for each other. You supposed to pick ordinary-looking folks and pretty-up their gene pool. Like money. Money shouldn't marry money... need to spread it around."

They all laughed as Jaz fingered the magnificent cappuccino machine from *Rare Finds*, yet another surprise wedding gift from her husband. When Mr. and Mrs. Chandler returned from Lake Tahoe, thanks to Mrs. Meucci, the ornate piece of furniture sat perched on the kitchen counter taking up most of the space. Now, the intricately carved façade and the intoxicating aroma perfumed Alta Vista.

"Can I have another cup of Joe?" CC asked.

"You are going to be in a caffeine-coma by tomorrow," Sloane said. "Give her water."

Jaz eyed the clock. "Is that the right time?"

"Yeah? Why?" Farrell asked.

"You all have to get up outta here. My man. Excuse me. My husband will be home soon." Jaz started picking up the remnants of all the bad food they'd consumed over two days. "I don't care where you go...but get out of here!" Jaz began singing Dr. Feelgood. "Don't have time to sit and chit and chat."

Jaz successfully pushed them out of the door.

"Well, just use us up," CC said through the wooden door after it closed. "I love to hear that girl sing." She followed the other two down the steps.

Jaz had time to clean the apartment and herself. Taking a quick shower and preparing for their bubble bath for later in the evening. She'd gone to the florist for a pink rose and picked up their favorites from Aloutte's for dinner—whenever. By the time Qwayz's key turned in the door, Jaz, already clad in her baby-doll pajamas with a rose clenched between her teeth, draped herself over the sofa.

"Welcome Home," Jaz managed dramatically and Qwayz threw his head back and laughed before jumping over the back of couch and devouring his wife. "Humm. Make me feel like Paradise."

And he did. Sweaty, satisfied, they lay in one another's arms, synchronizing their breathing as they recovered. "Missed me huh?" Jaz teased.

"You have no idea."

"What'd you bring me?"

"I just gave it to you."

"Yes, you did. Notice anything?"

He looked around the apartment until his gaze fell on Jaz. "I apologize Jaz-of-mine. I'm horny and wiped out. Although you took care of one of them. Just one more game and it's over. I'll be back to normal. Promise."

"I don't want a 'normal' guy. I want you."

"You got me, girlie." He rested his forehead on hers and feigned snoring and being asleep.

"Flesh to flesh. No jacket."

"What? Ohh." He held his head. "Ohh, nooo."

"It's alright."

"What do you mean 'it's alright?' We've been too careful all these years and we wait until we get married to be sloppy." Jaz watched his mind blaze with panic. "OK, maybe it'll be

OK. Maybe the Lord will give us this one time. We are not ready to be parents. Law school and you—"

Jaz smiled. "I got you covered." She held up a round container and watched curiosity claim his face. "You've been so loving and giving and I thought 'What can I give him?' And I thought of making love…without a raincoat. First time for you and me. So, I give you… us… a diaphragm."

"I didn't feel anything."

"That's good."

He started laughing from relief. "Talk about March madness. How? And why didn't we think of this before?"

"I'm a married woman now. I went to Mrs. Cooper's and I'm sure CC's gynecologist and got fitted. Ta Dah!" Qwayz was still chuckling. "So, what do you say? A keeper?"

"I say, let's take it from the top. In our marital bed this time." He grinned widely and said, "Show me you know me."

They made slow, deliberate love until nature took completely over as Qwayz drew in a chocolate drop and then posed suspended over her as he rhythmically dove deeper and deeper into her love of him. Jaz felt Qwayz rush into her like a river strong, causing inner havoc, spasms, a sensation she had never known. Cascading, rippling, rolling…flesh-to-flesh. Echoing all through her; there was no place she'd rather be. Honey devoured hazel as Qwayz melted into her in every possible way, filling each pore with his love. They smiled at one another without speaking. No words necessary.

"That was exquisite. Supernatural," Qwayz panted, rolling from her to lay beside her. "What'd you think?"

"A little messy. But so worth it." He reached for her hand and kissed her fingertips, both staring at the ceiling. "I believe the beams are blushing."

~*~

364

Many of the same spectators from the last big game reconvened for the Stanford/UCLA game; the last of Qwayz's college career. Without the hype of Magic vs. Midas from the previous year, Qwayz put on a razzle-dazzle show. "So, they'll really miss me," he told Jaz. She watched her husband sprint up and down the court, his magnificent bronze legs in those little shorts, arms rippled and glistening with sweat, and all she could think was, *that his body, heart, mind and soul are coming home with me tonight.* All Qwayz's boys showed out from all phases of his life from the Dragons, Mag 7, Roosevelt High School, Watts, Raw Cilk and Stanford plus the smitten "public" he didn't even know.

For Jaz, the game was over in a flash. AJ jumped to his feet at the Stanford victory. The teams exchanged the sportsmanship ritual and jogged off the court. It must have been die-hard Roosevelt Rough Riders who began it. A familiar chant from their side: "Qway-z! Qway-z! Qway-z!..." like a rhythmic African tribal chant. People stopped leaving and stood in place and joined in. "Qway-z! Qway-z!" AJ stared as the entire colosseum began stomping, rocking the bleachers and clapping in sync. Prompted to do so, Qwayz jogged out. The crowd went wild as they continued cheering and chanting. Qwayz did one victory lap around the court. He bowed, sent up a kiss to Jaz, before he jogged out again.

"Aunt Jaz, why are you crying?" AJ asked caringly.

"Tears of joy," Jaz said and hugged a puzzled AJ.

Grownups, AJ thought.

Despite Lew Alcindor being named Player of the Year, the cover of *Sports Illustrated* featured a picture of Stanford University's Quinton "Magic" Chandler as he "Kissed Basketball Good-bye." The article entitled "Trading Courts… Basketball for the Courtroom."

A congratulations card from Gladys Ann to Mr. and Mrs. Quinton Chandler arrived in the mail. "Our first," Qwayz said proudly holding it up. "You all beefin'?"

"Why do you say that?" Jaz asked.

"Haven't seen any fat letters from here to Howard recently."

"I'm a married woman now. I don't have time for childish things." Jaz hadn't shared with her now husband that her then best friend had actually questioned her decision to marry at such a young age. *Who the hell asked for her advice?* Jaz thought. Sharing the best news ever with her best friend and, instead of jubilance, she questioned her. What made it worse, Gladys Ann knew Qwayz. Knew their history together. Just because she and Jehson hadn't lasted past her freshman year, didn't mean diddley for her and Qwayz. She could see if Sloane or CC had questioned their intentions, but they were elated, full of congrats and best wishes…but Gladys Ann? A disappointed, hurt and pissed Jaz only thought, *Gladys Ann should know better.*

"By the way, I have a new keychain." Jaz pulled out a Lake Tahoe souvenir chain and replaced the Best Friends one Gladys Ann gave her at the Oasis.

"Nice." Qwayz eyed his wife.

"See. Happily married woman, now."

"Yeah? How happy," Qwayz's hands slipped up Jaz's inner thigh.

"Let me show you."

~*~

Hello," Qwayz picked up the phone as Jaz and Akira disappeared into the bedroom after their outing.

"Hey, man. Sorry I missed your last game," TC admitted.

366

"Yeah. Why is that man?" Qwayz accused jokingly. "I shoulda loss."

"But you didn't. Jaz around?"

"Always. Wanna talk to her?"

"No."

A puzzled Qwayz detected a decided sharpness in his buddy's voice.

"I'm hurting man," TC whispered. "I need you to come down here."

"OK. Where are you?"

"At home. Don't bring Jaz," he hedged. "Don't want her to see me like this."

Jaz came out and Qwayz said, "I got to make a run to L.A. I'll be back after a while."

"What? Now?" Jaz asked.

"Yeah."

"Who was that on the phone? Everything alright?"

"Don't know yet. Will call you."

"Call me? I'm not invited?"

"Not this time."

"Why aren't you looking me in the eye? What's going on Quinton Regis?"

They went on for a few minutes until Qwayz realized he was wasting time and wasn't going to get away without a plausible explanation.

Partly distracted by TC's uncharacteristic demeanor, and Jaz's asking him questions, he finally told her that TC asked for him and he's going. She said, "Not without me."

"He specifically asked that I come alone, Jaz."

"The hell you say. I either ride with you or drive myself. Your choice."

Qwayz watched Jaz throw things into her suitcase realizing it was easier not arguing with her if she would end up going anyway; expending unnecessary energy and hurt feelings spared.

"Spring break is coming up, we could wait until then," Jaz suggested.

"I can't."

Once Jaz realized that Qwayz didn't know why TC wanted him, the ride to L.A. filled with loud silence. "Where are we going?" Jaz asked Qwayz as he navigated the pristine neighborhood with the manicured lawns.

"His house. He bought awhile back when his accountant said he needed to spend more money."

The lamppost shone brightly as they went up onto the porch, rang the bell a few times before Qwayz began knocking, followed by pounding on TC's carved Mediterranean door. They looked past the neatly trimmed boxwoods to the driveway where the custom van and Porsche, outside of the garage, stood parked and unwashed. Not a good sign. "He's home," Qwayz pounded again.

"Maybe's he's entertaining and doesn't want to be disturbed," Jaz hoped, both afraid of what they would find inside.

Finally, the door creaked open; a single ray of sunlight lit a column into the dark room. A sweltering thick, stale air assaulted their nostrils as their eyes adjusted to the lack of light. Jaz followed Qwayz as they waded through undistinguishable debris on the floor and opened the drapes revealing French doors. The backyard with its neat hedges and flower beds, and the patio with furniture surrounding the brick barbecue pit conspired to keep the secret of the atrocity hiding inside. Jaz let Akira out and watched her frolic for a few seconds.

368

Jaz turned from the pastoral façade to glimpse her brother for the first time. Involuntarily, tears sprang to her eyes. She refused to blink less they fall as she watched the shadow of a man being supported by his best friend. His beautiful coal-black hair that sent shivers up the spines of many girls now hung as long and unruly as drugged-out white boys in Haight Asbury. His famous, expertly groomed goatee—the pride, joy and signature of his genius, often stroked for confidence and effect—lost in a scraggly, full beard that hid his smooth, Indian-brown complexion.

"I'll start on the kitchen," she said, her voice low and gravely as she began stacking the Chinese cartons with decaying food and a half-eaten, moldy pizza, still in its box.

"Hey, brother," Qwayz unsuccessfully tried talking in a casual tone. "How 'bout we take a bath, huh? Been awhile?" He led his brother-friend to the bathroom, sat him on the commode and began washing out the tub to fill it with fresh water.

Alone in the kitchen away from view, Jaz let silent tears flow as she alternated between wiping the counter and her nose; wiping out the refrigerator and wiping her eyes.

"He's in a bubble bath," Qwayz said from behind. Jaz turned into him and just cried. Qwayz rocked her, blinking back tears which refused to return to their source.

"What happened?" Jaz managed after a few minutes.

"I don't know. I can't imagine what would break a man like TC." He brushed away the unending wetness from Jaz's eyes.

Qwayz checked on him constantly between helping Jaz clean the living room and the bedroom. TC remained there for hours replenishing the cold water with hot as if exorcising a demon from his mind and body. Afterwards, when Qwayz stayed with him for hours talking, Jaz joined Akira in the yard.

"She really loves wide open spaces," Qwayz said, pulling up a chair from the glass table with the umbrella center.

"Our next place must have a fireplace in the bedroom and a yard or at least a balcony for Akira."

"And your flowers."

"Did he talk to you about what happened?"

"Some." Qwayz grabbed Jaz's hand. "Not hard for another man to it figure out. Kinda running on psychological empty. Nowhere to gas up so to speak. The women in his life, his world... are gone."

"I cannot believe that my brother is having all this over any woman. Pick one of the thousand waiting in the wings."

"Not that simple. If something were to happen between you and me. No holds barred flat out, no way back, burn all bridges over—I'd be just as destroyed. Of course, you'd never know it," he teased. Jaz smacked at him playfully, happy for the relief. "It's more than Ronnie's dying, LeLani's leaving and the reporter picking career over him."

"I should hope so." Jaz shifted in her chair. "Hurting my brother aside, I am proud of the sister who has goals and dreams and sets about achieving them. But she hurt my brother...so, she's dead to me."

Qwayz chuckled and asked, "Who said it's a thin line between genius and insanity? I thought TC had erased it."

"You think he's crazy?"

"No. But he's had a crisis of faith. He's had a phenomenal life. Everything came so easy for him. Things have never 'not' worked for him. There is a first time for everything and this is his first time. He thought he was ready for a happy love-life with marriage and kids but the one he picked said 'no dice.' He looks at his boys, you and me, Scoey and Tracy and wants

370

to know why not him? TC has no faith in his future right now. It'll pass once he realizes who he is again. Once he stops trying so hard to get everything he wants… like he always has."

"He's had no experience coping with adversity." *Mel said the same thing,* Jaz thought.

"Now he has. Other cats of his ilk get a little weed, drink, snort coke, throw back pills or shoot poison into their veins. Make their world alright until they come back and when it gets heavy… take another synthetic trip. Musicians are famous for that. TC's not like that."

"Wish he would smoke a little reefer."

"You know he don't play that. Never has."

"I know. Athletes. I need to go to the store. There was nothing to salvage in that refrigerator."

TC slept for eighteen hours straight, waking up ravenous, and Jaz cooked his favorite breakfast at 1 a.m., the trio's time clock all out of whack and none of them minded. They talked together, and Qwayz and Jaz took turns spending time with TC while the other napped. On the fourth day, TC felt up to going out and they saw "The Dirty Dozen" and "Bonnie and Clyde," ate Chinese food and walked the Santa Monica Pier where a couple asked for his autograph and told him how much his songs meant to them. Over the next couple of days, TC and Qwayz played basketball and worked on music and TC finally returned to the studio. An entire day went by and he didn't bother to come home at all. "You two better get back to school. Spring break is over," he said coming home from the studio.

"Kicking us out," Qwayz teased.

"You all cramping my style," TC teased. "'Sides, I want a doctor and lawyer in the family. Not going to tell your children I was the reason you two didn't finish."

"Don't have to tell me twice. Tired of your rusty butt and making quiet love with my wife."

"You all ain't that quiet," TC joked.

Jaz looked mortified as she let Akira into the back seat. She went to her big brother head first into his shoulder as she'd always done. "Bye" she looked up at him. "I love you. Always."

"Me, too. Qwayz, my man." TC accepted a quick hug from his boy.

"If you need me, bro, just call." Qwayz flashed his patented smile and hazel locked with dark obsidian pools. Qwayz revved up Reds. "Later."

"Much." They exchanged their finger-thumb salute and Qwayz burned rubber away from the curb.

"You think he's OK?" Jaz asked, waving until her brother was out of sight.

"I think there is nothing more *we* can do for him. It's on him now. A total reset."

"He'll be fine," Jaz mandated.

"I'm glad you came," Qwayz said, stroking her hand reassuringly.

"Me, too."

37

On an unbelievably crystal clear northern California day, Quinton Regis Chandler, a gorgeous black man in a horrible navy-blue cap and gown, received a BS from Stanford University. The program indicated he had graduated with honors and was headed to Stanford Law School in the fall.

Hep and Lorette Culhane reserved a suite of rooms at the Fairmont and Marc Hopkins Hotels, which were occupied by the Chandler family: Ma Vy, Hanie and, for one day, Denny as well as AJ and his parents. Aunt Selena and Uncle Zack brought Keely-J with them but Star convinced her mother, Keely, to travel the distance via first-class by train. Mel came for one day and TC sent his regrets with a promise, "I'll make it up to you later."

Jaz and Qwayz eyed one another with concern. "It's not the same, Jaz. He gave us a heads up. He's involved in something serious," Qwayz said. Jaz quieted her heart. "It's a good thing," Qwayz assured her. "Look, a graduation card from Gladys Ann. That's nice."

"Any money in it?"

"She better keep it. I hear D.C. is expensive."

Never once mentioning the apartment on Alta Vista, Hep tooled everyone around San Francisco as if they were tourists, proudly showing them the site on which Culhane Enterprises would be built in a few years. A trip to the Pier, Alcatraz, Sausalito and trolley cars rides rounded out the tour. "It's like the wedding we never had," Jaz said to her husband as they lay in their magic carpet of a brass bed. "My husband, the college graduate. Dad was so proud of you. Like you were his son." She wriggled beneath him. "You're the first one in 'our' family to get a degree."

"The ball is in your court. You are next."

A few weeks later on June 16, the kind of warm crisp day that is renowned in Northern California, Qwayz guided Jaz to their seats at the Monterey Pop Festival. Keely-J remained a few extra days before returning to Paris, and Star and Grandma Keely insisted that they take the 'long' train back to Colt, Texas; Keely loved the train as it reminded her of the trips with Papa Colt when they were young. "Now, they have locomotives, Ma," Star teased.

"She is so funny," Jaz said to Qwayz. "Mel said Lorette is going to stay with her and the baby for a month after it comes."

"Really?"

"Lorette must be trying to get to heaven. No figuring her. I thought she'd condemn and banish Mel for being pregnant without the benefit of matrimony."

"People change. Grow and mature," Qwayz said between acts.

"But she is going to stay in Hud's loft with Mel and the new baby?"

"Dig. How long before Grandma Lorette gets a suite at the Ritz for the duration of her stay?"

"And hires a nurse."

"Who are these clowns?" Qwayz asked of the current act on stage. "Covering a Raw Cilk song!"

"Imitation is the best form of flattery. It did win a Grammy. Next we'll hear it in an elevator."

"Oh, this is noise!"

"The drummer remind you of anybody?" Jaz asked.

"Dickie."

"Yep. I miss him. I kept up with him at Skeekie's who told me the Army reclassified him and he took his now able-body to Canada. Army is crazed for new fodder."

374

"What about his wife and kid?"

"Kids? Albeit from three different women. He didn't have the best role models in his life."

Qwayz side-glanced her and asked, "You know about that?"

"Yep. Once when Carter Hix ditched us at movies we walked home right past his house. His father yelled at us from across the street."

"Better be glad he didn't abduct you," Qwayz returned his eyes to the act on stage.

Jaz thought of her friend growing up in the House of the Rising Sun…or Setting Sun. Eating bologna and Velveeta cheese sandwiches on white bread with Jell-O for dessert if he was good. She chuckled and added, "He's doing comedy in Canada."

"I betcha he's good. That's a naturally funny cat."

"He was. Skeekie said that Dickie's wife told him he had a drinking problem. Without missing a beat Dickie told her, 'I have no problem drinking at all.'"

She and Qwayz chuckled before Jaz asked, "I wonder how old he was?"

"I heard he was so old the school asked him to leave. Dang!" Qwayz fanned the smoke. "You can get a 'contact high' just sitting here."

After Zack and Selena Fluellen and Dizzy Gillespie performed, Jaz was ready to go. The harmony displayed by the Mama and Papas kept Qwayz engaged, but Otis Redding commanded the attention of the crowd with his Southern soulful, raspy voice and energy expended around stage. Things continued to percolate when a white girl singer with Big Brother and the Holding Company outshouted everyone—a rough-and-tumble girl named Janis Joplin. Jefferson Airplane and The Who tempered Qwayz and Jaz again, but Jimi Hendrix and the Experience blew them all away. A mesmerized Qwayz was riveted by the guitar licks Hendrix perfected, making that instrument sing liked he'd never seen; Hendrix made the strings punch, soar and cry. A black guy doing rock. Jaz rolled with him note for note until he set his guitar on fire. She thought, n*ot sensational, but ridiculous. Like black folks burning Watts… their own property.*

~*~

As she reached for her order at the Purple Hippo she heard from behind, "Jasmine Culhane." She turned into the chest and looked up into the waiting, bedroom eyes of Solomon Noble. Taller than Qwayz, not as tall as her father but still the smooth, Hershey-dark chocolate, no cream, no sugar, coloring of her father, aunts and Gladys Ann. "Been awhile. How you doing?"

"Just fine. And yourself?" She couldn't stop grinning. Stop staring. Stop blushing. She felt twelve. She couldn't see his body under the colorful dashiki but she knew what was there was prime. "You're still around?"

"Grad school. Finishing up actually. My last year of a two-year program."

"Ah. What's your field?"

"Politics." He shrugged his massive shoulders.

"Figures. You'll be successful I'm sure."

"Got time for a cup of coffee? We can catch up?"

What? Her inner voice asked. He'd never said more than a sentence or two to her, although he had asked CC what her "situation" was.

"I'm married," Jaz blurted out, feeling really out of her league. To make it truly humiliating she wriggled her third finger left hand with the gold cigar band engraved with her husband's initials crowned by a ring of diamonds.

376

"Lucky man."

"I think so. We're both really lucky." You idiot, she self-chastised. Shut the hell up. Wondering if she appeared as doofus to him as she felt. She had no experience dealing with guys: She liked Joaquin because he looked like a movie star. Jesse Ramsey? Sheer convenience and Qwayz snuck up on her before she was hit with the thunderbolt. Still, she knew she'd better stay away from this brother.

"Well, if your status ever changes or you just want a cup of coffee, look me up."

"Good luck to you, Solomon Noble." Jaz threw up her head like Bette Davis in an old black and white movie and vamped out the door… not looking back.

38

"Have mercy, girlie," Qwayz said as he sat on the ottoman, while Jaz modeled her latest bikini for him.

"You like?" She pranced and pirouetted suggestively in front of him.

"The swimming hole will never be the same. We ought to go someplace else, too."

"Myrtle Beach maybe?"

"How far it is from Colt, Texas?" he wondered as a knock on the door interrupted them. "You expecting someone?"

"No, but they have lousy timing," Jaz snipped as she went into the bedroom to change.

Jaz reentered the living room to find Qwayz in the company of TC and her father. Her glee evident. "Three of the most important men in my life. Together in the same room. What an honor." She kissed them both before sitting on the arm of the club chair where Qwayz sat. "Can I get you something? Cappuccino, tea, juice?"

"Qwayz already asked." TC gave his boy credit.

"That is a most handsome espresso machine," said Hep, who went over to inspect it as Jaz gave him a brief history.

"If you ever want to part with it—" Hep began.

"We won't," Jaz said the trio knew it as a wedding gift from Qwayz. "So, what'd I miss? What are two moguls doing in San Francisco? Dad showing off his building site?"

"Something like that," TC said.

"Beau coo press and they haven't even excavated yet."

"Don't know what to make of the tallest, most elegant office building in San Fran," Qwayz spoke for the first time.

"So, what's your favorite part TC?"

"The express elevators to the executive suites—"

"And the way the top five floors will be recessed. Dad can zoom straight to the top and not ride with the regular folk."

"And there is going to be a uniformed operator and a bench so he won't have to stand for thirty-five floors."

"The three-story foyer with Carrera marble."

"Let me quote *Architectural and Interior Design* magazine, 'The Culhane Building will bring Park Avenue chic to the West Coast,' unquote."

"Let's go get something to eat. Dad's treat. You know who'd love to meet him?" Jaz asked Qwayz and they answered together, "Giuseppe."

"They love you and use only imported Triple O, Orsini Olive Oil."

"Hate to put a damper on but I have to get back to L.A.," TC interjected. "Dad's my ride."

"You all drove up here?"

"No. Charted a plane."

"Well, it goes when you say so, right?"

The males of the room fell silent.

"Next week we won't have any constraints. Colt, Texas awaits," Jaz beamed and was met with the same non-eye contact silence. "What gives guys?"

"We're considering a change in venue," TC hedged. "At least for the front end of the trip."

"I've charted a yacht, The Sea Goddess, to cruise the Caribbean for a few weeks," Hep said.

"Is that all? It takes three of you to tell me that?" Jaz laughed nervously, knowing her men too well. Jaz eyed the three men who would not meet her gaze and a sinking feeling claimed her. Qwayz was too quiet and, though Dad loves his building, flying all the way up here to show TC didn't ring true. Jaz's honey eyes searched hazel and the two pairs of obsidian black. "So, what is it you wanted me to know besides a change in venue for the trip?"

Her father remained resolute that he wasn't going to utter a word so it wasn't anything to do with Mel or Lorette. Jaz eyed the two "brothers," who seemed less mentally prepared but she knew their bond would take precedence, as Qwayz's gaze darted between her and an imaginary piece of lint on his easy chair. Qwayz, like her father, felt it was not his news to share. That left TC. Jaz faced him squarely, challenging him to stop stroking his goatee and spit it out. It was then that she noticed that his habitual solace was missing.

"Well, TC?"

Always amazed at his sister's smarts and deduction, he answered simply, "I won't be with you all on the last leg of the trip."

Relief washed Jaz's face. "OK? And you say women have drama." She didn't want to ask so she waited for him to tell her that he was getting married or something. Maybe he and his mystery woman, turned field reporter aiming for anchorwoman had decided on him.

"I'll be reporting."

"Reporting?" Jaz chuckled at the officialness of the statement thinking his fiancée wouldn't like to think… the flippancy drained from her face. "What do you mean 'reporting?'" A knot formed in the pit of her stomach, her psyche became flooded with unrelated possibilities. Neither Qwayz nor her father looked at her.

"Vietnam."

"What? You're kidding, right?"

Qwayz sprang to her side but was rebuffed. No one spoke.

380

"I've already finished basic," TC said quietly. "That's why I missed Qwayz's graduation."

"Basic? Dad, do something. Get him out of it. A doctor's note that he has bone spurs or flat feet like the white boys—"

"I wasn't drafted, Jaz. Besides how did you think I got the extra time for the cruise."

"This is a bad joke. Unfunny. Terribly horrible…" Jaz pleaded and her breathing grew shallow. Qwayz stood by the fireplace, his hand across the mantle while Hep sat rigidly. "Daddy?"

"We've been through it all, Punkin'. Before he went, while he was there, on the plane ride up, a few minutes ago…it's all been said."

"I suppose you knew about this, too?" Jaz accused Qwayz who did not reply.

"C'mon, Sis, be fair. They all talked blue streaks but you know the two of us. Once we decide to do something…that's it."

"But why?" Jaz's honey eyes melted into her brother's ebony pools of darkness pleading for an answer.

"It was kind of a revelation. A message from a higher power telling me to take some time. Take stock—"

"In Vietnam? That's what God came up with?" Her voice cracked. "They kill people over there. I don't know one person who has come back with everything he left with…not his life, his limbs, his mind."

"Then I'll be the first," he said, his attempt at levity failing miserably. "Basic felt good. I did what I was told. I didn't make any decisions. Nobody wanted or expected anything from me but a good day's work. It was a clean slate. I was just one of the GIs."

"They don't shoot real bullets in basic. If you want to commit suicide, why not just blow your brains out here and save the government the expense of sending your body parts home."

"Jaz!" Hep roared and jumped to his feet.

"What?" she spat back. "If you were any kind of father--"

"Jaz," TC said, taking in her venom, "Let's go for a walk."

"I don't want to go for a walk or on any death cruise." She jerked away from her brother three times before his strength and steadfast demeanor calmed her. "Please. Just the two of us. Let's get some fresh air."

Qwayz watched TC guide his sister out the door and then raked his hands through his hair and fired up the cappuccino machine. Soon the talk of Vietnam, death and dying was replaced by the fragrant aroma of freshly brewed coffee.

"An elixir," Hep deemed. "You know it's going to be awhile before she forgives you for knowing and not telling."

"Yeah. We'll get through it." He sipped the hot liquid. "Jaz heats up, blows off and cools down."

"You love her very much." Hep knew it, and finally realized it fully.

"She's worth more than anything else in my world. I don't know how not to love her. Not to consider her or think about her."

"I hope you never have to prove it."

"I hope I prove it every day." Qwayz looked at Hep evenly resisting the temptation to claim her as his wife. "It's reciprocal. I never want to be the guy she used to love. Never want her to stop loving me for something I didn't do. Besides, I know her. Understand her. She's not spoiled as many mistakenly think. She believes that anything you want, you can get—through hard work, perseverance, determination and

382

planning. Nothing is beyond her reach if she just sets her mind to it. She can thank her Daddy for that." Qwayz complimented His Excellency who smiled knowingly. "She's as naïve as she appears worldly. She's been sheltered and protected by you, TC and now me."

"It's natural to want to protect those you love," Hep began. "I had the same argument with my father about World War II. I didn't listen. I was younger than TC. Funny how history repeats itself through the generations. Fleeing to war... thinking it will solve everything, saving face, taking a break, answering your prayers... but a stupid choice then as it is now. Covering up losing a scholarship. Luckily, it wasn't a permanent solution to a temporary problem. Turned out OK. I want it to work out as well for my son. Parents protect their children the only way they know how. Papa Colt threatened Star; didn't work. So, he let me step in it myself; I couldn't wait to get back home. Even though my girl was married and pregnant by her husband... I had to go on. I did. But sometimes when we least expect it, the real world slips by us and snatches loved ones when we aren't looking."

"We need to teach our children resilience," Qwayz said. "Positive, bounce-back ability. Jaz has that but I'm afraid this lesson, even with perseverance and determination, are beyond our grasp. You cannot control other people's lives and their independent decisions hurt the most. Those choices we may never understand," Qwayz said just above a whisper as he continued to struggle with his best friend's decision.

As Qwayz spoke of both Jaz and TC, once again, Hep realized how very lucky his daughter was to have this man in her life. Essentially because of him, Hep did not uproot her and drag her to Connecticut and enroll her in Briarcrest Academy. She would have probably become an estranged, resentful girl by now. Instead, he sits with her boyfriend and a beautiful Iris Setter in a comfortable apartment full of love, values, and a cappuccino machine he'd love to own. Hep respected this boy, now a man, whose own family relied heavily upon him after his father's death, just as Hep now relies on him with this daughter. Qwayz'd lived up to his potential and beyond.

"I hope you understand how much my children mean to me. Do not take my obstinate stance against you personally," Hep told Qwayz. "I would have felt the same way if she were dating Sidney Poitier."

"Isn't he kind of old for her?" Qwayz teased and Hep laughed. "Gotta take Akira for a walk. Wanna come?" Qwayz asked and Hep obliged. They ended up eating at Giuseppe's where His Excellency posed for pictures with the owners and a bottle of Orsini Olive Oil. Qwayz proudly took Hep to see Jaz's award-winning model of South Hall still on display in the School of Architecture.

"She really enjoys those classes," Qwayz told him. "Almost all of her electives are in that field. She got into it during her visit to Paris."

"Still want to get you two to Italy before I leave my post."

"We plan to honeymoon there."

"Oh? Anytime soon?"

"Nope."

"Well, you have to let me gift that to you both. When the times comes."

"We accept." They chuckled.

They came in moments before the siblings returned. Jaz went straight for Hep's chest. "I'm sorry, Daddy." Hep winked at Qwayz, thinking he could have used Qwayz's insight when she was growing up.

384

"And you," she went straight for Qwayz. "I understand. Better than before." She encircled his waist. "I love you."

"I know," Qwayz teased while stroking her back. "I can't keep the ground from shaking, Jaz-of-mine. But I can hold you through it." He kissed her forehead.

"Well, I still think Vietnam is a helluva a place to go for clarity. But I hope you find what you need so you can come back to us. I love you, TC."

"What calmed her down?" Hep asked.

"My brother could always calm me down." Jaz hugged him.

"With the help of chocolate ice cream," TC added.

39

The cloudless, azure-blue sky complimented the calm, aquamarine sea without clashing as the cab rounded the sharp, narrow streets, emerging from their secret hideaway for the last three days on their way to the marina in Charlotte Amalie, St. Thomas. Qwayz and Jaz nuzzled, kissed and cooed all the way to the docks. "There's no way we can sleep apart for three weeks."

Qwayz peeled off the fare for the cab driver and said to her, "We're super lovers. How long was it before we actually made love in a bed? We'll find a way. Besides TC knows I sleep walk."

Upon seeing them in a distance, Hep stood and waved them toward the yacht.

"Here goes," Jaz intoned.

Smiles, kisses and hugs all around as an introduction to black neighbors from Connecticut who would be on board for ten days were made. A man nearly pumped Qwayz's arm off while spouting all of his basketball stats and triumphs in high school and college. *He'll be trapped on board with a 'fan'. Poor thing,* Jaz thought.

TC came over to the arriving couple, "Hey, man." They slapped five and did their point and thumb gesture. "They're harmless," TC whisper-warned of the Connecticut Cavanaughs. "Hey, Sis."

"You all look just divine," Lorette drawled, glowing in a coral-colored Cassini pantsuit sans jacket, currently draped casually over her chair.

"Are you all hungry? Want something to drink?" Hep asked so he could dismiss the ever-attentive steward.

"What's that?" Qwayz asked of the pitcher of liquid on the table under the deck canopy.

"Lemonade."

"That's fine. Thanks."

"No, thanks," Jaz said, and told the steward fumbling with their luggage, "You can put those in the same stateroom."

Her words silenced everyone. Smiles suspended in place and all that could be heard was distant chatter and the sound of the waves lapping lazily against the ship. Hep closed his eyes hoping that a scene wouldn't ensue so early. Lorette froze in the horror at the impropriety in front of their friends, as though Mel's pregnancy wasn't enough to bear. "Well, dear, we thought Qwayz could bunk with TC like the old days, and you can have—"

"I sleep with him now," Jaz relished the statement as Hep let out a slow breath on a silent prayer. Lorette's confused eyes stuck wide open while TC and Qwayz smiled.

"Relax. We're married," Jaz confessed and held up her hand with the rings. "Have been since Valentine's Day."

Congratulations abound as Hep pumped Qwayz's hand and ordered Dom Perignon for a toast.

"When did all this happen? He's a good guy," Lorette offered her daughter with a hug.

"Yes, I know."

"Children?" Hep asked, Qwayz on the sly.

"Lots I hope, but no time soon."

The Sea Goddess and their seven guests set sail with almost as many hands on deck to cater to their every comfort and whim. The trio, TC, Qwayz and Jaz, as inseparable as they'd been in their youth, romping from island to island, rummaging through quaint native shops, swimming at different beaches, dining on native fare, from turtle soup to old Man's

387

Wife fish. They plucked bananas, mangoes or breadfruit from their original plant homes. Early morning splashes could be heard in lieu of showers. Surrounding water converted into large aquariums as they snorkeled and swam with the fishes. The chef and his two stewards cooked exquisitely elaborate meals, which the trio enjoyed and danced off at local haunts with names like the Pepper Pot, Banana Boat or Slim Easy's. Many nights they retired to the stern where the three blended their voices in songs by Raw Cilk, the Drifters, Sam Cooke, the Temptations and the Shirelles.

The yacht coursed through gentle, bathtub-clear waters, first through St. Maarten, St. Barths, onto Antigua, lingering or moving on as the seven decreed. They spent almost a full week anchored in Guadeloupe in the vicinity of St. Justin and St. Michel while Qwayz easily sought and found Melie's parents, Elona and Vernal, with whom Vilna lived after the hurricane wiped out her parents and home; long before she thought about being Ma Vy. They shared stories about the courtship of "Butterscotch and Chocolate" as they were called. Vilna caught Big Q's eyes one day while she sold fare by the docks. A known rapscallion, Uncle Vernal indicated, "We were hesitant as to his sincerity when courting our Vilna. Word was he left St. Justin because he had run out of women to sample there."

"Like father like son," Jaz teased her husband.

"He put his eye on Vilna, 'the oldest virgin on the island' he called her, and the rest, as they say is history."

Driven to the house that his father built for his new wife, Jaz watched Qwayz quietly walk the five-room stucco house with the missing roof and the walls reclaimed by lush vegetation. *By island standards in the forties, this must have been solidly middle class,* Jaz thought as Qwayz explored and soaked up the essence of this home he never knew. The crunch

388

of his sneakers against the glass comingled with the hypnotic sound of rolling surf across a powdery soft beach right outside the window. Intoxicatingly soothing. Fresh, salt-laced air touched with humidity from nighttime showers coaxed everything to grow. Jaz wondered what could make a man leave such an idyllic haven. Restless, probably like her father leaving Colt, Texas, Qwayz's dad desired more for himself and his family. With news of Vilna's second pregnancy, he braved a new world alone, made sacrifices and accomplished what he sought. That same quiet enthusiasm for life and determination coursed through his son's veins as Qwayz tackled all his endeavors, mastered them with dignity and aplomb from sports to academia, graduating college from a prestigious white university; Qwayz'd inherited his father's foresight, vision and restlessness.

He reached for Jaz's hand and said in a low voice, "Did I ever tell you that I was supposed to have gone with him to get the ice cream? He told me to take my bath and put on my pajama's and we'll have it when he gets back." He walked a few paces. "He didn't come back."

"I'm glad you weren't with him," Jaz replied quietly.

He stopped in front of the car and felt her cheek.

"Me too."

Having cleared it with the local government, Hep had fireworks in the harbor before treating Qwayz's family to a banquet at a local restaurant. The next morning, they sailed to Grand Cayman, where the Cavanaugh's left the yacht to fly back home and Zack and Selena boarded.

The festivities proceeded with the lively Fluellens, stirring up more fun and chastising Qwayz and Jaz for missing their wedding. "I'm sending them on an Italian honeymoon when they say," Hep boasted. The Fluellens only stayed five days before returning to Colt, Texas and then back to Paris. Gone too quickly.

The trio traipsed around in a jeep by day and ate with the family at night, capped with a phone call to AJ and a bark from Akira. When the cruise ended, Hep rented a beach villa on Barbados that had four bedrooms flared out like an open fan, and The Chandlers scored a room with an ocean front view. The center of the house was completely open with a living room, dining room and kitchen. The home, dressed in sturdy wicker and glass furniture over imported tile flooring, which continued onto the covered portico with hammocks and a picture-perfect ocean, boasted both comfort and elegance. Hep flew Scoey in, which dampened the trip for Jaz. Not that she was sad to see him, but she knew with his coming the trip was winding down and her brother would soon be leaving. It was the four of them now. The trio plus the girl who went from being a tagalong to a wife.

"How does he seem to you?" Jaz asked her husband when they were dressing for the evening meal.

"Really? Resigned. Calm. At peace."

"Yeah. I find that so strange."

"In the end, it is his decision, Jaz. All we can do is love and support him through it. No matter how hard it is on us. And be there for him when he returns. A man's gotta do what a man's gotta do."

"Who are you? Gary Cooper?" She hugged him tightly. "I will *never* understand."

"Like Denny said, we give him happy memories so he'll want to come back. And when he does we'll throw him the biggest welcome home party ever."

"Muhammed Ali refusing to go and being stripped of his title and TC volunteering. It makes no sense," Jaz lamented quietly.

390

"Where's Scoey?"

"Calling Tracy."

"She could have come too."

"Have you met Mama Summerville?"

"I think the man's in love." TC laid in the hammock and crossed his feet at the ankles. "Maybe when I come back I'll go to Hawaii and look up LeLani Troop. But that'd be a rebound."

"Did you even think she was the 'real deal' and anchorwoman-wanna-be was the rebound?"

TC eyed Qwayz. "You know she was a field reporter doing assignments from supermarket openings to shootings in the ghetto. I just called her 'anchorwoman' since that's where she wanted to be. You know, supporting her dream."

"Mighty white of you, man," Qwayz joned and TC laughed. "I mean you said the last time you remember being content was with LeLani." Qwayz redirected the discussion and made his point.

"Yeah, like Sam Cooke sang, 'It's a mean old world to try to live in all by yourself.'"

"Amen."

"Besides, that ain't love like you and Jaz."

"Nobody's like me and Jaz," Qwayz clarified.

"Yeah, eye-to-eye. Heart-to-heart. Soul–to-soul. High school. College and beyond."

"That's the plan. But there's all kinds of 'love' and preludes to it, man."

"I want a woman in my life but LeLani Troop was a little too demanding."

"You think Jaz lets me get away with anything? Sheeeit."

"You like it. You need it."

"Damn straight I do." They slapped five and chuckled. "That's the difference between you and me. I know I got the best woman for me. Supposed I'd missed out on her? It'd be fun 'out there' but not worth jack. And not for long."

"Naw. I ain't ready for none of that. Settling down? Well, Uncle Sam has me for two years. I'll worry 'bout all that when I get back."

Jaz watched as the three laughed and took turns on a hammock, a beach lounge and a windswept palm tree whose trunk formed an ersatz resting place. Their voices carried on the tropical night air and Jaz could see the silhouettes slapping five or talking in hushed tones. Scoey returned to the "real world" and the guys took him to the airport.

Jaz took Scoey's place for the nightly beach talks.

"Problem is that you shouldn't make any life-changing decision before you're twenty-five."

"This is her Psych 101," Qwayz clarified for TC.

"Your prefrontal cortex is not yet formed. So, you have no sound judgment. You make bad choices," Jaz continued.

"Uh-huh. So, what's that mean about you and Qwayz being hitched."

"You see Qwayz and I …are magic. Nothing bad can happen to us as long as we are together."

"Uh-huh. Like Papa Colt once said, 'What a man feels in his heart he sees in the world.'"

"Qwayz's the optimistic-realist of this relationship. He wakes up each day wondering what kind of possibilities are out there," Jaz proclaimed.

"Opposites attract," TC teased his sister.

"What's that make you? An idiot genius?"

"Actually, you're more of a pessimistic dreamer," TC continued. "You dream big but deep down don't think it'll

392

happen." Jaz lunged for him and he ran away from her, grabbing the vacated seat.

In their suite Hep and Lorette watched the three down by the bent palm tree and hammock.

She sniffed and Hep brought her the tissue box. "You're doing real well, Lorette."

"It's hard to watch your baby boy get ready to go off where I can't protect or see him."

"He is a grown man."

"A good one. Like his father." She held Hep around his waist. "Where did all the time go, Hep? I always figured there'd be nothing but time for me to do everything... especially get to know Jaz better. Now she's married."

"He's a good guy."

"Yes. Thank goodness. Life is so uncertain. TC going off to fight. Mel pregnant and living with the daddy of her child-to-be. And Jaz... is thriving."

"She is."

"The child I had the least to do with raising turned out the best. What does that say for my parenting skills?"

"We should be proud of all of our children. They are unconventional but at least they're not druggies or engaged in illegal activities."

"I think that speaks well of us. And your family edict: 'Be who you are.' They are that."

"Yes, indeed. Now let's get some shuteye. We've got a man to take to the airport tomorrow."

Jaz hugged her brother, clinging to him the way she did during thunderstorms or when he would come from school and take her outside to play. Later to the Boys Club, the studio, beach parties and beyond. He'd always been there for her and was now taking a two-year sabbatical… to a place she could not follow.

"I'll be gone when you get up," TC said, wiping a stream of silent tears from her cheeks.

"No. I'm going with you to the airport."

"You've always wanted to go everywhere and I've taken you. But not this time. Please. I just can't take another teary goodbye. 'Sides I'll be back before you know it. And I won't mind if I have a little niece or nephew waiting for me." Qwayz choked with laughter. "Shit happens. Only don't name him after me. I'm saving Tavio for my own son."

"You wish," Qwayz challenged. "We ain't studyin' 'bout no babies."

"I love you, TC," Jaz took the play from them both.

"Love you too, Sis. Always have. Always will." The siblings double-cheek kissed and Jaz ran up the beach to her room leaving the best friends to their goodbyes.

Jaz nodded off and on, awaking several times in the darkness of the early morning hours. Seeing the black, cut-out images of two of the three men she loved most in her life. Jaz respected their friendship as the way things once were and always will be. The two of them. Brothers bound not by blood but by hearts and souls.

Sunlight bouncing off the whiteness of the stucco walls didn't wake Jaz but the distant whine of a car engine did. She sprang from bed and ran out to where her parents stood while Qwayz loaded the jeep and TC said his final goodbyes.

"Trying to sneak off, huh, Tavio." Jaz approached pulling her kimono to a close.

"Whew! Morning mouth," TC fanned playfully.

"The last memory you'll have of me… for a while." Jaz didn't mind the teasing. "Keep safe."

"Write often." TC pinched his little sister's cheek, wet again with involuntary tears.

"Where you going?" she asked Qwayz, smoke-screening her emotions.

"Pulled airport duty."

"Lucky you. You didn't come to bed at all last night," Jaz said, trying to prolong TC's departure long enough for him to come to his senses and ask his father to get him out of it.

"I'll make it up to you," Qwayz said and started the engine. TC hopped in and they pulled off.

Jaz watched the jeep round the driveway and go down the road until it was out of sight.

"Keep safe, TC," Jaz repeated quietly as Hep tried to rouse her for a big breakfast. "No thanks, Dad."

Another week of vacation was scheduled but Jaz couldn't stand being where her brother last was and was no longer. All the fun evaporated, replaced by the boredom of watching her father and husband's after-dinner chess matches. Jaz longed for California, for her apartment on Alta Vista, for Denny, Tracy, Sloane and CC. For all the familiar and reaffirming... for continuity and sanity in the wake of this madness.

"I wanna go home," she told Qwayz. Three days after TC's departure the Chandlers were L.A. bound.

40

Dry, hell-hot terrain churned as the jeep sped by and helicopters chopped the blue skies frothing up dust clouds that swirled around TC as he walked from the mess tent to the cot in his unit. The audios of Raw Cilk, Motown, rock and country music created a cacophony of sound as he ambled by certain sections. Music, both the escape and lifeline to back-in-the-real-world. He lifted his cap to let some air reach his scalp.

"Man, you still look familiar," Newton said, glancing from his face to the "Culhane" stenciled across his pocket. He'd been saying that since the new recruit arrived.

"Got one of those faces, man," was all TC answered in reply.

He'd been in-country for a few months, long enough to be officially introduced to Charlie on the search and destroy missions. He had shot his first man and watched him fall face down, sending up a plume of fine dirt. It stunned TC. "Kill or be killed, man. Simple as that," his lieutenant fresh from OTC said. This land and its people were like nothing TC had ever encountered, and the army, despite its training, did a poor job in preparing soldiers for it. More than not seeing or hearing "this bad cat," as Qwayz described Jimi Hendrix at the Monterey Pop Festival, TC'd missed hearing H. Rap Brown, chairman of SNCC, declare, "We are on the eve of revolution, Brothers." He could hear Raw Cilk hits and recall where he was and what he was thinking at the time he recorded it. He could hear the Temps call it all a "Ball of Confusion" and Edwin Starr bark the truth, "War! What is it good for? Absolutely Nothing." The poet James Brown's anthem "Black and Proud" escorted him to his cot where he flopped on the sagging canvas. More than the adjustment from luxury to filth, a round bed to flat, no support slats, from getting a cold chicken leg from your fridge or haute cuisine at a fine restaurant to undefinable eats in the mess, there was no peace and quiet; an uneasy chaos the norm.

Lack of control in his life. The making "sense" of the nonsensical things he was ordered to do. Fighting tooth-and-nail to take a hill with mounting deaths on both sides. Spending time up there only to vacate the hill in a week's time so that the VC could just walk in and claimed it again. What was that for? What was the dying for? At least in World War II, the soldiers advanced toward a goal, taking towns and progressing on. Not in this crazy jungle, where friendly slanted-eyes during the day became your enemy at night. You follow them until they disappeared. Vanished. Up trees, down tunnels, into thin air. The 102-degrees in the shade days and the frigid nights. The never-ending rain. The leeches. Boot-rot. Once he drank from a cool watering hole only to find a tiger doing the same from across the short expanse. *Holy shit! He* thought, staring at the animal while it stared back at him. Simultaneously, thoughts converged, *please don't eat me and look at the beautiful stripes on his coat.* The animal sauntered off, leaving TC thankful the tiger had already eaten and passed on him. Thanks to Papa Colt's teachings, he backed away making sure the animal wouldn't charge when his back was turned. The mere crazy madness of being in camp talking trash and playing cards one day, and the next being viciously fired at and watching your buddies being hit with bullets, scream and die; spun-around shot or limbs blown clear off…blood still pumping. The sound of the smooth zip of a body bag shipping someone home who would never have to face another day here.

TC fought to keep his mind right, his sanity intact in the midst of insanity. With a benign chuckle, he often thought of Jaz's remark, "Vietnam? A helluva place to go for clarity."

Sitting on the latrine, he asked himself out loud, "What the hell am I doing here?" *Exercising your right of choice,* he thought. Jaz right again… that prefrontal cortex had another year to form, but TC knew, once he got back, *exactly* what he was going to do and how. He picked up the black and white composition book that Qwayz had given him to write lyrics or capture a mood. TC was no longer confused. At least he could tell his children he'd served and come back to have them. TC chuckled. *That ought to make them laugh.* He also wanted to find Yudi; TC now understood what his friend went through and was willing to help. Jaz never discussed Yudi in her newsy letters, so he assumed he still hadn't returned. That would have been the first thing on her list to share.

TC received letters from family: his parents, Grandma Keely and Star, Selena and Zack and Scoey. Qwayz didn't write but piggybacked on Jaz's tomes. She wrote like he was down the street, catching him up on all the minutiae in and around Watts. Mel had her big head boy, Hud, Jr.—eight pounds and some ounces. TC couldn't imagine Little Mel with a big stomach. Lorette stayed at Hud Sr's two-bedroom loft as promised, complaining about the location and that it was just a big open space with a closet for the baby: No window; a child needs sunlight through a window. Lorette already hired a nurse and searched for a nanny for when she returned to Italy and Mel went back to work. Jaz wrote: "I give her a month before she has Mel moving back to her own apartment where Grandma Lorette has already put in a request for the next two-bedroom vacancy. Lorette doesn't care for Hud, Sr. Not that he just changed his name legally to reflect this role in this play but he doesn't 'act like a father.' Late nights or no nights."

Jaz admitted only seeing him once: "Fine indeed, smooth, licorice-black complexion, like Carter Hix but there's more to life than just good looks; the man is short on character. Good googa mooga, did I agree with Lorette?

"Now I have a man with extreme good looks and character," she continued. "You know him, don't you? With his first year of law school and no more b-ball games, we've turned into an old married couple for sure and love it. His books are abominably big and heavy but we remain as inseparable as you said. Nothing suits us better than to snuggle up in front of the fire and look at television; preferably, "The Rifleman." We hosted a fondue party for friends after I took the MCATs; we were still hungry. Qwayz runs with Akira in the mornings and we walk her in the evenings. For special occasions we still dine at Giuseppe's and Aloutte's but switch to Pier 39 when we have AJ. We're taking him skiing in Tahoe for his excellent grades. Our life is wonderfully mundane and predictable. We saw 'Cool Hand Luke' and 'In the Heat of the Night,' you'd like them both. All while trying to ignore that somehow, they elected Reagan governor of California; what a mess. We attempted to make ice cream one day… hilarious. It tasted nothing like the frozen dessert we all made on the back porch of Cherokee Ranch. We're going to Colt, Texas for Christmas so we can all talk to you at one time. You know where I wasn't going? Connecticut!"

His sister kept him flush with hot sauce, Red Hots and Tootsie Pops. Finally, Newt, seeing him sitting on his cot with his composition book in hand and the Tootsie Pop in his mouth, identified him. "Culhane! TC Culhane. Man, that's you!" Newt said loudly to the confusion of the guys around him. "Raw Cilk, man. Even without your porkpie hat and goatee. I remember your picture in *Ebony*. They did an entire

399

article on you man. That bad studio. The pad with the round bed. You got Grammy's and shit!" When the excitement leveled off he asked, "What the hell are you doing here?"

~*~

"Happy birthday to you!" TC laughed at his long-distance wishes on cassette tape from all his friends at the studio. "Wish you were here!"

"Me, too," TC said. Apparently Qwayz orchestrated an ersatz celebration with a big chair and a mannequin all dressed in black reserved for him in Studio 3 and folks had a high time in his honor. They sang, harmonized, cut up and joned, from side A to side B.

"Hey TC," a female voice said, "I came home because my father was ill and thought I'd stop by. They told me you were in Vietnam. Is that true? What are you doing over there?"

LeLani Troop, he thought, with a sly grin.

"I'm heading back to our fiftieth state but we have to catch up when you come home. Meanwhile, stay safe. See you, then. Oh, this is LeLani Troop. Bye."

TC could visualize Qwayz giving him a knowing grin in the background as he called up the next dedicator to the mike.

"Hey man," Scoey came in loud and clear. "When do you get your first R&R? Qwayz and I been talking about joining you… wherever man. We heard about Pattaya Beach in Thailand."

"I'll be damned!" Jaz interjected from behind. "Tracy and I aren't going for that!"

Everyone laughed and Scoey continued, "First beers are on me. Miss you, man. Stay safe. Later."

Although he had been sent a tape of Christmas carols, TC kept his birthday tape cued up and played it repeatedly as it captured the lovable, mundane chaos of home. At the end of the birthday tape they all sang, "May God bless you. May God
400

bless you. May God bless you…" when Jaz concluded, "We love you, TC" followed by Qwayz's voice, "Miss you man. See you soon. Later."

Two months later, the Boys Club Christmas benefit went on but everyone there felt the absence of its creator: Watts-ite extraordinaire, the Messiah of Music, Pied Piper of Mega-Hits, the boss, brother, friend and one of the 465,600 U.S. troops in Vietnam. They all offered a silent prayer of thanks that he was not one of the 9,378 killed in combat that year and requested that God continue to bless their "brother across the way."

The Christmas call to Colt, Texas hadn't lasted nearly long enough and the reception was scratchy, but everyone got their chance to say a brief "Merry Christmas" to TC in Vietnam. Knowing she wasn't going to get another chance to talk to him, Jaz disappeared to the front porch and Qwayz found her there.

"You OK?"

"About as OK as you are." She folded herself into his waiting arms. "It's harder than I thought."

"Think about how tough it is for him. We get to find solace in one another. He's alone in that wacky world of war."

"Sometimes I think he'll be OK and back before we know it and other times… it seems like forever. Like he's been gone for years."

"I know." He held her tighter. They relaxed in one another's embrace, a comfortable silence soothing them both.

"Did I tell you how good you look holding Hud Jr?"

Jaz grinned. "A cutie pie."

"You're going to make a fantastic mother. I'm going to give you more than four babies."

"Promise?"

"I'll do my part."

"Remember. No Tavio." They both chuckled.

~*~

Company E was deployed to divert an obvious major offensive against Khe Sanh, a Special Forces base, established to watch the Ho Chi Minh Trail. As the marines took possession of Khe Sanh, Company E moved closer to the Laotian border near the village of Lang Vei conducting operations from there while the marines launched air strikes on the Ho Chi Minh Trail, intending to destroy the flow of supplies to guerrilla and North Vietnam forces from the south.

Conversely, the Viet Cong, called Charlie by Americans, intended to isolate Khe Sanh and cut American troops off from reinforcements from Quang Tri and Dong Ha. General Giap surrounded the airfield, which lay in a valley, positioning anti-aircraft weapons in the hills and long-range artillery along a relatively safe DMZ that had been off limits to American bombers.

On January 21, 1968, the siege at Khe Sanh began only three days after the truce halting the bombing of Hanoi in preparation for the Tet Lunar New Year Holiday. Strategically, Charlie attacked at dawn with few causalities and destroyed the main storage depot and several helicopters. North Vietnamese launched attacks against the defenses of Lang Vei and what was left of Company E made its way to Khe Sanh with orders to keep that road open between the two points and "bail out the marines." On the 22nd, 1,500 reinforcements arrived at Khe Sanh and supplies were replaced by air. On the 23rd, 18,000 Communist Viet Cong lay under a cover of fog as additional troops and supplies moved along the Ho Chi Minh Trail, waiting for the dense visibility to lift so they could attack and capture the airfield. On the 26th, every available American aircraft flew missions over Khe Sanh, more than 450 on that day alone, many forced back due to heavy Viet Cong anti-aircraft fire. Finally, all American troops, whether patrolling the road between Khe Sanh and Lang Vei or fighting to reopen Route 9 between Quang Tri and Khe Sanh, were ordered to "fill in the gaps in defense made by the enemy and to fight to the last man if necessary."

With fog so thick you could chew it, battle-weary Company E made its way to Khe Sanh as ordered. The lieutenant on point was followed by Williams, Rankin and Culhane on drag. Having lost over half of their guys, with sporadic radio contact, rations and ammo low and morale even lower, the feel of death and finality surrounded them like a blanket of doom. The lieutenant raised his hand signaling a short break and they huddled within feet of one another. TC, behind a fallen tree trunk, pulled out his last Tootsie Roll Pop, popped it into his mouth as he readjusted the recorder with the birthday tape Jaz had sent. They had chucked most of their gear but TC held fast to this last bit of home. The lieutenant dispatched Williams and Rankin ahead and after a few steps, there were two pops, unlike the gunfire they had heard all week; Williams and Rankin fell like lead. TC rolled over on his belly, scrambled further under cover, surfacing with his gun poised in time to catch a glimpse of the lieutenant blown back by a bullet. TC froze, horrified. Certain, he had stopped breathing. Rifle poised in hand he rose and plastered himself against a thick tree. He saw no one. No movement. He stood rigid fighting to gather his senses, and control his fear. How long he stood there he wasn't sure but he was prepared to do so until kingdom come, if necessary. Scared, alone trying to harness his breathing, he mopped sweat from his brow and couldn't get his bearings. No clear direction under the lush canopy of trees. Finally, he heard voices, relief relaxed his body until he realized they were not American. Charlie was coming to pick the bodies clean. To mutilate him. Spike his head on a tree stump. To imprison him; Watts or no. Culhane or no. TC knew he hadn't the stomach to withstand the certain torture of a POW. He hoped for their humanity and that they would just kill him. Is this how it ends? In a jungle in Southeast Asia? He had people he loved and loved him back in the U.S. He prayed that his body would get back home. If he was going out this way, he sure as hell was taking some Viet Cong with him.

When they were close enough to smell, TC jumped out, startling them, yelling and firing his M16 killing seven before his body jerked and jumped with bullets several times before he fell to the ground. As the surprise Viet Cong commander ordered his men to fan out, a single sheet of loose leaf paper sprung from a black and white composition book, drifted down, landing inches away from the hand and open eyes of the black GI they'd just annihilated. "Home" scribbled across the top.

As TC lay face down in the rich, red blood of his own making, a muffled singing echoed from his body through the dense fog cover. A Viet Cong turned him over with his foot.

"May God bless you! May God bless you!" eerily emanated from the recorder the Viet Cong couldn't locate.

"We love you, TC," a female voice said.

"Miss you, man. See you soon. Later," a male voice said.

Spotting the recorder, the VC fired a single, silencing shot.   A haunting quietness rose in the mist.

41

At the American Embassy in Rome, Italy, a petite, elegantly attired woman collapsed onto the cold step at the bottom of an ornate marble staircase, rivers of black mascara streaked her face and, for once, she didn't care how she looked or appeared to staff. Her husband stood stoically by her, removed and in a world of his own before he reached down to help his wife to her feet. His face expressionless, resolute but damp with salty tears. The natural order of the universe destroyed; a parent should never have to bury their child.

~*~

Qwayz, Jaz and AJ dined at the Fisherman's Wharf, bought a week's work of goodies at Ghirardelli Square before setting out on AJ's skiing trip in Tahoe. Having already regaled them with "My Baby Must Be a Magician," AJ asked for his second favorite song for Aunt Jaz, "It's love that makes a woman...who she is." On the screechy high note, Qwayz and AJ laughed as Akira barked.

And the phone on Alta Vista rang...and... rang...

~*~

Zack held an inconsolable Selena in the upper apartment over the club, finally instructing Henri to announce to the audience that there would be no show tonight. Selena lay on her chaise lounge in abject darkness until the car was brought around and Zack walked her down the steps amid a meandering crowd who had never seen "Sassy Selena" in such an emotional, zombie-like state. Concern washed their faces as they asked, Was she sick? No. Her nephew was just killed in Vietnam. "Oh, yes Vietnam," they had heard of it but knew of no one fighting there. "The handsome talented composer who came to visit? Who wrote 'Beauty Black?' Who played for the Queen? What *was he* doing in Vietnam?"

~*~

"Hey, Hep," Star smiled into the phone at the sound of her brother's voice. "Are you here?" she listened while watching her mother put the finishing touches on the cakes for the church bake sale. "Yeah, she's here," Star said. "Ma." She handed Keely the receiver.

"Hello, son," Keely greeted.

"He's gone, Ma…"

"Who?"

Star watched her mother's face transform from rich, sun-kissed brown to pale white and back again as she listened to her son talk. Keely grabbed her head, her heart and her throat, thankful that her son couldn't see her. Tears spilled from her eyes as she spoke calmly, consoling her baby boy who had just lost his. They spoke for over thirty-five minutes when Keely finally said, "You bring him home. He belongs here at Cherokee Ranch with his family."

~*~

AJ skied rings around Qwayz and Jaz as Akira frolicked in the snow, the whiteness glinting off her rich auburn coat. They dined in the lodge before returning to their chalet where Qwayz built a fire and AJ fell asleep on Akira, and Jaz on Qwayz, who thought "all's right with the world" as he saw their star shining through the chalet's window. The next day they made snowmen, snow angels, sped down hills in a toboggan and took a sleigh ride on mountainous paths after dinner. Qwayz showed AJ his and Jaz's star.

And on Alta Vista…the phone rang… and rang…

~*~

Opening the door to their New York loft, Mel ran to the phone with Hud Jr. while his dad closed the door and bolted the metal locks. The jubilance of another standing ovation coupled with hearing her father's voice, soon washed away with the news of her brother's death thousands of miles away. Mel listened, hung up and quickly gave her son to his father and ran for the bathroom where she threw up heaves of bile between wailing cries.

~*~

"Scoey, did you hear me?" Hep asked.

"Yessir." He wiped his big hand over his mouth and asked, "Could this be some mistake?"

"I'm afraid not."

Scoey placed his head on the door jamb away from Tracy, not wanting her to see him crying. "What can I do?"

~*~

Qwayz and Jaz drove back to San Francisco in time to put AJ on a plane to LAX and called Melie and Aubrey with the flight information. They pulled into an open parking space next to Pinkie, stopped for the mail before they both started jockeying to be first in a hot shower. They laughingly scrambled up the steps, Jaz playfully tripped Qwayz and climbed over him and he pulled her back on the second floor. "Shush!" Jaz admonished as they passed the second-floor apartments and Jaz sprinted up to the third floor to their door. "I win! Home!" Jaz exclaimed and kissed him as he opened the door, both simultaneously trying to get through it like a stunt from an old comedy act.

She shed her coat, threw off her shoulder bag and ran for the bathroom. Mail in hand, Qwayz knocked on the door, "How about we share? A nice long bubble bath for two?"

407

"Nope. I've had enough of you guys and the cold. This is lady's choice and I choose solo."

Qwayz chuckled, "OK, I'm going to get Akira some dog food. We need milk. Anything else?"

"What I want from you cannot be bought from the store!"

"I'm gonna hold you to that."

"Please do."

Qwayz grabbed Akira's leash, attached it to her, left though the door and down the stairs…and the phone rang…and rang….

When Qwayz returned he unhitched Akira and picked up the ringing phone. "Hello?" He set the bag of groceries down. "Oh, hey Mr. C," he replied brightly, eyeing the closed bathroom door knowing Jaz was still in there. "Oh, yeah. We took AJ skiing in Tahoe—"

Moments later, Jaz bounced from the bathroom. "Wow! That was fabulous. I'm clean and prunie. Wanna help me plump the wrinkles out?" She paused brusquely in the doorway for effect but Qwayz didn't budge. "AJ's gone so we can engage in loud, noisy, sloppy, lovemaking," she teased but he wasn't biting.

Maybe he's tired, she thought so she suggested, "Why don't you take your shower now and I'll rustle us up something delicious to eat?" He remained transfixed by something outside the small, round, strained-glass kitchen window. Arms folded across his chest. Immobile. "Qwayz, what is it?" Jaz joined his gaze out the window but saw nothing peculiar, but then his eyes met hers. Honey locked with hazel. She'd seen that look only one other time, when the gang member came for Hanie.

"Qwayz, what's the matter?"

"Your dad called…" his mouth open but nothing came out. Jaz thought her father had blown her anniversary surprise,

408

their wedding picture in oil that was to be shipped directly here. "Jaz," he gripped her shoulder for support and it scared her. It wasn't the painting.

"What?" she implored as his face looked full and contorted as if it were going to explode, as if he wasn't breathing. "Qwayz what?" she screamed as her heart pounded uncontrollably, her breathing shortened. Her equilibrium failed her and a queasiness churned in her stomach. *And she knew.* There was only one thing her father could say that would hit Qwayz like this.

Tears sprang to her eyes, streamed down her face as the silent answers were heard and received. Qwayz, having fulfilled his responsibly, freely joined in the release as Jaz pleaded, "No... no... no... noooo!" Forehead to forehead, nose to nose. Honey on hazel, wetness to wetness, they sank to the floor entwined in one another's arms.

"Died in the TET Offensive. Instantly. Painlessly."

Jaz jerked at the idea that death can be painless.

"He didn't suffer. No torture. No POW. He lay in ambush and took out a few before they got him."

Jaz smiled through tears. "That's TC."

"He'll get the Bronze Star for Valor."

"I don't give a fat rat's ass about medals. I want my brother back."

Hep volunteered to go pick up his boy but authorities nixed it and Hep settled for being at the army base to receive him. When they finally spoke, Hep recalled Jaz pleading, "Just don't bury him in Connecticut. TC wouldn't like it. It's cold and he doesn't know anybody up there."

Lethargy, anger, confusion, disbelief, isolation all converged on the couple. The Black Student Union, Sloane, CC, Farrell and Hilson sent Jaz flowers. Jaz intentionally bypassed Sproul Plaza with all its demonstrations. Now her brother had been a causality of that dreaded war. Muhammad Ali had the right idea. Dickie fleeing to Canada had the right idea. Anyone who avoided this mess did. She wondered what ever happened to Sinclair Cosgrove. "Hell, no we won't go! Ho-ho! Hay, hay! How many lives did you kill today?" Something that meant nothing to her in 1964 was now front and center and screaming into her life.

St. Theresa's Church sat surrounded by a multitude of folks from all walks of life. All races, creeds, colors and ages pressed close to glimpse the flag-wrapped coffin of a fallen hero: The Prince of Watts, from elementary to high school and beyond. Guys from the pool hall, mechanics who worked on his cars, people TC'd helped get a leg up in this world. Stars and celebrities from all generations, those for whom he had written, arranged and orchestrated songs and those who had covered them. Thousands stood in orderly lines at Hodges Funeral Home to file by a closed casket with a picture of him in his porkpie hat, smiling with a Tootsie Roll Pop in his mouth. A young, gifted, talented black man who'd achieved the impossible, didn't believe in the word "can't" and didn't allow anyone else to believe in it either. Unselfish, he had invested in his community through, not only his Boys Club Basketball Clinic, but also the Christmas Benefit, the music program at Roosevelt, where he supplied instruments and donated his time, and so much more.

A parade of folks ascended the altar and spoke into the mike about Tavio Culhane's goodness and genius, an endless litany of praise. An oblivious Jaz didn't know that Dickie and Greg Minton and two-time Heisman Trophy winner Jesse Ramsey were in attendance. Z and Jaxson made sure a sound system was hooked up outside so all those who could not get into St. Theresa's could hear the services.

410

Photographers, who were barred from inside the church, captured pictures of the grieving family as they left: the ambassador in a tailored black suit; the mother in an elegant black, mink trimmed Adolfo with matching mink hat; the sister straight from Broadway in an African print; the youngest sister in a red coatdress with brass buttons; and her husband, the deceased's best friend and basketball star, in a black suit, red tie and Converse; his aunt, Selena, in her signature caftan and turban with huge sunglasses; and his uncle, Zack, in a charcoal gray suit as well as scores of relatives the press did not know. The family bypassed the throngs of mourners outside the church, and provided for them generously at the repast held in Club Oasis while they then flew directly to Colt, Texas for private burial at the family cemetery.

The residents of Colt, Texas attempted to be respectful and give the Culhanes space, but the dam broke at the service at Mt. Moriah Gethsemane Baptist Church where the crowd filled the church to overflowing, down the outside steps, near open windows, surrounding TC and the Culhanes with love.

"Seems we were just here for another Culhane," Revered Gassaway began. "Colt Culhane. A celebrated life of over 100 years. But today we are here for a much younger Culhane. A too young Culhane. Tavio Range Culhane who we all knew as TC. First born of native son Hepburn Culhane and Lorette Javier Culhane, TC started coming here as a boy and we all got to know him. Watched him grow. Tackled things we didn't understand but we knew him to be as special as his grandparents, founder Colt Culhane and his wife Keely. As special as his father, Ambassador to Italy, his aunt an international singer. His sister a Broadway star, so we know what special and rarified folks the Culhanes are. The genius TC could play anything he wanted on that organ when he

411

accompanied his grandmother. On piano, a little drums and horn. I'd like to think, like many others through the years, that folks came to Colt, Texas to be reminded of what love is. To get fortified for the world beyond here. I like to think that when they left here they took a little of Colt, Texas with them. That their experiences here gave them the confidence, strength and fortitude to endure anything out there. TC proved that to be so. His contribution to music is unparalleled from one so young. His music, the soothing balm for the ills of the world. His music penetrated all phases and all people of the world. The Queen of England and the Duke of Ellington were just a few of his fans. He never forgot where he came and gave back to those in his community that meant the most; both here and in Los Angeles. As Selena sings in one of her hit songs, 'He had the world on a string. Sitting on a rainbow.' Well, in January, that string snapped in a place called Vietnam."

Qwayz felt Rev. Gassaway's words vibrate in Jaz's hands and he held them tighter.

To Jaz, everything seemed so viscous, hazy, like they were just going through the motions, like it didn't really happen and TC was still here, somewhere on this earth. Like any minute someone would announce there had been a mistake. In matters of war, it happened all the time. TC himself could appear. Jaz looked back at the door but only saw Scoey's tear drenched face. *And now there were two,* Jaz thought. One member of the trio—beyond reach.

As the Reverend spoke of TC, Jaz thought of all the great summers and Christmases they had had here. Nurtured, loved, challenged and disciplined. She couldn't remember the last time they spent an entire summer here, nor the last time they all went to the Satin Doll to ring in New Year's, nor the last time she danced on the tops of her daddy's shoes. The last time they all sang into a mike at Champion Studios. There was a

412

last time for everything; you just don't know it at the time. Reba finished up "Amazing Grace" and Jaz wondered what a gift it must be to cry and sing at the same time. TC loved her voice. The first time he heard her sing—that might have been the first time he thought about recording. About building an empire. Making a mark in the music business. Private thoughts got Jaz through the service without dissolving into tears and evaporating away. Now, Qwayz held her hand as they walked up the hill to the cemetery. The cold ground had been turned up into a brown pile of Texas' finest waiting to accept the latest Culhane offering. The warm winter sun vied with the brisk swirling wind and landed on the cheeks of TC's grandmother, father, mother, sisters, his best friends Qwayz and Scoey, and his aunts. Here, TC will have the company of Papa Colt, a child uncle, an infant aunt, and an Uncle Range he had never met in a place he loved. Sun in the winter and shade in the summer and on a quiet Texas day, he could hear the faint tumble of the swimming hole waterfall.

The motion of Qwayz removing his hand from hers and approaching TC for the last time brought Jaz back to the task at hand. He unfolded a piece of paper with a poem he and TC had decided long ago that one would read for the other on such an unlikely and remote occasion.

Under the spiky branches of a leafless tree, Qwayz began in a strong clear voice, "Don't stand by my grave and weep. I am not there. I do not sleep." Qwayz recalled how TC needed little sleep. A genius like him, always awake. The nights he would sleep over after Coach C. had taken them to see The Platters or Sam Cooke, TC would be so hyped. "I am a thousand winds that blow," Qwayz continued as did images of their nights spent at the beach romancing girls behind dunes and around the bonfires and the ferocity of a summer Texas

413

storm. "I am a diamond glint on the snow." Qwayz could hear him saying, "I could use some snow. It's hot as hell here," when they were on Roosevelt bleachers revising the poem and admiring the legs of LeLani Troop as she walked by. "I am the sunlight on a ripened grain. I am the gentle autumn rain." Qwayz paused and looked up and over at the prairie and saw their young images riding horses, kicking up dust and the faint clang of Keely's bell summoning them for supper. "Do not stand by my grave and cry. I am not there. I did not die," Qwayz's voice cracked and he stood tall and strong and thought of another poem to paraphrase. "Laugh and talk of me as if I were beside you. I loved you and it was heaven here with you, my brother. Rest in Peace." Qwayz stared at the bronze coffin before stepping back to grab Jaz's hand again.

~*~

Valentine's Day and their anniversary came and went before Qwayz and Jaz realized it. Qwayz pulled into the space beside Pinkie and headed up the steps and presented her with a dozen pink roses. "Happy anniversary! Been a little distracted but you know you mean the world to me. And I love you."

"Me, too, you." She smiled, they kissed and later enjoyed dinner at Giuseppe's. When they staggered home and climbed upon the magic carpet of their big brass bed, Jaz scooted off and went into the seldom-used small closet behind the portable TV and its stand. "What are you doing?" Qwayz chuckled quizzically. "Need some help?"

"No." Jaz fanned him back to sit at the foot of the bed as she positioned then unveiled the oil painting of them on their wedding day.

Qwayz stood slowly unable to remove his eyes from the wondrous images. "Look at us."

"Just a year ago."

414

"It looks exactly like you. The hair, the ring of gardenias, your eyes, nose, those luscious lips…"

"Yeah, it's me. Look at how handsome you are. The skin tone, the Jeff Chandler jaws. Paul Newman lips. The Chandler nose, cheekbones. I forget how handsome you are. I don't see you with my eyes."

"Wow. We were so happy that day."

"And will be again."

"Starting with tonight." He drew Jaz to him and they rocked and looked at themselves. "We are a beautiful couple inside and out," he said, repeating part of TC's toast. "You all are going to have some amazingly bright and beautiful children—"

"No time soon!" they'd yelled together and laughed. "We are still newlyweds, aren't we?"

"We will always be newlyweds. You are my happily ever after," Qwayz said.

They made slow deliberate love that didn't belie that this was the first time they had done so since the news of TC. They'd laid in one another's arms, cuddled, affirmed life in one another's touch and sought solace from each other as best friends would. But the act of loving escaped them, had become inconsequential… until now. And they made up for all the loving they had missed.

The next afternoon they drove to L.A. and Qwayz took care of studio business while Jaz visited Denny.

"So, how's my baby brother?" Denny asked, serving her guest hot tea and homemade chocolate chip cookies.

"Mmmm. If that psychology thing doesn't work out you could open a bake shop." Jaz sat in the sunlight streaming through the window. "He's better. Coming around. It took us all for a loop."

415

"You all gave TC a good send off. Gave him a reason to come back."

"Lot of good that did," Jaz said sourly.

"I asked about Qwayz because you know my loving, control-freak brother hates when he's not in charge. TC's death brought back our Dad's. The poem he used at TC's stemmed from a conversation with our father when he was only six and wanted to know why we didn't have grandparents like other children. Qwayz asked if Dad ever missed his parents and Dad told him that they are not back there but are here." Denny touched her head and heart. "Always will be. I could see his little eyes trying to understand it. Dad said that as long as they are kept alive in your mind and heart, they will never die."

Jaz took another cookie. "Your dad was deep."

"A few weeks later, our father was dead, too. They were inseparable."

"I don't know who I'd be without him. Where I'd be. He is helping me deal with this. Whenever the skies get dark or the water too deep... he's there for me."

"You are there for each other," Denny said. "That's plenty powerful." Out of habit Denny glanced at her door.

"Any word from Yudi?"

Denny shook her head. "Not here, not his family. I know he's around. I know he hasn't left me."

Jaz eyed her friend without speaking.

"He came home once. Showered. Changed clothes and took an old picture of us." Denny eyed Jaz and confided, "I found him once under the bridge, sitting on a box. I slowed the car down to a stop. He looked at me. I looked at him. He didn't run or look away. Just stared. Then he shook his head slowly and looked away."

"Oh, Denny."

416

"Somehow I got the message that he had no intentions of coming back. Still… I haven't changed the locks. Just in case."

Jaz went to Denny who accepted her embrace for only a minute. "Those men of ours, huh?" She wiped an errant tear. "Like my brother," she abruptly changed the subject. "He doesn't do 'out of control' well. Dad's death, that thing with Hanie, and now TC. I'm sure there are others but he copes really well. He attacks everything because he has to be on top of the situation. He has to claim it, tame it and then he can function. He's no good with blind-siding. He takes the upper hand right away… sports, academics, dancing; makes everyone take notice while he sets himself apart so he can't be questioned. Doesn't matter if they like or don't like him, they have to give him his props. Respect him. All they can say is that 'he's good.'"

"He is in his realm with superlatives." Jaz took another cookie. "I'll just be glad when the reading of the will is over and then we can really get on with just loving and missing TC. Healing."

"There's one thing I've learned professionally and personally," Denny confided quietly. "Everybody's a little bit broken."

~*~

The Culhanes crisscrossed back and forth between Italy, California, and Colt, Texas many times before they now sat in the studio for the reading of the will. TC insisted that they be together. The room darkened and projector spots slithered across a silver screen. "This was TC's idea," Z said as he left the room, unable to watch it again. Zack chuckled aloud, recalling what an electronic buff his nephew was and how he liked updating equipment and taped everything.

417

"Hey folks," he began with a wide grin and a strong voice. Jaz shuddered at the image of TC consuming the screen, wanting to both cover her eyes and soak up every nuance of his handsome face. "Well, if you're looking at me one of two things happened. Either I made it back in one piece and I wanted you to know what a hokey idea I had before I left. Or I'm not coming back. I sure hope I am sitting there with you in the studio projection room with a bottle of Beaujolais. Hope I didn't buy it in Nam. Believe me I tried my damnedest to get back alive."

Lorette began weeping profusely and was consoled by her husband.

"Let's say I am not sitting there with my family and the guys. Sorry 'bout that."

Jaz chuckled though tears as Qwayz cracked his knuckles and gritted his teeth.

"I hope you all could make it." He shielded his eyes like he was peering into the room. "My Colt, Texas folks will get their own copy and I hope none of you beat me up yonder. If you did, save me a seat. I see Mom with some gorgeous designer black something with fur trying to outdo Aunt Selena in her signature caftan and matching turban. I see Qwayz, Zack and Scoey in a dark suit because dressing up ain't their thing. I know Qwayz has on Converse. I can dig it. Mel is in something wild, ethnic and aesthetically expressive with the gold ball in her nose and Jaz has on something red despite what folks will say because she knows that's my favorite color. And dapper Dad is always cool and constant. My executor whether in the States or Italy. I'm not leaving my parents a thing because they don't need nothing…but my undying love and eternal gratitude. You were the best parents for me. Having my father, my first ace boon coon, almost exclusively until I turned 12, and then the community…the

418

world needed him more. That autonomy came at the right time for me to discover and test myself. My parents gave me enough love, support, space and freedom to explore what I wanted. Didn't force me into college or anything else I didn't feel. Sorry, my last choice didn't quite work out. You do get first pick from my personal effects at the studio or my homes or cars. Second dibs go to my aunt and uncle, Selena and Zack, who also need nothing… at least not materially. The support and encouragement you gave me over the years… priceless. I would not have succeeded in this business without your unselfish encouragement in my life. Zack, maybe you'd want some of my equipment or gadgets and you are welcome to it. And Aunt Selena, I'd like you to have the masters and sheet music to all those pieces we collaborated on. Especially 'Beauty Black,'" he caught himself and continued, "And to my sister Mel, I give my first Grammy and when you get your own, and you will, you can give it to Mom and Dad. My Grammy for 'Night Moves,' goes to the Chandlers, Qwayz and Jaz. You know why," he winked and grinned.

"I have three houses: the one you all know about that I lived in and the two on either side that I bought after the '65 riots. They're rented to good people now. The one I lived in goes to Jaz and 804 goes to Qwayz. Maybe Ma Vy and Hanie will want to move, and 808 goes to Mel and Hud Jr; she can continue to rent it or move back to L.A. with Hud Jr whenever you leave that trifflin' Negro. If you have already? Congrats! Since it is specially outfitted, I'm leaving my black van with the studio. And my black Porsche I'd leave to Qwayz but I can't get him out of Reds. I've tried, so it goes to Scoey who loved, washed, kissed and cared for her as much as I did. I'm feeling he might be ready to upgrade the Impala. Although we had some times in her," TC paused for effect and grinned.

"Beach parties, bonfires and blankets. And Scoey, if you decide to sell it give my dad first crack. He loves old cars. In the glove compartment is a check for you my brother enough to cover your law school tuition and fees for the next two years and seed money for your first office. From Mrs. Lloyd's Park View first grade class right up to the present… you were always there. I'm proud of you, man. Don't be alarmed that the check is signed 'Paladin. Have Gun—Will Travel' it's good." Both TC and Scoey laughed.

"My money distribution is filed in a separate codicil. This I can tell you right off the cuff, I've left a trust for Hud Jr–he's gonna need it–and for the Watts Boys Club to be given in yearly increments. Let it be known I have no children of my own. None. I was careful, so don't fall for the okey doke. Have one of those paternity tests if anyone comes out of the woodwork claiming otherwise. Hmmm, I guess now it would have been nice if I wasn't so careful. Not that Qwayz and Jaz's children will need a thing but I've set up trusts for them—all four of them. Let's see Q5, Heath Shane, Amber and Tallulah," he teased, they all laughed. "And the other four Qwayz will convince her to have later." They all chuckled along with him.

"In the event these funds are not needed by the Chandler brood, I've made alternative provisions for a Fine Arts Scholarships for aspiring musicians with talent, and funds at Roosevelt High School under the Chandler-Culhane Program. Yeah, Negro, I put you first. Alphabetically and all."

"This brings me to the hardest thing for me to leave behind. My baby. Champion Studios. The dream I made come true. Impulse says leave it to Qwayz… my brother, best friend, in-law, co-creator, fellow writer and artist, who loved it almost as much as I did but that would be unfair to him as I know he has other plans and it would be more of a burden than a

420

blessing. He has a permanent seat on the board, but I bequeath Champion Studios to the guys who are running it now. My trusted and talented partners in crime Zion and Jaxson, a talented duo reminding me of Chandler and Culhane…same commitment to hard work, innovation and good music. With the studio goes the van and any memorabilia that the family does not want. Taking a lead from my father, the buildings in which Champion is currently housed and Club Oasis, one each, to my sisters but handled by my father. I prefer Jaz take Champion because she wouldn't try to put Z and Jaxson out like Mel would." He chuckled as did the mourners. "I'd like those cats to stay as long as they like. Besides what has already been bequeathed to Selena Fluellen, all solo and groups cultivated by me during my career are to remain status quo. Royalties on the two labels: Princess and Punkin', and on which Raw Cilk was released, ownership therein and all the master's and original sheet music goes in its entirety to the man with the music and lyrics…Quinton Regis Chandler, IV. Now you get my share, too. Who else deserves it?" TC fidgeted with this pen and gritted his teeth, biting back emotions. "I'm goofin'. All this is written up in legalese.

"I'm sorry I didn't live to have children of my own or to see Hud Jr. grown up or the six kids Qwayz wants and the four Jaz agreed to give him. Or to see you graduate from college. You'll be the first of our family Jasmine Bianca Culhane. I'll be there but not so you can touch me. So proud." He hunched his shoulders. "I had a good life. The Lord had other plans for me. Rest easy. I'm with Papa Colt and Grandpa Javier. I'm in good company. I hope."

He aimed his eyes straight into the camera, "Life is short. Shorter than you think. Make it sweet. Make it count. Try to get along with one another…Mom…Jaz…It's the last time I'll

421

ask." He cleared his throat. "Love is rare and I come from a long line: both sets of my grandparents Culhane and Javier. My mother and father. Jaz and Qwayz. Scoey and Tracy. Finally, I am confident that I would have found one or two wives myself. We don't have tomorrow but we sure as hell had yesterday. I'm not really gone if you keep me alive in your memories. Please, please don't mourn me—what a colossal waste of time. I made my decisions and I apologize if they negatively impacted you, but you need to get on with your lives. I'll be seeing you soon enough. 'Til then I'll be looking in on you all. Love. Peace and happiness. Love you! TC peace-out." He offered their classic finger-thumb gesture to Qwayz and Scoey, but ended by tucking under his thumb and raising a two-finger peace sign morphed into the black power sign fist. Both Qwayz and Scoey gave it back... then the image went black.

Jaz thought how that one gesture epitomized their entire lives from Mag 7 to present; the trio now a pair and their lives will never be the same.

May we all love and revere those who are still here;
May we all remember those who have gone on ahead.

Epilogue

The woman sat with her back against the Koa tree on the soft white sand facing the expansive Pacific Ocean. Having played in the tumbling blue water which tired him out, the little boy had climbed up into his mother's arms and fallen asleep. A soft, sweet breeze caressed her cheeks as silent tears fell into his dark brown curls and perfectly matching long eyelashes… like his father's.

She was going to tell him when she visited her sick father in L.A. but he had gone to Vietnam. Vietnam? She wanted nothing from him, just thought he ought to know he had a son and that she'd loved him when they were in L.A. Ronnie was no threat, neither were the other women he'd occasionally had. He'd said they meant nothing to him, therefore they meant nothing to LeLani. But the reporter posed a gargantuan threat; it was hard watching your man fall for someone else. When she discovered she was pregnant and then decided to keep the baby, she left. No need to complicate or destroy four lives.

She had a good job at the bank, already had one promotion and anticipated more. Her mother cared for her son during the day and LeLani's banker's hours put her home by 3:30 p.m., so when he started school it would all work out. But now TC was dead. Opportunity lost. There was no need to disclose his parentage now. Father "unknown" would remain on his Hawaiian birth certificate. She and the spirited, handsome little boy would be just fine.

The Golden Rules To Live By In The 1950s-60s

Family First

Do unto others, as you'd have them do unto you.

Pretty is as pretty does.

Don't put off tomorrow what you can do today.

Always remember your "please and thank yous."

Don't lie. Don't cheat. Don't steal.

Honor thy father and mother; Respect your elders.

Live and let live.

Never dim your candle so others may shine.

Always Do *Your* personal best.

Remember to finish what you begin.

If it's worth doing, do it right.

If you can't say anything nice about a person...say nothing at all.

It's better to be thought a fool than to open your mouth and remove all doubt.

Sticks and stones may break your bones but words can never hurt you.

No one can make you feel inferior without your permission.

Never be afraid to ask. All they can do is tell you "no."

Everyone who *comes* with you can't *go* with you.

424

Count your blessings and be thankful every day.

"They're just jealous…," explains a mother to a bullied child.

Personal Favorites:

It takes a mighty good man to beat having no man at all. (aka, you can do bad all by yourself)

Sometimes you're the windshield and sometimes you're the bug.

To insult me, first I must value your opinion. (aka, consider the source)

The difference between a good day and a bad day is your attitude.

You don't learn anything by doing it right.

You're not going to like everyone and everyone isn't going to like you.

A man may ruin your lipstick but never your mascara.

In the name of James (Brown, the poet) my all-time favorite, "I ain't asking you to give me nuthin'. Just open up the door… I get it myself."

98573010R10259

Made in the USA
Columbia, SC
28 June 2018